BAZUMEL

CHRIS BONNER

D & T PUBLISHING

Bazumel by Chris Bonner
Edited by Jamie LaChance
Cover by Ash Ericmore

Bazumel

I don't know who this is for
~ Chris Bonner

"What I've dared, I've willed; and what I've willed, I'll do! They think me mad—Starbuck does; but I'm demoniac, I am madness maddened!"

Herman Melville, Moby Dick

"First Molech, horrid King, besmeared with blood

Of human sacrifice and parents' tears

Though for the noise of drums and timbrels loud

Their children's cries unheard that passed through fire."

John Milton, Paradise Lost

PROLOGUE

The boy and girl followed the bend until they could see the tombs. Their fingers searched the cracks as they tried to find footing along the rock face. The boy gripped the shelf overhead to cross a gap, slipped, and one of his arms flailed as he tried to right himself. The girl laughed as broken branches and egg shells rained over him. She crossed with a series of nimble movements.

"It's not funny," he said, smearing bird droppings onto the rocks.

She grabbed his other hand, tugging him along through the brush. The stench spiced his nostrils and set something soft and rancid on his tongue.

"He lives there?" asked the boy.

The girl nodded.

"Why do you want to see a man that lives among the dead?"

She wrinkled her nose. "Are you scared?" She held tight despite the sweat in his palm.

"I'm just seeing how much longer."

She giggled. It was nice to hold her hand. He let her lead him on.

The damp air hummed with insects. Enamored with the scent of decay, they made dizzying circles, occasionally landing on faces and hands. They passed through some high weeds and on the other side, its sudden proximity startled them.

Browned moss clung to the hewn stones. The slab jutted overhead, giving it the appearance of a stern browed monolith. Its mouth was wide and high, black as Sheol but even less inviting.

The girl pulled again but he'd planted his feet. "Aren't you coming?" She looked back and smiled. Her eyes didn't seem as confident as her words suggested.

He stared at the void before them. "There?"

"I want to see him."

"Are you mad? We don't even have a lantern." His next words were whispers. "He's a demoniac."

"They tell that to children so they'll listen. There's no demons in Israel."

"That sadducee rubbish has gotten to your head."

"Suit yourself." She wiped her hands over her cloak. "Sleep well knowing I'm more of a man than you'll ever be."

She stood at the opening. He could see the darkness around the folds of her garment spread as she walked, like ink consuming parchment.

A long groan came from inside.

She stopped. "Hello?"

"Rachel... *Rachel,*" the boy called.

Another moan. She retreated a step. Then turned to look back at the boy with a mouth that mimicked the opening behind her. Her eyes were wide yet full of excitement.

She held her hand out to him. He shook his head.

The groan that followed was high and carried longer. Dark shapes burst from the shadows and fluttered past, chirping and squeaking as they brushed against them. She swatted at her head and shrieked. The boy crouched and hid his face in his arms. The moan expressed pure agony. It seemed as though the tomb was a wound in the earth crying out.

"We should go. Rachel. *Rachel.*" The bats seemed to be inside him now, flapping at his organs and struggling to leave.

The girl waved a hand back to silence him. Her eyes were on the tomb.

She stepped forward until all he saw was a light patch of her garment, the color of bone under a full moon. She took another step and disappeared.

The boy didn't breathe. Even the grasshoppers and frogs seemed reverent to the moment.

"Does your mother know you're here, Rachel?" The voice was a deep, reverberating rasp.

"He knows my name," she whispered back to the boy. "Hello? Do you need water?"

"Water won't quench the flames."

"What does that mean?"

"Dry brush. You kindle at the first spark."

Metal slid over stone.

"I can't see you. Are you chained?"

"It's the chains you can't see that are binding."

This voice was different. Higher. It prickled the boy's neck.

"How do you..." The boy saw the white of her tunic again. At the edge of the shadows it looked like a tuft of wool submerged in dark water. Its outline, along with the girl's head, faded in and out of darkness as she moved.

"Rachel, come back."

"Is that our little priest?"

The boy's heart became a heavy, burdensome thing at those words. He couldn't move. It wasn't just what was said, but the voice and intonation. The voice of a man who'd taught him what it meant to be a Levite. Who he helped bury, whose bones he'd helped gather and put in an ossuary. In a place that wasn't much different than here.

The silence that followed made the boy feel the tomb's darkness was leaking out into the world, seeping into his thoughts.

Rachel screamed.

He saw it.

Saw *him*.

The flash of sallow skin, swallowed up by black as soon as it came. He wanted to lie to himself.

Eyes without color, white as the stones around it. The face contorted in a smile contrary to all things holy.

Rachel screamed again. Her cry was cut short as something snapped.

The boy flinched. He stepped back, shaking his head. Piss trickled down his thigh. Wet the leather of his sandal.

"Rachel?"

Nothing for a moment. Then, a whisper, "Aaron?"

His heart echoed in his neck, his temples.

"Aaron. Help!"

He took a small step. Shuffling his feet.

"Help."

Metal scraped stone again.

He froze. Thought of the eyes. The snap. A face that smiles in a sepulcher.

"How do I know it's you?"

"She's fine, little priest."

Saba? His grandfather's voice. It left him cold. He thought of the stories, how many nights he was lulled to sleep by that voice.

"I liked holding your hand, Aaron."

"Rachel, just… come out," he pleaded.

"He's already shown me things. Things you need the darkness to see."

He didn't respond. The voice of his grandfather returned. "You'll see more than she can, Aaron. Glories only the house of Levi can see."

Something shifted. His stomach turned. There was movement at the edge of the shadows. It was subtle, hard to notice in the black, like a ripple through tar. He strained to see. Aaron wanted to say he wasn't a boy, to encourage himself to take heart, be a man. The puddle of piss he stood in drowned the thought. His eyes were playing to his nightmares now, surely. The way children recognize monsters in the cloaks their fathers hang by the threshold.

He didn't turn away, he couldn't. Something broke the dark surface, a slow point of light rolling like a shimmer. Skin. Darker than the flesh from before. Rachel's face floated forward, pushing from the depths. Part of her stomach protruded from the black, the soft flesh near her breasts. *Where is her tunic?*

"Come, Aaron."

Aaron felt a numb alchemy overtake him, the mixture of panic and the culmination of boyhood crashing together.

"Come see the holy of holies. The glory of Levites." He watched her hands slide down her stomach. She shifted and her hands disappeared. He could barely make the blur of her face. She moaned.

Aaron's manhood stirred to life. He was appalled his body would betray him in such a way. Rachel giggled. But not like her laughter from before. There was something off, something that made him squirm inside.

"Rachel." His voice was a low whimper.

"Show me your little priest." More laughter.

Aaron didn't move. Her skin rose in points from the dark, slowly, walking forward and exposing herself with beckoning arms.

The cold, squirming thing the giggles brought could no longer remain dormant. The way her neck sagged, as though it were suddenly much too heavy for her body. Eyes as dull as the beasts that pull plows.

He ran.

He heard Rachel–the Rachel thing's voice, his Saba, screams and laughs and hissing and a long sputtering bray that brought squeaks and the beats of leathery wings fleeing from the caves after him.

C H A P T E R 1

S W I N E

The pig's heart beat faster than the man's. Pressure built through its chest and sides as it worked, every beat a call to war thrumming through the barrelled torso. Bazumel didn't notice the burn of tired muscles, he ignored the organs throbbing, failing in their intended purposes. His stocky legs struggled to keep pace with the others.

He'd planned to round the corner to give himself space from the edge, but the enormous belly took some getting used to. His hoof hit a rock and he stumbled, tried to regain his footing, but one of the others clipped the hind leg. Bazumel fell, scurried to his feet to keep from going over the edge.

A torrent of pink flesh swallowed the path. Their hooves shook the ground. The pink bodies bottlenecked, smothering the hillside, the shapes of individual animals lost to one another. The portion of the precipice where Bazumel struggled broke free. Swine and earth splashed down, the shallow water below a hungry gullet with rocks for teeth.

Bazumel's head struck a boulder, the heavy body's momentum bent the animal at the neck. The fat bodies of his companions rained down around him. Cracks and splashes and muffled squeals.

Sprawled over the rocks with his head turned from his hooves,

Bazumel twitched. The porcine body, like a soft clay figure dropped, contorted the way impact demanded. A wrinkle circled the ruined neck. Dark bruises spread into pale flesh like spilled dye.

Bazumel stared up at the precipice. *HE* was standing there. After sending them to the pigs, and inevitably the water, *HE* stood over them, watching until they drowned.

Their collective voices had begged to enter the pigs. *Anything but the abyss.* And *HE* had obliged. Bazumel was ashamed of their cowardice, but there was no point fighting. This latest mercy, sparing them endless darkness to dwell in these filthy creatures–a gesture he found particularly revolting. *HIS* lackeys and *HIS* onlookers were up there, arms crossed, looking down their noses.

Bazumel hated them.

The animal's mouth opened and closed. Its legs kicked without Bazumel's consent. The body was dying. Bazumel looked up at his maker. A twitching insect watching the thing that crushed him.

HE watched them fall before. The first had transpired in an instant. They were pummeled, humiliated. Every gem and diadem adorning their bodies scorched and torn away. And *HE* had stared down at them then. Bazumel shuddered. Whether at the memory or with the dying body he couldn't tell.

Fell like lightning.

Bazumel didn't know how long he laid there. Among the archipelagos of swine, half submerged, mixing viscera into water. The rest of their band, the majority, had continued down the slope until they hit the water. They stayed below the surface until the bodies expired. The sun rose, fell, and rose. A few started to float after the third day.

When a host's body dies, Bazumel's kind typically return to where they've been. They abide in planes beyond man's reasoning or perception. Humans sometimes brush against these boundaries in rituals. Dreams and hallucinations that thrive on paranoia and fear, prayers to idols, all provide perfect opportunities to slip back into the physical world.

This time was different. Perhaps it was the drop, short as it was, that reminded them of their state. Or the prospect of future glories for the bright ones, which ultimately meant more shame, more humility for them. Regardless their reason, they stayed. Bazumel and the strong ones refused, and the worms always follow the strong.

They waited in the corpses. With half his head submerged, an ear and eye to the ledge, Bazumel meditated on his former triumphs. Though wrapped in the machinations of *THEIR* will, in a way incomprehensible to even his mind, it felt good to be an agent of wrath. He thought of the women of Israel boiling their children when the Assyrians came. The pride he'd taken in his duties to deceive kings. He'd Inhabited statues and relics for centuries, haunted areas visited by death, convinced peasants to sacrifice children. They bled for him.

Some time later, hooves scraped and clicked against rock. The others regrouped around Bazumel, their stench sour in the damp air, but welcomed.

They tugged and nudged him from the rocks into the water. Ears, snouts, and black eyes poked from the surface. These bodies would move as long as they deemed necessary, unhindered by exhaustion, broken bones, death. Until they cast these bodies aside, or *HE* commanded them to leave.

But *HE* wouldn't. There were more important things to worry about than wayward messengers. Bazumel heard one of *HIS* pets break into praise when they entered the pigs, "He *even shows mercy to unclean spirits.*"

HE is glorified in their humiliation. At their expense.

Once he was off the stones and into the water, Bazumel swam. If you could rightly call it swimming. His head was turned halfway around, forcing part of his face below the surface. Cut by his own hooves when he kicked, head bobbing as he paddled, the skull and spine held together by an isthmus of skin and ligament he felt tearing with every movement. Water flooded the holes in his flesh. He eventually crept along the bottom, thrashing through weeds. It took longer than the others, but he followed the gradual lift of the bank and eventually found shore. The sun bled into the sky and sank behind the mountains as Bazumel rose from the water. Weeds clung to tears in his flesh, water drained from gashes. He looked his comrades over.

They were many.

Clouds of flies swarmed about. Acrid decay and rancid water tingled in their snouts. Days spent in the water warped them the colors of clouds set to burst, their bloated bodies morbid caricatures of the pigs that boarded the ark. The corpses who fell with Bazumel were confined to whatever rigid and broken movements their bodies allowed.

Marduhl tried to calm the herd through a dislocated jaw. Words came shrill and cracked due to a hole in his throat. He saw Bazumel rise from the water and trotted over, squealing. Bazumel snickered, his mangled snout spurted water.

"I thought you were lost." Marduhl raised his legs and brought them down. The spiral tail bounced as he pranced around Bazumel, snorting and throwing his head back.

Bazumel tried to turn his head right. Marduhl giggled at the cracks and pops the bones made.

"Try to get a hold of yourself." Bazumel's jaw hung open, jowls frothed with cobwebs of slobber.

Marduhl grunted. "We need to find another body."

Bazumel gave up his attempts to return his head to normal. "I don't want to shove up into one body again."

"We don't want to draw attention."

"Where do you think *THEIR* attention will be?" With his crooked head, tendrils of weeds hanging, and waning sun reflecting red in the water dripping from his flesh, Bazumel made a monstrous sight. "I'm done slumming in caves and carving beggars with stones."

"Should we find another herd? Until we find the right host."

Drool hung from Bazumel's upturned jaw. "You're perfectly fine as a beast aren't you?"

"Maybe you'd be more comfortable as an owl?"

Some of the others laughed. Bazumel squealed. The sound surprised him. He tried to rear back on his hind legs, but collapsed. Marduhl laughed again, but this time Bazumel lunged forward, using his upturned mouth to bite into Marduhl's leg. Marduhl yelped. "Don't forget this broken body's only temporary."

Marduhl lowered his eyes. Some of the rotting herd had gathered around them. They snorted and kicked at the dirt and Bazumel promised bloody tidings for the Israelites.

CHAPTER 2

A MEETING OF SHEPHERDS

Elijah couldn't make out anything to his right, and some of the people to his left were obscured by the spot growing over his good eye. He moved to see through their head coverings, most dull and greyed with sweat. Murmurs rippled through the onlookers. A baby squealed somewhere.

The Rabbi's voice was resonant and carried over the crowd. He spoke of the dangers of pouring new wine into old wineskins. Broken cisterns. Before he'd compared his coming (strange, since he was already there) to virgins waiting until it was too late to borrow oil. *What would happen if they didn't get oil, if he came to them in the dark?* Could they not borrow from a neighbor? Spectators blurted questions. Lauded the Rabbi with praise, which swelled up from certain sections of the crowd. They begged him to touch them. To touch his cloak. He did. They did. He kept to his stories. The Rabbi answered their questions with his own, and their arguments were pulled apart like the peels of spoiled fruit. Some of the men around him grunted approval. Elijah looked at their faces, relieved when he saw a young woman with two boys beside her with an expression of bewilderment.

"This is the one who flipped the money changer's tables?" The man who spoke had a beard a bird could nest in.

The man he whispered to had his son on his shoulders. "Remember the demoniac, the one they chained up in the tombs?"

"In Gergasa?"

"I thought it was Gadara." The man with his son on his shoulders shrugged. "Debra says he was filled with them. Like wasps. The demoniac was terrified of him." He pointed to the Rabbi.

The great beard tilted. "This is true?"

His friend shrugged. "I wasn't there. She said he begged to go into a herd of pigs."

"Pigs?" The bearded man looked as though he'd sniffed something awful. "Then what?"

"He waved his hand and they went into the pigs." The man let go of his son's shin and made a shooing motion to demonstrate. The boy teetered. Elijah brought his hands up to catch him, but his father had grabbed his shin again just in time. "They ran into the water and drowned themselves."

"Debra saw that?"

"No. Her husband told her. Apparently his friend knew someone that was there."

A grunt made the beard twitch. "It's always someone else's story with you."

The man with his son on his shoulders shook his head. "I'm just telling you what I heard."

"Tasty morsels," teased the beard.

"I'm no gossip."

"You're at home around a loom, old man."

Someone bumped Elijah. He turned to confront this rudeness, but the man who'd walked into him was pushing on, moving through the men and women, who turned scowling in his wake. He held one side of a mat. On it lay a thin girl with crooked legs. Skin clung to bone and her cheeks were hollowed. The man holding the other side winked at Elijah as they moved on.

"Step aside!" called the first man.

"Make a path!" the second added.

"He thinks he's Moses," came a voice in the crowd. Some of them laughed.

They set the girl down in front of the Rabbi. Elijah couldn't see his face. Gasps passed through the onlookers. A voice that had to be the Rabbi, since no one else would be so brazen, said, "sin no more."

Sin no more.

The crowd closed back in around them. Elijah shouldered through to get closer. Stepping past a large man, he saw the girl through the gaps in spectators. The Rabbi was helping her stand. She rose and stood on her own. A flame flicked to life in Elijah's breast. Her body rocked side to side. Although half covered by someone between them, and obscured in his poor sight, it looked as though she was dancing.

She was.

The girl spun. Arms out, hopping, spry and mobile, her legs no longer brittle twigs. She jumped and kicked and scissored as though she had to savor the moment for fear she might wake on the mat to find it all a dream. She raised the mat over her head and threw it. Then fell at the Rabbi's feet.

The crowd, who only a moment before was understandably silent, began heaping praise. Warmth filled Elijah's chest. Hope made him weightless, the edges of flapping wings brushed his insides as his heart provided a beat fit for the girl to dance to.

People screamed. Closed in around the girl. The men that accompanied her began pushing people back. The one who winked at Elijah grabbed a man and threw him to the grass. When the Rabbi raised his hands they were still. Silence only lasted a moment however, for a shrill voice cut through the calm. "Rabbi! Lay your hands on my husband, we need a baby!" Elijah smiled, feeling sympathy for a man that would hear a baby cry alongside that woman's voice. Others followed. "My mother is sick! Have mercy on us son of David!" Elijah couldn't make out anything the Rabbi said now.

He forced his way to the front. There was a woman at the Rabbi's feet, holding his ankles and wailing. "Daughter," he said, "your sins are forgiven." He had a plain cloak and wrinkles under his eyes. His eyes were almost too dark to notice the pupils. They held no malice, but when they fixed on Elijah, cold sweat broke over his skin. Elijah dropped his eyes, heart still pounding. He thought God's chosen one would be someone handsome. Nothing in his appearance seemed noteworthy. The thought filled him with shame.

"But she's a prostitute," came a woman's voice to Elijah's left. The Rabbi searched the crowd, silence trailing the sweep of his gaze. "How can God forgive this woman?" Elijah had to turn his head to see her through his good eye. The woman was old. She'd let bitterness twist her face into a permanent frown, accentuated by her many wrinkles.

The Rabbi's face softened. He ignored the old woman and cupped the prostitute's face to bring her eyes to his. Something passed between them. She held his wrists, nodded, and kissed his hands before rising and turning. She left with her chin raised, as if she meant to sniff the air. Tears connected her eyes to her smile. She shook with sobs, her silence betrayed by her body. Excited murmurs rose up among the bystanders again.

Elijah glanced back, smiling. The old woman's wrinkled face gave her the appearance of a thumb submerged too long in water. Elijah's cheeks burned at the thought of such things in the presence of the Mashiach.

Could he really be the Mashiach?

Word of this man's miracles had spread with brush fire speed throughout the region. Whatever type of man he was, he could heal a crippled girl's legs and restore the muscle, make prostitutes weep with joy without so much as a mite, and prevent riots with the move of a hand. Regardless of whether this Jesus was truly the anointed, *He could fix Elijah's eyes.*

The rabbi in Bethpage had quoted the Tanakh. *Then the eyes of the blind shall be opened, and the ears of the deaf unstopped.*

Elijah's mind returned to the present. The Rabbi stared at the old woman. There was no malice, nor satisfaction in his voice. "The kingdom of God is like a banquet the noblemen and their wives were invited to. They tarried, yet they still expected seats of honor. They arrived at the dining hall and discovered peasants had taken their places. They begged the host to let them in, but it was too late. They were thrown out into darkness. Where there was weeping and gnashing of teeth."

The old woman's eyes widened. Behind her scowl a war seemed to take place. For some reason Elijah thought of the seeds choked on the thorny ground the Rabbi mentioned earlier.

Elijah wanted to fall at his knees and beg, implore him to restore his sight. Composing himself was growing difficult. Sweat trickled down his lower back and made his skin itch beneath his tunic.

Before he'd left home, Salome told him the spot on his good eye was larger. Since that day he'd been terrified, fretting constantly about it, asking people he spoke to the day before if it had grown overnight. He didn't have anyone to ask here.

One day soon he'd wake up and even the haze would be gone. He would wake up in darkness. And there would be no one to help him.

When Elijah looked up from his daydreaming, the Rabbi's eyes were on him. He breathed deep, trying to compose himself, but a surge of emotions he'd held down rose like a cistern filling with water. He went forward, knelt and sobbed.

"Walk to the village," Elijah looked up again. The Rabbi's face didn't soften with Elijah's tears. Not like it had for the whore. Or even that bitter hag. A jealous twitch stirred in his stomach. "Cover your eyes with mud, then rinse them in the water." Elijah nodded. Blinked. There didn't seem to be any humor to the man. He waited for something else to be said, and when nothing came he rose slowly and turned to walk away.

Elijah took a few steps, walking as though a dream strung him along. The Rabbi's voice broke through his daze. "Leave the woman and follow me."

Elijah froze. The Rabbi's tone was sincere. The voice of a man entreating his friend to give up a vice corrupting his soul. On the journey south, Elijah thought of all he'd do to keep his sight. What he wouldn't do. Could he kill a man? Would God expect him to slaughter a village like Saul did the Amalekites? To offer up a loved one? His name was Elijah after all, like the great prophet. At the time, hot needles danced in his face when he realized how self righteous he was being. *Who was he to think God would ask anything of him?* But now a sacrifice was required. A sacrifice he hadn't come prepared to make. Something pulled at him, tugging at his heart in the secret, dark places where feeling triumphs over reason. All he had to do was turn around. Surrender his sins to God.

Elijah shifted his feet. The miracles he'd seen and the things he witnessed burned in his mind. He knew without a doubt the Rabbi watched him. He tried to turn and face him. But he couldn't. Not all the way. Not without thinking of her. The way her cheeks grew with her smile. The smell of her hair. When the sun hit her eyes and drowned her pupils in globs of honey. Elijah stood with half a shoulder turned, trembling.

Leave the woman and follow me.

Salome. *His sin.* Elijah shook his head. A tear rolled down his cheek. He turned the rest of the way. Wrinkles of concern lined the Rabbi's forehead now. It made everything worse. Elijah shook his head again, then turned and ran.

CHAPTER 3

VILLAGE

On the eastern shores of The Sea of Galilee, a small village resided in the shade of the nearby hills. This village was like many others. Stone houses and retaining walls stacked in multiple stories, with patios on top where families sat in the evenings sharing stories of their fathers and of their prophets. Sheets and garments fluttered in the wind as laundry dried. Livestock roamed, fenced in by thin branches stripped and carved into crooked barricades. The smell of bread filled the air, and the rich, watery scents of hyacinth. Something foul lingered too, rolling from the hills with the breeze.

The villagers went about their business. Carrying stone vessels and buckets to and from the nearby well. Farmers with sheaves in their carts, urging their animals in preparation for the sabbath.

A family reclined in the grass on the outskirts of the village near the stone wall. Grapes and bread filled their flat baskets. Their son chased a small lizard with a stick around the sheet they'd laid out. Their daughter stood a ways off, watching the hills with a hand shielding her eyes.

There was a mass sweeping down the hills, gaining on the shadow it cast in the grass before it. The girl couldn't tell what it was, but saw the plume behind it.

The little girl squinted, her parents oblivious. Someone strummed a lyre in one of the houses on the other side of the wall. They laughed when the musician plucked the wrong note. As the mass drew near and approached level ground, the girl pointed up at the hills. "Pig!" she cried. "Pig!" The father stood with his brow furled. They were heading straight for the village.

It was the busier part of the day. Cool enough to get the women and children out of the houses.

The woman screamed. They grabbed their children and ran toward their house, abandoning what they'd brought. The man and woman scurried through a gap in the wall, shrieking. Their neighbors stared, perplexed.

Moments later the herd spilled through the gap in the wall. The wood fence along the house on the corner toppled over as they trampled into the yard. An old woman had been tending to her laundry. She fell on her back and the pigs poured over, tearing her throat and face. Chewing fingers, squealing at the futile attempts she made to shield herself.

They moved into houses. Up and down stairs, tearing through courtyards, only stopping long enough to dispense with whomever they saw. The herd burst through the fences where their livestock was confined. A man in a house nearby was chased onto his roof. He leapt when they followed. He laid in pain at the bottom, clutching his leg. The herd swarmed over him a few moments later.

Soon silence fell over everything. The pigs laid in hay, on the thatching of roofs, sprawled on the low tables where families ate together. Could one of the villagers still see or comment, they'd surely be outraged by the unclean beasts wiping their bodies where their food went.

Bazumel walked through the houses, watching his companions chew bones or grind their backs into the stones covering the ground with their eyes closed. Blood and mud splotched faces and jowls. He surveyed the damage, smirking at the villagers' remains. He walked over the rags and bones of what used to be a woman and cocked his crooked head. One of her eyes was gone, along with a considerable portion of her cheek. Her mouth screamed silently. Forever. He bit into her nose and slurped it down. The big belly rumbled. He lowered his snout and ate more.

They stayed in the village that night, picking off a drunk and a fisherman who wandered home after dark. They rose together before dawn, heading toward the nearby forest.

Less than a furlong from the village, the herd happened upon a farm. An old man lived alone with his animals. The pigs tore through the house, smashing possessions, goring the man. Behind the house, a white goat kicked its feet in the dirt, threatening the pigs. Bazumel stopped them before they fell on the creature. "No," he said. "This one is mine."

CHAPTER 4

THE COST OF DENIAL

Elijah ran a long time. He passed fig trees and stone walls, some intact and managed well, others with holes and crumbs of bricks beside them. Houses were packed and plastered together, roofs sagged, soft and dented with holes in the thatching. Stakes sectioned off animals, where they loitered and bleated near their troughs. The protests the beasts made at their work broke on the distant hills. Faces of loved ones and memories streaked by, coalesced with the signs of life in the village. He finally collapsed past the houses, but the blurred images of priests, Salome, the expression melting over the Rabbi, was all around him. He breathed in heaves, tears glossed his eyes.

Leave the woman and follow me.

He'd left stunned, wondering whether the Rabbi really was the Mashiach, *if* there even was a Mashiach. There was certainly a presence to the man. According to the rumors he had a command of the Tanakh that drove the Pharisees mad, embarrassed the Sadducees, shamed Levites. And he knew the hearts of men. But the Rabbi's followers looked upon him with a fondness that made Elijah uncomfortable. They revered him. Almost to the point of idolatry. Would they expect that from him? Elijah would never follow a man in such a way. What self respecting Israelite would clutch a man's ankles and kiss his feet like, like…*a whore.*

Daughter, your sins are forgiven.

Elijah fought the creeping certainty the Rabbi was everything they said he was. It became an itch, burning at his scalp, boring into the mind, screaming a refrain, *leave the woman and follow me.*

"No...No no no." Elijah's head drooped and he shook dirt from his cloak. Dust swirled up around him.

"Are you alright?"

Elijah was startled by the voice. Just a boy. His tunic was torn and filthy, the eyes lacked the excitement a child his age should have. None of the insatiable curiosity children have for the world. The face of a life burdened too soon. There were many children with faces like this. Elijah's certainly had been. Probably still was. He dropped his head again and tried to wave him off, affronted by the similarities between them. The boy didn't move. He looked down at Elijah, head canted like a dog.

"Are you hungry?"

Elijah looked up. Stared a few moments, then shook his head.

"You were talking to yourself."

Elijah slapped the dirt. The effort was feeble. He laughed. Tried to gather himself, but once he started he couldn't stop, cackles rolling like rocks, gaining momentum.

"What's wrong with you?"

Elijah's head jerked up, laughter replaced with something darker. "One day, everything you'll ever need will line up on two different paths and you'll have to choose. Whatever you choose will come at the cost of the other, and you'll spend your whole life wondering if you made the right decision."

"I just asked if you were hungry."

But Elijah was mid soliloquy. "Or maybe you won't choose. You'll go on believing you don't deserve either. That it's the lot God has for you. You'll go on, caught in a netting, writhing like a fish."

"Why don't you just choose one?"

Elijah looked up, eyes wide. Then laughed again.

The boy didn't move. "Can't you draw lots? Or let a stranger decide for you?"

"It's so simple for a child."

"I'm not a child."

Elijah clicked his teeth. "That's one of the advantages of youth. You act before you think, but at least you act, you don't just cower in fear, let your thoughts whip you into a cave." The boy stared at Elijah, his expression blank. "Ok kid." Elijah sighed, trying to keep his frustrations at bay. He sat for a while like that. When the boy finally sighed and turned to leave, Elijah ran his hand through the sand and found a pebble. "Ok, wait." The kid turned. "We'll try it your way." Elijah shrugged like a man already full of regrets. "If God truly rules heaven and Earth he'll make the right choice." Elijah put his hands together behind his back. Then he held both fists out, looked up at the boy and nodded.

The boy frowned. "You shall not put the Lord your God to the test."

"You said to draw lots."

"Not like that."

Elijah rolled his eyes. Nodded to his fists again. The boy's arms came out from his body a little and dropped, like a bird shy to open its wings.

Elijah decided left, then right. changed his mind a hundred times in the span of a breath.

The kid tapped the fist on the left. Elijah nodded, slumping into the dirt.

The decision was made. Wasn't that why he'd come? Seeking something from God. That, and of course… *His eyes.*

Elijah sprang to his feet. The boy nearly fell over as he streaked past. "Raca!" shouted the boy.

He ran, outer cloak wrapped in his hands, darting through a crevice between two houses. He broke into the open and knocked over a man pulling a small cart. Elijah muttered apologies, breathing hard, and was on his way before the man responded. As he ran, Elijah scanned the ground for the mud the Rabbi promised. The smell of shit was strong, which even the welcomed scent of bread wafting from the houses couldn't help. As hopeful and certain as he was of being healed, he processed the smell as an omen. A blessing wrapped in foulness. He pushed this from his mind, breathed, pumping his legs. His lungs burned. Elijah hadn't moved like this since he caught a man trying to steal one of the sheep. He passed a well with pieces of its stones broken off, and caught a glare from some puddles of water on the ground. Elijah fell to his knees in one, water splashed up around him startling people nearby.

Some of the villagers watched as he scooped mud in his fingers, smearing cold muck over his sockets and eyelids. He laughed, slathered his face, rubbing it into every crevice. Giggling like the senile.

Elijah paused, unsure whether it should be happening. *Does the mud need to set? Should I wait for it to dry?* He laughed again, high and cracking.

He was taught the God who provided the widow more oil day after day, who split the sea and closed it on Pharaoh's army, could heal an affliction like his with fire if He chose.

When things like this were said, *if He chose,* it always made him uneasy. He'd ponder why God chose to do what God did. Why his life, the lives of most of the people he knew, were spent rowing against the current in a river of tears, just for a few smiles spread out along the bank. He pushed these thoughts away.

Elijah stooped over one of the puddles and splashed his face. Wiping furiously, already regretting how much mud he'd used. Once his eyes were cleared of mud he blinked. His bad eye was blurry.

Blurry! The darkness was gone.

Elijah repeated the process in frantic motions, scratching his skin with the coarse sand in the mud. This time, when he wiped mud from his bad eye he could make out the shapes of the people and structures around him.

His eyes watered. He couldn't tell if it was all from crying, which had started when he noticed the difference in light, or if it was just the reaction of parts he hadn't used in so long. The stirring of dead flesh. He washed his eyes once more. His vision cleared after.

Elijah blinked. He looked down at his hands. Then around. A bird hopped and skittered behind the trees a ways off. He could see a tiny red patch on its chest and the colors in its tail feathers.

Elijah fell back to his knees. This time, crying aloud, unhinged. He stayed that way a while. His chest felt light, free, as if stones had broken up from around his heart. The words of the prophet came to mind: *"To open eyes that are blind, to free captives from prison and to release from the dungeon those who sit in darkness."*

Elijah finally stood, brushing dust and clumps of mud from his cloak. He turned and stopped. The Rabbi sat on the edge of the well. He had a chunk of the chipped stone in his hands, chiseling it into something new. Elijah was stunned. The light feeling in his chest was gone. His stomach sank into the puddles.

CHAPTER 5

FALSE PROPHETS ABOUND

Saul prayed. The thunderous supplications shook his phylacteries like figs ready to fall. His arms were raised and his eyes were closed. From the carefully woven garments, all 613 fringes bolstering the seam in testament to righteousness, to the subtle knell of pharisaic bells; he looked, and felt, very much like a prophet.

He bellowed paraphrased passages of the Tanakh. Learned through strict repetition as a child, chewed over, ruminated upon so as a man he'd mastered the ability to incorporate the prophets' sentiments as his own. Now their hearts melted as hot metal, malleable with the scriptures as his hammer, beating their volition to whatever shape he desired. His skin tingled with a crowd under his spell.

A farmer asked him to pray for a wayward son. Saul wept for the boy, priming tears from a reservoir he'd dug into over the years, inexplicable apart from attributing to all the times he'd willed through the urge for tears of his own.

The man who prayed before him was a Sadducee. Funny lot, the Sadducees. Poor students who ardently claim literal translations, yet don't believe in the resurrection, afterlife, spirits, and even miracles. Wealthy and officious hypocrites. Saul heard a whisper nearby, "he prays like David." The compliment set Saul's face and ears aflame. He was certain the Sadducee heard this. The old man's consternation brought Saul considerable satisfaction.

His prayers reverberated from the walls. Once he finished, a widow fell to her knees before him. She buried her face in his garment and wept. The hag's spectacle drew attention. Saul held her face in his hands. "Ask God for mercy. Repent, and perhaps his wrath will turn from you." She nodded, sputtering a few sobs and bringing a hand to his. Saul heard coins rattle in the Tzedakah. His heart swelled. He patted the old woman along and scanned the crowd.

Saul was distinguished and meticulous in every mannerism. His face was composed of sharp angles, too precise and chiseled to allow warmth, radiating intelligence. Green eyes and wild feathered brows, along with the peculiar groove that split the center of his forehead and darkened with his mood, made sinners squirm. Saul was a head taller than almost everyone in the synagogue. He stood proudly, attributing this trait to divine favoritism. He'd been set apart from birth to study the law and the prophets. Even as a child, the rabbis would practically swoon when he recited from the Tanakh.

Saul checked his robes, adjusted the phylacteries fastened to his head and forearms, tightened the belt holding his robe in place, and began his rounds.

He made his way to a familiar face. "James, how have you been, old friend?"

"I'm well, Saul. My son is studying hard." His hands were on the boy's shoulders and his dirty face beamed. The child's face was dirty too. Saul held his revulsion, put his hands on the boy's shoulder and gave a feeble squeeze. "Much of the law has been written on his heart."

Saul's brows rose. He looked from the boy to his father. "Then I suppose he'll have no problem blessing us with the Shema." The boy did, stumbling on a part where his lisp made an endearing replacement for hearts, which made the Synagogue hum with laughter.

I could recite the entire Torah at that age.

Saul wrinkled his forehead to show he was impressed. "Out of the mouths of babes."

"My son wants to be a Pharisee."

"Oh?" Saul looked down at the boy.

"Like Simeon Bar Jonah."

Saul smiled. If he'd clenched his teeth together any harder they may have broken off and lodged in the boy's face. He left James and his son to approach an elderly man he'd known since childhood. He had favorable dealings with the Romans and a small fortune inherited from his parents. The old man's arm lurched forward, shaking. He made a few slow, labored pats on Saul's back. "It's worse, Saul. My hands." The old man put a hand to his chest, the knuckles bulbed with spots covering his sallow skin.

"Ask God to take the pain. Seek his face in your turmoil. You are in my prayers, daily."

"I'm going to see the Mashiach. He can heal me." The old man had a hopeful gleam in his rheumy eyes.

Saul's lips were straight as the horizon at sea. "The man who speaks to God as though he were a member of his family?" He made a series of clicking sounds. "A man pompous enough to declare sinners, whores no less, forgiven?" The old man's eyes dropped. Saul's lips relaxed. "My friend," continued Saul, "you've been deceived." His green eyes passed over the people around the synagogue. "Yes," he nodded, "many have been deceived by this man."

Saul turned to the crowd. "Moses gave us the law. Taught us to write it on our hearts, to chew the word as the cow grazes." He put a fist to his breast. "I've devoted my life to meditating on the Tanakh. I've followed the law stringently. All 613 precepts." He pointed to the long fringes at the end of his garment. "I've kept my eyes to heaven like a farmer hoping for rain. Waiting and studying, combing the scriptures for signs of his coming."

"He heals the invalids they bring to him." This came from an older woman leaning on a stick, whose back bent and bulged.

Saul fixed her in his gaze. The woman cowered a little, which pleased him. "You've seen this?" The woman shook her head. Saul's face appeared commiserate. "Yes, I can see why you'd want to believe such things. Tell me, can he heal your soul?"

"He's said to forgive sins."

Saul shook his head again, laughing under his breath. "A stonemason that forgives sins." His point was validated by the laughter that followed. The woman melted back into the crowd, hobbling on the staff she used.

"We are the children of Israel," added Saul. "I am a Benjaminite. Not the most prestigious of the tribes, but one of you, nonetheless. Our first king was a Benjaminite, though he fell. Jeremiah, taken into exile, was seen worthy by the most high to be his mouthpiece. We were small, yet we blessed Jacob." Saul was turning slowly as he said this, making sure to look into the eyes of as many people as possible. "The law has remained the same. Following Moses is how we show the most high our love for him. This man would have us abandon our love." Several grunts and indistinguishable words passed among the audience. "Who among us has put this prophet to the test?"

There was a pause. While future plans and schemes for political power fluttered in Saul's mind, he heard a voice say "why don't you?"

Saul's back straightened. The members of the crowd standing near the speaker shrank away. It was a man named Lucius. A butcher. His father was a gentile, his mother the daughter of a prominent Levite. He moved from Thessalonica when he was already old.

"Very well," Saul's hands went behind his back. He paced, not looking at anything in particular, a concentrated strain softened the jagged stone features in his face. "Tell me, Lucius, how do I go about testing this man?"

Lucius shifted his feet. His eyes darted around the Synagogue, as if struggling for something safe to land on. "I don't pretend to know more than I do."

"Ahh," Saul nodded. "This man, who pronounces woes on Pharisees and the everyday man. You know he commits these miracles on the sabbath? He doesn't observe the ceremonial cleansing rites? He defiled the lesser temple and called the priests harlots?"

Lucius blinked. With his eyes low, he replied, "there's so many pronouncements for a man you haven't met. That's all."

"Oh, but he's met my brethren. Hoshama Bar Joezer said he has forsaken the law of Moses, and he claims a new law has arrived."

"All I mean is if you want to test him you should be the man to do it."

"And again, how does one go about testing a prophet? This is a place to learn such things, after all." Saul watched the strength drain from Lucius's face and tried to keep his own pleasure subdued. It was in the Torah. Something a child learned at synagogue. Your father didn't teach you?" Lucius was flustered. "Oh, my apologies." If an expression could be somber and malevolent at once, the Pharisee's face embodied it. Saul motioned for the boy who'd recited the Shema. "Young man, can you tell me what the law says about testing prophets?"

The boy's gaze drifted slowly right, the way men's do when they search their memories for lost treasures. The answer glowed in his face a moment later. "If a prophet speaks in the name of the LORD and what he predicts doesn't come to pass, he is false."

Saul hooked a fist through the air, smiling. "You see-"

"But if he prophesies something bad and we repent, He can show mercy. That doesn't mean he's a false prophet."

Saul's smug expression mimicked the proud father's. "And if a prophet is proved false?"

"He shall be stoned." The boy answered as if the act were a favorite pastime among children his age.

"Ahh, Lucius," Saul waved a bony finger at the crowd. "You

could learn from this boy." He ruffled the child's hair. Lucius looked as though he'd carried a millstone up a steep and muddy hill.

"I will test this prophet." Prophet was pronounced with sour disgust. "I hope you'll bring the stones, Lucius."

Saul stayed and spoke of the state of affairs in Israel. The Roman occupation, the temple, a recent outbreak sweeping over Galilee. And of course, more about the false prophet. The crowd thinned some time later. Some stayed to talk with Saul about personal dilemmas or ask for the interpretations of difficult passages. The boy and his father were among the last to leave. After everyone was gone, Saul picked up the Tzedakah to load onto his ass, which he'd affectionately named Balaam.

A Pharisee must set an example for the children of Israel. When among the people, Saul's behavior was always exemplary. He moved in an even temperament. Reproached sin when he saw it. Sniffed it out when suspected. Sin was the scourge of Israel. David, Soloman, Aaron-so many of the great prophets failed in their obedience to the most high. And how would his people fare any different without guidance? The true meaning of the Tanakh was his to wield in the fight against these new schools of thought. The Sadducees and their maligned views of the afterlife, that stone mason pretending to heal lepers, charming his fanatics and sending them about to plague the rest of Israel.

Saul knew that, like him, this man claiming to be Mashiach had to have ulterior motives. *Miracles.* How had he done it? He'd met men–smart men–who vouched for the miracles he performed. The teachings were radical. What self respecting Jew could believe the law had changed?

He'd made a commitment to follow everything Moses prescribed. And he did, in public. What he did in private was his business. Perhaps the thing that infuriated him most was that he hadn't thought of it. *Changing the law. Ha!*

Mashiach. The Son of David, the anointed, chosen of God. Why couldn't Saul be such a man? God granted him the propensity to learn and memorize with such ease, but providence had directed him to the dark corners of Israel's forgotten villages. A father with a hand of stone and a mother with a stomach made of wineskin. Saul wasn't from Judah. That was why it was the stone mason–or rather, why people believed his claim. This Jesus was from a pockmark in his country's soil. Nazareth. Saul had been. The Seraphs can smell Nazareth's shit from the firmament. And this young and ugly man whose reputation hasn't diminished, though he deals with whores and gentiles (at least the Pharisees and scribes had the sense not to do this in public), he was fortunate enough to be born into the same tribe as David. It wasn't fair.

Saul mouthed an apology, eyes oriented above him. *Where is your blessing, Addonai? your face I've sought.* Though he toiled, wrestled every jot and tittle, scoured the scrolls of his fathers for the truth in the prophets, he would never be more than a teacher to peasants. He'd never sit on the Sanhedrin.

Saul went to the Tzedakah, shook, smiled at the coin's song. Money certainly elevated his mood. The widow had played her part. Lucius and James's boy were an added bonus. With this maybe he'd finally have enough to build that addition for Netanya. The retaining wall and excavations would be costly. Getting the stones down the hill was another problem altogether. But if he had that built for her, maybe then she'd give him some peace.

Saul thought about the stone mason, this supposed Mashiach. Perhaps he could be hired to build the additions to his house. *That would humble him.*

Saul smiled, mind in another place, fantasizing of leaning against his new retaining wall and criticizing the stone mason's handiwork. "Where did you study the Tanakh?" he asks. "What did Malachi say about tithing?" He questioned the false prophet. Asked how his friend the baptist was.

Tugs on his robe cut the fantasy short. He flinched slightly, and turned to the black gaps of the widow's smile. Her breath seeped through so foul he was surprised he couldn't see little trails of yellow smoke. By now the sun was low, the shadows thin fangs stretching from the objects that gave them life. Baalam brayed as Saul led the woman briskly into the shadows by the arm.

"What do you want?" His voice a harsh whisper.

"What you promised!"

"Keep it down, you old bat."

"Bat?" The widow laughed, closer to lunacy than anything akin to real humor. "The bats are the people who believe your pig fodder. What's in those phylacteries, you bony bastard, the last mites of all the grandmothers you've swindled?"

"Shut your mouth or you won't get so much as a shekel."

"And when this matter meets other ears?"

"You'll get your coin, woman. But if you keep approaching me here you'll ruin it for both of us."

"I need to buy oil." Her lower lip hung out and she slapped lightly at the seam of his robe.

Saul snickered. An ugly sound, how a rat would laugh. "With how many coins I've given you over the last few months you should be selling oil outside of the temple."

"I hear you're paying me less and spending more on harlots."

Saul snatched her arm and the widow yelped. "Here." He shoved some coins in her hand. I don't want to see your pruned face anymore." He shoved her, she toppled over and grunted. "Owwww!" She howled.

"Shut up."

She tightened her lips and counted the coins. "This isn't what we agreed on." She looked up, seething.

Saul shrugged. "We don't always get what we want, do we?"

"I'm going to tell everyone here what you had me do." The old woman spat and rubbed her face. "Charlatan. You won't be able to enter a synagogue in a gentile territory when I'm done with you." She spat again. "Pharisee."

"This is what I get for trying to help you." Saul's eyes, stern and malevolent, made the woman crawl backwards. He advanced. She tried to turn, but he pushed her down with his foot. Through sobs and choked whimpers, she pleaded with him. Saul cornered her into a narrow space beside the synagogue. There he found a large rock. The woman had risen to her knees. He raised the boulder and threw it once she started to run. It struck high on her back.

"I've got your coin, bitch." Saul brought his foot down sharply, satisfied by the protest her bones made. "I'll be damned if some shekel chasing whore sullies my reputation." The woman groaned as he raised the boulder.

The holy man did his work there in the recesses beside the synagogue. Balaam helped carry the Tzedakah and their former accomplice back to where they'd come from.

CHAPTER 6

LAMBS FOR THE SLAUGHTER

Petra cringed. The underbrush was thick, twisting with thin branches and littered with bits of crunching dry wood. Two of his sheep were missing. They were hungry, and would likely continue to wander while his anger simmered and his voice grew hoarse.

Every twig that broke replayed a fraction of his childhood nightmare. His worst memory, which also happened to be the earliest. In it, he's running toward the open door, the sunlight outside's a blinding white square. His brother's cry startles him. If Petra hadn't stopped, things may have been different. His mother might have smiled more with two broken sons than she had after Aaron. Aaron and their father were on the roof, trying to patch the thatching for the next time it rained.

The snap is a clear, horrible sound, like dead timber breaking in the path of a bear. Aaron's a step beyond the threshold, contorted. A wounded bird. The afternoon's so bright his blood glistens as it muddies the sand. Petra sees his older brother and vomits. Some splashes on his leg. It shouldn't matter, but to Petra, this somehow makes him culpable. Aaron doesn't notice. Never notices anything again. His mother screams. Petra's pushed into the wall as she runs by.

He hears that snap over and over now, in small maddening measures. Sees it happening.

Crack. Aaron? Snap. Are you alright? No sheep. A bird screeched and sounded like his mother's cry.

Focus.

Petra pushed through dead vegetation. The dry branches bent, some broke, some scratched his face once he'd let go and they whipped back to their original positions.

The foulness in the air made him spit. Probably animal carcasses nearby. Gnarled branches warned with invalid fingers. He was off the path, but there were tracks a ways back through the crushed leaves. They were round, and if it was a track, it may have been cloven. Hard to tell. He pushed on, angry at himself for leaving his staff. For losing his sheep.

The smell pressed at the back of his throat, threatening to summon his breakfast. He took shallow breaths, in and out through the nose.

Petra heard something. For a moment he thought it sounded like the bleat of a lamb in pain, and heat surged through his chest. He straightened up like a startled doe. *Bleating? No. Not lambs, more shrill. Dogs?* That wasn't it either. He moved the naked branches of a bush aside, tearing its roots from the loose sand. Squeals? Maybe it *was* one of his lambs, caught in a thicket like Abraham's.

He listened for a moment, canting his head, statue still. The skin on his face itched from whatever insect's legs explored his cheeks.

Snorts?

Petra pushed forward, oblivious to the branches tearing garment and skin. The dead trees shook and pieces broke away as he trudged up the hill. Snorts, squeals, grunts, clearer as he climbed. The smell an ember of sulfur lodged in his nostrils.

He made it to the top in a sheen of sweat, making no effort to quiet his steps. It was hard to see through the underbrush. Barren branches and scorched bark made the dead trees look like piles of charred bones. It thinned out a little as he walked on. He stopped when he caught movement. A pink and white mass passed between jagged branches. One of his sheep. *They took the wool?*

He rushed forward, ignoring the twigs and branches. A shepherd protects his flock at all costs. If only he'd brought the staff. There were tiny cuts all over his exposed skin, his heart beat violently, pounding in his temples. Pink and purple masses crept through a gap in the dry foliage. The stench filled his throat.

Petra broke through to the clearing and gasped. Tufts of bloody wool covered the ground. Bloated pink bodies lay in heaps over one another. Lying about, sleeping. Some walking. A small group was gathered around a bloody mass. Their snouts tore and shook the flesh free with furious motions. Wool rained, bloody patches of clouds falling. A chorus of insects swarmed from the pig's festering bodies. They looked…no, it couldn't be…

Petra stepped back, reaching his arm out for the same tree he was just leaning against. His head spinning. When he reached for the trunk he missed, fell back, and landed on a broken branch jutting from a downed tree.

Pain seared through his back. The pigs devouring his lambs squealed when they noticed him. Squeals and scurrying hooves advanced. Petra screamed.

CHAPTER 7

TRAVELERS

They wait in the trees. Their flesh withered parchment, cloy with death's scent. Naked branches tremble in their presence. God had forgotten this place. Where cloven feet tread.

Down the southern road, matted with dry blood and crawling with lice, Bazumel devised ways to fill his wicked cup. Irises set in ossuary squares peered at the world, the surrounding eye dark as dying sleep. His horns extended past the back of his skull. Being this creature's host was better.

Marduhl inhabited a new body as well. The shepherd who came for the lambs. The torso was wrapped like a child's swaddle to keep the organs from spilling. One of them tore the cheek before Bazumel stopped them. The young man's screams were invigorating. He enjoyed hearing him beg for his life. Marduhl was happy to be the proprietor of such mercy. He was asked inside, with some guidance, after the shepherd surrendered.

They made an odd pair. Traversing the country road searching for suitable subjects. People with position. Power. Susceptible minds. Most of their companions still roamed the Earth as swine.

"Marduhl, you must do something about your face."

Marduhl felt his cheek, dabbed the spot with his fingers and inspected them for blood. The dark globs of dried blood resembled chunks of raspberries in the beard of a messy eater. "What can I do?"

"That flap of skin, for one. Do you suppose anyone will stop if your face scares their children away?" Marduhl shrugged. After prodding around a bit, he found the flap of skin and tore it away, tossing it to the ground like a dead leaf. Bazumel bleated and rammed him in the thigh. Marduhl's legs went out from under him. He tumbled down the little bank sloping up to the road. "You idiot, I can see your jaw through your cheek."

Bazumel hopped down the bank and stood over Marduhl. His nostrils flared, hooves scraped the ground as if preparing to charge again.

"You said to do something about it," Marduhl whined.

"I didn't say to carve another socket."

"We just need a body."

"Just need a body." Bazumel spat, then shook his head violently, thrashing horns through the air. "We can't settle on corpses. You're falling apart. The others are festering and a village will smell them 10 furlongs away. We need meat that lasts. Willing recipients."

"Where do we find those?"

"We find the dejected. The hopeless and forlorn are simple enough. Clay in our hands." Marduhl looked at Bazumel's cloven feet. "Focus, fool." The goat feigned to charge. Marduhl flinched and covered his face. "Sad is easy, angry better."

Bazumel hopped up, left then right in a diagonal path up the bank. Marduhl climbed slowly, trying to gain traction as he did. Bazumel looked down, watching him. "You remember the story?"

"Yes, yes."

"We'll make it work."

Later they came upon two men in a cart pulled by a weak looking ox. Bazumel bleated. Marduhl limped along, twisting his face in a snarl to be convincing.

"Peace," called the man from the other side of the road. His ox stood its ground, bellowing and shaking its head back and forth.

"Picccs," Marduhl returned. This earned a subtle thud from Bazumel's horns. "I'm only having fun."

The cart was filled with wares. Its wheels squeaked too loud to hear most of what was said until they came near. One of the travelers was an enormous man with a bulbous nose, red flames for a beard, and a brickish forehead. The other was older, his ears drooped along the side of a comical, exaggerated face that looked to be partly melted. "Are you ok?" asked the big one. The cart rose when he climbed out.

"There were some bandits a ways back. They took our cart, all of our supplies. We've been on the road for many days. We have nothing left."

"I'm Shem," said the old one. He'd climbed off and came around the other side while his friend waddled over. "My friend is Abijah." He nodded, wheezing as he approached.

"I'm Petra."

"Are you bleeding?" asked Abijah.

Marduhl shook his head. "One of the men struck me with a goad." He held the tool in his hand, raising it to show the weapon responsible. They'd stolen it from a farm farther back. Bazumel decided to lather it in blood. They'd laughed about the surprise they left the farmers."I bled for a long time, but it stopped. Many have passed but none have offered to help."

Shem shook his head. "How the children of Israel have strayed."

"You must be tougher than you look," said Abijah. "I'm surprised you managed to wrestle that free."

"They had me cornered. If Bazu-" Marduhl paused. Bazumel's head whipped up from the grass he was eating to glare at Marduhl. Marduhl flinched, playing it off like it was pain. "Baza. If Baza hadn't charged I'd be dead."

"He's covered with blood," said the old man.

"He gored one of them with his horns."

Both men looked the goat over. "Baza, ey? Your name may be hateful, but you're a good boy." Abijah went over and scratched under the goat's chin. Bazumel's teeth clacked loudly and Abijah snatched his hand away. "Bathsheeba's tits!" he brought his knuckle to his mouth, already bleeding.

Marduhl slapped Bazumel on the hindquarters. The goat turned and Marduhl stepped back before the teeth took the nose from his new face. "You're horrible," said Marduhl. He smiled and wiped his hands. "He's wary of strangers now. He's been through a lot in the last few days."

"All is well," said Shem. "I see why you named him such a thing. And Abijah should know better than to put his hands near an animal's mouth he's never met." He turned to his companion and frowned, then back to the man and goat before him. "Poor Baza's coat's stained with those men's blood." Bazumel's head was low, eyeing the old man. "I know better than to venture on petting you, boy." Shem put his hands on his knees. "Baaa-zaaa." Bazumel huffed and bleated back, lowering his head and kicking dirt behind him with his hind leg. Shem laughed. "I don't think he likes my goat voice."

"Enough talk," said Abijah. Let's get you to someone that can help you. Then we'll feed the beasts. Men's knuckles aren't a fitting meal for goats." He looked at his hand. Then held it up to show Bazumel. Bazumel turned and sniffed along the side of the road. Abijah scratched his head. "If I didn't know better, I'd think your goat just rolled his eyes at me."

"I hope you're not hurt badly," said Marduhl.

"I don't think I'm in any position to complain, seeing the state you're in. If you could see your face, my friend, you'd bless the most high you were alive." Shem brought strips of linen to wrap around Abijah's hand. By the time he finished the material was already soaked red.

They moved some of their things aside. As Marduhl and Bazumel approached the cart their ox kicked his feet and bellowed.

"What's gotten into her?" asked Shem, grabbing the reins. The ox had to be beaten to get Marduhl near the cart. Bazumel walked beside them. Marduhl had a rope tied around the goat's neck. After they'd gone down the road a ways, Abijah started singing. Marduhl groaned.

"Surely, my voice isn't that bad?" Abijah laughed. A few minutes later he was singing again. This time, Bazumel rammed the side of the cart. The items they'd packed rattled.

"It must be bad," said Shem. "Even Baza hates it."

"He hates everything," said Abijah. They both laughed at this. Marduhl moaned and Abijah patted his leg, still singing.

"We'll be there in a few hours. Just lie back and imagine you're following Moses out of Egypt. Marduhl winced and groaned louder. "We'll get you to someone that can patch you up, good as new."

The song continued. For the man and goat, the words conjured awful memories. Salt sprinkled over sore wounds.

Who is like you—

majestic in holiness,

awesome in glory,

working wonders?

Halfway through the song, Shem joined in. Their voices rose, singing like drunkards. Marduhl clenched the handle of the goad. He squeezed, then released. Bazumel bleated to get his attention. Marduhl fumed, muttering obscenities under his breath. Bazumel rammed the cart again.

Shem turned his head. The goat was close to the cart, bearing teeth. The animal made strange noises that sounded almost like whispers. If Shem didn't know any better, he'd think the goat was reprimanding his master. The man was clearly in pain. Abijah's voice was cracking and terrible. His wasn't much better. The goat made guttural, and sometimes human like sounds.

Abijah let out a cry, then gurgled. Shem turned, "What's going on back the–" the sharp end of the goad jutted from high on Abijah's chest.

"Shut your filthy mouth!" Abijah fell forward. Marduhl had a foot on Abijah's back, tearing the goad free with a sucking sound. Abijah wheezed and twitched as blood puddled beneath him. Marduhl raised the goad and brought it down again. He pulled it free and stared at Shem

Shem prayed. Opening and closing his mouth while trembling at the sight before him.

"Fool! You can't control yourself long enough to get anything done." Shem couldn't believe what he heard. The goat had spoken like a man. "I should have brought Sanayel!"

"Saneyel's incompetent. That idiot would have left you at the farm and headed straight to a brothel. Or sodomized these idiots! I can't sit and listen while my enemy is championed before me."

Shem leaned back against the front of the cart. "E-e-enemies of God. Ashmedai!"

Marduhl laughed. "No. But I know him. He did a good number on you gullible clumps, making you think he was a king."

Shem brought his leg over the side to flee and fell.

"Where are you going?" said Marduhl, still laughing. "We require strapping bodies for the revolution." He stood on the cart with one foot on Abijah's back and the goad toward the air like a flag that lost its banner. His head was to the sky, laughing in shrill, sickening cackles.

Shem stood, clutching his chest.

"Marduhl, you'll give this withered corpse a heart attack."

Shem turned and ran.

The goat tore around the other side of the cart, kicking up dust. The old man pumped his arms. Before he got very far, Bazumel took his legs from under him. Shem flailed his arms and rolled over the goat's back. He laid moaning.

Bazumel brought his mouth to Shem's ear. "We'll make good use of those old bones." Marduhl had hopped down from the cart, now standing over the old man. Shem tried to crawl away and Bazumel rammed him in the side. The old man felt the bones in his ribs give. Marduhl winced at the sound.

CHAPTER 8

THE BLEAK SHADE OF DREAMS

At times the screams we make in nightmares seep into the waking world.

Elijah woke with shallow, shuddering breaths. His sweat shimmered in the moonlight. He looked around, relieved to be alone for that pathetic moan. The guilt was still with him, tangible, weighty as a millstone resting on his chest. He swiped spikes of hay from his beard and hair and wrapped himself in his tunic as his breathing slowed.

Something to do with the Rabbi. Visions? Seraphim? No. Profane imposters of the beings Ezekiel and Isaiah saw. The fear they described was certainly present, that same knee wobbling terror the prophets suffered, vibrating through his spine like the pluck of a chorded instrument; God's finger strumming notes of horror. Or was this guilt? Was he paranoid enough for such things to haunt his thinking? Maybe his base nature, that which should reflect the divine image–had cracked. He was now covered with filth and beyond recognition.

Elijah shook his head. How pretentious to assume prophecy would fill the dreams of a dejected soul. There were no burning bushes for this shepherd, no ram in the thicket to substitute the required sacrifice. His eyes were healed only to see the horrors of sheol. And his stiff neck would spur him to insanity.

Thinking of what he'd seen in the dream made that millstone heavier. Flames, splashes of burning liquid so prevalent in the dream, ash as loose and pervasive as dust–acrid in his nostrils still. He rummaged through his bag for the cloth Salome gave him. Held it to his mouth and breathed her in.

Elijah could make out things in the dark now. His acuteness of vision made his healing worse, bonded him to his waywardness and inability to follow. He'd spurned the gift. Wasn't responsible enough–no, strong enough, to handle the consequences that went along with what was done for him. To him. Now the hole inside grew and ate its way outward. To such a man, every blessing's a bitterness, joys are soured. Soon, the hole would engulf him, and he'd numb to those feelings distinguishing man from beast.

He brought the cloth to his face, smothering his mouth and nose, inhaling deep. Her scent. His heart began to settle. It brought shame now, too. Made the hole inside pulse, call out to consume him.

Through the gaps in the ransacked structure he'd taken shelter in, the moon was large and bright. Shadows fell through the cracks. The shapes and patterns stabbed into the planes they fell on, like angry scribbles from a child's hand. Their fractured and jagged lines took on the forms of the things in his nightmare. Something scurried across the floor and brushed his leg. He started a scream–but caught and subdued the sound in his throat. It was low, too weak to register to anyone else and choked by the whine of wind through the gaps in the wall before him.

He could still see the eyes. Burned into his vision like the sun becoming a blue and green blur after your eyes close. It was vivid. The eyes everywhere. Gashes that blinked with red and gold irises, each capable of looking in independent directions, closing to make the skin smooth. Wings extended from knobs on their spines. As many wings as a spider had legs, he thought. He didn't count. They were black, solid things, with flecks of gold peeking through where they weren't charred. Their bodies sleek, supple, sinewy. Dexterous hands that tore at him and pulled flesh from his body like cooked meat. And faces. A man's, a pig, a lunatic goat. In the nightmare, his body healed almost as quickly as they tore his flesh, and they continued the process again and again.

Elijah put his face into the cloth and wept. An ugly, pitiful sound. Even the wailers attending a funeral procession would scowl at him.

He didn't have a clue what to do, no ambitions to return home. He feared the inevitable confrontation with Salome. Dreaded the thought of carrying on his life as though she didn't exist.

Was the nightmare a threat of some kind? Is this what would happen if he went back to her? He caught the scent again and longed for her.

The Rabbi had been waiting by the well. He didn't say much. Didn't need to. Elijah fell to his knees before the man, just as he'd vowed not to, assured himself he was beyond. He cried harder than he ever had.

Then the Rabbi, this Jesus, had warned him. He told him the Kingdom of Heaven was costly. Sometimes, he said, he wished people had never heard these tidings. For these, It would be better if they'd never existed. The stonemason told Elijah though his vision was better than ever now, he was blinder than he'd ever been.

The holy men always speak in riddles.

Maybe the Rabbi was right. He wished more than anything to feel like he did before. Now that he knew all this, going back to Salome would come with a burden. A burden, he thought, too heavy to bear. Being with her. He would think of the blessing he would miss out on. Leaving her to join the Rabbi and the others would only leave him with a new hole growing, in the shape of Salome's laugh. A wound curved in the crescent of her smile.

The part that confused him more than anything was that deep down, where subtle intuitions steered a man from his core, he understood he belonged with Salome. But the rabbis and Pharisees, every teacher of the Tanakh, taught not to trust in feelings. What does Addonai say? It was funny really, in a depressing sort of way.

A few days ago he thought he would be blind soon, and would be forced to live alone in darkness thereafter. Things were less confusing then.

Miserable and sorry for himself, he sat in the darkness until the blues and greys of dawn cleared. Then he rose, dusted off his things and walked. Still far from home. Drifting. Alive, but in many ways, already feeling quite dead.

CHAPTER 9

MUSINGS OF THE UNCLEAN

The things in the pigs grew restless. Their clearing, once flourishing, now laid waste with moribund vegetation. Fragments of fallen trees redolent with death. Its scent, its presence, its intention. Belphegor inhabited a porcine body weighing nearly 17 talents. He laid on his side, the great belly rising and falling, flesh succumbing to the slow devourer, decay.

Before their fall, Belphegor was a being of importance. An agent of the most high's wrath. His happiest times were spent wielding a blade that laid waste to fields of men with single strokes. The ash that rained after! Piles, smeared into rock and floating like dark motes. Embers of the half thought shapes of men crumbled in his wake. Belphegor was a proud messenger. His genius now languished in the body of this snarling obesity.

Some of the lesser creatures were still called upon to disrupt or confuse. Whether peasants or the will of leaders, this was their primary use now. When *THEY* needed something done that required deceit or malice to complete. Confuse the tongues of this ruler, put it in the fool's heart to murder his subordinates, muster a spirit of ambition so he'll kill the king and inherit the throne. Such subterfuge wasn't appropriate for *HIS* noble messengers.

God remains righteous after sending the wicked to do wicked things.

Belphegor was conflicted. He didn't care for Bazumel's plans. But he was a part of this, even if his portion was begrudgingly executed. Second in command of a festering pig brigade. A proud Centurion in the legion of swine. Snorts leavened his laughter. One of the pigs nearby raised his head, something like a grin turned the snout. Belphegor snarled, "keep ogling, I'll make you my concubine. Over one of these logs you'll squeal like a pig really birthed you." The other pig huffed, then turned away and lowered its head again.

Belphegor inhabited the body of a large sow that had just given birth. The one he chided didn't know he lacked the tools to carry out these threats.

He'd made this discovery a few days earlier. A group of piglets (the least of their ranks were forced to possess the infants of the herd) began to suckle while he slept. He drove them off, barking, cursing demon and maker. But a moment after they dispersed, the brutes were prancing, squealing, pressing shoulders into the dead brush, where they rocked to scratch their putrid backs. *Pigs shall be pigs.* Belphegor sighed, lowering his head. His jowls bubbled out to the sides under his weight. He soon flopped over and dozed again.

Belphegor woke once more to tugging. He grunted, swinging his head side to side. When he went to roll his girth so he could stand, he crushed one of the piglets. Some foreign sense of worry passed through him. This fading maternal sensitivity revulsed him. In his exhausted state he toppled back over. Two of the little ones were still attached. Belphegor pondered on the base needs of all living things. They needed food. Therefore, they needed the provider of food. The humans, but even more so Belphegor's kind, needed purpose. An impish trick from underhanded providence. While thinking these things over, he found the release of milk provided a rush of warmth. Calmed him. Settled the mind.

Now, he laid still. Allowing the least among them to feed. "Not so much damn teeth."

"Looks like you'd be the one bent over a log, Belphegor." Snide as ever, Abaddon trotted down the slope. Snorts and squeals from the others welcomed his arrival. Some perked up and pretended to be diligent, especially the sentries. "You'd do well bearing children, at least. Tell me old friend, how are you at making bread?"

"You scour the dregs of humor Abaddon. I don't care anymore. Mongrels need to feed and I think clearly with them at the teat."

"You've fallen smoothly into your new habitation. The accuser would be most displeased."

Belphegor's tail rose and fell again. "When is he not displeased?"

"You'd defy him, Belphegor?" Abaddon's eyes had a gleeful spark. "I must say, I didn't figure you for the rebellious type."

"You forget from where you've fallen, Abaddon."

"Ahh, and I thought we fell with him."

"And what will he do if I defy him? Torment me for eternity?" Belphegor let out another high pitched squeal of laughter. He shot a glance at the pig he threatened earlier.

"Fair point." Abaddon approached Belphegor and plopped his fat belly down beside him. "I think Bazumel has some fun in store for us."

"Fun?" The sow's jowls shook. "Hard to beat self mutilation in a cave. Something about the sounds of bats that stir the insides."

Abaddon laid next to his friend in silence. After some time he looked over. "You've been thinking of *THEM*."

"Ha! You're omniscient now."

"I see it in your eyes. It's natural to think of that time fondly, it is what we were made for."

Belphegor raised his head. An ear twitched. "Supposedly."

"Meaning?"

"What should be clear is our real purpose. We made our decision to rebel because *THEY* designed it so. In as much as he made the accuser beautiful, he gave him unsurpassed wit, with no humility to balance. Pure genius and unbridled vanity. He led us to the lake of fire, skipping. As designed."

Abbadon rose on his front legs. "You're saying I had no part in my rebellion?"

"Do *THEY* control all things or not?"

"I have thoughts. I feel."

"Who gave you that mind? Your true body?" Abaddon didn't say anything. "It was decreed before the foundations of the world, before the first of us came forth singing their praises."

"So they intended for us to defy them?"

"Abaddon," Belphegor chuckled softly, the way a patient parent would a child. "Was it ever really much of a fight?"

Abaddon blinked. Looked down. "No."

Belphegor brought up his front legs and rolled over. The piglets squealed as the weight of his ample belly rolled onto them.

Abaddon still had his eyes on the ground. "Why would *THEY* make me just to suffer?" The contempt was evident in his voice. The muffled squeals of piglets continued.

"Glory. It's all glory. Satan is supposedly the proud one. Yet *THEY* condescend to the levels of mortals, just to rise again and hear praises. Besides, you know what will be written. We're but clay, Abaddon. Some clay is made for destruction, some to be instruments of *HIS* glory. We're clay just like the others. It doesn't matter how the pottery shines."

Belphegor laid back down. The piglets adjusted. He wasn't angry. There was an apathy inside, beyond caring or being offended, beyond feeling. The realization that his entire existence was subservient to the professed attributes of another, and that somehow, despite how ugly and unfair this was, and it was, *HE, THEY,* that confusing mixture of personalities encompassing one, would remain blameless for their crimes against him. Belphegor had known this for a long time. He looked at his friend, lost in grief himself, and felt the closest thing a demon could to pity. He decided to play his part. To join Bazumel's cause with more than mere ascent.

"I know the way you feel," said Belphegor. Abaddon raised his head. "I realized all this after the rats were taken to Babylon. Who do you think poisoned the King's head to kill Zedekiah's sons and sear his eyes after he watched? That fool still wanders the abyss blind, groping and calling his sons' names. I used to mimic their voices calling for help and laugh as he wandered in circles. It makes you wonder why he was made. Why anything at all was made."

"I remember that well. There was much use for us then."

"There will be use for us again." Belphegor stood. A few piglets fell, some still clung to the teat, legs kicking. "I will be a sword in the mouth of liars. Blades in a hornets nest."

"I'm glad you're with us, old friend. Could you talk to Bazumel? He's much too proud to admit it, but we could use your mind."

Belphegor grunted. "I'll see what I can do. For your sake. Yours alone."

Abaddon rolled on his back, legs bent over him. He rolled and used the twigs and wood to scratch himself. "It's good to have powerful friends."

CHAPTER 10

THE WAYWARD PHARISEE

Saul scraped his brow with the back of his sleeve. His mind pondered proverbs about slothfulness, toil, the poor and those that prosper. The spade's crisp stabs in the soil and the shush of pebbles supplied a slow rhythm in the heat.

It was the sabbath. Work was strictly forbidden on these days, and Pharisees, especially sticklers for the law like him, were held to standards beyond what most dogmatic men considered reasonable. Some of his friends tied ropes around their waists to keep from traveling past the 2000 cubits permitted on the sabbath.

But Saul's work was necessary. That old bitch, who'd really been quite effective while they worked together, while she knew her place, would have exposed everything. His main concern was if anyone saw. He held a stirring animosity for the woman even now. Blamed her for his Sabbath errands.

He wasn't very concerned about upholding the law anymore. Not in private. He didn't pray much while he was alone either. There's a hardness of heart a man develops when he goes against what he professes. The rigors of life, his perpetual sense of failure, the Sanhedrin's disapproving vitriol, his wife... He was tired.

Saul packed the dirt over the top of the mound and smoothed it out. Ignorant of how shallow the grave was and what kind of scavengers it would attract. Not that it mattered, no one would miss her. And no one would wander this far into his property. Even if scavengers found the widow and dug up her severed remains, his servants would tell him respectfully, subtly. They'd mention soil depths perhaps.

If Saul were to tell the truth--to anyone, a concept that seemed like a novelty for at least the last ten years–he didn't want anything to do with the law, the Sanhedrin, this nascent craze over the Mashiach.

Or God, for that matter.

Saul had been a faithful Pharisee his entire life. Days spent in diligent prayer and memorization, meditations on the Torah and the prophets. He'd taught Jacob, sweet inquisitive Jacob, all he knew. Saul's first wife died giving birth. The boy saved him from sorrow. The two were inseparable. Studying by candlelight, traveling for the passover, meetings with the elders. When he was eight, Jacob recited the blessings and curses, Ebal and Gerazim, verbatim. He'd like to see James's son try that.

They were happy. *Were* happy.

Old Soloman once said, "there's nothing new under the sun." Apt and quaint and wonderfully glib. Since a child, death had been a distant relative, the type that stopped by at the most inconvenient times, whose cold fingers clamped around those he cherished.

Memories were all he had now. Something he focused on now, allowed to seep into his pores and take root in his heart. The anger he felt now began its slow kindle, added to with every misfortune, every disappointment poured from his bitter cup. Until rage against his fellow man, against Pharisees, against the law he'd squandered his life for, and against God Himself, all rose in the pyre of his heart, consuming an effigy of Jacob and offering a column of black smoke that spoke to him like the Tabernacle clouds in the tent of meeting.

Just before Passover, some years ago now, he'd been meditating on the goodness of El Loheim, how he was but a sheep in His pasture, resigned to be content with his lot in life. He went to the field, calling for his son. Past the wine press, past where the greedy nag was buried presently. "Jacob," he called. "Jacob!" Saul walked to the tall grass in the back of his lot. He covered his mouth when he saw him. Stained rags. Eyes open. The hair Saul's fingers ran through while he told him stories was streaked and clustered with dried blood. He'd been run down by a bull. When Saul happened upon his body, the flies were already spreading word of the banquet.

And for a while, attribute it to faith, that deep and unwavering naivety, Saul still loved his God. He cried to the Lord like David, day and night. As it were, Simeon, that coiled serpent masked in friendly smiles, dealt the final blow. Saul was slate–no, destined–to join the greater Sanhedrin. After his wife and son, it was his last hope at accounting for something. Something more than a local Pharisee policing nearby villagers for violating the Torah. He wanted to make them proud, to one day see their happy faces in Sheol, join them in the resurrection with a life that had mattered.

Simeon began the discord. *Saul was not mentally fit. Saul was incompetent with the scriptures. Saul's mind, after losing so much, couldn't handle the responsibility of joining their ranks.* Set in his ways, Simeon brought the matter to the Levites.

Humiliation does little to convey the sentiments those events produced. He brought a healthy goat, an ox, and several doves to be sacrificed. As was custom. The Nasi, that sniveling idiot, broke the news. Saul of course could stay with the local Sanhedrin, let his talent and knowledge spoil in obscurity. But he was not fit for the ranks of the 71. Maybe later, if he stayed faithful, and one of the members moved on.

Simeon accused Saul of pilfering alms from the Tzedakah. Not overtly, his claim was subtle, more an allusion to Saul's public perception. Saul was rich because he, like his father, was shrewd and industrious. After the loss of his son, he found new ways to spend his time. His standing prayers and stern preaching earned him reputable esteem. He began teaching the Law for a sick rich man who housed orphans near Capernaum. Saul had grown fond of many of the children. Then the man died, and his widow eloped with a legionnaire whose service had ended. They left for Damascus without a word. The orphans were sold to Romans. With this loss, Saul's heart finally withered. He'd been blamed, in an indirect way. Simeon convinced his Sanhedrin associates Saul's lack of oversight all but delivered the children to the hands of sodomites.

Gossip cuts through the land in many inlets. Simeon made a worthy adversary.

After Jacob, Saul preached for a purse. Without moral quibble. Saul felt he'd given enough. And since then he'd made a fair pile of shekels over the years.

He'd learned life could be enjoyable apart from the law. If only for the brief pleasures his actions provided. Thinking fate was dictated by divine plan made his suffering an intolerable and volatile throb, slowly rising. His contempt was a seed planted in the same soil as Jacob's grave. The bull was slaughtered, of course. Not as a sacrifice, privately. He'd slit the throat and watched its pitiful measure of intelligence drain from its eyes.

It was his right to get something back. This God, the God of Abraham, Isaac, David, who delighted in bull after bull, goat, dove, slaughtered and scorched for His pleasure. *Sacrifice.* What about Jacob? Was his life a pleasing aroma? Leave a man alone to brood after stripping him of everything that matters, and what do you expect? The time neared for others to sacrifice. Saul would facilitate. Perhaps Simeon had something pleasing enough for his LORD. He seemed fond of that pretty little wife.

Saul was smiling now. There were big things coming for him.

If only he knew just how big.

CHAPTER 11

FATHER AND SON

James walked the road with his son. The wonders they'd seen remained lucid, the Mashiach's voice triumphant in their minds. As they walked he tested the boy's knowledge of the Torah and prophets and quoted the respected commentators. Ephron answered, never raising his head from a branch he peeled in his hands.

He loved him.

Blurred heat rose on the horizon from dark shapes that looked like rocks.

"What is it papa?"

James smiled. "A portal."

"What if we walk into it?"

"We'll go somewhere else." Ephron stopped. James looked back, laughed. "By the time we reach that spot it will move somewhere else," said James. "He leads our way."

"What if we catch it?"

"We'd see signs and wonders."

"We already have."

James nodded.

Ephron walked with his head down, still picking at the branch. "But do you think it goes anywhere?"

James shrugged and ruffled Ephron's hair. The spot where the road faded into haze began to sharpen. Something was up there. They couldn't make out what, but it appeared to be moving. The desert did this from time to time. Even in fertile areas, when the sun is right, the whole land can reflect as though it were water. It gets a man seeing things. James was seeing things now.

He thought of the wisdom he'd heard from his son a moment before. *Anything was possible.* Ephron was remarkable. Every son is remarkable in his father's eyes, of course, but even the Pharisee Saul agreed. And that curmudgeon even denounced the man James saw heal a leper. He shuddered to think of the danger one must subject himself to in criticizing God's anointed. The Rabbi had said something interesting: *He who has ears to hear, let him hear.* Perhaps Saul just didn't have the ears.

After Saul denounced the man, James resolved to find out for himself. It proved well beyond expectations, and he was looking forward to another talk with the man. James would convince the Pharisee the stonemason was the coming one.

The road ahead sloped down gradually. The blur spread and broke over the shapes on the ground, lost under the high sun. He ignored his gut, pushed childish notions aside.

"Are they closer?"

"It's an illusion, Ephron. The light will do that when it's bright enough."

"Something's moving, Abba."

The boy was right. The bright haze still engulfed the end of the slope where the hill flattened out. They walked farther and everything shifted. What he'd thought were rocks came alive with movement, breaking apart, distinguishing themselves and pulsing as a mass of collected things, still partially obfuscated in the heat.

The ground trembled under their feet.

"You smell that, Abba?" Ephron covered his nose.

He did. The stench of livestock, intermingled with something spoiled. Meat. Death.

"Abba! They're pigs!"

James couldn't yet tell. Age had warped his sight. Ephron tugged at his father's cloak, hopping up and down. "There's men too. And a goat! A white goat! Why do they smell so bad, Abba? There's so many pigs."

He saw them now. Dead sprint, grains of sand winking in the plumes billowing behind them. A multitude of swine, stepping forth from their amorphous shapes into clarity. The rear of their herd still lost in the blur.

What were they running from?

They neared. James could make out a cart pulled by an ox. It staggered as it ran, drifting side to side, ready to collapse. There were two men in the cart, the skinnier whipping the animal furiously. Toward the rear of the stampede, a man on a horse galloped. James heard them now. Squeals and snorting, the discordant drum of hooves on the ground, stirring a hum James felt rise into his feet from the soles of his sandals.

James and Ephron watched in a daze. Then the ox staggered and collapsed with a burst of dust.

When the ox fell the cart turned sharply, teetering and spilling the thin man with the whip and a large man with red hair from its side. The herd stopped. Some of the pigs tripped and stumbled over one another, hooves sliding in the dust. They gathered around the ox. The large man rose, James could see his arm twisted in the opposite direction. He grabbed his wrist, pulled hard, then shook his arm and opened and closed his fingers. No sign of pain on the man's face.

James grabbed Ephron and took cover in a cluster of rocks. They climbed onto a boulder, lying low so they weren't seen. The herd was quiet. James hadn't seen the white goat at that point, only heard of it from Ephron. He watched as the goat went to the ox, shaking its head, motioning toward the fallen animal with its horns. Its fur was stained the color of old armor rusted in the sun. *Dried blood?* James's heart thundered like the ground beneath the pigs' hooves. He cursed having a son in his old age. They wouldn't get far if they were chased.

"Abba?" James put a hand over Ephron's mouth. One of the pigs standing a little ways off from the herd turned in their direction, cocking its head. The goat motioned again with its horns. A large pig fell over. Then all was still. The tension in that silence permeated everything, crept under James's and Ephron's skin and prickled their napes. Ephron jumped when the ox's legs spasmed. The animal twisted, contorting its body, its great belly bulging toward the sky as it arched its back. Dust swirled up around it as it rolled, grinding horns and hooves through the dirt.

When the dust cleared the ox was standing. The two men helped ensure its harness was fastened into place. The larger of the two, who had twisted his arm, used his hands as though nothing had happened. The goat trotted over and rammed the skinnier of the two men. Both cowered after.

This goat chastises men.

Pigs snorted and the group circled, then began advancing. The ox's strength was renewed, no signs of exhaustion now.

"What is this?" said James.

"Abba, they're coming."

James shook, mouthing words that barely broke from his mouth. "Be strong and let your hearts take courage. Shelter in your wings. I will give great praise to the Lord. I will praise him in the midst of the throng." He held Ephron tight.

The pigs neared. Closer, their smell became unbearable. Ephron vomited on the rock, James wiped his face with his cloak and patted his back, trying to calm him. James looked back at the herd and cold panic broke through his insides. Some of the pigs were staring up at them. They hid their heads.

Grunts and barks and squeals followed. James dared a peek and saw black eyes fixed to the boulder. They passed, and most turned to look their way as they spread along the path. They were in a horrible position, for as the swine rounded the path, the top of the boulder came into clear view. They looked into them. Smirked if that were possible. He knew it somehow, and more than anything he wished he could tell this to another man. Ephron's words returned, *Anything is possible,* and James shook with a sob that sounded a lot like laughter at its end.

"Abba, I'm scared." The rock where they stood was wide, though no higher than a man. They were exposed. James hadn't taken the shape of the terrain into account. If only he were a father who could survive the wilderness.

The herd circled them. Murmurs, low at first, a hum of voices rising in a maddening peak. A closer look at the bodies revealed their deformities. Festering, hooves and putrid flesh, the stench assaulting them and closing them in, bringing bile to the doors of their throats.

"Abba." Ephron's voice was lost in the swarm of noise. James held his son, covering him with his garment. His eyes welled hot with tears. Flies hummed around the corpses, because somehow, that's what they were, cadavers that breathed and communicated amongst themselves.

Man and swine led by a goat.

The men in the cart's eyes were unlike any he'd seen. Blank, glossed, like the animals. One look and James knew no evil was beyond them. Fear for his son took hold, wrenching in his chest. The pigs' eyes were different too. Harbored a cold intelligence.

The goat stepped from the hoard and approached the boulder. He leapt up, and in two swift movements stood over the father and son. The black slits in its amber eyes appraised them. A piece of skin dangled from one of its horns. Blood had dried in its beard, which danced while the jaw worked. The red stains were darker up close. It had been a pure white animal at one time, a beautiful creature. It was covered in viscera now, filthy, detestable. The lip curled and it spoke. "James. You should know the perils of venturing off alone in a dangerous land."

"Baal…zebub."

The goat, the pigs, the men–all laughed. The sounds they made weren't cackles, nor was the goat speaking in a tongue he recognized. But still, James understood them. Their laughter was cruel. The goat cocked its head. The flap of skin twitched from its horn. "No, no. But we're old friends. I shall send him your regards."

"Abba." Ephron's voice was low. He was shaking, whimpering.

James closed his eyes, began to mutter a Psalm. "My God, I call out by day-"

"And you do not answer!" The goat snarled. Spittle foamed around its mouth. "Let me tell you a little secret, James. *HE* never does. What would *HE* think of your sniveling?"

"How do you know me?"

"I know you, James. I see through you. Through your spineless body to the futility of your existence. These pigs are hungry, James. Not that we need food to keep going. But it does make everything easier." His hoof scraped the top of the boulder. "Maybe we can work out a deal."

"What?"

"Give yourself to us. Renounce God and offer your body willingly."

"No." James squinted teary eyes, clutching his son tight.

"Then you'll watch the pigs devour your son. They'll start with his fingers. Then the little toes. Then chew off any chances of you ever being a grandfather."

James held Ephron tight against him, shaking his head.

"I grow weary, James." The goat nodded to the sea of pigs surrounding them. They piled together at the sides and climbed over one another, spilling over to the top of the boulder in moments, until their mouths were snapping at the precipice.

"Wait!" The goat turned to him, waiting. "You won't hurt him?"

"You won't have to watch any of that. I can only imagine what

75

kind of effect that would have on a father."

James rose, squeezed his son and kissed him. Then he pried Ephron from his legs and pushed him aside. The boy protested, reaching for his father. James shook his head. Ephron sat with his hands around his knees, trembling and ducking his head.

In a voice more fitting a serpent than a goat, Bazumel said one word: "Worship."

The old man knelt before the goat. He brought lips to hooves, recoiling at the filth. Bazumel brought his snout to the old man's ear, whispered something. Then Bazumel raised his head, looking over the pigs. "Who will it be?" One of the little pigs in front volunteered, but Abaddon came up beside him, snapping at it. "Ahh, yes." Bazumel brought his head back to James. The lips moved. The man nodded.

James fell forward. The pig collapsed after. Hosts often struggle against the change. The mind ceases to function, the body writhes, and a silent war takes place inside. Abaddon was no ordinary possessor, so the change came quickly. The man rose, dusting himself off.

Ephron looked up into the face that was once his father's. Now a stranger with dead eyes and a smile that made his flesh cold. "Abba?"

"Abba's gone, boy." Abaddon grabbed Ephron's arm, pulling him to the edge.

"You promised you wouldn't hurt me! You promised my father!"

"What makes you think we're obligated to tell you the truth?"

Ephron looked up, eyes darting left and right. Abaddon dragged him to the side of the rock and tossed the boy into the waiting swine.

Squeals drowned his frantic screams.

CHAPTER 12

STUPOR

Elijah slept in a field. Morning revealed a wineskin beside him, empty, with the patch of ground near its opening stained. *Like blood.* He wasn't a drunkard. This feeling in his head, like rocks thrown at his temples from the inside, the spinning world, all seemed to crescendo. It pulsated in sharp waves of pain. He sat up, then rolled over to vomit. There was a squeeze in his stomach, a tight fist forcing everything out. When he finally opened his eyes he saw the grass around him. His clothes. This wasn't the first thing that had come up.

He had the dreams again. Every night now. This time one of the creatures climbed into his mouth. Despite its great size, and the many wings, it shoved its way through his screaming orifice, forcing itself down his throat while he gagged. From that moment on he was stricken with a cold paralysis. His body became its slave, moving where it wanted, speaking the parasite's words while he panicked internally, voiceless and immobile. Elijah could feel the creature's intentions. He recoiled at its satisfaction, and his own excitement, as it used Elijah's hands to choke an adolescent girl. Others joined. Took turns in unspeakable acts of torture. Somehow the mind inside him--greater than his own–made him share in its joy. The girl's suffering brought the being immense pleasure, as did Elijah's.

Elijah cupped his face in his hands, weeping until he wasn't making sounds, like a child hitching for breath. His throat burned from vomiting, his stomach was tight, throbbing. Elijah's body was as deflated as the wineskin. It was foolish to think he could drink the dreams away. The cup of wrath is more bitter than any wine.

It all served as a strange lesson in contentment. Perhaps he should have made due with his impending blindness. A strange punishment for acting on hope. He thought of Salome, the texture of her skin, the oils in her hair, the curve of her face; Elijah felt resentment building for the Rabbi. Perhaps it *was* better to have never known him.

The village he'd come from was still a day and a half's journey. Not a soul cared for him there other than Salome. He pictured her, worried over his whereabouts, oblivious to everything that had changed. How would she react to the terrible burden he'd been dealt?

Elijah wanted to crawl into the hole of the wine skin and drown in the grape's nectar. To be forgotten.

There were a few boys in the field, neglecting the crops they tended, laughing and throwing stalks of grain at one another. Placing a palm on the ground, he stood. All the blood in his body rushed up to his head.

Elijah staggered away, still drunk, leaving the wine skin and his cloak. Hot mouthed and thirsty, he made his way toward the well he'd seen the night before. The amber glow of morning soaked the leaves while the birds sang. Their song brought a sharp pain through Elijah's head.

The well was already crowded. The people came early to avoid the heat. Elijah shuffled to the bucket. He waited, the wine from the previous night a nagging finger jabbing at an open wound.

Two old men were arguing beside the well. The older of the two, with a bald spotted head and wisps of hair draping his temples, pointed his staff at the other as he spoke. "I saw him. The man drives out demons." That word settled into Elijah's stomach. He thought he might vomit again.

"Tricks of the eye. He's a two bit sorcerer that will rob you for your last denarius." The man who responded was in rags. His teeth as scarce as the coins of the alleged victims.

"I saw him. Heard him!" The bald man's fist shook in the air and the strings of hair followed. "The man makes bread from nothing!"

"Stuffed in his sleeve. Why would God make bread to show his might? Bah!" He swiped his hand dismissively. "Every woman in Israel does these miracles."

"Do you forget the manna in the wilderness? Is it not written–"

"You can read now, Zachaeus?" This brought laughter from the others around them.

They droned on. The noise and the annoyance over what they said made Elijah's head spin again. The word Mashiach made his stomach turn.

"I'm going to see him."

"Don't give him any money."

"He doesn't want money," said Elijah.

The two old men, and the bystanders, turned their heads. Elijah's face was flush, wrinkled as a dry grape. His clothes were filthy, stained with vomit and whatever else had seeped from his body, or drifted by and splattered on him during the night. He was in only a tunic. When he saw their faces Elijah realized he looked like a beggar.

"We don't have alms to give, boy. Go to the Synagogue for that."

"I was going blind. The one eye I could still see from was fogging over. I went to see the Mashiach."

"Your eyes look fine to me." The missing teeth gave the old man a lisp.

"He healed them." Elijah made his way around the men and leaned against the well.

"You see! You see!" Said the bald man to the other, he heals the blind, he-”

“Does anyone know this man?” The sparse toothed man’s tone was incredulous. “How do we believe the words of a boy who looks as though he’s crawled out of the whale’s belly?”

“I don’t care if you believe me or not.” Elijah realized his words were slurred. The people around were a blur of faces painted with different emotions. “If you can’t pay the price, don't go.”

“What do you mean?” asked the bald man.

The gap toothed one’s face brightened. “You see, he charges for these miracles.”

“He might ask for something in return, but it won’t be money. Unless it keeps you from righteousness. It may be something you’re not prepared to give. And if you can’t give him what he requires…” Elijah looked down at his feet. They were chalked in dust and blistered. “You’ll wish you were dead.”

Elijah was still leaning against the stones. He took the bucket from a woman waiting nearby. She grabbed his arm, but he pulled away and chugged the water down greedily. None of the crowd commented, still pondering his words. Disgusted at his lack of decorum. When Elijah drank his fill, he dropped the bucket. It knocked against the bricks. If the woman hadn’t reached out, it would have plummeted into the water below. Elijah staggered forward a few steps but felt dizzy again. He turned and vomited into the well.

The villagers fell on him.

CHAPTER 13

THE WITCH

The path home rose steadily. The old woman pushed a cart that splintered her fingers and sent burning pain through her lower back. Her head was down, lower lip quivering as she mouthed contempt for her neighbors.

One of the rare occasions she came down to the village. The sun seemed to focus on her clump of crooked bricks more than the surrounding homes. The thatching on her roof glowed bright white in the afternoons and made its holes conspicuous. In the summer she could practically bake bread on the floor. In the rainy season she sloshed around her house like a bog.

Recluse isn't the appropriate title for her. Hermit is slander for the misunderstood resolved to solitude. She belonged to the rare breed of women maligned for maternal failings and already guilty under the judicial rumors of zealots who see portents in every gust of wind. They call her things like medium, sorceress, witch. Stone worthy offenses at minimum, were they proved. The village developed a healthy fear, which she soaked up from her summit like flowers do rain.

The same women that stare up at her house and gossip knock at her door. They bring sacrifice, hoping she'll solve the mysteries weaved into their lives. They inquire for dead husbands and children. Beg to make dry wombs fertile. Or barren. For crops to flourish.

Look at the woman for any length of time, especially meeting her eyes, and you wouldn't think witch. You may surmise something was off. It's not her bones or the shape of her face or body that makes her appearance unsettling. She has the makings of a woman that should by all accounts be attractive, were you to have met her when she was younger. What's soured her over the years is her scowl. How the crevices networked in tiny lines around her mouth and eyes, and the wrinkles continued through her skin to her tiny black heart, which had shriveled with the years of disdain and the hypocrites' smiles. With all the rumors that climb her steep hill.

From where she sleeps she hears them. Their footsteps, the squeaking wheels and hooves. She feels the jars of water and oil rattle. There's a fire going at her house already. A cauldron filled with salt, some plants she plucked from the Jezreel valley near Molech's shrine, and something that once crept outside her garden with the nasty habit of barking.

She lays down at night and hears everything. Quiet discussions in back alleys, their lies, the private whispers of inflamed lovers. She knows their shameful secrets. She feels their eyes on her house during the day.

You shall not suffer a witch. She's talking to herself again. She would be stoned if we could find a reason.

When she concentrates, thoughts come in broken fragments. She gets enough to understand their feelings toward her. They're easy to interpret. And manipulate. Over the years, she's learned to show people things. She conjures images to plant in people's minds. They see it. Feel it. They'll even smell it if the images are ghastly enough.

Even her name lacks the redeeming graces of pleasant conversation. Chuldah. It has a hard edge, almost lewd in its pronunciation.

The gossipers are out. Their voices a scab in the ear, a din like being in a room filled with flies you're a step too slow to swat.

She had nearly pushed her way to the top of the hill. Two

women stood in the path near her house.

Chuldah's head was still down and her lips were parted. She walked until she reached their shadows.

"Why doesn't that young girl in your house help you?" said the first woman. She was tall with crooked teeth.

"Or does she only leave at night to entice our husbands?" This came from the second woman, who may have been pretty if it didn't always look like she'd sniffed something terrible.

Chuldah looked up, her lip slightly raised on one side. "She came home very late. Singing. I didn't want to wake her. I never know where she goes at night."

The second woman put a hand on the cart. "Who is she?"

Chuldah turned on the woman. She removed her hands.

Chuldah studied their faces. To the pair blocking the path, her eyes were like a dark cloud choking out the light. The tall one shifted her feet, took her hands from her hips and stepped back.

"Does your husband know you lie in bed most mornings thinking of his brother?" Chuldah's question was met with bewildered eyes. The tall woman blushed. Chuldah laughed. A single burst of sound, not having much mirth to share with the world, for a witch must be frugal with her humor. "You worry about where your husband's eyes roam, while you pine like a stray in heat. Does that warmth come any more for your husband?"

The woman's mouth hung open. Chuldah knew this experience would likely fuel her on for some time. Supply some false sense of adventure peasant minds grasp for. This was a woman who found the friction in other people's lives more interesting than her own.

"Is the woman a harlot?" The second woman had a round face, cheeks with black splotches, worn like a badge of honor for her domestic efforts. Chuldah had seen her with her children waddling behind like ducklings, their faces bothered by the same stench that plagued the mother. The longer Chuldah looked her over, the more her animosity grew.

"You're more concerned for the women that enter my house than the men that roam from yours."

"What can we do if our husbands stray?"

Chuldah shrugged. "If you can't please a man he'll find someone who can." She pushed her cart into motion again. The mother duck waddled in front and put a hand out to stop it. "We're not going to stand by and let your guests cast discord he–"

"Another word and I'll pin your tongue over my threshold you Jewish dog!" The woman nearly fell from the path. Chuldah put her shoulders down and shoved forward. As she passed the tall gossiper, she turned to address her. "Do you know what your husband's doing now, Jewess?" Worry washed over the woman's eyes.

These women. Israelites. Descendants of the inbred tribes that slaughtered her ancestors in their conquest of the land. Their God promised them milk and honey, and a righteous excuse to overlook the blood it cost.

Chuldah hated the Israelites. Hated the God that structured their lifestyles even more.

A sheen of sweat covered her skin by the time she'd traversed the hill. She put the cart beside the wall and wedged a stone beneath the wheel. She brought the vessels into the house, then moved toward the shade in the back to avoid the heat. Speculation over the woman in her house brought a wry smile.

When Chuldah's visitor came down the hill their association never crossed the people's minds. Her appearance captivated the men, and while the women were swept up in the immediate scandal of her appearance, the coincidence between her presence and Chuldah's absence, their murmurs about witchcraft, the righteous indignation–were temporarily quelled. Chuldah made them see what she wanted. Her purposes began as strictly monetary–her alter ego really was a harlot of sorts–but once the gossip floated up to her bright corner of the hillside, she resigned to increase the visitor's presence for no other purpose than tearing the social fabric of the little community.

The door to the shanty on the hill was closed for some time that afternoon. Once it opened again, the visitor stretched her legs, striding into the sunlight, turning heads as though they were pulled on an elaborate network of cords.

There was a sharp pressure in her chest. Quiet anger built as she passed people tending to the mundane tasks of life. Their poor attempts to ignore her were discovered when she caught them looking up, eyeing her. She despised their dirty faces, the dirt caked in the hatchings of skin, their grime filled folds of flesh. They were an unwavering attestation to monotony. And not just their lives or faces, even the dwellings. Misshaped bricks built up haphazard homes, streaked where mud dried. The colors began to look the same as the years went by, like the skin beneath a tunic the sun rarely sees.

She stopped at the gate of one of the women that had blocked her cart along the path. Mother duck.

Chuldah stretched her hand out. An old man lurched by and nodded but didn't take much notice. Most of the villagers regarded the woman Chuldah projected to the world as something scandalous. A woman that lacked modesty. The men who weren't interested in matters of the flesh didn't care. If Chuldah would have come down as her normal self, no movement would have gone unnoticed. It was irritating, but it amused her how much they thought of her.

She stretched her hand over the gate and opened her fingers, twisting at the wrist and methodically testing their dexterity. Something dropped from her sleeve in the sand and scurried off. Several more plopped down after, their impacts brought little sighs from the dirt. A moment later they were unrolling, pincers snapping, legs stabbing the ground to push them on. Their tails loomed dangerous and high, stingers poised. Heading for the woman's clothes. The clothes of her children.

Chuldah made her way back up the hill at an unbothered pace. Seeing the village with less atrophy now. Her actions sought a valuable and superfluous lesson in humility. As she walked, smiling to herself, a scream peeled through the little village. She laughed, then spread her hands in front of her and watched her fingers like a child.

The inside of Chuldah's house was a dark oven. It reeked of old sweat and all the concoctions scalded into her pot. Bars of light fell through the holes in the thatching, dust swarmed in their glow so the house looked like a prison housing something that thrived in darkness. She hummed to herself, took a box with carvings in a script that looked to be inscribed by a bird's feet and sifted through the contents. Bones of dead mice and birds she'd scrounged from owl pellets, pincers of scorpions and the dried and hollow cadavers of insects, reptilian ligaments, and the moldering pelts of some small creatures no longer distinguishable. She used a pestle and ground up the sharp angles of heads and skulls into fragments, pressing until they were crushed into powder. Chuldah lowered her head and closed her eyes, mumbling incantations few living ears would recognize, words spoken from tongues that had long rotted from mouths. She sighed, thinking of Jezreel, nearly a day's ride away. Her people, the deep recesses in the cliffs where her master was still venerated.

There was leisure there, but something about her presence in the village had an allure that tingled in her skin. She was the Philistine among them, a role ripe with derision, with a glory she coveted. Here she was the woman the Jews warned their sons about. The hair of a thousand Samson's, every botched circumcision in Israel, the smile over a man's throat that opened wide enough to swallow a rock–she wanted to be a blade for them all.

When she'd finished her ritual, she scattered bones and dust, dumping the contents of the bowl over an area of stone she'd cleared with her forearm.

What's this?

Chuldah's smile stretched as far and wide as the stars.

She crossed the room, rummaging through her trinkets and boxes. She squealed when she found her pouch and looked inside. Then, sitting with her legs crossed, she gathered the contents of the bag in her hand, muttered something to what she held, and spread it over the floor.

An omen.

Chulda clapped and fell back on the floor. She kicked her heels on the ground like a little girl, laughing.

Something was coming. Something terrible. Something she would appreciate. There would be many more women screaming once it arrived. She would head to Jezreel and wait.

G I V I N G   O V E R   T O   Y O U R   P A S S I O N S

Saul loaded Balaam for their journey. The ass brayed, Saul laughed and rubbed its back. He sympathized with the creature, every cry and haw were expressions of rage against its creator.

The last few days bustled with commotion, and now, finally, the debris cleared and peace settled over his house. Life moves like the cyclones that pop up from the sand. They come, stir up the world around them with their brief spurts of violence, then vanish as quickly as they came. The morning after he'd buried the old widow, he sat reclined, sipping wine and reflecting on his life. His wife returned from her little trip in the peak of his relaxation. Hurt that Saul had not accompanied her, but lacking the brashness necessary to directly confront him, she'd commenced with her subtleties.

"What did you do while I was gone, Saul? Did they till the soil? Did you have them plant anything?"

Oh yes, I planted a withered old log beyond the garden. She's not buried all that deep but I doubt there's enough rain for her to take root.

"Saul?"

He blinked, "yes?"

"Have you heard a word I've said? You haven't said much since I came home. Or before I left. If you'd express to me your needs every so often…"

Saul's mind shifted back to the old woman. How the heat tingled over his skin as he raised the boulder. How the murder's proximity to the Synagogue, the calm walk from the village, the sweat that broke his brow while he dug her grave, made everything all the more satisfying.

"Saul?"

He thought of another woman he'd like to pummel with a boulder.

"We haven't seen each other. You know they've found people dead on the roads? Torn to shreds. It looks as though they were eaten by packs of dogs. How would you feel if it were me?"

The year of Jubilee comes early.

"One was a pregnant woman. People are going missing. The only thing they've found were pigs. There were hoof prints everywhere. Remember Lydia and her husband?"

"Yes, yes, the lady with the drooping ears." Saul waved his hand, urging her on.

"She passed." She waited to see if Saul cared. "He has a new wife already. We got along well. We went to the market and all those young boys," she laughed and shook her head. "You couldn't scrape their eyes from her with a hoe."

The woman was a never ending blade. Extending into nothing, cutting everything it came in contact with, never reaching a point.

"The Romans are investigating. They think it's a madman on the loose. The baptizer from Herod's dungeon resurrected, they're saying."

"Are they?"

"Oh, you know how these women gossip while they're mending. Tasty morsels."

Tasty morsels. That comment was the final spark. Saul was soaked in oil, ready to ignite at the slightest provocation. It never stopped. She droned on about people, things she remembered, her mother, her father, her cooking, her mother's cooking, her weight, her bitterness over everyone else's weight, her bitterness that Saul didn't gain any weight.

What was she good for? That feeling, that sweet serenity the widow's death gave him, stirred in him. She moved to the other room, still talking. Still seasoning his life with irrelevance. The woman is supposed to be a man's rib.

While she was in the other room talking, Saul rose. He looked around the house. There was a thin knife near where they cooked. He remembered the stone, however, and felt the knife was a coward's weapon. There was a clay bowl, hewn stone, certainly heavy enough for her. None seemed fitting. Natanya had to be special. Saul's heart drummed a chant for blood. A thousand little points played in his hands. He walked outside. The sun was high and blinding, exposing everything in a white hot glare. He found it lodged in a stump. A sliver of glory shone brilliantly along its curved blade.

For all I've sown, I shall harvest. And he had sown. His boy. Miriam. Years of study, pointless striving under the law. For listening to Natanya all these years. Her voice still buzzed from inside like an insect in a little jar. He grabbed the sickle. Squeezed the handle, taking in the heat emanating from the leather after baking in the heat. He ignored the pain. Welcomed it as a sensation that not only informed him of vitality, but served as a rite of passage.

Saul stood for a moment, knowing his life would never be the same after this. He was like a drunkard trying to resist the wineskin in his hand. But the taste of blood was sweeter than any wine he'd ever known.

He walked back into the shade of his porch.

"Are you listening, Saul? Why are you holding that?"

The stroke was swift. Never possessing much athleticism or strength, the accuracy of his strike came as a surprise. Her hands clutched her throat, trying to plug the gash he'd made. Crimson covered her knuckles. She sputtered, fell on her knees as though Saul was the God she'd been sacrificed to. Natanya fell forward.

Saul had a warm numbness in his chest that spread to the top of his head. A physical sensation accompanying happiness was something he hadn't felt in a long time. He sat, sipping wine again. Several hours later, good and drunk, he got up to put her in the ground beside the old woman. He buried her far from Miriam and Jacob.

When the shadows stretched over his land and the sun's drowsy lavender soaked the sky, Saul packed the earth over another grave.

Now, saddling Balaam, loading the Tzedakah, he smiled to himself, singing an old Psalm his mother used to lull him to sleep with. He was arranging some of his garments and wine when a noise behind him startled him. He yelled when he saw the two men in the grass. A stab of fear pricked his heart.

One of them was James. Funny, he'd never seen the man without his son. The other was a large man with a fiery beard. Both had unsettling smiles, as rife with death as the ground behind his house.

"Hello Saul," said James. "Already packed I see. Good, good."

CHAPTER 15

HOMECOMING

Elijah limped home as the sun sank. Clouds of bloody wool hung overhead like soiled bandages, floating dreamlike toward the mountains. Elijah figured, judging by the way his cheeks felt when he touched them, they were probably the color his face was now. He paused at the colors of the fleeting day, admiring the beauty, yearning for home, and would have praised his creator for such a sight if it wasn't so physically revolting to do so now.

After the fiasco at the well, some of the men of that town, as well as some of the older women, took it upon themselves to mete out their punishment. Branches and stones, kicks to his body. He could've mistaken spit for rain. He staggered through the village, passing Salome's house. He heard her voice, asking one of the servant's something. His stomach leapt. His tunic was torn, skin burned burgundy beneath, shreds of wool stained where he dabbed blood from his nose and mouth. After walking barefoot, he tore his covering to tie into strips around his feet.

Adding to his shame, he could smell the unwashed odor of his testicles and armpits, wafting up when the breeze was to his back. He wouldn't see Salome now. Besides, Samuel and Hannah were there.

His house was more pathetic than ever. Everything stuffed between the beams sagged. Its walls had stones set in uneven rows that made little gaps and resembled a mouthful of jagged teeth. Inside was damp, and if he didn't do something soon, it would probably smell worse than his body before long. He collapsed on the mat and said a prayer. *Please, anything but the dream. Just black, hollow sleep, please.*

He woke to prodding. Pain spread through his ribs. It made him cough, which brought his body curling in on itself like a newborn. He felt someone shake him, then drifted back asleep.

Then came scattered sounds and glimpses of reality. Something wet being wrung out, a song, prayers. When the voice prayed he groaned. He wanted to scream, but something in his side felt broken. A lot of things were broken. His will, his body, the sense of reality and grounding he had to all of creation.

Later, after he slept, Salome's face blurred into focus. She had a damp cloth, dabbing his chest with the edge. He was wrapped in something that provided a cool tingling sensation. She put a finger to his mouth.

Seeing her brought a dull ache. The wounds he'd received came alive, and his want stirred low in his stomach. Hot little coals danced in his cheeks, like he was nervous again. Set to do something he knew he shouldn't and couldn't fight very long, yet exhilarated for the opportunity to rebel.

Her eyes calmed him. Dark and searching, they never faltered. She was a woman set in her intentions. Even the things she did which their people considered scandalous, she owned, never flinching at a choice she'd made. Not like him. Seeing her again made him know he couldn't part with her. It was time to live with his choices too.

And Elijah knew that if this Jesus really was the son of God, he'd already known his decision before he made the request.

How was that fair? Why even put it forth?

"I have to get back soon," she said. One hand caressed his head, the other held his hand. Elijah squeezed. His grip feeble. She brought a sponge to his mouth. He coughed on the bitter mixture. "It will ease the pain."

Elijah scanned the room and found his things had been moved around. Shafts of light intruded through the window. Salome's face behind the motes of dust looked like a celestial figure behind a sky full of stars. His reverence to this image was blasphemous, but if he was forsaking his god by staying with this woman, he may as well allow her to take the honor of being the sole idol.

"Your eyes!" The way her mouth hung open, her childlike wonder, brought those loathful feelings back. "You're healed! What was he like? Did he speak like Moses?" When Salome said Moses her hand curled in the air and her voice assumed a mock baritone. She laughed at herself, but saw Elijah's misery and her smile fell away. "Ohh," she cooed, "I know it hurts." She sat and stared at him for a while. Her brows were raised, mouth tight. Her concern tore him apart inside.

A few moments later she left. Elijah moved his arms and legs. Got up on his elbows. Even breathing was uncomfortable. He wheezed when he exhaled. He sneezed later and it felt like a blade forced through his rib cage.

This was going to be harder than he imagined. He got up and walked around. The soles of his feet were sore and stung, his knees and ankles ached. After walking around the cramped space a few times, he collapsed on his mat again, exhausted. And slept.

Salome returned later. Elijah was still on the mat, he'd drifted in and out of consciousness, mercifully spared the recurring nightmare for now. She brought a lamp. They sat in the flickering shadows. His adoration for her glowed like the fire she carried with her.

"Are you feeling better?"

Elijah shrugged. His skin itched where she'd wrapped his wounds.

"Who did this to you?"

"Some fools mad about their well."

She shook her head, as if she didn't know how to interpret. "You met the Mashiach?"

"I don't want to talk about him."

"But your eyes, they're clear."

"Yes."

"So he was the Mashiach, this Jesus?"

"I said I don't want to talk-" Elijah groaned. Raising his voice brought pain screaming through his ribs.

"That's what you get. Don't raise your voice to the woman that washed your ass." Salome sat on the stool, leaning over him, smiling. She looked at his hands, humming to herself.

"He's ruined everything."

"Who?" she asked.

Elijah turned away.

"Who ruined everything?" Silence spread between them. Salome shifted on the stool. Their conversations were always fluid. He'd never felt uncomfortable around her.

Tears ran down Elijah's cheeks. He wanted to tell her. But Salome was a virtuous woman. He feared she would end things if she knew what the Mashiach said. And to make matters worse, he knew that he should. Did Salome love him enough to forsake God as he'd done? He moaned, more now from this internal torture than pain, and she came over to caress him again. She kissed his head. Elijah turned to her, and Salome kissed the trails of tears. Then brought her lips to his. She laid on the mat beside him and waited until he was asleep.

When he was snoring, she covered him, kissed his forehead and left for her house.

CHAPTER 16

THE EVER DIVISIVE IMA

Samuel's bed was against the wall in the corner of the room. Hannah was arranging the varied jars and pottery on the table beside him. She must have done this dozens of times a week. Seeing the woman hunched over, the bulge in her back a ridge beneath her clothes, and hearing her clatter, brought an eager tension to Salome's chest. She sighed, waited for the old woman to move along, and began arranging the things she'd moved.

Hannah turned her head. "Is that you, child?" With her head cocked to the side, the candle cast her elongated nose on the wall in the black shape of a perched vulture.

Salome smiled, finding it fitting. "Yes, Ima."

"It's late my dear, where in Heaven's watchful eyes have you been?"

Subtlety made Hannah's tongue a dagger. The gossip around the village had obviously grown, and although Hannah was practically blind, she saw more than she let on.

"I enjoy the night, Ima."

"They wander about in darkness, while the whole world is shaken to the core."

Salome blew air from her lips. Hannah's head cocked at the sound. If the hag's ears were any sharper, she may have heard Salome's eyes roll. "How's Samuel?"

"He spit up on himself earlier. Glad I'm here to keep after him."

Salome ignored this. "And the backs of his legs?"

"The same, more or less." His skin was pooling. The legs were just twigs now with knobby knees from the years of inactivity. "It's not as if he'll jump out of bed and follow his wife into the night any time soon."

"If only he could," said Salome under her breath. She walked over to her husband. Caressed his cheek with the back of her hand. It still hurt to see him this way. His fall from glory came from a high summit, and now the rubble of squandered potential laid the foundation of their home. Sometimes, she resented him for what had happened. Even considering the nobility of the act.

"Joseph brought yeast and oil, and that farmer's boy brought a flask of oil." She looked up with a smile. "For you. You should see the way his eyes light up when he asks if you're here. And how they dim when I tell him no. If I didn't know any better, I'd say he's trying to take Samuel's place."

"He's a boy, Ima. If he found a goat with breasts he'd chase it around spewing poetry." Hannah cackled. An annoying, choking sound Salome found fitting for a shadow vulture.

"Ohhh My Samuel was so handsome," she said. Her hand was on his brow. "Curse those Romans. If only he'd been born a coward!"

"He was prepared to give his life, Ima." Samuel moaned. She thought of Elijah. And how Elijah's groans engendered compassion, but her husband, this broken shell of a man, brought forth resentment. She tried to reason this away. This was her life now. The life of so many women, dying in slow silence. Even a man in a prolonged death bed kept her manacled. Almost 9 years now. It was a sentiment she'd only shared with her sister and God, but she'd prayed for him to pass on. To just die. Not just for his sake, but hers. And after the shame, the resentment and bitterness, and the frustration at the futility of her daily existence, she realized she didn't feel bad about it anymore.

"Hmpf." The old woman kept watch over her son. Wiping spittle from his mouth. Salome stood with her arms crossed, looking down at Samuel, lost in thought.

"I heard the Shepherd boy came back a few days ago. Did you know he sold his sheep?"

Salome frowned. "No."

"They say he was beaten. There's been a lot of talk about bandits on the roads."

"Oh?"

"That boy's always been trouble. I knew his grandmother. Poor woman had to raise him. She had a strange smile. It never felt safe to leave the house unattended while she was around."

"She was always sweet to me." Salome would have preferred that woman as a mother in law, even if it meant she'd had to give up her own legs.

"Hmpf. It makes you wonder, though. Why a wicked boy like that, lying with every hussie from Tyre to Jericho, gets off walking. And my boy, he tries to protect his people from the invader's idolatry and ends up like this. All bones draped in skin."

"Samuel hears you. And I don't think he'd wish this on anyone."

Hannah nodded. "Samuel was a man of God."

"Samuel's still alive."

"You call this a life?"

Salome sighed. "His heart still beats."

"Perhaps Samuel hears the rumors about you."

"And what rumors are those, Hannah?" The old woman turned back to her son.

In the years Samuel was healthy, he'd kept his mother at a distance. She moved in with Salome after Samuel's accident, under the guise of helping, and tried to control things as soon as she arrived. She played the victim. Hannah was a wealthy widow, Salome a helpless wife stuck with caring for an invalid everyone admired. Her role became a public symbol of honor. The wife of the man who fought back. The symbol meant nothing to Salome, drowning daily in the monotony of service. Fighting back had never done anyone good.

"What rumors, Hannah?" The old woman didn't turn. "You know, sometimes our outlook on the world is ugly because of our own ugliness."

Hannah turned back to Salome. She couldn't bear her daughter in law's eyes, and turned quickly back.

"I think I'll go back outside," said Salome.

"You carry the scent of *outside* in with you."

"Maybe I'll go roll around in the flowers, then. About time this place smelled like something other than salve and stale breath." Salome stormed off.

CHAPTER 17

VALLEY IN THE SHADOW OF DEATH

In the Jezreel valley, in a place the ancients once referred to as Endor, a progeny of worshippers survived through the generations. Their order recruited in the shadows. They communed with the dead and mixed things forbidden to marry. Much blood had been spilled there for their gods. Through their cunning, sorcery, and questionable fiduciary endeavors, they endured. These people merged with the populace over time, passing the secrets of their arts to one another in private, blending like drops of poison stirred into a stew.

After King Saul's debacle with the witch of Endor, the Kings that followed sought to route their kind from Israel. If it weren't for the wayward kings, some of David's own sons, and those seeking the same forbidden services as Saul, the Israelites would have succeeded.

Their enclave lies on a dry plain, wallowing in the shadows of Mt. Tabor. There's a cleft seldom traveled, both for its shape and for the legends it's inspired over the years. If one knows where to look they can have access to the dwindling society that still haunts its caverns. They worship the old gods of the Philistines and Canaanites. Molech, Baal, and for the scribes familiar with such clandestine and nefarious groups, there is another. In Canaan he was Dagon. But those who walked before them, who migrated west along the Euphrates and gave their pregnant women and crops to the fire in his name, he was called Belphegor.

In the charred marrow of Israel, Belphegor reigned.

The esoteric nature of these cults demanded the strictest scrutiny. If the average Jew discovered them all would be lost. With worshiping the old gods came all the blood letting, child sacrifice, and lascivious rituals the prophets denounced.

Belphegor expected his welcome to be rich. Plump children and open gashes. He would have use for them. Much use.

The man, once called Petra, followed a goat and a large sow into the cleft. The inside was rancid, gore had set into its rocks over the centuries. Too damp and suffocating to explore at leisure. The three paid no notice to the trivialities that bother mortals.

The cleft led to a chamber centuries old. In the center lay the shambles of a fallen idol. A broken tribute to Molech. Two shallow trenches ran along its sides, sloping in a decline to allow blood to flow toward the deity.

Marduhl crouched and put a finger to one of the trenches. He brought it to his lips. "There's been blood here recently."

"Good," said Belphegor. "They're still faithful."

"We shall see," said Bazumel. The three walked on.

It was easy to see why most men wouldn't have explored here. The walls grew closer together the farther they walked. Marduhl had to stoop. Belphegor barely fit. Bazumel's horns skidded off the walls.

They pressed on through a narrow corridor devoid of light, with no sounds but the squeaks of rodents and the drip of water somewhere in the dark.

Eventually they saw the dancing shadows of torches. The three emerged in a large cavern with sharp stones lining the ceiling and floor. The effect was like climbing into the mouth of a giant leviathan. There were people inside, huddled to the stones. Soot covered faces and sackcloth adorned their thin bodies. Many were missing teeth. The walls were decorated with crude paintings of large figures devouring bodies. The bodies were small and large, some infants, all thrown into the creature's open maw. Flames rose up behind it.

The colors had faded over the years. Painted in blood and excrement, mingled with the secretions of men and women.

Marduhl kicked an old man lying against the wall. "Where's your priest?" The man groaned and raised a limp hand ushering them on.

Deeper into the cave, the walls spread apart and it brightened. The air was worse, redolent with a catacomb smell and mildew. The stench was the perfect deterrent. It would repel any unwitting mortal from coming this far. Belphegor was pleased with their dedication to remain secluded.

The three could feel the tragedy here. The lives cut short, the sufferings. It came to them as sweet supplications. Many of the abominable acts were done to their glory, after all. And these people detested the God of Israel. They bled, and made others bleed, for them. Their names would soon bless the lips of priests as they held their blades above their heads.

The three were powerful here. The peoples' sentiments and bad intentions hummed through their bodies like lightning in low clouds. Belphegor felt as though he'd ascended again. The piss and shit and blood surrounding him was his own golden city.

The path wound around a bend and led to an opening without any rock overhead. There were a handful of men and women, many standing naked. Their heads were low, and they had gathered in a semi circle around a hole where something was burning. In the pit, a raised knee was burning, accumulating black flakes like layers of feathers. Judging by the amount of coals outside the pit, and the streaks of blood in the sand near the opening, whoever it was had been thrown into the flames alive. The bystanders were chanting low from their throats, in the language of the Philistines.

The three watched. Beside the people was a pile of clothes. After some time, Bazumel broke their silence. "Belphegor, you've really outdone yourself this time. The Accuser will be most pleased."

The sow's chin was high. The black eyes gleamed. Whether it was pride or some nefarious resentment was inscrutable to all but Belphegor and Heaven.

Their moment was interrupted by a scream from one of the women.

"Do not fear," said Belphegor, coming forward. "Your God has come. Go and gather more for the kindling. I want their smoke to reach Heaven."

"Baal zebul?" said one of the men nearby.

"I folded Baal's legs behind his body and gouged the eyes from his back," the demon's snout twisted in a snarl. "The old ones will know my name. Tell the witch Belphegor is home." The coil of the pig's tail bounced, the ears twitched. "Tell the young, Dagon requires blood."

The people fell to their knees. One of the men pulled a blade and dragged it down his forearm.

"Very good," said Bazumel. "Very good."

CHAPTER 18

ELIJAH'S GUILT

Elijah's strength returned after a month. He still grimaced when he pressed his side, but now he could sneeze without daggers, breathe deeply free from a spear through his side, and bend to pick things up without reeling in pain. His rib tingled at odd moments, and a numbness spread from the injury. Elijah interpreted even this as an omen; Eve's primordial form burning at the adulterer's irreverence.

Salome made visits, each time waking him in the night. She was cautious. Rumors were honey in Israel, and women like Hannah licked their lips at gossip. Salome brought him food, attended to his wounds, sang sweetly in his ear. All the while Elijah sulked. She teased him for his moodiness, attributing his gloom to the injuries. "Rescued from a life of groping in the dark and you don't smile when you see me." She gestured dramatically with her voice low to mimic Elijah, "the one soul that's shown you any love." He grunted. She kissed his forehead and laughed.

Elijah haunted the pastures his sheep once roamed, contemplating whether to tell her what the Rabbi said. A part of him insisted his hesitance diminished the purity of his love. He tried to bring it up, the burden flitting at his lips, but each time Salome's face suppressed the urge. His secret sank to his belly.

When Elijah was a boy an old man visited the synagogue. A traveling rabbi, preaching throughout the region. Dusty as a tomb from his journey, with torchlight for eyes and a mouth like the trumpet of heaven, he expounded on the commandments. The preacher castigated the throng for their sins, beseeching them to repent with tears in his eyes. Men and women moaned at their wretchedness, clutching garments, kneeling, crying out, smiting their breasts, and tugging hair. Elijah looked around, bewildered at the frenzy infecting the crowd. This was the contrition of sackcloth and ash, what the prophets spoke of. The old man scrunched a face with more lines than a scribe's parchment, and leveled his bony finger at Elijah. "You have a secret, boy, a hidden shame!"

Elijah shook his head, glowing coals in his cheeks.

"It takes root in you. Grows as quick as weeds. Careful lest you're tempted to think you're clean." The old man turned maddened eyes on the crowd. "Beware those who take the justice of God for granted. Who hear of His perfect judgment without trembling. Of his mercies, yet remain unstirred."

He looked back at Elijah and shook his head woefully. The preacher turned again to the crowd. "When gold and silver are put to the fire, their imperfections float to the surface, all the scum accumulates there. Consider this for yourself, are not men the same way? Truth is the purifying flame. What heats the forge of a man's heart, cleanses impurities, and summons the luster beneath to glory. Lies, betrayal, omission, all pollute the metal of a man. Cheapen the value of the ore in question. But honesty," his bony finger pointed skyward now, with one eye wild and searching, the other squinting as if incredulous of the other's accusation. "Truth burns away dross and slag and every impurity from the metal, so its resplendence shines forth. It is the truth tellers that shine. Tell the truth and scrape the dross from your souls!"

Elijah's chest tightened. He had secrets, what boy his age didn't? Another boy, who Elijah developed a bitter disdain for, under no other rationale than the whims of young jealousy, carried around a carved figure of a man on a horse. Elijah was too old for such toys. But it had been carved by the boy's father. Elijah hated the boy. His sanguine disposition, the fact he had a family (Elijah's parents were long since dead), the way it stuck to his body like an extra ear. One day the boy left the little horse unattended. Elijah snatched the carving, broke the toy to bits, and scattered the pieces. He'd felt guilty after, especially hearing the boy's cries. But never told a soul.

Now, the man's finger, the preaching. *He knew.* Somehow, *he knew.* His dross now tarnished his sense of righteousness. Elijah was far from gold or silver. Even iron. He was more an earthen vessel, slathered with a clear finish to mask the cracks beneath.

Elijah clung to the preacher's cloak and wept, confessing all. He was instructed to apologize to the boy. To make amends. Elijah assured the preacher he would, giving his oath. He never did. But after, Elijah went to extremes to show the boy kindness.

Holy men speak in riddles. *Parables.*

Elijah's father even spoke this way. He painted the world with analogy, through everyday items and the wisdom of shepherds. This, with the preacher that left such an indelible impression, made the stories and parables Jesus told all the more poignant. Though he couldn't understand most of the parables, they reminded Elijah of his childhood.

Which only made him feel worse.

What was his life now but a set of choices he was terrified to make?

The dreams had returned, and now featured some sort of tribunal where the verdict was guilty, always, and decreed without hesitation. He saw the faces of the people he loved, most of whom were dead, mouthing the words. Elijah walked through his village, turning from his neighbors' eyes. He passed a little girl and her mother outside a fenced enclosure. Too far to hear any words, but their lips made the same motions as those in his dreams. *Guilty guilty guilty.*

He made his way between houses, deciding to pass near Salome's, just so he could nod her way. They lived in a large home with extensions added on over the years. It was only the three of them and their servants. Salome said it was a lonely place after Samuel's accident.

Salome was pregnant when Samuel had his accident. Accident, of course, is a kind word. A kindness the Romans didn't merit in any real sense. Since he'd been rich, and a powerful man in their stain of the world, the soldiers did suffer repercussions. They were beaten publicly. A mother's spanking compared to Samuel being trampled by Roman horses. Their shrine had still been constructed. An idol raised up clear, a Babel for the Israelites to loathe. After Samuel, no one dared to say or do anything.

Elijah saw Salome's face while the Romans were beaten. She stood tall, her dark eyes embers set on high cheekbones, hair fluttering. He recognized her strength then, before even her beauty. It was several years before they spoke, more before he ever saw a smile. And now he was the reason that smile returned. A rare flower blooming in secret. When she told him that, it became his proudest achievement. He was a fool for not telling her.

Elijah rounded the corner and saw her house. Salome and Hannah were outside, the old woman barking at the servants. They were preparing for a trip. Samuel was on a litter. The servants raised him into their covered cart. Hannah saw him watching, squinted to see who it was, and waved.

Guilty.

"Elijah, how good to see you." Her words were full of venom, his name slithered from her mouth and up his spine.

"Hello Hannah." He smiled, aware how the rest of his face betrayed his lips. He nodded to Salome and addressed her formally with a nod.

"Oh, you're so cordial, Elijah. Just like your father."

Elijah's blood practically boiled. "Going somewhere?"

Hannah smiled. Her teeth the tan color of the stone walls around the village. "Our little talk inspired me, Elijah. I'll admit I didn't believe at first, but seeing your eyes convinced me. We're going to bring my Samuel to the man. This Jesus will heal him, I know it." She turned to her daughter in law. "Salome is ready to feel safe in a strong man's arms again." She put an arm on Salome's. "It's been so long, dear."

"It has Ima." Salome smiled. When Hannah turned back to Elijah, worry crossed her face.

Elijah's pulse was heavy in his neck, as if the old widow was jabbing her dirty fingernails into the side of his throat. He tried to swallow, panic clogged his throat like wet wool. "I hope he can do the same for Samuel as he's done for me."

"I know you do, dear. Things are going to be much different around here when we return." A smug smile mushed the center of her wrinkled face. "I might even ask him to heal my back." Hannah looked at Elijah, still with that horrible smile, then flashed it at Salome. "Oh, I almost forgot!" She hobbled up to her house for whatever she'd forgot.

Salome mouthed something to him, still quiet with the servants present. It was some small reassurance, but the only thing in Elijah's mind was *Guilty guilty guilty.*

"Safe travels, Salome." Elijah stood there a moment, hoping no one would notice his legs shaking. They couldn't talk here. Not around Hannah's servants. He turned and walked home. Heavier than he'd ever felt.

Elijah was undone. As if sewn together crudely, the old woman had plucked a thread that led to everything unraveling. His hopes spilled out on the ground like fish from a torn net. His every aspiration now laid about him choking, flopping in their struggle for life. Elijah walked on in a daze.

Hannah had been in to check on him the day before. He thought this strange, she'd always had a nose upturned and a condescending aura. She asked about his eyes, seeming surprised when she beheld his face. This he thought strange, since he couldn't remember her ever looking him in the eyes. But regardless, he told her about the man, how unimpressive he appeared. How he made the mind and heart burn when he spoke. Unless of course, he burdened the listener with some impossible task. Elijah was gripping his stumbling block now, and he could feel his fingers slipping. The old woman had come along to wrench them away, and they'd snap off in her hands like dead branches.

When he told her about his eyes being healed, about washing and rinsing in the mud, he saw something. Her own eyes, already rheumy, seemed to shine.

He should have been sharp enough to put things together. When a woman who's never so much as looked at you other than to scowl or raise a suspicious brow takes interest, it should raise concern. Perhaps he could have discouraged her from going to the Rabbi.

The thought sickened him. Would he really deny a mother the opportunity for her son to be healed, just for his own selfishness? Is love something to lie for? Would that keep with its ideal? What would the Mashiach say?

He knew what the Mashiac would say. *Leave the woman and follow me.*

Guilty guilty guilty.

If Salome would have asked, he'd have smothered her husband on his mat to have her. To really have her. Maybe *his* love operated like that. Maybe not God's, not Jesus's, probably not even Salome's, but he wasn't perfect. Just a poor shepherd trying to pluck some happiness for himself. And if it's commendable to die for the ones you love, which no one denies, who's to say there isn't nobility in killing for them?

Elijah was smiling to himself. Walking off beside the village, he'd passed his house. The depths of his own depravity surged up and dirtied him. He was a wretched thing. Lenin used to wipe up soot. The worst feeling of all was the certainty he had now. How right the Rabbi had been. He should've never returned. He didn't deserve Salome.

Elijah was a Shepherd. He had no business waxing on like this, leave that to the scribes and pharisees. His world was wool and animal scents, bleats and howls, the dangers of wolves. And with a growing sadness, he realized he wasn't even that anymore. The sheep were gone. He'd given up his livelihood. There were proverbs written for people like him.

CHAPTER 19

THE NOBLE PHARISEE

Inside a synagogue south of Sychar, a crowd of eager Jews gathered around the steps to hear the Tanakh explained by the talmudic expert and respected Pharisee, Simeon Bar David. An honored member of the greater Sanhedrin, and one of the few detractors among their ranks in support of Jesus Bar Joseph, the Nazarene, who many believed to be the coming one, the Mashiach, the son of David. This set him at odds with his peers, of course, but Simeon remained unperturbed. God's ways, after all, are nothing like man's.

Simeon was elaborating on the meaning of a passage by the weeping prophet concerning the new covenant. He'd provided a particularly brutal historical detail, where in the siege before the exile, some of the women ate their children to survive.

A woman nearby gasped. An angry crease formed between her eyes. "They're wombs were never worthy of the seed. I hope their breasts shriveled and their husbands left them for sheep!" Some of the bystanders laughed.

"You'd be surprised what a person will do when they're hungry," said Simeon. "You don't think these women said they loved their God?"

"It's one thing to say they love their God, it's another thing entirely to show it." The woman sat with her forehead back and chin raised. Outside, a donkey brayed. One of the children covered her ears.

"Just let him get on with the lesson," said a tall man with deep set sockets. He seemed anxious for the sermon to end.

"Ahhh," said Simeon, putting a hand up to quell the excitement. "Our people perish for a lack of understanding."

"More from Jeremiah," said the woman. Clearly impressed by her own knowledge of the scriptures.

"Yes, yes, you were saying one's actions should be good, yes?" She nodded. "And what kind of actions should accompany the talk of our love for God?"

"Alms." There were satisfied grunts and the whoosh of garments. "My husband and I give a tenth of the grain we harvest to the widows and orphans, as well-"

"I didn't ask," said Simeon. "Alms. Good. What else?"

The woman looked off, deep in thought. "Refrain from work on the sabbath." Simeon nodded, urging her on. "Bring sacrifices, teach your children to love the Lord."

"Before or after you eat them?" The woman's eyes narrowed. "I'm kidding. When I saw the Mashiach we talked for many hours. His comprehension of the law and the prophets far exceeds my own, and he's half my age. He told me the law can be summarized in the Shema. And for the life of me I can't find any reason to think he's wrong." Simeon held a phylactery in his hand and shook it in front of the woman. "That's what's important. Your knowledge won't save you. All you've ingested, if not used with your heart and mind to honor the Lord your God, will amount to nothing. The words you've chewed like cud to memorize will be seen as no different than if your son's remains were festering in your stomach. The Lord sees all." Simeon, seeing the woman on the verge of tears, relaxed his shoulders. "I don't say this to deride you. I only want you to be careful when you cut down your neighbor. Watch yourself first and always, it's God's duty to judge, not ours. I dare say you wouldn't want that task." The woman nodded. A tear rolled down her cheek.

She flashed a shy smile and curled into herself.

The onlookers sat in awe with Simeon's teachings. "Where were we? Ah, yes, I think it's important to understand the Babylonians' treatment of our people during the siege. They were brutal, but not like the Assyrians. That was a far worse fate. The Samaritans lost many. And they suffer to this day, because our people have hardened their hearts and do not accept them."

"Let those half breeds suffer," said the man with the deep set sockets. He crossed his arms and leaned back.

Simeon stretched his arm toward the man with his palm to the ceiling, looking around at the crowd. "You're all rather wrathful today, aren't you?" Simeon started to explain the hypocrisy in the man's logic, but he stopped to look behind him when he noticed the open mouths before him. A man had staggered into the synagogue. His tunic was stained with blood, the skin on his head blistered and peeling from sun exposure. Simeon recognized him. A widower from Bethsaida named James who almost never left his property without his son by his side. His every waking hour was devoted to that boy.

Dread sank into Simeon's belly. The crowd around him murmured, a low, ominous sound. Simon held a bundle in his arms. Something wrapped in linen with stains all around it like a pattern of brown roses. The smell hit Simeon's nose and cold sweat followed. He heard a gag from one of the women nearby. Simeon trembled, aware of what James held before he accepted the reality in his mind.

"Ohh God," he moaned under his breath. Then, as if the thing in the bundle heard, some of the cloth slipped away and a little arm dangled free. It was missing some of the fingers.

"My son!" James's voice seemed ages older. He knelt on the Synagogue floor. Laid the body down in front of the people there and sobbed.

His wail was terrible. Simeon shuddered. He thought for a moment that something about this cry seemed off, but Simeon put the thought away. Who was he to say how a man should sound grieving?

The donkey brayed again, louder than before. Both man and beast's cries to Heaven went ignored.

Simeon knelt beside James and embraced him. Touching the man unsettled him. Simeon was physically revulsed. For a moment, he thought he might vomit. The feeling passed and Simeon laid his hand on the bereaved father's shoulder. When he started praying, James turned, shaking him away. "What will God do? What will you do? This is *His* doing!" He shook a fist in the air and looked to the ceiling above.

The way he said *His*, as if James spoke of some scurrying thing in a cave, unnerved. The Pharisee, renowned for his eloquence and understanding, for always providing some moment of learning through a clever analogy or story, said nothing. What comfort can you be at a time like this? *But this is when they come.* They want to be near you because they think you're close to God. As if a man devoted to the scriptures had access the common man didn't. But if the Mashiach taught him anything, the idea of one man being more worthy of access than another was rooted in arrogance or ignorance. Often both.

The people stood now. A woman behind James had a hand over her mouth. There was murmuring again. A little girl hugging her mother's knee cried. The donkey brayed.

For reasons Simeon couldn't discern, the donkey made him apprehensive.

The woman that brought up the mothers and their children tugged at Simeon's fringes. "Can we take him to the Mashiach? He was south of here a few days ago, surely we can catch up."

Simeon's eyes widened. He'd seen the man revive a dead girl with the wailers already carrying on. The Nazarene dismissed them all. When the wailers were gone she rose at the sound of his voice, her body completely restored.

If he could do that for the girl…then perhaps… But this boy. That arm was mutilated, and judging by the smell he'd been dead for days… *No.* Faith is what mattered. When the impossible rears its head, a man of faith must wrestle with it until it receives the blessing, like Jacob. Simeon rose and cupped the woman's face. "Yes! Yes! He can do anything." Traces of the joy burning in his chest while witnessing the miracles tingled through him. "He said a mountain can be moved. We must follow him south-"

"No." James's voice was low. Something dark clouding his face.

"No?"

"This was *His* doing."

That awful *His* again.

The people huddled around started talking. They all chattered, voices reverberating from the high ceilings and columns. Simeon shook his head. "No. There must be some mistake."

"You think I'm lying about my son?"

Simeon looked down at the heap of bloody rags. "This is not God's work."

James laughed. A callous, dead sound lacking warmth. "He's not God's man. You've been fooled. We've all been fooled." James stood, sweeping the eyes of those gathered around him. We were heading back home, south of here. *He* was there. An old woman came with a curve in her spine. He straightened her body. There were others. We shouted to God. We were so full of hope, the children cried Hosanna. We stayed until the last. I was curious, naturally." James sighed, shaking his head. His breath hitched. "My ruin came when I looked for them after. I saw this Jesus draped with whores and tax collectors, drunk and lewd. He and those fishermen were engaged in the foulest debauchery my eyes have ever seen."

"A man who heals the blind can not be a sinner."

"You use his own quotes to defend him. It's a fool's circle. He pretends to be God."

"You're not well, James." Simeon put a hand back on his shoulder.

James pushed him off, Simeon nearly fell. "The maggots squirming in my son's flesh attest to his cruelty. I bear witness against this man. Saul Bar Azareel was right about him!"

"Saul? What does that serpent have to do with any of this?"

"I saw them in the darkness. In the hills where no one could see. Harlots dancing naked around their fire." James heard gasps from the onlookers. He turned to them, voice rising. "They let out blood to Molech. What the Sadducees say is true. He performs these signs in the name of Baal-zebub. I heard his prayers with my own ears."

"What prayers? This is ridiculous."

"The truth rots before you, yet you deny its stench."

Simeon shook his head. The people were confused, his heart pounded within him.

"Ephrahim and I, we approached to find the meaning of it all. I questioned him and when I heard him call upon the gods of the Philistines…" He lowered his eyes. "I rebuked him. But He is strong. He cursed us, and a bear came forth from the trees like Elisha did to those boys all those years ago. I begged him to heal him. To heal my son." James whimpered. The people standing around moaned, some crying, and comforted James.

Simeon could see their demeanors change upon touching the man.

"There must be some misunderstanding. I know this man, I can assure you, if some confu-"

"There's no mistake, Simeon." The voice came from the door, low and resonant.

Simeon whipped around to the speaker. The sun was low, his shape in the door made a black figure in the blinding white pouring in behind him. "The only mistake was the Sanhedrin finding you competent enough to join its ranks." His face came into view when he stepped forward.

"Saul?" Nothing made sense. *Ephrahim?* Both these men being here together now…*Bears?* "Why are you here, Saul?"

"I tried to warn the Pharisees about him. He corrupts our law. Dines with sinners. Now James can attest to his vileness."

"I don't believe it. I don't believe anything you say."

"Then believe the power of God!" Pointing with the staff he carried, Saul fixed his eyes on the bereaved father. "James, do you believe God can raise your son up? Not just in the last day, but here and now, in the presence of these many witnesses? That the God of Abraham and Isaac can snatch him from Sheol and reunite you?"

"Yes," James's voice was low, breaking. Simeon didn't trust it.

Saul went to the bundle on the ground and waved the staff he held over it. "My child, I say to you. Rise!"

The heap of stained rags, that bloody swaddle, started to shift. Some of the soiled strips rose with the movement, fell away as they loosened. The Synagogue held an electrical tension. The people covered their faces, gasps and muffled prayers rose up. There were cracks, bones popping into place as the bundle undulated like a worm moving. Some of the rags were caked on, hardened by the dried blood. When the body began to writhe, the dry strips had to be pried apart by James. "My boy...Oh, my son my son." He was weeping. The boy sat up. Linen fell in strips, the stained rags as hard as unleavened bread. James wrapped his arms around the boy.

"Abba?"

The crowd huddled around to see. They proclaimed the goodness of the Lord. Simeon listened to their comments. "It's a miracle! Saul has raised the dead. Could this Pharisee be the real Mashiach? What does this mean?"

Simeon tried to quiet them. He put his hands on the boy's shoulders. "Who did this to you, what happened?"

The boy furled his brow. Blinked. "I...I...His head swept the room, dazed. He looked from face to face, then stopped. "There was a fire... Women... Abba covered my eyes. They had no clothes. He told me to wait and he went to where the men were sitting. With the naked ladies. Then I heard a roar...and...and..." The boy screamed, turning back to James. "Abba!"

James threw his arms around him. He sneered at Simeon, then, in his boy's ear, still glaring at Simeon said, "nothing will hurt you now my son."

A man exclaimed, "praise be to God God performs signs and wonders through his prophet, Saul!"

James looked up, smiling, lines of tears shining on his face. "Saul is the anointed one! Saul Ha Mashiach!" The people came down from the steps and gathered around the Pharisee. Holding his arms, asking things of him. Stroking his robes and turning the fringes in their fingers.

Simeon sat, overwrought with these events. The crowd enveloped Saul, and after a while they followed him outside. They left the synagogue and Simeon heard the donkey's bray again. As the father and son left, the boy turned and waved. The boy's sly smile, with the splattered blood and stained teeth, fit well with the rest of the marks on his mauled body. The hand that waved still lacked portions of its digits.

Could a man like Saul really be *the Mashiach*? Simeon sat staring at his hands. This boy still had the cuts and deformities from the bear that attacked him. It must have been a small bear. When was the last time Simeon even saw a bear? Where? *South of Bethsaida,* they said. *Three days ago.* God would have no problem summoning a bear, would he? The boy, Ephrahim. How many times had he met the boy? Would he not have remembered the boy being named after one of Joseph's sons? That would have surely been peculiar, seeing as Simeon's family was from Gad.

Three days.

It's been two days since the Sabbath, the day before he traveled home from the northern village where he'd gone for fabrics for his wife. Zebedee's boys said they'd left Tyre and Sidon and were heading south. Those boys are from Bethsaida, there's no way they would've mistaken that. The Mashiach was headed to Jerusalem through Samaria, according to some of his disciples. Apparently they'd cut right through Samaria on their way north, an act many considered scandalous. Simeon too, at first.

And the boy's name…What was it about the boy's name? *Ephron!* His name was Ephron. In 58 years, he'd never heard Ephron used for Ephraim. But how would James forget the name of his own son, his only begotten?

They were lying. Had to be.

But one thing was true. He'd smelled enough bodies to know the scent of death. And those wounds at his side. A boy wouldn't survive that. Not with those rags smothering his mouth, bleeding like that.

This whole business was foul. And Saul's presence assured him so. He'd held a grudge against Simeon for years. Where it began, he couldn't say. But he knew the man was hurt and bitter. He'd lost his wife and son and somehow managed to blame all of it on Simeon. Simeon recognized his instability, his inclinations toward outbursts. Though Saul was remarkably erudite–he was brilliant–they decided he lacked the temperance for the Sanhedrin. Saul campaigned against Simeon ever since. Starting rumors, trying to frame him with harlots.

"Woe is me," Simeon muttered, bitterly. He rose and went to the door. Outside, more people had gathered around. James held his son on his shoulders. People were raising their hands to touch him. Simeon crept closer. Saul was speaking.

"Hear O' Israel! I was in the wilderness. Contemplating my miserable life, searching for a purpose in my old age. The sky darkened. Clouds rumbled and the ground shook. I saw the flaming chariot that swept Elijah and Enoch to Heaven. I tried to flee. My knees shook like Samson's pillars, this old bladder barely held in its awesome presence. Adorned in gold and emeralds, sapphires, resplendent as the desert sun. I saw the throne room brothers, like Ezekiel and Isaiah." The people listening were fully engrossed, smiles and cheers followed every exclamation. "I fell on my face and asked to die." Saul said this with a tremor in his voice.

"Seraphim flew all around. Eyes and wings and all colors…so bright. I saw two men in the chariot. One with a tunic of coarse hair, eyes of fire. I knew he was Elijah. The other had a great white beard. And eyes that searched your very soul. He presented me with this!"

Saul raised his staff in the air.

Bewilderment swept through the crowd. Even Simeon's heart twitched in excitement at his claims.

"He told me to go. Preach the new covenant to the true children of Israel. The marked ones of God, who walk in his law and precepts. Who don't covet idols or this stone mason, Jesus. Moses spoke unto me. 'You, Saul, though you are no one. Not even fit for the Sanhedrin. I anoint you. Take my staff. It bears the same sign as I was given so long ago to lead my people from Egypt.' "I fell to my knees again, but our father, Moses, rebuked me. He said I am to unite the tribes. And together we will rid the land of the Roman plague and restore our glory."

The crowd burst with cheers and praise, their hands stretched over one another for Saul. Simeon was irate. "Enough!" he screamed, moving toward them. "Enough!" There were too many between them for Simeon to get close. They fell silent, turning to him. "You believe this swindler? He travels the villages with his Tzedekah, which no one knows where the proceeds end up, robbing the poor widows of their last mites. He spends his sabbaths scraping the dregs of Roman wine skins. I know a prostitute in Nain he visits twice a week." Simeon looked around at them, eyes pleading. "There's a reason this man wasn't allowed a seat on the Sanhedrin. And you tell me this is the man God chose as his anointed?"

The people looked around at one another. Confused faces searching to anchor their certainty. In front of a low wall behind Saul, Simeon caught a glimpse of two men. One was a large man with red tufts of hair in his beard, the other old and gaunt. Their eyes burned into Simeon. A white goat was beside them. Its snout low, as if anxious to charge. Some of the fur on its chest and back was stained a rose color. Simeon thought of the bloody bandages and swallowed hard. The animal seemed fixed with the same intent as the men. It looked angry. Simeon ignored the cold tingle coursing through his body, the fear trying to grip his mind. He made a silent prayer for courage.

Saul raised a hand. The din of the crowd teetered off, and once they were settled he began again. "This man seeks to denounce whom God has favored, allow me my defense. I'll admit, before this happened, I was not the model Pharisee. I sinned, again and again." Saul's eyes swept the crowd. He had a somber smile. "When I lost my wife and son, I became bitter. Jealous of those who seemed to rest in God's favor." He sighed, rubbed his eyes. "I've done many things, even some of the things this great scribe attests to. I am but a man. A sinner. But who among us has not sinned against Heaven? Did not David, who God so loved, lust after Bathsheba and send her husband to the front lines to be killed? Did Jonah not run from his calling?" There was a collective sigh from the listeners. "Yet God found use for the prophet. And even now we reside in the belly of a great beast. But God is merciful. Thankfully, more so than that man." Saul stepped onto a large stone and held the staff level with the ground. "As I said, Moses gave me a sign for those who don't believe."

The crowd was silent enough to hear the rod fall. Then a woman screamed, and they erupted. The villagers jumped up and down, shouting glory, lavishing Saul with compliments and reaching their hands out to him again. Saul smiled, hunched over, reaching down to touch the onlookers' hands.

From where he stood, Simeon saw the serpent coil around Saul's arm. Then straighten as it headed to the ground from where he'd held it. Simeon's heart shrank. The crowd roared when Saul raised the staff again.

No. None of this was possible.

Simeon scanned the crowd. The men beside the goat were no longer standing there. From the corner of his eye, Simeon caught the large man with the red beard making his way around the spectators. The older man closed in from the other side, already close. The goat's eyes were still locked on Simeon. He felt cold inside, as though he'd breathed in frigid air. The goat raised its chin slightly when Simeon looked its way. He turned and ran.

Simeon was far from his home in Capernaum. Most of the people he knew here were faces from the Synagogue. The friend who invited him, a young scribe intent to make a name for himself as a scholar, was swept into the hysteria as well. *The rod of Moses. Ha!* Overweight and breathing hard, Simeon pumped his legs. His head covering slipped. He ran on, throwing up dust.

The houses were sturdy stone structures. His belongings were all at his companion's house. Though he'd been here again and again, knew the city, he couldn't find his way now. Not from here. He was a man who lived in his head. Too focused on his musings to pay attention to his surroundings.

Oh my God. My rock, my bulwark in times of trouble. Comfort your servant. Give him strength. His pulse drummed steadily, shaking throughout like the tambourines at the feasts in Jerusalem. While his mind raced he found solace in the fact he had spoken up. He'd make a stand. Even if it meant death.

Simeon stopped. He breathed in heaves, hands on his knees. Something clogged in his lungs rattled loose as he coughed. No signs of the two men. He walked on at a quick pace, keeping alert, searching for anything out of the ordinary. Simeon thought of the goat. It's cold fascination with him. The way it stood when the others left. As if it bid them leave.

The scapegoat. The creature the tribes laid hands on, announcing their sins, transferring them to the animal to send it into the wilderness with a crimson cord around its neck. Full of their sins, carrying them away while another was slaughtered in its stead. Is that not how the animal seemed, brimming with every wickedness imaginable? He'd trembled under its gaze. It was somehow worse than the men following.

The goat's come back from the wilderness, full of our sins, ready to punish Israel for rejecting the Mashiach. It was white once, now stained. Like Adam.

Now, questioning whether the goat had something to do with Saul's new mission, Simeon thought he may be losing his mind.

He tried to focus. Moving through houses, running then walking, in unpredictable paths. He tried to sort things, but the neglect he'd shown his body made concentration difficult. How could a fool like Saul change a rod into a serpent? Or, perhaps more accurately, how could Saul cast such an illusion?

This morning life seemed so simple. The Mashiach. The Kingdom of God. Passover around the bend. Now he'd seen a dead boy raised and still doubted it being good, saw a man whose evils he was well acquainted with claim he was the anointed one. Whatever was happening, was it really that strange to think the goat was playing a part? Simeon hurried on. He picked up his pace a little. Trying to manage his energy.

Once he'd gone a considerable distance, he turned around and made his way back through some of the houses. He wanted to circle back toward the synagogue. All of his things were close by, and he could find his friend's house from there. There must be someone left in this place who wasn't blinded by Saul.

But they would be waiting.

He descended some stone stairs that wrapped around a section of houses. He could see the trees beyond the village, the arid land beyond that. Perhaps the woods and the wilderness were better than the whims of the mob.

Simeon stood, thinking over his next move. He started down, but when he raised his head he nearly tumbled over the steps.

In a flat patch of sand at the bottom stood the boy. *Ephron*. His hands were behind his back, one of his toes carved a divot into the sand. He looked up and smiled. A thin, scarce curve that looked grossly out of place on the face of a child.

"Hello Simeon," said the boy.

"Ephrahim." Simeon's breaths were heavy. He stepped into the clearing, staying a good distance from the boy.

The boy laughed. "You're sharp, old man." He shook his head, smiling to himself. The gesture was something an adult would do. "That old fool can't even get his son's name right."

"Who are you?"

"I am the beginning of the new Israel."

"What do you want?"

The boy stretched his arms out, revealing a short scythe in one hand. He swung it in slow, eccentric movements, grinning at the clouds. "What do I want? What do I want? What do I..." He stopped and dropped his arms. "I want to be a stumbling block. To bring the temple down, brick by brick. To fill Galilee with blood. I want to see the forests and crops throughout all of Israel turned to ash." The child waved the scythe while he spoke, accentuating his demented soliloquy. "I want the people to worship the old gods." The boy smiled. "The fun ones."

"Dybbuk," said Simeon.

"Finally, one of you with sense."

"The scapegoat too, then?"

"The scapegoat?" After a brief pause, the boy nodded. Oh, I wouldn't worry about him. Not yet. He has more important things to handle than fat old Pharisees."

Simeon closed his eyes and prayed.

"Call your friends, I'll call mine. We'll see who comes." Simeon heard sniffing. There were huffs of heavy breaths and snorts, something hard clattered against the stones.

Simeon looked up as a deluge of swine washed over the steps above. Bellies and jowls shook as they crammed together, some stumbling and causing others to roll until they spilled out, snapping and twisting to turn upright in the sand. More rounded the corner, breathing hard and snorting.

"Leave the face and fingers this time," said the boy.

Simeon was already running for the trees.

CHAPTER 20

THE REDEMPTION OF SAUL BAR AZAREEL

Saul turned the rod in his hand, passing it through the spilling light. He rubbed the shallow grooves of chariots and Seraphim etched in the wood, scrutinizing the foreign inscription and marveling over details. Obsessing over its effect. Well crafted, certainly, but the Torah never mentioned carvings adorned Moses's instrument. So Saul first held the artifact with doubts, until the staff seemed to quiver slightly in his hand, and a subtle convulsion thrummed through his body. Whether this was due to paranoia plaguing the replicators of such a sacred object, or its innate power bestowed upon the wielder, who could interpret? But Saul was dubious anyone would believe this was the very rod which transfigured before the burning bush, bled the great Nile, summoned swarming clumps of gnats, and cast pervasive night; no Israelite with his wits could entertain such outlandish claims.

And yet, that which could never become a snake, did. It was like one of the hooded vipers that coiled dormant in the depths of traveler's baskets, rising to writhe with music. It was long as a man, with snippets of the abyss for eyes and a burning wick tongue. Saul felt its scales against his skin as it slithered around his arm. A small splinter burrowed in the web of his thumb from when it hardened back into wood in his hand.

Saul smoothed over his robe, turned his lips in a weak but fond smile, and leaned the staff against the couch. He looked around, absently rubbing his head. The opulence here tempted satisfaction. The staff lay across an ivory and bronze framed couch, upholstered with fabric Saul didn't recognize. The food he ate, garments worn, the libations served–everything embodied wealth and extravagance. All but the inhabitants, who increasingly disturbed and evoked Saul's unease in profound new ways. But they *needed* him. And did not Saul deserve these things, after all he lost?

He sat high, thinking of possibilities. Saul beckoned a woman standing over in the corner, then picked from the tray she held. She shook, rattling the clusters and nuts. Her eyes were bloodied, round and wet as the grapes, vines for veins.

"Stop your sniveling, you sound like one of the pigs." The poor girl nodded. Saul kept his eyes on her. She still had welts. Hearing her screams had made him wince. Seeing singed his cheeks, sent shame festering hot in his belly, ignited his loins. To display such pleasures, indifferent to spectators…it seemed bestial.

What manner of beings were these? Can they really be the Sons of God?

They were unfathomably shrewd, penetrating the hidden machinations of the mind. Strength and unquenchable hatred made them capable of vileness surpassing even the Philistine shrines.

The high places had returned to Israel.

His shudderings aside, Saul longed for such ferocity. Position and wealth were not enough.

They promised him their strength, once his purpose was fulfilled. The witch would teach him things. Occultic secrets spoken in privileged circles, esoteric mysteries from depths normal men couldn't fathom. Her powers were rumored to stem from Jannes and Jambres, the Pharaoh's sorcerers who turned their own staffs to serpents after Moses. The two supposedly stayed in the Hebrew encampments after their return to Canaan. The magicians scavenged wayward jews from the multitudes to pass their knowledge. Saul wondered why Moses had never dealt with them. Perhaps the old command about suffering a witch wasn't as strongly enforced as the writings implied.

The woman, Chuldah, though repugnant to the senses, was remarkably astute, charm leavened with malevolence. She sought pleasure in the suffering of others, yet operated with a dignity, an almost noble air. She claimed the medium who channeled Samuel as an ancestor.

Chuldah delighted in the pigs. Saul watched her roll through mud with them, laughing like a child. Despite these displays, the knowledge he'd learned in such a short span was truly incredible. The Pharisee was invigorated to learn again. And on the cusp of transcending his loftiest ambitions, broaching things previously restricted solely to the Levitical bloodline. This Bazumel, the goat who oversaw them all, required a high priest. Not only that, but an intermediary for the Romans.

Saul's enemies were dwindling. Simeon had escaped, but Saul wasn't worried. Ephron (or whoever controlled the boy now), lost him in the village near the villa. Apparently, while the cart transporting his foe wormed up the hill to the villa, the old man rolled off into a ravine, tumbling, picking up speed as he fell. Saul pictured Simeon's fat body rising and thudding at each impact, breaking and bruising, colliding against trees and rocks with heavy grunts all the way down the steep incline. Ephron didn't notice he was gone until they were at the gates. But the pigs were on his trail. Simeon was to be presented alive. And hopefully he still was. Saul wanted nothing more than to see the agony of his dying breaths, to watch life dissipate from his eyes. To think, his enemy, staring down destruction like a fly swaddled in silk for the spider's jaws, only for some fortuitous wind to blow and tear the webbing free, robbing the spider his sustenance. Robbing Saul his vengeance. *Crawl now little one, I'll squash you soon enough. For now, like a good fly you abide near corpses, whose kind you'll surely join.* According to what he'd been told, Simeon's stomach was torn open by the swine (a fate Saul found delightful for such a devout man), so he couldn't have gone far. Simeon would be with them soon enough. Aspirations of joining the Sanhedrin seemed beneath him now.

"Playing with your stick again?"

Saul's head jerked up. Chuldah. She sounded amused.

He'd been rubbing the carvings in the wood again. "It's really a remarkable thing."

She laughed and shrugged. "There are those that are blind, those that see the world as it is, and those that can make the blind see what they wish."

"Are you saying I'm blind?"

"Are you not?" Her tunic was loose and Saul could see part of her nipple. It was bluish purple, like the skin of a man that drowned.

Saul looked up. What he saw brought him upright, and the staff fell to the floor. He wouldn't have believed the witch was before him if not for the laugh. Her wrinkles, pocks, chipped teeth, all were gone. The woman before him was decades younger, her skin smooth and perfected in the sun, breasts full with youth, eyes green as fertile land after rain. Chuldah giggled. She stepped forth and brought Saul's hand to her breast. Encouraged a firm grip with her hands and eyes. Saul trembled as she stooped forward and traced his thigh. His lower belly heated to life like a boy on the cusp of manhood. Chuldah searched beneath his tunic, not having to swipe his hand away with much force to dismiss his resistance. He looked at the girl with the tray. She'd dropped her eyes. Chuldah cupped him, made the old curmudgeon feel all of a man again. She put her arms around his neck and pulled him close. "Aren't you?"

Her lips touched his before the bite of her breath. It was sour and hot, the acrid smell overwhelming. He knew before he opened his eyes, but she held him close. Saul squirmed and spat on the floor, shoving her away and wiping his mouth.

Laughter snapped her head back as she sat down on the floor. "Ohh, the blind never really want to see, Saul."

Saul picked up the staff. He stood, scowling, thought of cursing the woman, then turned to storm off. He stopped before a second step.

This was a different room. The candelabras, fine woven rugs, gone. A fetid animal fur lay where the rug was. There were smears beneath where it slid over grimy stone. The crooked tables and chairs looked like an amateur painter's attempts at decor lacking perspective. The couch a haphazard blasphemy to craftsmanship. And the smell. The wet damp vinegar sting of soiled linen. A vagabond stench. It mingled with the livestock odor from outside, where he could smell *them.* Their death. Filthy creatures. Frolicking in excrement, snorting through the world drunk on blood. One thing Moses *was* right about; unclean is the perfect description for a pig.

"You don't like what you see, Saul?" Chuldah was young and beautiful again. "We want you to have these things. But beware complacency. Empires don't begin with riches. They're stolen from the weak."

Saul looked around the room again, wrinkles lining his forehead. The security, the sense of accomplishment he'd enjoyed only moments before; nothing seemed tenable. Chuldah watched him.

"You can have it all, Saul. Every desire your wicked little heart imagines."

The goat pushed the door open with its horns a moment later. He scanned the room with menacing acuity. Chuldah bowed her head. Saul saw the girl squeeze her eyes shut, her lips swallowed up in the thin line her mouth became. The goat advanced, its head high, horns thrashing with its haughty approach. He crossed the room and hopped up on the couch, letting a hoof dangle. The leg shook like a man tapping his foot impatiently.

Saul hoped he wouldn't have to hear its voice again.

Chuldah rose and approached the woman with the tray. She stood in front of her a moment, appraising her. At length she smirked, then slapped the woman. The tray clattered on the floor. One of the grapes rolled and hit Saul's foot.

Saul bowed to the goat and swept his arm, attempting an elaborate greeting. He turned to leave, but stopped when he heard the voice.

"Don't lose heart, Saul. I'll make your enemies your footstool."

"Yes," said Saul, back still turned. Its voice turned something loose in him, as jolting as the thought of biting into maggots. "I need air."

"Your eyes are open now. We can teach you these things. To commune with the dead. To make your voice irresistible. More than party tricks with sticks and snakes."

Saul turned with staggered steps, unaware the squares in the goat's eyes sought to be ossuaries for his soul.

Let me in Saul. The voice permeated mind and ear. Like the horrible suggestions of inner thoughts made without conscious effort. But these could not be averted by shifting focus. *So much pain, there. So much loss. I will return to you what was stolen. Let me in. Be at peace.* Saul relaxed. The top of his head tingled. He sensed something strange. He tried to regain his faculties, but giving way to its influence spread warmth throughout, the feeling like the first pleasant tidings of wine. He heard screaming. It seemed far off, Chuldah had the woman, beating her with a broken chair leg. Laughing and old again.

What is it you want? Saul looked up. Beside the goat stood Miriam and Jacob. *His son. You can see them again. Trust me. As you trusted me when I promised you Simeon.*

Saul mumbled, "Simeon is still free."

"A fish in a net is not free."

Saul's family smiled. They reached for him. He could see Simeon, lying in the brush, suffering.

Yes. Trust. Hadn't it been long enough since he'd felt that feeling? And what did it profit him to trust God? What had God ever given him but disappointment, loss, the stern and unrelenting law? Tragedy after tragedy and a cup of bitterness that never passed from his lips. He'd let go and be like James and his boy, wherever they were. *Wherever they really were.* A flicker of worry hollowed his chest, but the warmth returned at once.

They're free, Saul. This thing, this maligned Seraphim… knew his thoughts. Was he not more of a God than the God of Jacob and

Abraham had ever been? This was his ram in the thicket. The salvation of his son. The redemption of his name.

I watched the mountains form. I am your God now.

Saul closed his eyes. *My God.*

CHAPTER 21

THOUGHTS OF AN INVALID

Samuel listened. It was all he could do. Their voices, highs and lows, pleasant and tortuous. Laughter, complaints, moans. The spectrum of sighs–he somehow understood women better without talking. Quiet whimpers, covetous whispers. Bickering. Prayers. His wife and mother's were hard to bear, both stricken with the affliction of religious sluggards; always giving problems to God, never doing anything for themselves.

Now he could do nothing for himself.

Nothing but listen.

His mother sat at his bed for hours, lamenting the whore his wife had become, detailing every lewd rumor she heard, or invented, waiting for Salome to run off with the shepherd. Samuel laid in wonder over his mother's words. She told him, without much humor in her face, Salome's hips call vagabonds from the fields. That Salome probably slept with half the village. She's beautiful, but her beauty is from a dark place. You can tell by her eyes.

Rumors weren't surprising. Samuel couldn't speak, couldn't clean his backside. At least Salome tried to comfort him. Sat by his bed and sang rather than chewing on his feeble bonds to life. He wished more than anything he could feel her. The caress as she washed him. He loved getting glimpses of her face. She handled the wretch he'd become with such merciful placidity. Samuel wanted to give her some sign of care. Gratitude. Show he wasn't angry. For now, he could only moan lightly and swallow soft food. He had tried to speak. Tried for so long, but would begin coughing, which hurt his throat (this excited him at first, the prospect of feeling). Swallowing became increasingly difficult, and the pain only intensified. Samuel hadn't made a sound in years.

No way for a man to live.

His broken body was a prison. In his strength, Samuel stood a head above the other men in his village. His body—Samuel and his body had that strange disconnect now—had pleased women, shamed men, bested warriors. Now he was alone to think, and his thoughts were divided. Misery built on the bitterness within. Encouraging animosity toward his wife, his mother, the pity he loathed to see in their eyes. The sounds of their voices. It was always there, ready to pounce on him in weakness. The other voice, which came in times of great stillness, encouraged contentment with his lot in life. This voice was faint, for what man could find peace in such a state? But Samuel tried to keep it foremost in his mind. As the other raged louder and louder.

Not a night passed he didn't long for death.

The ultimate mercy. In Sheol, he'd no longer hear his wife's name dishonored. Despite her infidelity, Samuel still loved her.

Samuel's yearning for death was strongest when his mother sat by him, droning on, venom dripping from her teeth. The queen of fraudulent smiles, she pursued the villagers, wringing secrets from their pores. Samuel eventually realized anger achieved nothing. And in his state, it had no opportunity for release. His feelings were irrelevant. His mother was angrier than he'd ever been, her way to blame Salome for what happened. Samuel was still her claim of relevance in the world. Poor Hannah, the widow of a miser and mother of a valiant son. Left with the burden of an invalid to care for and a wayward daughter in law. She viewed herself as the personification of womanhood. This vision, or whatever name the facade she wanted to live behind assumed, had been long ago trampled, along with Samuel, by Roman horses.

His reward for standing up for his people. Real life is nothing like the scriptures. Samuel went head to head with the Philistine giant in full faith, and Goliath simply brushed the stone away and proceeded to stomp on his body until all that remained was a sackcloth of broken clay.

But there was no feeling sorry for himself, despite his mother's tears and curses. He'd known about Salome long before his mother brought the rumors to his ears. He knew the scent lovers leave on one another, how she dropped her eyes, even to him, broken there as he was. He heard the guilt in her voice when it began.

But Salome never pitied herself. Never aired remorse at being stuck with an invalid. He was thankful for that mercy. And if she was angry, who could blame her?

Life on his back taught him many things, slowly and painfully. His hurt was worse than merely physical; worse than the hooves. The Romans' laughter.

His mother's rage, and self pity, began to make her detestable in his eyes. If this Jesus could heal him, this Mashiach, as they'd said, he'd take Salome and leave. Get as far as he could from his mother and her forked tongue. Tyre and Sidon, near the sea maybe. That sounded nice. If he got the strength back in his bones, and his loins, he'd make love to his wife on the sand by the beach. Like no Shepherd boy ever could.

He couldn't blame him. Who wouldn't want Salome?

And Salome's body still hummed with the pleasure's of youth. Such a woman needs touch. Companionship. Like this, nothing existed for him beyond the edges of his mat. So if the boy helped her in her own affliction, so be it.

Now, Samuel could hear the wheels squeaking. The servants' laughs, his mother chiding them for it. Her fake affection toward her daughter in law. Salome knew she was spiteful, vindictive, backbiting; yet still it was "Ima this" and "Ima that." Samuel knew this was in deference to him.

From time to time, he thought he felt a tire hit something. His head shifted. Salome righted him and fed him bits of figs and the paste she always made him. To feel her skin now. If he could do more than flap his pathetic jaw and try to move the food to his teeth with his tongue.

Death, or life, may providence choose. But choose soon, the torment encompasses all.

CHAPTER 22

SALOME'S DILEMMA

Salome and Hannah reached a hillside village near the river while the canopy above peeled to stripes of azure and lavender, the host glinting far off. They decided to try and find an inn before dusk. The houses seemed empty, reposed silently in the looming shadows, each door and window black sockets in skulls. One of the servants poked his head past a gate on the outskirts of town. He turned back to Hannah shaking his head and hurried down the steps to join them. Garments hung stiff on a line. Even the breeze abandoned the place. They walked on.

They heard a faint chant. Low and indistinguishable. Whether it was singing, or reciting something repeatedly, they couldn't tell yet.

Hannah looked at Salome. The old woman's worried face sought something. Reassurance, or a plea to turn back.

Salome shrugged. She no longer cared. The old woman made her comments, alluded to what would happen once Samuel was strong and on his feet again, criticized her every move.

Salome was torn over Samuel. Optimistic he could walk again, with all the wifely duty and affection she could muster. But another part of her, a part shelled in and clawing for happiness, hoped it wouldn't work. She could be stoned. And Samuel would surely be after Elijah once Hannah started in his ear.

Up ahead a boy stood in the road, scraping patterns in the dirt with a short scythe. A few pigs laid nearby. They witched their noses, raising their heads to see what came near.

"Strange place for pigs."

"Yes, Ima."

"And what's he doing with that? It's not a toy."

Salome didn't answer. She approached and stopped once she noticed the boy's neck. Red and dark with thick scabbing. Something smelled awful.

"Young man," called Hannah.

The boy looked up at her, grinning in the fading light. "Yes?"

"Where is everyone?"

"They've gone to see the Mashiach." He grinned and carved the ground with the scythe.

"Where is he?" Hannah couldn't contain her excitement. She approached the boy, but stopped when she was close and her weak eyes could make out his face clearly. "What happened to you?"

"It was a bear. My father found the man Jesus in the woods with whores. He cursed me and the bear attacked."

Hannah's hands went to her chest. "You poor child. He did this?"

"Are you deaf and blind?"

Hannah flinched at the boy's reply. The old woman backed up a little. "Oh, well… I'm sorry. I just thought…"

The boy stood, stretching his arms overhead. He rolled his eyes, some of the skin on his face and arms exposed tissue beneath. "You thought *He* was the Mashiach. Does this look like the work of God?" He stretched his arms so they could see more of the mutilation.

Hannah shook her head. Still clasping her hands together at her bosom.

"How are you still standing?"

The boy looked up at Salome. When his eyes met hers she felt cold bumps spread over her skin. "The true Mashiach has been revealed. I was resurrected."

"The true Mashiach?"

"Yes, I'll take you to him."

CHAPTER 23

DREAMS

Elijah's nightmares returned. These were different. He sat at the head of a table, on one of the stools the Romans use. There were 12 seats. Hundreds wedged into a banquet hall, breathing over one another's shoulders to see the table. Candlelight splashed their shadows on the far wall, so it looked like black figures clawing their way out of the darkness. Shapes moved independently from the forms that cast them. Horns and wings rose and widened along the stones, tendrils coiled.

The guests smiled. Revolting, untrustworthy perversions, the way boys grin before dropping a lizard in a girl's hair. Salome was on the table. Nude, sweat glistening on her dark skin, smiling toward the ceiling. An old man in Priestly robes sprinkled her body with herbs and rubbed oil over her. He did this slowly, keeping his eyes on Elijah with a pervert's smile, enjoying his task. Salome moaned when he caressed her modest parts. She was soon louder than she'd ever been in his bed, and a stab of jealousy pricked Elijah. The old priest prayed, and a large blade was brought into the chamber carried by a little girl. The priest cut her into 12 pieces, then divided her parts out to each of the twelve seated around the table. While this occurred, the story of the Levite and his concubine was read by the little girl who brought the blade. Once they'd eaten their fill, Elijah included, they rose from the table and walked out of the hall in procession.

In most dreams, Elijah remained a spectator. This was different. He could feel the strain in his mind from resisting, trying to force his hands down, to keep them from coming back to his mouth. The top of his head was alive with hot little spikes. Even in his thoughts he was not alone. Something inside laughed at his resistance. He could sense its malevolence, the ease with which it moved his limbs, cast him aside to assume control.

Elijah snatched the girl who brought the blade by the hair. He couldn't scream, but felt the pleasure the thing inside him derived from her torment. He pulled the girl's head up. As a tear rolled down her cheek, he woke.

Elijah was panting on the floor beside his mat, soaked in sweat. He laid there a while, trying to grasp reality again.

What did these things mean? The things from his earlier dreams, deformed seraphims as best he could tell, were somehow connected with those seated around the table. He knew this. Unsure of where this certitude came from, but also aware the others at the table were not mere men. Their smiles gave it away. Like him, something drove them on from inside. Perverted grins over unwilling clay.

Salome.

She hadn't been in any of the previous visions. *Visions*, yes. These were far more than mere dreams. The Mashiach, these creatures, his indecision with Salome. Something dark was coming. Salome had gone south with Hannah. And if Samuel was already healed, he'd probably kill Elijah when he saw him. The old woman would encourage it. Elijah sat with his arms folded around his knees. He sat that way for a very long time.

When the sun was high and blazing, he dressed and prepared for the road. Feeling rather stupid to leave his house because of a dream, but helpless to resist.

CHAPTER 24

GONE TO MASHIACH

The boy, Ephron, had climbed into the cart after Hannah, leading them along the forgotten byways of Israel. Several pigs followed behind their whole journey. When they stopped for the night, the animals wandered about, sniffing the air and grunting now and then. Salome woke up in the night and the boy was awake, looking up at the stars, still holding the scythe. It took several days, but they came to a small path near the river Jordan and veered west. It was another day before they arrived.

The houses were built atop a hill, along a path that followed a curved incline. Some men and women walked about the village, carrying on with their errands with cisterns and garments in hand. They seemed weighted down, troubled by some unspoken sorrow. Ephron stopped to chat with another boy near the outskirts of the village. The boy only had one leg. Salome noticed he had the same detached mannerisms as Ephron.

Watching them, their expressions seemed beyond those of children. But then again, they'd been through horrible things by the look of them. Salome was following a child with enough meat ripped out of him to stop a horse. He was walking, laughing, showing wit far beyond his years. Every time Salome felt anxious the kid would turn, grin at her, tell her something a father would say to his little daughter. This miracle child frightened her And he stank, too. She didn't care how much perfume he doused on his scalp.

And the pigs. They were strangely colored, smelled awful (even for pigs), and watched you. Their black eyes followed every movement, while their mouths chewed, whether there was food in their jaws or not. Wherever the boy led, the pigs trotted behind.

She tried to catch up with Hannah while they climbed the hill. "Ima," she begged, tugging on her sleeve. Hannah turned slightly, eyeing her over her shoulder, hoping to trudge on and ignore her. Salome tugged again and Hannah stopped.

"What?" she hissed.

"I don't like this." Hannah rolled her eyes and went to turn and walk on, but Salome pulled her arm. "Something isn't right."

"Look at the boy, he's still walking. He should be dead. He's a miracle."

"He smells like he *is* dead."

The boy turned and stopped. He was a ways ahead of them. "We're almost there."

"I have a cramp." Salome winced and held her side. When Ephron turned and walked again, she turned back to Hannah. "Why would the man that healed Elijah attack a child with a bear?"

"Elijah." That name in Hannah's mouth was like rancid food coming up. "You would be thinking of that...that sheep loving sodomite, with your husband at the cusp of walking."

"None of this feels right."

"You'd know all about following your feelings, wouldn't you?" Hannah brought her face to Salome's. Hot breath accompanied her words. "When Samuel's well again, your frolicking is over. I have the right mind to have you *stoned*. We'll see if you remember your husband once he's walking." Hannah pushed her back, nearly sending Salome down the hill.

When Salome looked up the boy was grinning, a trail of saliva dangled like a cobweb in the wind.

She slowed and walked beside one of the servants. They climbed the path in silence. Once Salome heard the boy and Hannah talking, she whispered to Hannah's servant. "Something isn't right about this."

"That boy is wrong."

"About the bear?"

"About everything. That's no boy."

Salome nodded. "If anything happens, we'll take Samuel and go. Forget what that old bitch says." He turned and looked her over. Then nodded.

They passed unlit houses. The shells of homes. Pigs squealed somewhere nearby. The moon was low, a flat denarius with the face scratched out. *A bare mineral that lacked the image of its maker. Like the boy.*

"We're here." They stopped in front of a large gate. Beyond were palms, a stretch of grass, and farther on several buildings, the stones of which were evident in the moonlight. An enormous pig lay in the yard, watching. Others darted around the grass, squealing and snapping at one another. The stench here was worse. There was a sweet tinge that made Salome fight back gagging.

"Is it safe?" asked Hannah.

"Don't worry about them," said the boy. Hannah smiled.

"These are unclean," said Salome. Hannah turned and glared at her. "The Mashiach lounges near unclean animals?"

"We're all unclean without his blessing." Ephron smiled. "But I'm surprised a woman like you would look down on someone because of who they associate with."

Something twitched in her chest, like a lyre plucked too hard, sending a discordant note through her bones. *He knows.* Hannah's teeth were black and grey in the ambient light. Salome saw the joy in her eyes over these words. They moved through the gate.

Salome lived in a house her neighbors envied, and was considerably wealthy for an Israelite. She'd visited homes of notable Pharisees, a tax collector Samuel did business with whose home overlooked the Sea of Galilee. Before his accident Samuel did business with some of the misers Herod ate with. The villa surpassed them all.

It was a series of connecting buildings annexed by courtyards. They were led through corridors with gentile sculptures, antiquated weapons arrayed across bright frescos of pagan deities in battle. Hannah's mouth hung open as they were led through room after room.

A demure young woman met them at the door. She tightened her mouth and tucked her lower lip in, as if something pertinent burned inside waiting to be told. Salome tried to draw something out of her other than the descriptions of what rooms were used for, but she dropped her eyes and left after leading them to the baths. After, they were brought to rooms to refresh themselves and led to a banquet hall.

More extravagance. The affluence had a nauseating effect on Salome. With the villagers outside and the beggars she'd seen along their journey, it all seemed wasteful. They ate on decorated pewter plates, leaning over tables with designs etched into the surfaces, its wood a brilliant red luster. Bronze and stone goblets, wine skins on the tables stacked against one another, many already empty and dented hollow. Wine flowed from the corner of a table where men jostled cups and plates as they laughed.

Shadows played on the faces of the men in the far corner. They sat brooding, as if impatient for something that would never come. With them, her eyes devouring Salome, was a thin woman with green eyes, wearing a Jerusalem of gold. She was breathtaking.

They were given wine. Hannah refused at first in her ostensible piety, but after a slight nudge her mouth nuzzled the wineskin like an infant on its mother's teat. A fatted calf was brought to the table, seasoned with herbs redolent enough to cloud all memory of the stench from outside. The sight of the vegetables made the inside of Salome's mouth come alive, she could already taste faint traces of the oil. Her stomach flipped.

There were Romans too. Already slurring drunk. A taller man

with a cleft chin sat with an old Jew with large ears and a face that sank to the ground. They were in the middle of an intense conversation and the Roman's eyes weren't moving.

Coy faced women poured drinks, likely concubines. Salome leaned over to Hannah and the boy, who had come back for them after the baths. "Where's the Mashiach?" she said. A hurried lilt in her words. "I want to see the man with my own eyes."

"Be patient," said Ephron. "That time will come."

The woman in the Jerusalem of gold rose and walked over to them. She never turned her eyes from them, moving with a determined grace that exalted whomever she approached. Every eye followed as conversation lulled.

"I'm Chuldah." She was all the more striking up close. Exuding poise and confidence, her green eyes flashed and her smile stopped the men's hearts. She took Hannah's twisted fingers in hers and smiled. Despite her aversion to her mother in law, Salome found the woman's willingness to caress the gnarled hands endearing. Hannah's eyes, though they darted to the crown on Chuldah's head and back, seemed full to burst.

The old woman threw her hands around Chuldah's neck, sobbing. Chuldah patted her back. Patient, cooing. "Wait and see. He'll take care of everything." Salome felt tears well in her own eyes. She really did want Samuel restored. Despite whatever consequences.

Chuldah took Hannah's hands and stood back, smiling. "Welcome." She bent to put her arms around the boy, still without the slightest trace of disgust. For this, Salome was ashamed. She'd been horrified to even look at him.

Chuldah came last to Salome. "My darling, you are radiant." The way her hand caressed Salome's face brought bumps down her arms. The feeling was difficult to interpret.

"I'm Salome."

Chuldah's hands went to her bosom. "My peace," she said. She looked down at Samuel, lying on the mat near Hannah. Chuldah bent and cupped his cheek. "Your suffering will end soon. She let her fingers glide over the features of his face. Then led Salome off by the hand. She walked after Chuldah as if it all were a dream.

Something about it was dreamlike. She couldn't place what it was exactly, but as she and the others were led down the corridor, past rooms and through a portico lined with torches, with the leaves of distant trees and marble buildings splashed in moonlight, she got the sense of her body moving on its own, as if being lured on by awe rather than her own volition.

Chuldah talked as they walked. About the former owners and their generosity, how it was given to Saul Bar Azareel for his ministry. The proprietor was a retired Centurion turned tax collector, who had trained a number of others and garnished each accordingly. The gracious host was still here apparently, much of the wine and food provided by him enthusiastically.

Salome stopped and watched the vineyard. Something was running. She heard crunches, the thrash of fronds deep in the grass, a squeal of pain.

There. She saw them. From a distance, she thought they were wild dogs, until she caught the shape of fat bellies and the gleam of the little hairs along their backs under the moon.

So many.

She turned and walked after the others.

What kind of man guards his home with swine? Who would claim to be a prophet from God and surround his home with unclean animals?

"Chuldah," said Salome. "Why are there so many pigs?"

Chuldah's disposition seemed to change then, but only slightly. A squint in her eyes, shifting of the lips that could have indicated a hundred little things beneath the surface. "The law is changing, dearest. All His creatures are acceptable. The lion will lay with the lamb, the pig with the man." Chuldah laughed. It was a sharp sound, not unpleasant, but seemed to teeter on breaking. She turned and walked on. Hannah passed Salome and looked back over her shoulder, smirking.

Whose creatures?

Everything looked pristine, opulent. But it still smelled foul. The scent of cooked meat wafted out from the hall, but the filth remained beneath it all, left a hint of itself in every other scent.

They made their way to another door at the end of the portico. Samuel moaned. Salome went to attend to him, but Hannah hurried and stepped in the way and put a hand on his head. "Soon we'll walk together through our vineyard, Samuel." Hannah wiped her eyes.

The next room was more modest. Less Roman. Men reclined around a table, watching as they entered.

"They've brought a man to be healed," said Chuldah. She had a smile on her face Salome didn't like. She waved her arm in a slow arc to present the man they'd come to see. "This is Saul Bar Azareel. The man who will deliver us from Rome and restore us to our former glory."

He nodded and smiled. "Chuldah always reminds me of the weight on my shoulders."

Chuldah walked over and stood beside Hannah. She looked around while Chuldah introduced them. Salome caught the reflection of the men at the table in the Jerusalem of gold. It flashed, metallic and amorphous, but looked to her as though wings stretched open behind them. She turned back to the table, then back at the Jerusalem of gold. It was gone.

When she looked up Saul was watching her, reclined at the table. She squirmed under his gaze, and felt a great wave of relief when he motioned to one of his attendants. "Bring the man," he said.

Hannah urged her servants on, apologizing for their slothfulness. They laid the mat on the floor. Saul rose and knelt beside the invalid.

He ran a hand over Samuel's face. "He's tired." His face raised to them. "Tired of lying helpless while his wife yearns for strong arms to hold her. Tired of no one in the village being inspired by his sacrifice." He looked at Hannah. "Tired of bitter words. Most of all, he's tired of pity."

Salome wanted to like the man He was older, handsome, although his cheeks were high, brows and nose angular, which made his disposition fierce. He had the look of a warrior. But he seemed to see clearly into Samuel's pain. Salome knew without a doubt her husband would feel that way, could he express it. Samuel was the most self-sufficient man she'd known, he loathed anyone feeling sorry for themselves.

The man they called Mashiach stooped to Samuel's ear. He crouched low, whispering.

Samuel groaned. After a silent pause, Samuel's chest rose. The hair on Salome's arm stood. Then the air shifted, as though a cold draft burst through, Saul's robe rose behind him and fell, and flames twitched from the candles and lamps. Some were quenched. Salome heard the cracks. She listened as bones popped, bringing a hand to her mouth as his body bent and rose.

CHAPTER 25

THE ROAD

The annual pilgrimage to Jerusalem chokes the roads with travelers. Watch them from the city walls, and by the eve of the passover they're trails of dusty ants, meandering down the routes from Jericho, Lydda, Arimathea, with cargo roped to carts like giant crumbs, funneling into the city's gates. There's a current in the air at this time. The devoted Israelites and those that find a spark of religion for the festivals unite, merge in the chaos. Alms come with them, in an assortment of forms. Coin, of course. Bulls and oxen led by hand, doves, goats, lambs, fat and ready for slaughter. A pleasing aroma for the Lord of hosts.

Many sins must be atoned for, after all.

Elijah headed south. He searched village after village, asking anyone he could about Salome. So far, nothing. And no word of the Nazarene. She could be anywhere. The horizon was unforgiving, a wide open promise of despair. He searched along the coast of Galilee, deciding to hug the shore where the terrain allowed.

He found a small cluster of houses near the sea. Too small to be a village. A man stood facing the water, talking to himself.

"Hello," called Elijah, waving his arm.

When he turned, Elijah took a half step back. The stranger's eyes darted from Elijah to the houses, then back to the water. He looked briefly at Elijah, then checked over his shoulder and out at the sea again. "Stay off the roads."

"It's almost passover. Everyone will be heading to Jerusalem soon."

"They're out there."

"Who?"

"The unclean." He couldn't keep his back turned from the water for long.

"Have you seen women come through here on a covered cart? They would have had servants. An invalid with them."

He shook his head. "The road's no place for invalids. They can't run."

"Did something happen to you?"

"They came out of the water." He turned to the shore, sweeping his hand. "The demoniac said they drowned. They came out of the water and it was covered with them."

"The demoniac?" Elijah nodded to himself, preparing to leave.

He stretched his hand over the shore again. "All of it."

"Where is everyone?"

The man swallowed. Galilee winked behind him. He turned to Elijah and shook his head in small, but vigorous movements.

Elijah couldn't get much more from the man. He passed the houses. The inside reeked of fish. He didn't bother going in. A net lay torn, white in the sun. As though the fishermen laid it out to dry and moved on with their lives.

The sun was dropping. Elijah wouldn't sleep here. He turned and pulled his cloak over his shoulders. He looked back before he got too far and the man was still facing the sea. His hand came up pointing, then fell limp to his side.

CHAPTER 26

THE VILLA

Salome hadn't slept. The Mashiach, as those who accompanied Saul were fond of calling him–Salome couldn't bring herself to say it without a sense of unease–insisted Salome and Samuel take a room at once. He waved them away, "enjoy your privacy." Salome was relieved, Hannah seethed. Samuel stood in a stupor, watching his hands open and close.

They were leaving, arm in arm, led by the boy Ephron, when the voice of one of Saul's men carried after them. "Ahh look how she leads him away. Hopefully it hasn't withered off." His companions laughed.

Saul burned up their mirth with the look he gave. "Act like the pigs and you'll sleep with them." His voice prickled hairs on Salome's neck. Her heart beat faster.

Strange and crude humor for a disciple of the anointed. She was thankful for Saul's defense of her modesty, nonetheless. If Samuel had been right of mind he may have killed someone. She was thankful for that as well.

They were brought to their room. She watched him, not ready to believe what her eyes affirmed. He sat on the bed, glossed in a shimmer of sweat. Samuel looked over his body, turned his feet, tested the mobility of every limb and digit.

This wasn't so strange. After years of immobility, languishing on a mat, it must be a shock for the body to finally obey the mind. When Saul told him to rise, the pops and snaps his bones made were dreadful. Even the lewd man who made the comment flinched at the sounds. He stood and looked around, trembling. Something like terror wrinkled his features. Then his eyes widened even more and he spasmed, collapsing before them. After that, he was calm. He showed an indifference to his mother Salome had never seen. He walked away from Hannah mid sentence, hardly heeding a word. Salome was tempted to feel sorry for the woman.

Rather than rejoicing over this miracle, Salome suffered a growing nausea. Something still didn't feel right, regardless how she tried to reason or sympathize. Her husband still had the body of an invalid.

She wasn't sure what she expected. But when Elijah told her about the stonemason, who the people here seemed to loathe and discount as a fraud, all of his healings–according to Elijah–made people whole again.

On those withered legs, Samuel's body would bend and snap off at the knee if the wind blew strong enough. But he had the same austere presence as before. The dignity hadn't left his eyes.

They talked. He hadn't spoken in years, but the things he mentioned, the comments he made, seemed so trivial, as if he was already bored of the intimacies partners share. But perhaps secrecy comes as a guard after living in one's head for so long.

Samuel laid behind Salome and pressed into her. She hesitated at first, feeling a pang for Elijah, and confusion over who she would betray by the act. She decided, not without fond memories of Samuel's body rocking with hers, that she'd betrayed herself long before any of this, so it didn't matter. He rolled onto her and she smiled, welcoming the familiar sensitivities, inviting him in. It happened three times that night. He was callous. No remnants of tenderness in his embrace. Nothing like before. Just slick sweat and scents of arousal, slaps of skin, grunts, both pleasurable and painful. He continued, impervious to her needs. She put a hand to his frail chest to push him back, which he ignored. Nothing how she remembered him. When she got up to relieve herself later in the evening she was sore.

Samuel was a tender lover when they married. She attributed the vigor he assailed her with now to her infidelity, and took the crass and vulgar things he whispered in her ear, the lewd impetus of every stroke, as propitiatory. After, she loathed how alive it made her feel, how his degradation enthralled her.

The man beside her was a miracle. She wanted to be happy for him. Searched for some sign that he was happy. After lying so long, shouldn't he be excited just to stand? To feel the air? To speak to his wife? Perhaps he was so accustomed to living in his head movement felt foreign. Regardless, she had to find him again, the man who stood up to the Romans. For all these years she had hated and cherished him for it. But now she saw her role. She would draw him from whatever darkness he inhabited, delve into the catacombs of his mind to unearth the fragments chipped off along the way and piece together the bones so that broken part of him could walk again too.

Then, that hulking shadow cast from the monolith her sin had become eclipsed everything: *what about Elijah?*

She was a married woman. She'd *been* a married woman. But now, her husband could speak. Could walk. Could love–with some work. She recoiled at the thought of Samuel inside her again, then felt ashamed at her nature for yearning for it. She loved Elijah. By no means had Samuel been the man of her dreams. She'd learned to respect him. Admire him even, eventually love had bloomed and life with him became easy. Then, more difficult than she'd wish upon anyone.

A woman can't love two men. Not in Israel. Salome was no harlot. But Samuel was not himself. Still, duty, oaths, these things must supersede selfish desire sometimes.

She laughed to herself, watching Samuel's shoulder blades press into the skin on his back, counting the knobs of his spine. *Is that what love is, to forgo desire for another's sake? In that case we're all doomed.*

When Salome was a little girl, a scribe visited their synagogue to teach the women. They studied Solomon's description of a good wife. The girls memorized this over the following weeks. "This is the standard for the women of Israel," the scribe said. The grey streaks in his beard somehow attested to his authority. The man went into Solomon's descriptions, the strong hands, flax, hands that "grasp the spindle." He commented on Moses's books too, detailing the role of submissive women and the admonitions against adultery. He even went so far as to point out a homely looking woman from the crowd. "Charm is deceptive, beauty is fleeting, but a woman who fears the Lord is to be praised." He pointed at her and told her these things. And the woman smiled.

He's calling her ugly. Little Salome did her best to hold back her laughter at the time, but she'd snorted. She was asked to explain herself, and she made the mistake of being honest. Why, in a society beholden to truth, should it be so difficult for a woman to express her own?

She was disciplined. When she came home, her father took his turn. She couldn't comprehend how a woman could stand there and hear a man degrade her appearance in such a way and smile. She asked her cousin about the men's study. They had focused on David and Goliath. Courage gained through faith. None of those boys would be warriors. Herders, farmers, a few stonemasons or carpenters maybe. Where were *their* instructions in chastity? A man had no evidence for his virginity, so it seemed vital to teach them something similar. Or did it matter? These were thoughts of a young mind, before she knew how the world was.

This idea of the noble woman never settled with her. Consider the source. The oracle mentions King Lemuel, who the scribe insisted was Solomon. The words came from his mother. The first line describing the ideal bride warns Soloman not to spend his strength on women that will ruin kings. This comes from the woman who bathed naked in plain sight of David's house, which inspired her husband's murder, and gave her a permanent place in the King's chambers. *Women like me, son. Stay clear of women like me.* But that part of David's life wasn't in the men's study.

If she were to choose a woman to idolize, why not Rahab? Although she was a prostitute, she risked it all, simply because she heard of the God of Israel's triumphs. His flock was tearing through the land of milk and honey, smashing idols and casting down false gods. Her faith redeemed her. She lied to the Canaanites, hid the spies, and was thus spared. She was immortalized in the law, and forever engrained into the minds of the Israelites.

Salome appreciated how normal Rahab was. One could call her a whore. But she was a woman with children, and Salome knew several prostitutes. Some of them had attended those same types of lessons with her. They became what they were as the troubles of their lives seeped into ugly and irreversible crevices. And the same men who denounce them are the first to bring them coin.

Solomon's model wife was not the ideal vision of a woman's aspirations in her eyes. It was the culmination of a woman's expectations in a world where men were kings and any man's wife was a few poor decisions from becoming a whore. Even the way it was framed was to bring the man glory.

Elijah recognized this. He never sought her out of personal grandeur, as a way to make himself look better. Samuel came to her father with a contract. He was certainly infatuated, but there was always the certainty in her mind that their union was built on status and image more than her personal worth. Samuel looked better with a woman like her on his arm. A few days after consummating, he told her she reminded him of the woman Solomon described. That night she cried after he fell asleep. Salome swallowed it up, like women learn to do most things. But on the days when her fulfillment seemed a high and lofty thing she couldn't grasp, these sentiments returned and brought her sighing at the world outside, scanning faces for signs of a love without agenda.

After Samuel's accident, Salome woke one morning vomiting. The nausea hit her and she recognized the implications immediately. They'd been trying for years, but after Samuel's accident, the great comedian intervened. She walked every day. Through the hills, climbing the rock faces. She tried everything she could. Her predicament at the time, and her future, where a son or daughter would come into this world and see their father in such a way, was unimaginable. And her existence would count for nothing but feeding helpless mouths. The predicament, along with her selfishness became too much to bear. One day she stood over a precipice, letting her toes hang over the edge, trying to build the courage to leap. She didn't. She couldn't.

Eventually, Salome stopped the strenuous activities. She accepted the pregnancy, although couldn't bear the thought of Samuel's mother poisoning a susceptible child's mind.

In the end she lost the baby, and the rabbis told her God was teaching her humility. Part of his perfect will. By that time she'd wanted the baby. She reasoned she would no longer be alone in the world. She'd prayed daily. But Providence had other plans. Salome never thought of her maker the way the Pharisees described him.

She learned to live with her grief and her lot in life. Time went on. Her days became misery and monotony.

One day, she went to a spot she hadn't been since she was a small girl. She looked out at the grass and flowers, thinking of her father, who brought her there, and of all the people that surrounded her now. Elijah found her slouched on a boulder, wailing with her face in her hands. His sheep were somewhere bleating.

What do you say to a man who sees you weep?

The thing women say before they know better, when they think they're the reason the world has trampled them underfoot. "I'm sorry."

"Sorry for what?" asked Elijah. She flinched. His face bore no guile. "Does a cloud apologize for raining?"

It made her laugh. She shook her head.

"Imagine if they held their rain forever. It would black out the sun and the flowers would die." For the first time in who knew how long, she smiled.

Herder's wisdom, he called it. What an interesting outlook on life. And he was the first man she'd known that didn't seem to want her as a means to something else. They met there on the rocks, time and time again. But never touched. Not at first. Elijah was reserved. Before long she told him everything. Her sadness, that great weight pulling her legs down while she tried to surface for air. The child she'd never raise, the bitterness and regrets of a life where she was forced into roles she didn't want and couldn't escape.

Elijah's skin was dark and smooth, with none of the wrinkles bitterness brands into the face after one's left to brood. It spoke to his character. His simplicity. She found herself thinking of him. Often.

As the years progressed, Hannah never sheathed her sharp tongue. She became a pestilence, recalling Salome's every fault. "Perhaps if you'd spent more time attending to your husband, and hadn't strained yourself on those walks you took…I don't mean you meant too, of course…there's no way you could have known your body wouldn't hold it… When I was a wife I took great pleasure in tending to my husband…" *Yes Ima*, she'd wanted to say, b*ut your husband could walk.* "If only I had more help to care for him…I'll never have grandchildren."

Something in her snapped. The next time she saw Elijah she put her lips to his before saying a word.

The affair began as a means for independence. To be the kind of woman she wanted to be, on her terms. Forget the "praises at the gate."

She was a hypocrite. She'd admired Elijah for his perseverance, for his simplicity, his near inability to be duplicitous. And she was using him as an escape.

Yet she loved him. Loved him in a way that fluttered in her stomach still. Just thinking about what she had to do brought a rotting feeling through her.

None of that mattered now. Samuel was back, and there was no way out. She'd deal with Elijah eventually. Although she hoped she wouldn't have to face him, not after all he told her she meant to him.

When her mind wandered back to the present, Samuel's head was turned toward her. His smile looked out of place, like the result of some wound you wouldn't expect to find. He put a hand on her thigh, letting his fingers spider up her leg. She closed her eyes as he tugged her closer.

CHAPTER 27

FACES IN THE SAND

The last time Elijah traveled, he'd felt lighter. Hope does that to a man. Anxiety added weight now, became a burden Elijah could never set down long enough for a moment's rest. Sand pelted his face, the sun blurred persistent overhead, nature itself opposed him with all her wiles. No one he met on the road or in any of the villages and scattered houses had seen anyone like Salome and her party. Nor was there any word as to where the Rabbi was last seen.

Dust obscured the path forward. He kept his head low. Granules hurled through the air and moaned like ghosts. He set his shoulders, trekked on. There was an apprehension building, that hair raising awareness watchful eyes provide their prey. Elijah turned back the first time this feeling came. The curtains of sand abated and revealed a figure. His arms and legs extended casually, as if he strolled the shore on a pleasant day. He disappeared with the next gust. Elijah looked back later and he was there again. Brown cloak fluttering behind like a torn sail, the face swallowed under the hood. Elijah stopped this time. He waited, but the man never came into view. He continued on, checking over his shoulder ever so often.

Later that day the feeling came strong, something cold brushing his nape. When he turned, the cloaked man was close. Head up, gait unperturbed by the rough collisions of sand. This time Elijah stretched his legs out, pulling his cloak closer over his face and barreling on with his shoulders down.

The sand subsided later that afternoon, and for the rest of the day there was no trace of the man. Elijah slept a little ways from the road that night. When he woke, there were indentations in the ground beside his head. Partly obfuscated by the wind, which had been mercifully calm during the night, divots, large and small, heading away from him in pairs and curving off back toward the road.

He tried to convince himself the marks were from a rock moved, or footprints from when he got up to relieve himself. He knew better.

Elijah spent a good portion of the morning looking back, finding nothing. He asked the travelers he encountered whether they'd seen Salome and the others. Those ones who answered hadn't. After a few hours a dot appeared on the road ahead of him. He advanced and the shape proved a man, moving along with a heavy gait. The man lurched forward, struggling to stay on the road. All he had were his clothes and a staff. No bag slung over his shoulder. No water even.

Elijah followed. The man walked as though drunk, swerving along the path and drifting left and right. Before long he was staggering, kicking up dust. He slowed, slugging along without bending at the knees, until finally turning. The staff fell first. He faced Elijah with his arms limp and his body seemed to convulse. He looked like a brown blade of grass in the wind. He fell on his back.

Elijah reached the stranger, whose eyes were still open. He looked up, covering his sun warped face with a weak hand. Elijah propped his head and poured water in his mouth. He coughed and spurted water. "I was just resting." He smiled, an expression the sun carved in a dried out branch.

"You'll be resting in Sheol if you don't drink." He did. "Did you run into trouble?"

"No."

"You ran out of water?"

"Didn't bring any." The man sat after a while, elbows on the insides of his knees.

"Do you not understand what the wilderness is?"

"Of course."

"Yet you brought water?"

"Everything I need will be provided for."

"By who?"

"El Loheim."

"You would have died if I didn't find you."

"Who's to say you weren't supposed to find me?" The man shifted and brought his knees in to rise.

Elijah watched him stand. The stranger took a step and fell on his face. "That was planned too?"

Lying with a mouth half full of sand he mumbled, "I make peace and create evil…"

Elijah looked him over. Then in the direction he was headed. He contemplated leaving him there, then threw his bag down and sat.

The stranger laid there while Elijah sat nearby, bringing him water occasionally. When he felt he'd waited long enough, Elijah walked over and prodded his ribs with his foot.

The man coughed. Opened groggy eyes, confused for a moment. He leaned on his elbow, looking around. "I'm Absalom."

Elijah sucked his teeth and laughed. "Of course you are."

"It was my father's idea. He thought it would make me resourceful."

"Yet here you are, dry and hot as a camel's ass."

"You've looked for water there?"

"I don't have time to wait for you."

Absalom's face had a questionable look. He picked sand from his teeth. "You don't have to."

"I don't have much to give you."

Absalom laughed, "you don't have to give me anything. You

came when you were meant to, did what providence prescribed. For that you'll be blessed." He looked up. "What's your name?"

"Elijah."

"We'll get you a camel fur tunic."

"And we can hang you from a tree by the hair."

"Have you thought of using your humor for good?"

Elijah didn't answer. He paced, looked off toward the city of the prophets. The arid landscape attested to its proximity.

Elijah sat and ate with Absalom. They shared bread, which Absalom blessed. Elijah learned Absalom had gone through Judea after the Mashiach sent a number of his disciples forth. Absalom wasn't one of them, he'd taken the initiative–whether foolishness or faith–to venture off into the wilderness in the same manner. Elijah admired the faith of the man. He'd been strong where Elijah had failed.

"Thank you for the water, Elijah."

Elijah turned to look off at the rocks and depressions in the land. He sat beside Absalom for some time. Absalom offered to pray for his journey, Elijah shrugged consent. He fought back tears, then rose. Absalom stood and they embraced. Elijah sighed, pulled his bag over his shoulder, retrieved Absalom's staff and handed it to him. He left him some bread and a small skin of vinegar and wine, as well as a small amount of money remaining from the sale of his sheep.

Absolom praised God, Elijah turned and walked.

He looked back and Absalom was sitting, head to the sky with his arms to the side supporting him.

Elijah looked back over his shoulder many times that day. For both the man in the cloak and the man he'd left. But if a name were ever a sign to leave a man behind, surely Absolom was that. That night he slept farther off the road and didn't make a fire. He dreamt of Absolom walking. The cloaked man walked in the shadow behind him.

He met a husband and wife the next day. Foreigners. Both were grey with spots of age and rode camels, pulling a third behind them with birds in cages and sacks of trade goods fastened to its back. It pulled a small cart behind it, with a tarp secured over it against the elements. Elijah didn't like camels. They made him nervous. In his experience they bit, sometimes spat. The last time he'd rode one it stepped onto a pile of boulders. The animal maneuvered them casually, with surprising agility for such long legs. Elijah swung with it and hugged the animal's neck so he wouldn't fall, shrieking as though the mountains crumbled around him. This couple said he couldn't ride the old camel, apologizing and offering him bread and wine.

He walked alongside them. They sang quite often, but Elijah didn't mind. A pleasant distraction from Salome, the significance of his dreams, the man he'd left sitting in the sand.

"The Mashiach will be in Jerusalem for the Passover," said the husband. He was a dark, leathery complexion, still lighter than Elijah, seasoned under the desert heat in the many caravans he reminisced on.

Elijah nodded. "Let's hope so."

"They say he heals," the wife added.

"Your bunions will be as smooth as a tadpole, dear."

"I'll smooth you with a rock if you don't whet that tongue."

"You know I'm kidding, Doris."

"I'm not Mahalel. Besides, this man has no interest in my feet. And I'm sure he doesn't want to help remove them from your backside. These bunions would hurt much more on the way out." She looked down at Elijah. His head was down, kicking rocks off the side of the road. Doris looked at her husband, then motioned toward Elijah.

"Why are you going to Jerusalem, Elijah?" asked Mahalel.

"I'm looking for someone."

"There will be so many people coming, how will you find them?"

"I don't know," said Elijah.

Doris sighed. "It's a woman."

Mahalel laughed. "Of course it's a woman." Elijah turned away, embarrassed. Doris giggled and brought her hands to the camel's hair, twisting it in her fingers.

"You're married to this woman?"

"No."

"Engaged?"

"Doris, I don't see how this is any of your business."

Doris bit her lip. Elijah looked up at Doris after a moment and shook his head.

"Your lover?"

"Where is your shame?"

Deloris rolled her eyes. "They're just questions, if he doesn't wa—"

"She's married to someone else."

Doris's hand went to her mouth. Mahalel scowled at her.

"I don't care what you think about it." Elijah's eyes were fixed ahead. His head high.

The three were quiet for a while. The only sounds the swish of the animals' mounts and their pads scuffing along the road. "My father had a saying," said Mahalel. "You never know what's in another man's bag." The old man dabbed his brow, running his hand through his hair and wrapping his head again in his covering.

"I've thought about that my whole life," he continued. "I never heard him denounce another man, even if they broke a commandment. And we were Jews among the goy, ehhh?" He glanced at Elijah. One brow curved like a child's drawing of a bird. "When I was small I pointed out the things I saw, like any child, and he would ask me if God knew." Mahalel nodded, smiling. "He asked if I wanted to judge sinners, if I wanted that burden." Mahalel shook his head, not focused on anything particular now." He laughed. The cough that followed like crackles in a fire. The old man brought a rag to and from his lips and hid it quickly, but not before Elijah noticed red spotting.

"It was an early lesson that's done me well," continued Mahalel. "Keeps me out of trouble. You stay younger by avoiding the unnecessary burdens in life. Your love life is an unnecessary burden for me to fret over."

Doris sighed. She looked at Elijah, yearning for a glimmer of young love. "Tell me about her."

Elijah looked down at his feet. The old couple waited. Something shook a dry bush nearby. Elijah felt the pressure of the moment pass and breathed deeply before he began. "I used to go to sleep at night dreading the morning. I knew the next day would be the same. Wandering hills picking the droppings from my sheeps' wool. Slipping into darkness. Alone." He kicked a stone off the road. "Since meeting her I've wanted tomorrow every day. Until she left. She's really the only person I have now." There was a small tremor in his voice. He pushed it down. "Now I'm not sure about tomorrow. I have to go, but tomorrow might be the day I find her. And I dread it. I don't think I'll like what I'm going to find."

Doris cooed. "Do I make you yearn for tomorrow Mahi?"

The old man tugged the reins and brought his animal astride his wife. He leaned over and kissed her. "I yearn for the day not to end. For I'm not sure how many we have left together." He patted her hand. Then leaned over toward Elijah and brought the camel out a little. "When you've been married as long as I have, sometimes it feels the day will never end." Doris swatted at Mahalel. The old man nearly fell to the ground laughing. He coughed and the camel turned its head to snap at its rider. Elijah laughed too. It felt strange, he hadn't for weeks now. Not since his eyes were healed.

The three traveled on. Elijah finally felt at ease. Like he'd dropped something heavy behind him. Doris had a laugh that sort of barked, but made everyone else laugh harder. The old man slapped the animal when he cackled until it turned its head back and snapped. Once he loosened up, Elijah laughed until his sides were sore. The old man and woman loved to play with one another. Doris talked about the sounds he made in his sleep. Mahalel described the women that were jealous of Doris when they'd married–the golden heifers, he called them.

Elijah thought over his own life, where he would be at that age. This vision held his shriveled body, his only companion the shadows his form cast. Loneliness would follow him into old age. His most faithful companion.

If he would have followed the Mashiach when they met, this whole thing may have been avoided. Salome wouldn't be traveling to whatever omen his dreams promised. He wouldn't be plagued with the guilt of two opposing ideals ripping his mind and heart away from one another.

There was a quiet certitude Elijah recognized in Mahalel. Though he seemed overly jovial on the surface, his wife rested in this strength. The shade of his love shielded her from a wicked land.

Mahalel and Doris had heard the rumors. They had each other, however, so they rode on with their heads high. Fearless. Mahalel's trust in providence made Elijah uncomfortable. Since the Mashiach, any contact with the devout spawned a tinge of anger in him. He couldn't speak or hear about God now without rising agitation. A precarious position for an Israelite.

The hills and mountains surrounding their path echoed their indictment on him. All of creation screamed the same. *Ichabod. Ichabod. Ichabod.*

The three fell into the rhythms of the road. The camels' motions and Elijah's steps became a traveler's song. They enjoyed their silence as much as the songs, reserved to their individual thoughts. Before long Elijah began thinking of the man he'd met on the road. And of course, the man he hadn't. He'd left what he could. Was it enough? What did he owe the helpless? What would Mahalel have done? What would Salome want him to do?

Guilt bit down, shook him until the pangs drowned the

confidence in his decisions. Elijah stopped and looked back at the blurred perspective shrinking behind them.

"Jerusalem's that way, my boy," said Mahalel.

Elijah stood in awe of how the land could change so drastically. So suddenly. Veils of sand hid his hand from his face a short time ago. Now, although ample desert stretched west and south, he could see the border where fertile land carpeted foothills toward the Jordan, the shade of clouds spreading a dark quilt to smother the land below, mountains and hills like broken teeth.

Leave the woman and follow me.

Elijah looked back again at the road they'd traveled. Mahalel and Doris were ahead, their camels canted to the side, the third threatening to walk off on its own. He turned finally, following them on, putting the man behind him for a moment.

Later, Mahalel showed Elijah what was under the tarp. They were vendors as well as pilgrims. Perhaps more so. In Jerusalem they would capitalize on the crowds. There was a large kiln Mahalel was hoping to sell for a hefty price, pottery, garments of rich colors, even a blue shroud. The old man had fit a staggering amount of wares in the cart and on the camels. Elijah helped move everything from the camels that night to allow them some reprieve.

Elijah laid awake after they fell asleep. Who would fill his head but the man he'd left on the roadside. Overhead, tendrils of dust encrusted with gems reminded him of mortality. Convicted him of insignificance. Elijah wondered whether Absalom's eyes could still open to appreciate such things. His guilt eventually proved too much. He rose and led Mahalel's camel from where they slept, shushing the animal until he'd gone far enough to climb on without waking them. The camel cried out, but when Elijah looked back neither moved.

They slept like the dead.

CHAPTER 28

ABSOLOM

Nervous with the movements of the high standing animal, Elijah held tight, spurring the beast on and squeezing until his fingers throbbed. The morning was making itself known. Grey streaks repelled the distant shadows and the horizon glowed like a dying fire stirred back ablaze. He passed the grandeur of creation with an irritated nod, as if it were a piece of information he was aware of, but could not consent to its glory. As it were, a man lay dying. Or in its throes.

Elijah hoped to find Absalom and make his way back to Mahalel and Doris before they'd gone far. There was a chance they wouldn't go anywhere. This probably wouldn't be the case, Mahalel was a man of initiative. From the stories he told in their brief time together, and the way his wife reacted to his statements, this much was certain.

Elijah's mind drifted back to his purpose here.

For a moment he despised Salome. That she'd climbed to his section of the rocks and talked to him, disrupted the perpetual monotony he'd found contentment in, only to fool him into thinking happiness was attainable. The sacrilege of these thoughts struck his conscience and made his heart a heavy stone. Should love make breathing harder? Heat through his skin, the faint quiver before her touch, the hollow sizzle of his insides in anticipation of seeing her alone, of stealing glances or modest words in public. Riding on, he interpreted this as prophecy from his body, a sign God's man was wrong about Salome.

Was happiness attainable for an Israelite? The slavery of the Egyptians, the humility Assyria dealt, dragging pregnant women through the streets with hooks in their mouths. Even the prophets. Ezekiel saw the glories of God, yet had to cook his excrement and spend his days tied and bound to fulfill a prophecy. David, Abraham, Noah, Jeremiah–why should a man come into this world to suffer?

Elijah knew lepers. Women with children who died only days after birth without wound or ailment. Men who had seen war, whose eyes never left the battlefield; the sight that became their undoing remained like the colors after staring into the sun. God made things of great beauty and terror. The mountains humble and inspire, and may yet crumble upon the admirer at a sound. Or the sea, for all its majesty, its depths harbor unspeakable horrors. No Israelite wants his body buried in the sea.

But with all the sour, there's sweet. Creation sang its truth before him there. The same song it has and shall continue to sing. The sun shall rise again. Regardless of man's bitterness or consent.

The day was bright and clear. Elijah squinted. There was something on the side of the road up ahead. He told himself it was a boulder, even as optimism waned with his approach. When the shape came into focus, describing what he'd taken for stone in the familiar color of a dusty cloak, angst clogged his throat.

What resembled rock, then a hopeful pile of rags, Elijah knew, was a man. He got closer and slid off the animal, nearly toppling over before he got up to run. He fell to his knees and lifted him by the shoulder so he could see his face. "Absolom!" Elijah gasped, fell back. The chest was cavernous now beneath his shredded tunic. He carried the gossip of insects. Face and limbs were picked clean.

Elijah stood with the back of his hand pressed to his mouth for some time, teeth to knuckle, trying to process what laid before him.

Absalom had departed in faith, without so much as a wineskin. He had given himself to God. Then the desert.

The wineskin was there beside him. There was water too. He could see the curve of animal prints in the sand, curving and breaking in eccentric paths.

What could have done such a thing? Elijah took the water and mounted the camel. He headed toward Mahalel and Doris, praying for their safety as he bobbed when the camel walked over rocks. His jaw trembled and the wilderness seemed larger than ever.

CHAPTER 29

THE PERFECT HOST

Chuldah led their visitors through the portico. One hand traced the vines creeping over the grooves in the columns, the other carried a lamp fashioned from a goat's skull. Its glow, with the light from the torches, distorted shadows into gaunt conspirators with blades for limbs.

They'd arrived late from the Roman Proconsul's estate near Judea. Laughter reverberated from the colonnades. Chuldah enticed and entertained, her myriad charms on full display. The witch's head was high, hips swinging minds into adolescent fervor. The moths and flies were fonder of the men than her.

The Romans were already drunk. The jews were too polite to comment on something as trivial as a stench, pervasive as it was. The odor from the cellar lined their throats. Its subtle sweetness, which always seems comical amid the wretchedness of decay, suffused into what spoiled. A pig burst into the light from the torches beyond the portico and one of the older jews jumped. This proved hilarious for Rome.

Chuldah led them on, nodding at their comments. She opened the doors. Smiled as the men gasped. Seasoned beef tantalized their nostrils as soon as the doors opened. Past the vestibule they saw meat, wine, and women.

Chuldah turned to see their smiles. The Roman emissary, a heavyset man whose scowl faced the opposite way from a crooked nose, stepped forward. "I am Livius." He spoke a choppy Aramaic. Livius dwelled in the Judean province for some time now and had acquaintances with both Roman politicians and high ranking officers, as well as Herod and some of the Sanhedrin. Livius introduced the people around him.

Chuldah's Mashiach watched Livius with an air of indifference. The Pharisee proved the perfect host for her master to inhabit. Sharp features, an intelligence implied by the angular nose and cheekbones. It was the face of a dignified man, handsome enough to be winsome, but with enough scars and dissymmetry to imply the capability for violence. All without alienating him from men like the ones before him. Bazumel had placed the Roman's heart on the scales before he'd said a word.

"I'm Saul-Bar-Azareel," he stood, as if to display a grandeur implicit in his very presence.

"We hear there's some dispute over the real identity of the anointed."

"You must mean the stonemason?" Laughter sang from the master. Chuldah was mesmerized with his casual grace. She'd only heard him laugh at the suffering of others, never in a social setting. Of course the ancient ones could command a room. She was foolish to ever doubt.

"We hear he's causing quite a stir throughout the provinces. The Governor is concerned he'll be another Macabee."

"I wouldn't worry about the Stonemason. After the next Passover, he'll only be a myth."

"I'm surprised you're not on your way to the passover. Isn't it customary in your religion to travel south this time of year?"

Bazumel smiled. "We belong to a new covenant. There's many things we do differently here."

"I see." Livius traced his thumb along his belt, checking over his shoulder at his companions. They searched the faces around the room. Bazumel's followers didn't share such delicate social etiquette.

Chuldah noticed the old woman who came with the invalid staring. She smiled. The woman smiled back and dropped her eyes. The hag stood whispering to the man she thought was her son, droning on about whatever insignificant events make up such lives. Chuldah didn't like the invalid's wife. Too curious. So she took great pleasure in Saneyel's possession of the invalid. The invalid's mother was even worse. Solely for how draining her conversations were. Question after question on Jewish customs, what parts of the law she was expected to observe now, where her son had gone off to, what she could do to help. By Chuldah's reasoning, she was due for an accident any moment. They had already taken care of her servants for their inquiries. Many that labored in the villa had been taught similar lessons.

Dagon's plan, the one they called Belphegor now, was ingenious. With Saul filling the sandals of a religious zealot, they could merge into the outside world, spread their influence throughout the diaspora and beyond. Something big was coming, according to the master. Something that would draw followers and keep them praising, even in the face of death. Their religion would be an indulgence in everything the law forbid.

Debauchery, far and wide.

The guests drank and mingled, and the master stood off to the side with Livius. One of the Romans stooped over Marduhl. His hands were on the shoulder. The ancient one stared up at the man through the eyes of the boy he inhabited. Unafraid.

Words passed between them. The Roman's voice rose and he banged the table. Marduhl smiled. The Roman's cup fell over and wine puddled on the table.

Chuldah heard the Roman's voice as she approached. "You won't speak to me like a servant."

"I'll speak to you like a fool. Servants can realize when they serve no purpose."

The Roman's shocked expression melted into fury. Chuldah put a hand on the Roman's arm. "Let's not ruin a good evening with threats."

She had a rotting detestation for unfounded confidence. The Roman looked up at her. An ugly thing. His nose looked as though a bull's hoof flattened it against his face. The ridge below the center of his eyes had a crease deep enough to sip water from. "He needs to watch his tongue if he wants to keep it."

Marduhl laughed. The voice was high, ridiculing. Chuldah tugged at the soldier's arm again. "Let the boy be. Surely there's things for men to occupy themselves with here. I'll show you where we keep the good wine."

"I don't care about wine, the boy must be taught a lesson."

"You can play with him." With this she pulled at him again. "Or you can play with me."

The soldier didn't deliberate long. He took a long look at Marduhl, then rose and followed. Chuldah lit her goat lamp in the vestibule and traveled down the portico with his hand in hers.

"Where are we going?"

"Somewhere the others can't hear any screams." She smiled. The Roman laughed. Halfway across the portico they cut through the columns into the clearing.

"What's that smell?"

Chuldah pulled him close. She put a finger to his lips and brought her hand to his groin. "Do you want to turn around?"

The Roman shook his head.

The building behind the estate was dark. The stench overpowering.

"What is this place?" He used his garment to cover his mouth.

Chuldah smiled. "It's where we put the meat."

"That's some lantern. Who made it?"

She raised her arm and brought it level to her face. Ran her hands along the horns. "It's just something the master didn't need anymore." She shrugged. "I found use for it."

"It's not off putting to your guests?"

"You're here aren't you?"

He smiled. Then put his arms around her and felt along her backside.

"Not yet," she said. "Come." Chuldah led him closer to the far building. There was a large tree that looked like a man stooping forward from the dark to listen.

"Is that a pig?"

"It's not a cat."

"It's enormous."

They walked around the animal and paused at the door. It was a cellar. These were common with the Romans. Jewish homes had them if they were wealthy enough. The door creaked open. Chuldah made sure the lamp's light was shielded by the wood.

"It smells like a stable down here." His lips turned in revulsion. "A stable where everything died." He made a weak attempt at laughter.

Chuldah nudged him on. He turned and looked her way apprehensively, then began down the steps. Something shifted below them and he stopped.

"What was that?"

Chuldah ran her hand along the side of his face. He stood canted, facing neither up nor down. "Those are your new gods."

She brought the lantern up. Its soft glow exposed the bottom of the stairs, where a drove of hungry mouths waited. Piled atop one another, jowls and bellies pressed and bulged by the weight of the horde, pink flesh scabbed with abrasions and rot. They yipped and snorted, excited at their offering. "What is this?" The Roman spun to flee but Chuldah was ready. She stabbed him in the side. Then shoved him down the steps. The pigs fell on him before he finished his descent.

The hungry passel went to task, squealing approval. Chuldah stood at the top of the stairs and smiled. She could feel them. Sense their otherness. It sent a charge through her. Enthralled with the beauty of death unfolding, she stayed until the man was gone. Which didn't take long.

These were small favors for him. Her body, her mind, her life. An honor. She was not inhabited. She chose to serve willingly. If her mother could see her. Communing with Dagon. Watching Molech delight in a blood letting. Carrying the seed of a new race.

Turned heads welcomed Chuldah back to the banquet hall. Livius sat beside Bazumel. The man was drunk, tilting a stone vessel and letting it roll on its edge in semi circles. Her lord said something and the fat man's hand slapped the table. The lit wicks on the candelabra flinched. His laughter seemed a bad note in an otherwise pleasant tune.

She scanned the tables. The invalid's mother was gone. The other Romans passed wineskins to one another, shouting obscenities. Women draped their shoulders and batted their eyes to keep them drinking.

Her time had come.

Chuldah stepped to the center of the room.

"Peace." The room fell silent. "I present to you the Son of David. The true Messiah of Israel. Saul Ha Mashiach!"

Bazumel stood. His eyes belied the pride he held.

The guests echoed Chuldah's words. "Saul Ha Mashiach! Saul Ha Mashiach!"

CHAPTER 30

CARVED IN A TABLET FOUND IN THE NORTHERN JEZREEL VALLEY

Oh Bazumel, mighty are your works. Scourge of innocence. Fetid breeze of plague swept bodies, a nation's redolent cry. A shadow descends on the land, the petals wither while every green thing languishes.

You crossed the naked thresholds at passover, caused atrocities the prophets never dared transcribe. The rage of nations kindled when embers fell from your mouth.

With your rage the Earth trembles. Your temper darkens clouds. Your wisdom confounds sages. Your patience watched rivers shape cliffs. Our refrain is the cries of anguish your enemies make at your feet. May blood soon stain the horse's bridle. Sharpen your blades. Bazumel reigns.

CHAPTER 31

CRUCIFIER

Claudius grit his teeth at the rasped cackles coming from above them. With his thumb, he found the notch where the bones join together at the wrist. The legionnaire beside him knelt on the prisoner's forearm while Claudius pried the hand open, positioning it so the wrist was flat against the beam. The condemned struggled until Claudius raised his cudgel. The man's eyes were wide, darting between Claudius and the others while his chest rose and fell. Claudius reached back and the boy that accompanied them placed a long nail in his hand. He found the spot on the prisoner's wrist again, and felt his pounding pulse. When Claudius placed the nail the man squirmed. One of the soldiers brought his thick soled caligae down into the prisoner's face. His head snapped back. Laughter rained overhead while blood poured from the man's nose. Claudius found the spot again. "Hold him." He placed the nail's point on flesh, noticing his own heart beating faster.

The man suspended over them made deep laughs that should've been impossible in his state.

The mallet clanked against the head of the nail, every strike accentuated by the prisoner's screams. It took five strikes. The soldier holding the forearm turned away. Blood streamed onto Claudius's arms and made a muddy slush in the sand beneath by the time the arm was nailed to the beam.

The heckler above continued, undaunted.

"Shut your mouth or we'll break your legs early." The legionary looked up at the last man they'd crucified. His voice cracked with his response, which only brought more fits of laughter. It was louder, teetering on hysteria. The voice rose and went silent while his mouth still opened and the body convulsed.

"Take them out and do it again, they're crooked!" said the crucified man.

The man next to Claudius rose to deal with him but Claudius put a hand on his arm. "Let's finish here, first. Ignore it."

The soldier lowered his head to Claudius's ear. "How can he do that?"

"He's a lunatic. The man's too mad to feel anything."

The man whose arm they'd just nailed to the beam thrashed and cursed. He was tied down. All he could do was roll his free arm a quarter turn beneath the ropes. They moved to his other arm to repeat the process. He sobbed and begged. His chest rose and sank in quick, shallow spurts.

The laughter was maddening. The soldiers did their best to ignore it.

The ankles are the difficult part of a crucifixion. Some nail the feet separately. Claudius saw this as a lazy alternative. He used a long nail, crossing the ankles before piercing the soft portion where the tendons meet between the shins and feet. Sometimes the condemned is unconscious at this point. Not this time. As they moved down his legs, he switched between sniveling and cursing. The laughing man didn't help. Claudius reached back for another nail. They crossed the ankles and he let the mallet fly.

TINK.

"He'll never dance the same!"

TINK.

"HAHAHAHAH."

TINK.

"Does this remind you of the Rhine, Claudius?"

Claudius missed the nail, smashing bones and tendons. The prisoner wailed.

Claudius looked up at the man they'd already crucified. He was smiling, head cocked like a curious bird. Even in his emaciated state, his demeanor seemed belittling. He laughed again, rolling his head and closing his eyes to let the sun wash over his face. After a moment he looked down at Claudius. "You would have died at Baduhenna if you weren't such a coward. Look at you now." The mauled face snickered and he clicked his teeth. "Can't hit a nail twice the girth of your pathetic prick."

Claudius went cold. It was humid near the water, despite this the shock made his skin feel dry. He looked at the mallet in his hand. Shaking too much to hold it steady.

It's not much of an inconvenience (unless you're the unfortunate soul being crucified) if the ankles are shattered during crucifixion. If the nail goes all the way through the job is complete. Once the body's brought upright, the arms are stretched on the lateral beam and the prisoner is forced to push themselves up by their legs to breathe. When the body hangs without support from the legs they suffocate quickly. It's much harder for the condemned to push themselves up on broken feet. This man would die fast.

Claudius normally explained this to the condemned. The entire process, what they'll likely experience is laid out for them in exquisite detail. He offers wine (the poor quality, reserved for low ranking soldiers and prisoner's bartering their lives for information) and gets to know them a little. Savors the fear in their eyes.

Claudius enjoyed this aspect almost as much as the end result. There was always a sense of satisfaction at the end.

But the man laughing was different.

The one sneering down now was not the man he talked to before the crucifixion. During their discussion beforehand, he'd sat serenely. A dumb sheen glossed his eyes like an animal while his mouth hung open. The laughter began with the torture. Claudius realized something was wrong when he laughed at his lashings. The flagrum whipped through the air, tearing flesh from his back and face. The fool only laughed, even as his eye draped from the socket and skin was torn away. The worse they beat him the more he laughed. After many lashings, his head drooped. The soldier attending him grabbed him by the scalp to check if he was still alive, and when his face came up the lunatic spat a stream of blood in the soldier's face. They beat him again. He laughed all the same.

Claudius knew the man was mad when they brought him. But he was shackled and subdued. He'd seen droves of tough men become lambs here. The lunatic was found alone in a village. Every one of its inhabitants had been slaughtered. The men who reported the atrocity, battle hardened veterans in their own right, were clearly shaken by the scene.

Their description certainly disturbed Claudius.

Bodies gored and mutilated. Profanities scrawled onto walls in blood and excrement. The man was found naked, soaked in blood, striped with self inflicted gashes. A man's skin draped his shoulders like an officer's paludamentum. The villagers who found him reported he was singing psalms, exchanging the name of the Hebrew god for harlots and rodents. For some indiscernible reason, a number of dead pigs littered the Jewish village where they found him. And although he sang from their holy books, the men who brought the matter to the authorities claimed the lunatic ate from the pigs' bodies and rubbed their blood over his skin.

He went willingly.

To Claudius, crucifixion was an art. Fresco cast in viscera. He wove the bone and glass into the flagrum himself. He used it. Flicked his wrist, heard its whip through the air, the thud of hard edges lodging into flesh. He reveled in their screams.

Claudius had witnessed many deaths. Fields soaked in blood, heaped bodies accumulated in Roman campaigns. But this man was something new entirely. He enjoyed suffering, and remained unperturbed by the most gruesome torture imaginable. The reversal was distressing. It transferred power from the executioners.

Claudius frowned at the broken foot. He breathed deep, ignoring the laughter. After composing himself, he straightened the nail to strike again. They finished. Hoisted the prisoner up. His body bounced slightly as the vertical beam slid into its hole. He screamed, much to the delight of some of the attending soldiers. Claudius looked up at the man's misery. He was already using his ankles to push himself up and alleviate the pressure in his chest. Claudius watched the awkward way the man's knees turned when he pushed and felt phantom traces of pain in his own feet.

The young legionaries laughed and threw chunks of bread at the man. They took the vinegar sponge on the end of the pole and shoved it into his mouth until he gagged. The crucified lunatic grinned wide. Some of his lip was torn away, making his smile all the more obscene. Impossibly wide.

Claudius shook his head. He watched the lunatic. The ruined eye left a gaping socket that cast a permanent wink. Claudius had the boy attending them pick up the mallet and nails. He leaned over to him. "Do it quickly before they're done. You don't want them to take you back to the castrum when they get bored here." The boy nodded and started gathering everything up to put in the battered loculus slung over his shoulder.

The condemned men were of little account in his eyes. The last man they crucified had wronged a centurion in northern Galilee. Apparently he refused to pay taxes, which to Claudius seemed modest, comparably. The fool was given multiple warnings, yet refused all the same. Men of principle without power often amount to little more than stiff necked fools. What were these ethics worth now, writhing in the sun? Tomorrow after his legs were broken and his body finally slumped, they'd stick him through the ribs. The men would watch the fluids in his chest spill to the sand like a punctured jellyfish.

Claudius considered piercing the mad man now.

What did he know of Baduhenna?

The boy wrapped the bag up in his arms. The metal inside clanged as he passed Claudius. He ruffled the boy's hair before sending him on his way.

Claudius climbed the steps and looked back. The sky resembled a smoldering furnace. The crucified made a staggered line of human trees along the beach. The scene struck Claudius as ominous, but he quickly pushed his superstitions aside.

He made his way back to the limestone awning overlooking the harbor. When he was well out of reach of the guards he leaned against one of the columns and closed his eyes, letting the breeze meet his damp skin.

Four more years. That would make 25 since he'd begun as a legionary. When that time comes (longer than most of his friends had even lived) he'd receive land for his service. There had been close calls. An arrow in Idistavisto under Germanicus, the blade to his side in Beduhenna. Where he'd lost Adronicus. That idiot stuck to the timbers didn't know a thing. And he'd be dead soon, so his opinion wasn't relevant.

He couldn't escape his words, however. They hung there, nailed to the timbers he built up in his mind to shut the lunatic out.

Four years and he'd have a colonia south of Italy. A small group of legionaries he'd fought with as a young man had pledged to combine their allotted lands and live out their retirements together. The idea was proposed beside a fire after a hard day's marching. Claudius was nursing his blistered feet when Adronicus made the suggestion. They all agreed. It's foolish for men of war to plan futures; they often don't see much farther than the tips of their spears. All but two of the original six who made the pact that night were gone. Claudius would make his home there even if he were the last.

Caesarea Maritima would likely be his final post. He dragged a foot behind him now, another parting gift from Bedahunna. His gait made marches of any considerable length nearly impossible–but he'd seen fighting, had bled rivers for the empire, and he was savvy with any weapon or tactic. The Praefectus made some arrangements. Claudius had been a centurion, faithful, recognized for gallantry fighting the Germanics near the Weser River. So they found a use for him. Claudius couldn't accept early retirement. War had been a faithful spouse for longer than the time he'd been alive prior to becoming a legionnaire. The beaches here were certainly better than the snow where they'd fought the Tungris.

Claudius made his way to the stoas, his mind as choppy as the Mediterranean slapping against the jetties.

You would have died at Baduhenna had you not been a coward. He couldn't shake these words. The mention of the Rhine could be a lucky guess. But Beduhenna was different. A black mark of shame in an otherwise commendable service. A shame he never mentioned. Which no living man knew.

Their cohort's support of the auxilia had brought them into thick woodlands. Trees rose into a grey overhead that masked their tops. Adronicus was run through by a spearman on a horse. Claudius crouched over his friend. He recognized the eyes, death's hands already around him. During the skirmish, a Tungri rebel swiped a blade along the back of Claudius's knee. A coward's swipe. He dispatched the man in a fit of rage. Hit him in the face with his helmet, swinging until his arms felt heavy and the legs stopped twitching. Were it not for the wool lining his legs, the limb would have likely been lost. The legionaries that remained charged ahead. There was no hope in these desperate advances, Claudius knew that much.

At that moment, Claudius could think of nothing but their colonia. With Adronicus and the others dead, his mind searched for reason in their squandered lives. Some purpose other than a senator's whims or a general's flanking strategies. He stayed in the trees, lying beside Adronicus's body. There were no witnesses. No questions. It had only been him and the corpses. Steam rose from under him. From his body beneath the armor and his blood trickling into the snow.

The shame didn't come until later. When comrades commented on his wounds, or young legionaries told battle stories, he'd sit silent. Those who have known war–its ugly truths, not the patriotism and jingo fantasies created by men with unblemished skin–don't need to talk about what they've seen. It is a private thing. Shared in the fraternity of experience. Told through the wayward stares of haunted eyes.

He justified these actions to himself. He wanted to stay alive for the others. It would have been a waste to die there. But the other part of him, the fledgling echoes of a soul singed by the fires of combat, knew he should have rose and ran forward. He fell victim to the struggle for preservation scourged by so many men of war. And despite how many times he'd risked his life, certain he would die thundering into battle, Beduhenna did make him feel like a coward.

Sometimes he felt guilty being alive. Wished he could return. To give his life alongside Adronicus. Perhaps there's some colonia waiting beyond the grave. Where the six could rest together with sound limbs and healthy bones.

Claudius.

He turned to look around him. *Who calls me?*

Has life been squandered hiding your head in holes?

"Who are you?" Claudius looked around. The crucified men were black shapes in the distance.

Such a waste of good blood.

Claudius looked around again, then began walking. He walked as quickly as he could, until his wounded leg burned from the exertion. He laid on his bed. Draped a forearm over his eyes and tried to sleep.

Your crimes are written in the snow. Your colonia will be a dung heap.

Claudius did sleep. A short lived rest. With dreams of nails and hammers. Massacred villages, trees…pigs.

He sat at the end of his bed, face in his hands. After some time he rose. He walked along the stones. Beside the pools and stoas, letting his fingers search the grooves in the stones he passed. There were torches lit over the path, and all that could be seen from the beach was the white surf beneath the glow of the moon. Its reflection on the dark water. He removed one of the torches and walked to the spot where the men were crucified.

Claudius heard wheezing, cracks of fluid filled lungs. The birds that gather at the water and run from the surf were picking at the bodies. They perched along the lateral beams.

"Please…"

Claudius looked up. The last man they'd crucified was wheezing. His legs shook. The voice shards of glass smothered in a whisper.

"I can't…" The voice took on a high pitch. "I can't listen to him any longer."

"I can't listen to him any longer." The lunatic repeated the man's whimpering. It was the exact tone used a moment before. Then laughter again. It seemed louder at night. The birds taunted him.

Something moved in the sand. Heavy huffs and snorts. Claudius swung the torch around. There were two pigs at the foot of the lunatic's cross.

"Kill him, Claudius. It's been days, has it not? Since the last time you killed a man?"

"You know nothing."

"We know all, Centurion. You shame the memory of Adronicus. Your colonia will be a dark hole, where you'll burn from flames you cannot see. Scream from lungs that never tire."

"I'll break your legs. You'll be in the pits before lunch."

Something brushed against Claudius's shin. He looked down and screamed before he caught himself. It was a pig, nuzzling against him as though it were a cat. He pushed the animal with his good leg. It walked off a little. Claudius looked back and another pig bumped into the back of his legs. He fell to his knees in the sand.

"They'll help you learn your place, mortal."

Claudius looked up. He'd dropped the torch in the sand. Its flame was almost gone, a glowing stone. Something splashed his shoulder. For a moment he thought it was rain, until he realized whose cross he knelt beneath.

Disgusted, Claudius tried to rise to his feet but one of the pigs rammed into his side. His face hit the sand. He laid there. The pig's snout loomed over him. The lunatic's laughing returned.

"Let me be your god, Claudius. You Romans have so many, what's one more?"

He shook his head. Tears stung his eyes. Granules of sand crunched in his teeth.

"I am a benevolent deity. Forget the lifeless eyes of your comrades. You don't want to die here. Eaten by pigs, soaked in piss."

He shook his head harder, like a dog throwing water from its fur.

"You'll run again, Claudius. I can make you a centurion again." The smell of death fouled the air. Salt mingled with the sour punch of decay. Claudius gagged. On his knees, hands in the sand, he wept.

"Place your troubles at my feet, child. I will bring you glory."

Claudius managed to whisper "no." The sound was barely audible.

"Come. Adronicus awaits."

Claudius curled up in the sand, bringing his elbows and knees close. One of the pig's snouts was wet against his ear. He heard a voice, but it reminded him of the subtle whispers in a man's head. The dark thoughts that rise up before you think better of them.

More whispers. Great and terrible. Sweet and sour. Kind and cruel. There were cracks above him. He looked up. The lunatic was barely visible in the ambient light. He had torn one of his hands free from the nail.

Claudius felt called. The urge as strong as a sexual deviant before succumbing to his lusts, or a drunkard returning to wine. He grabbed the remnants of the torch. The ash, veined with embers thin as hairs, crumbled in his grip, searing his palm and fingers. The pain reminded him he was alive. Of old wounds acquired in man's noble purpose. Claudius shoved a handful of the smoldered ash into his mouth, raised his eyes to the man peeling himself from the cross, and laughed.

CHAPTER 32

THE SHADOWS OF THE PORTICO

The stench outside was not something normal noses grow accustomed to. Shadows lined the stone path like fallen trees, the blues and blacks of deep night as dense as any foliage. The perfect place for a person to stand and hope anyone wandering by didn't hear them breathing. The chirps of crickets seemed to increase in frequency, nearly keeping pace with her heart.

Salome was quite certain Samuel hadn't slept in the days they'd been there. They laid at night together, her head on his chest, waiting for nostalgia to meet the forgotten solace his strong arms once provided. Twigs and vines made the man up now. His frame seemed to her brittle, as if he would shatter like the gentile's pottery were he bumped hard enough.

She couldn't distinguish the rise and fall of his breaths. On one of the rare occasions his eyes closed, she searched along his throat below his chin, trying to find the heart beating.

Salome shrieked when his hand clamped her wrist. "I couldn't tell if you were breathing." His smile was unlike any he'd shown before, more a predator's lip curled back than the expression of pleasure or enjoyment.

"You stir me to life, darling." Then he rolled over on top of her, pressing into her. Before Samuel was injured his body was firm, sinewed, sculpted from his labors like the statues of Roman heroes he so despised. But now he had hay needle legs and feeble arms, and the knobs of protruding bones left bruises. Samuel told her things while they laid together. Vile things. Degrading comments even a prostitute would try to stifle were they told them. And for such a frail example of a man, he gripped her like manacles. Somehow, despite his shriveled state, his strength had grown considerably.

When Samuel finished he laughed. Salome curled up away from him. He spoke when she addressed him, but he generally ignored her until he was ready to use her body again.

That wasn't all. Samuel was crass outside of their intimate moments. Cynical comments and questionable innuendos made up most of his conversation now, making Salome wonder again how much Samuel knew of her affair. Perhaps it would explain the missing tenderness. This man was an entirely different person. Had Hannah told?

More than likely. Probably before he was even healed.

Healed. In this case the word required exposition she wasn't equipped for. She imagined replanting a fallen tree, only this time, when the trunk was raised, instead of the fruit and water of a vibrant and fertile thing, the limbs and branches were barren and stuck out with sharp barbs. That was her Samuel.

Life at the villa made her increasingly uncomfortable. The unsettling words and deeds of its many inhabitants, the deformed products of healings, the stench outside as tangible as the bricks that made up its walls.

And their leader, Saul. The man they called Mashiach. Congenial enough when engaged, but his flint eyes and the natural scowl of his face seemed prone to relapse at any moment into the glimpses of a turmoil only hinted at. There was never a misplaced lilt in tone or loss of composure in the brief time she'd observed him, but she knew without a doubt the man was dangerous. This was purely intuitive, the notion didn't come without its doubts, but she could sense it, like being near some sleeping predator and hoping not to rile it to action.

She figured this unpredictability, the danger she sensed, is what was needed in the Son of David to rally the children of Israel. Goliath wasn't killed with hospitality, after all.

Saul bar Azareel performed wonders. That fact remained indisputable. Samuel could walk now, and she couldn't expect Saul to heal a man's bitterness, could she? The day before, two men brought their friend's body. Saul leaned over the cadaver. Spoke into the ear. The leg twitched and the body seemed to shudder, as if shaking off chains they couldn't see. Now he walked among them. Laughed, joked with the two friends that carried him there. Still, there was something about his expressions and mannerisms that seemed off. Perhaps the knowledge of what it's like on the other side warps a man. To Salome it seemed like he was trying on his skin for the first time.

The scriptures described miracles, recounted the Lord's works as joyous, well springs of jubilant tears and the source for shouts, spontaneity, and dancing. Nothing of the sort occurred here. A man rose from the dead and Saul's disciples behaved as though he'd done nothing more profound than slip into a pair of sandals.

And the way the resurrected man's friends smiled the day after made Salome wonder if they wished they'd let him stay dead.

Saul was a man made of sharp edges in a sea of tender flesh. He revealed personal things about strangers, knew the intimate sins men take to their deaths. And not only the violations of commandments and infringements of the law, Saul knew motives. Their greedy and malevolent considerations in the heat of passion, fantasies of impulse. He could sniff out a man's depravity in ways that could drive the listener mad. Salome kept her distance for this reason, not wanting to bring Elijah to light. Not with Hannah lurking. Not with Saul already leaning over Samuel's bony shoulders to whisper.

She sighed the syllables of Elijah's name.

Salome let her anxiety take rein. She imagined Saul telling the drunks in that room about Elijah. The details smeared in sweat, serenaded by their panting. She envisioned Hannah's smile spreading, Samuel's chin low as he glowered. Her nature scared her. The pleasure in forbidden lusts, the sweet tang of Eden's fruit on her tongue. As much as she genuinely cared for Elijah, and she did, she loved and adored the man; the act of adultery itself had enthralled and burned in her.

An adage from her mother came to mind: fretting over uncertainty is a frivolous endeavor. She settled some, breathing to try and keep her heart from rattling out of her body.

For now her focus was here. Was there room for two Messiahs? Did the stories of Jesus mar this man's image in her mind? Why were they so different? Both performed wonders. Had followers willing to die at their beckoning. *Does God build a house divided?* Is Jesus that much different from the man they revered here? If he was anything like Elijah described, then emphatically yes.

They seemed antithetical to one another.

She had no idea how long she'd stood in the dark of the portico thinking these things over. The acrid smells nipped at her palate. Her focus returned with the sound of old metal. Ancient hinges pained at opening.

Salome crouched, turning to the land behind. The shape of the building behind the main house rose into the dark above it, capped in shadow. Beyond the columns were fronds and sharp plants that made crossing the shrubs with any subtlety impossible. She moved from the portico a few steps until only a finger touched the column she stood by. Something moved and she froze.

Swine.

The pigs moved about the yard with labored breaths punctuated by snorting. Snapping at one another in the dark.

Whenever she saw them an unsettling tremor began in her gut, spreading like a slow wave.

The door ahead was still open, letting out light. Between the crickets and the fury of her own heart in her ears, she thought she heard laughter. It may have been a whimper, but the pigs began an uproar, chanting squeals and snorting like the chatter of an angry mob. Their commotion reverberated from inside the cellars.

The cellar was said to be a Greek triumph, the Hellenistic remnant of Roman relations with fellow gentiles. Now it was filled with unclean animals. They festered in there, stinking and shitting, rolling and playing in their filth.

She remembered pigs as intelligent creatures, inquisitive, even cute in their own way, despite admonitions to their uncleanliness and her people's derision toward them. These seemed nothing like the pigs she saw as a girl. Except for the huge sow that laid near the cellar, they rarely came out in the day. But they were brought into the clearing and sacrificed. Each time this coincided with the performance of one of Saul's many wonders. None of the healings offered what the Psalmists described.

Why swine of all things?

"They're fascinating creatures."

Salome shrieked. She turned to face Chuldah with a hand over her chest.

"You scared me," she said, breathing as though she ran a great distance.

"Smarter than they seem." Chuldah's head was cocked slightly. Her smile a slight curve.

"Yes, I heard them in the brush. I couldn't tell what they were at first...my eyes took time to adjust."

"You've wandered out alone."

"I wanted some fresh air."

"This is what you consider fresh air?"

Salome laughed. "No," she dropped her eyes. "I just wanted to be away from everyone for a moment."

Chuldah's brows raised and her smile widened. The expression struck Salome as a caricature of empathy. She walked to Salome and they joined arms at the elbows. "Come, let's gossip for a while, shall we?" She began walking, Salome was pulled along.

"Gossip?"

"Yes. So much is happening now. A shift in momentum is coming for Israel. The son of David will bring us back to glory." They passed a few columns before Chuldah turned to the other structure beyond the clearing. Salome understood this to be a Roman temple of sorts, its white stone mostly masked in shadows now. Chuldah whistled. There came clicks, labored breaths, then two of the pigs grunted as they emerged from the darkness and trotted to Chuldah. They stopped once they noticed Salome. Then their grunts intensified. They squealed and raised their front hooves. "I don't think they're very fond of you." Chuldah's face was turned to them, Salome couldn't interpret her expression.

Both of the animals were filthy. This wasn't surprising. The coloration in their skin, however, their smell, and their posture made them appear as though they'd already died. Her heart was beating fast.

Unclean.

"Are they sick?"

Chuldah turned to her. "The herd is sick. They share an infection. The bodies begin to rot, poor creatures. It makes them stink. The disease is totally harmless to people. But we keep them here so they're away from the other animals."

"Other animals?" Salome had heard a donkey bray the night before. It sounded greatly distressed.

Chuldah laughed. "There *were* other animals. They just don't seem to last as long as the pigs. They can be very affectionate. They'll never forget a kindness. Or cruelty." Chuldah knelt and one of the pigs approached. She scratched below its chin and it grunted. Salome got a better view of the animal. It was warped different colors, patches of hair stood in random spots like burnt grass in its scabbed skin. The spiral tail bounced as the animal turned in a circle, grunting and squealing.

Salome nodded and looked down.

They continued on. After a dreadful silence, Salome decided

gossip might be fitting. The sole reason she'd been outside the portico was to gather some information about this place. "Saul seems confident in your abilities as a host and caretaker."

"If I'm to do something, I do it well. He shares my philosophy and recognizes our shared traits."

Salome nodded, then cleared her throat. "Can I ask you something?"

"Of course." She patted Salome's arm. "Just us girls here."

"Why the pigs? The sacrifices, caring for them. The way you beckon them. They seem like pets."

"The master feels a special kinship with them."

"With pigs?"

"Yes." Chuldah glanced at her and smiled.

"But... they're–"

"Unclean?"

"Yes. Moses declared them unclean. Yet they're sacrificed here regularly. This man, Saul, they call him Mashiach–"

"Saul bar Azareel *is* the Mashiach."

The response was curt, Salome could feel the tension in the woman's body. "I just want to understand. I grew up with the law of Moses. An affinity for pigs is the last thing I'd expect from a prophet of Addonai." When Salome mentioned Addonai, Chuldah's body seemed to tense further, as if mentioning the name was a cause for revulsion.

"You're familiar with the prophets, the lion and calf lying together. Jeremiah's promise of a new covenant?"

"Yes."

Chuldah turned to her, somewhat abruptly. "You're quite fortunate, really. If only you understood our roles here. We are witnessing the birth of the new covenant. Don't let swine be your stumbling block."

Salome tried not to appear flustered. There was an aggressive tone beneath Chuldah's cordiality. She heard some of the pigs scurrying off to their right, grunting, as if to conspire in the dark. She decided to press on this nerve and see how far she could take it. "How does Saul share a kinship with them?"

Chuldah sighed. "They're outcasts. Put out of the fold by Moses. Saul sees the stigma they endure, the way they're labeled, treated like dirty things. How could something *God* created be unclean? Were they not loaded into the Ark to mate with the rest of the crawling things and beasts?"

Something in the way Chuldah said God. Salome decided to press this issue further. "El Loheim made all things for man to enjoy. I suppose that makes sense." Salome grabbed Chuldah's hands. They were warm and damp. "Besides, I've always wondered what shellfish taste like."

Chuldah returned her smile. She nodded. *She doesn't know what I'm talking about.* Salome smiled. The role of thespian had been altered. "How does the other man, this Jesus, come into play with all of this?"

Chuldah's face dropped. She pulled her hands away from Salome's. "He's a fraud. He dines with whores and casts out unclean spirits in the name of Ba-al zebub." A few of the pigs were lying in the grass not too far from where they were standing. At the mention of Jesus's name, they sprang up and darted off into the night.

Salome decided not to comment on the harlots or the Romans. "So I've heard. Ba-al zebub and Molech. All the worthless chaff the Philistines revered." There was another outburst from the pigs. Chuldah's eyes narrowed, almost imperceptibly. She seemed to catch herself. Salome could feel tension between them. "They say he heals illness, raises the dead. Is it possible there are two prophets in Israel," Salome decided to test the woman's knowledge further, "like in the days of Ezekiel and Malachi?"

"That stone mason is a fraud! He's nothing like Saul bar Azareel. How would a false prophet bear the staff of Moses? Saul has seen the holy ones. They came to him. Your own husband stands. Walks! You should grovel at his feet!"

The false correlation between Malachi and Ezekiel seemed to escape her. It could have been a result of her irritation, which, if Salome was honest, was in some ways understandable, since she revered the man so much. Still, a prophet of God who sacrifices pigs? Her suspicion seemed well founded. This didn't please her, but sank into her gut like iron. The implications made their own frantic squeals and grunts within her. Salome smiled, nodded, concentrating on her appearance, quelling all worries for the moment.

Silence passed between them. After some time, Chuldah smiled. "I'm sorry. I'm passionate about his ministry. This, Jesus," *did she squirm saying it?* "He threatens everything we stand for." Salome stopped. Her face illuminated by some new epiphany. "Come, let me show you something." She tried to lead Salome into the clearing, but Salome pulled back.

"I'm sorry for upsetting you. I'm just so confused. It's different than anything I've ever known. I must be getting to bed. Samuel and Ima will be worried."

"It will only take a moment." The smile, the heightened sense of congeniality, everything was wrong. She pulled her from the portico. Salome saw the dark outline of a pig rising to its feet.

"I've been gone far too long." Salome pulled her hand away and turned toward the portico with a thousand apologies, walking briskly to the door at the end. She stopped. Then realized Chuldah must be watching. Had to be watching, and would scrutinize her every movement and mannerism going forward. She began walking again, mulling over the thoughts that brought her pause. *What has happened to Samuel?*

CHAPTER 33

ABBADON RETURNS

With the brine of Caesarea Maritima at their backs, the three, along with a handful of swine, headed out, following the fleeting heat shimmers and thin whirlwinds that rose and died unexpectedly.

Before their departure, Abaddon stood on the breakers with the others, admiring the pozzolana, finding the repurposed ash Herod used to construct it poetic and rich in a cosmic sort of irony he kept to himself. Any meaningful symbolism was soon lost. Streams of urine brown as a rat hit the water and the pisser's laughter ate up the bloody dawn. They felt wind, then jealousy for man's sensitivity to creation's touch. They cursed man and his God there. The glories of creation and the surrounding architecture proved to them adequate examples of the hubris of each.

The boy's loculus swished with every step, the nails inside clinked in a delayed rhythm. The lunatic dragged a broken foot without falling behind. The nail that pierced his ankle hadn't been removed, it bent when his body flopped over after tearing his wrists free. His skin was caked crimson and there were holes in each wrist. The bone wove into the flagrum mutilated a once handsome face. Abaddon took the flagrum. The mallet the Roman used for crucifixions swung in his hand. Roman armor covered his chest, the Plaudamentum thrashed behind, and the galea, stolen from one of the officers, which Abaddon thought looked gaudy, bounced slightly with his gait. Its crest plumed in alternating red and black bristles of dyed horse hair. He enjoyed this new body. The gleam his armor cast foretold their approach.

Abaddon was pleased to shed the old man's carcass. Not so much to cramp into the body of a pig for the last portion of their journey, but spending epochs in a void of unquenchable fire prepares one for the setbacks in a life of flesh. After entering Claudius, Abaddon crept to the prefect's assistant's room. There, he whispered in his ear what Belphegor had advised. The man, like so many of the Romans, was a deviant, navigating the moral world with a broken rudder. He would obey when the time came. For now, the prospect of a feast, with insurrection as the dinner conversation, would haunt his dreams.

The boy attending the crucifixions walked with Abaddon and the lunatic. His sardonic grin and malevolent stare profaned childish innocence. This was interrupted occasionally by relapses, when the boy inside, the real boy, rose wild eyed to the surface. His face turned to Abaddon, who now assumed the face of the one man in Caesarea that had shown him any kindness. Abaddon stared down like a warrior looming over a conquered foe. The boy sensed the change. He turned away, bewildered further by the pigs beside them. When the boy noticed the lunatic he stopped. This greatly amused the lunatic, who brought the gaping wounds in his wrists to his brow, and with his remaining eye and black socket staring at the child through the holes before pulling them away quickly, like the games fathers play with toddlers.

They shoved him forward and laughed at the puddle at his feet. The swine stopped and lapped at the suds in the sand before scurrying along.

It was simple to coerce the boy to surrender. Roman slaves were pitiable, timorous from the hardships and cruelties they suffered, most often lacking the will or self assurance to deny any advance. Like most of Adam's progeny, coercion was only a matter of finding specific avenues. For a strong will, the demon must discover a man's sin, enthrall him in it, let him wallow in the effects of its pleasures;

then set it before his eyes so it's there when he turns his head, in his bed at night, as soon as he opens his eyes in the morning. For the boy, it was a simple matter of hierarchy. Promises of citizenship, grandeur, mirages as exaggerated as a spot in the senate were whispered in the secret corridors of his mind.

The boy found them conspiring beneath the cross. He'd been on the beach, knees tucked in his chest, sobbing over the soldiers' debauchery. Roused by the lunatic's laughter as he pried his body from the nails, he went over to where they stood to investigate. His need was recognized at once.

Abaddon saw something in the boy he identified with. They both strived for something they couldn't explain, with no possibility of attainment. A will is of little accord. Not in any meaningful sense, for creatures like Abaddon. But for the boy, ignorance over his own agency could at least allow the illusion of happiness. Puppets seldom notice their strings until they're wrapped around their throats.

One of the weaker ones pounced on the boy. The worm slid into his subconscious, pressing a bloody snout to his little ear, filling his heart with delicious promises. The child probably saw himself as Caesar.

The child fell victim to his own naivety. He was subjugated so long that any semblance of power could raise him up. Abaddon thought of their plans, established long before the rocks they kicked along the way crumbled from cliffs. Before the jagged points of mountains tore from the earth and rose to stab at the clouds.

The feeble ones among Bazumel's fold are the most destructive to their hosts. They prey on fear, feast on the sparks roaring through the brain when minds succumb to delusions. Lovers of pain, paranoia, recurring nightmares, the turns in the gut and hot needles in the face from panic delight them. It's all strong and irresistible drink. This is why weak hosts go and wither away in forgotten places. As the rational mind peels and wilts, the possessor's grip tightens, strangling any vestiges of personality or memory. A man is consumed slowly. The leaching of souls is a foul and methodical business.

They walked. Through harsh white sun, night chilling sweaty

skin. Blurred shapes of mountains came into focus and villages came and went.

Later, the boy inside assumed control again. When he came to, his arms and legs burned. Crippled by exertion and the sun's persistence. His stomach screamed. He feared his tongue may turn to dust if he spoke. They'd walked with nothing but the few things they'd brought. He staggered, feeling the sting of chafed skin where the strap of the loculus rubbed slow abrasions in his skin. The boy picked up his head and saw pigs trotting, looking up with snapping jaws. The world spun. He collapsed.

Abaddon carried the boy on his free shoulder. The Roman and the Lunatic didn't speak. There was no need. After so much time in the void, languishing in burning waves and choking on ash, then being tethered together in the man, they knew one another, like an elderly couple in the dusk of life. The boy and the crucified lunatic would prove useful in spreading their message.

Bazumel awaited. His new capacity was the antithesis of *HIS* preaching and healing, casting their brethren to the abyss. While they've possessed temporal bodies, *HE'S* been born as man. *HE* grew, feels pain and yearnings, temptations to sin. Where *HE* preaches kindness, abstains from the lusts of flesh, their dogma begets indulgence, the destruction of the temporal world.

The Accuser *must* be pleased.

Bazumel was the prized son. Instrumental in *HIS* wrath. How many times was he chosen to bear his sword against the enemies of the elect while Abaddon watched, pining for action? How many of the women that would bear their children now were his? Bazumel's pride rivaled only The Accuser's. But only in The Accuser's case did it seem merited.

While Bazumel was certainly powerful, his flaws were evident under scrutiny. One-upmanship, snide rebukes, his tendency to sabotage a coherent plan if there's not enough lauding, if he's not venerated above all. Bazumel was competent, but unpredictable. His will, while iron, would be his downfall. A heavy thing submerged would pull him down. If the Accuser's pride was his undoing, how could Bazumel survive his own?

He'd resigned to listen to Belphegor. For now he'd abide in the shade of Bazumel's swelling head, at least for the time being. Until the soil was ready. When the Prefect's assistant would warn his superiors. None of them knew. Not the two with them, not Bazumel, who viewed Abaddon as nothing more than a competent lackey. Not even the Accuser.

Belphegor's propensity to scheme could never rival the hands of providence, but even the Accuser, whose compliments were given like a miser's last shekel, gave the obsequious seraph his nod of approval. Abaddon had witnessed Belphegor thwart well thought plans as casually as a flame eating parchment. Bazumel now took credit for all of Belphegor's schemes.

Abaddon had his own interests in mind. When the Romans came, and they would come, Abaddon would fight against them with the others. That way, were Belphegor to somehow fail, Abaddon wouldn't be punished by Bazumel. And when Belphegor asked why he'd fought, he could attribute his behavior to his fondness for war.

Abaddon was quite pleased with himself by the time they reached the villa. They approached through the vineyard. The retaining wall had crumbled.

They entered through a gap in the bricks. In the clearing behind the portico, a crowd had gathered. An even mixture of Jew and gentile. Bazumel wore a blue garment. There was something red stitched throughout, its fringes shook along the hem like tiny tendrils. His head covering was a brilliant white, contrasted with the robe it hovered like a solitary cloud. His back was turned. In his hands was the rod the mortals thought belonged to the prophet. When he turned, Abaddon smiled. On Bazumel's chest was a gold plate with gems of different colors. The Urim and Thummim. Haughty Bazumel adorned like the high priest.

He marveled at the cleverness of such a ruse. The mortal's Messiah wandered in peasant's clothes, a simple tunic and cloak, as a man with an ordinary, uninspiring face. Bazumel sought the items tradition had claimed lost, assumed the body of a man that seemed fated to lead.

The crowd watched their priest, savoring his words. He told

them of their deliverance from sin. Not through the plucking of eyes, the ascetic endeavors of Essenes, but through a life of indulgence. He used the scriptures masterfully. The promises of new covenants and deliverance were expounded. The staff was thrown in the dust. It coiled, shimmered with scales, hissed at them.

Abaddon carried the boy to Bazumel. The prophet explained a parable about a scorpion given respite from the sun, and the faith it used to cross the road with birds overhead. It all sounded like nonsense to Abaddon, who thought Belphegor should have assumed the role of the Mashiach.

"I seek the one they call Saul," said Abaddon. Some of the crowd dispersed, seeing it was a Roman with rank speaking.

"I am Saul." He stood taller.

He really does enjoy this.

Abaddon set the body before him, awaiting a miracle.

That night, the fallen held counsel near the cellar. While discussing their plans, Bazumel and Belphegor began to bicker.

"You'd rather give yourself to maggots than help your comrades."

"Comrades," huffed Belphegor. "Flies about shit we are. Following the great dung beetle Bazumel."

Bazumel's face darkened. "I'd sooner build a kingdom among the dung heaps than fester in darkness again."

"The bird with broken wings believes it's free. The floating fish brags at how it swims."

"Speak plainly, sow."

Belphegor raised his head from his front hooves, eyes narrow and livid. "Every step we take, the movement of all things, from dreams and despair, to the direction tongues scrape palates to form sounds–he oversees all. Our role here is frivolous. You gather fools for a feast that was planned before you were made. You still take pride in the rebellion he fostered in you."

"The feast was your idea."

"And its purpose will be for *HIS* glory."

"So you'd propose we do nothing?"

"I propose we live in reality."

"My rebellion is my own. I have purpose here. Which I experience without coercion."

"You've worn your shackles so long you no longer notice the chains."

"Like you've grown accustomed to the piglets at your teat."

Belphegor's head turned slightly. "You shouldn't taunt me, Ahavel."

"What have I said about that name! Bazumel, my name is Bazumel!"

The suckling piglets scurried off. Marduhl backed away. Belphegor rose, knees cracking.

"You've grown complacent in that wretched body!" roared Bazumel. "You belong in the swine you inhabit!"

Belphegor had turned for the cellar. He looked back over his shoulder at Bazumel. "Says one cleft foot to another."

"I covered my feet in *HIS* presence. I routed armies! You were a pawn sent to bewitch mediums."

"You underestimate your adversaries."

"Show me one worthy of fearing. I am an instrument of wrath. Who did he call to turn the Nile to blood? To blot Egypt's sun?"

"Which you never fail to remind us. If only I could find a body without ears." Belphegor laughed and headed down the cellar's stairs.

Bazumel looked after him. After some time he slammed the door and headed back to the villa. The staff, which Bazumel left against the cellar, transfigured and slithered through the dust on its belly after him.

MAHALEL AND DORIS'S FATE

Mahalel rose in the night to relieve himself. The ground was cold, the wind biting. One of the camels bellowed. They slept near the cart, a ways off from where he and Doris wrapped themselves in their cloaks and furs. He turned to them. Standing their strange way, nodding in exaggerated arcs, their heads resembled branches swaying in the dark. They moaned and grunted, and were now beginning to buck.

He shook himself clean and walked over to calm them.

Mahalel circled the cart, staring off into the desert in search of what startled them. After putting them at ease, he went back to where he'd slept. Doris snored, unbothered by the camels. No surprise, they'd have a better chance waking the rocks. The young man had abandoned them a few days earlier. Mahalel looked back at his remaining camels and shook his head.

Mahalel had searched through their stock, checked his ledger. Besides the camel, everything they'd brought was accounted for. *Was the boy running from something?*

He stood in the wind with his hands on his head. The land felt more desolate now, his injustice brought a profound sense of abandonment. They cut their losses. They still had the two camels. Could still carry most of what was packed, though their movement would be hindered somewhat. He'd been ambitious to bring so much anyway. Though he was still angry, he worried for Elijah's safety. Doris had liked him. As had he.

Something startled him from these thoughts.

The camels again.

Voices. Harsh, raspy words scraped through hewn tongue and cheek. He tried to distinguish the sounds, place a dialect. It seemed unintelligible. Only he could recognize a pattern. Mahalel spoke Aramaic Greek. He was familiar with some of the old tongues the priests studied. This was different.

A chant. Although absurd, Mahalel couldn't help but feel they were incantations. They came from all around, like the songs the grasshoppers and crawling things sing at night. Somehow it all merged together, possessed a singular voice.

This tongue held place in men's ears. It was present in their inception, before roots clasped soil and everything walking was named. It coerced wayward hearts in the shadows of alleys, pushed hot blooded men further into passions. It would goad the affairs of men until their light flickered out.

The language of the Accuser is the song of man. They drift into sin at its lilt.

Mahalel.

Somehow the foreign tongue became intelligible now.

What is it you want, Mahalel?

The old man trembled. The insoluble mysteries of this sound's origin bore into his mind. *What delights you, Mahalel? Let us commune. Your problems will be forgotten. The blood you cough, honey.*

Mahalel's eyes watered. He clenched his jaw, his knees were wobbling pillars in a violent quake.

Let me in.

"Who are you?"

I am the end of sin.

Mahalel's jaw worked slowly. No words came. The camels moaned and grunted, bellowing loudly.

There was something there, on the edge of sight. Mahalel blinked.

The half moon glowed enough to distinguish a shape approaching.

I am the end of your sins.

Mahalel couldn't interpret what stood before him at first. He could sense the danger emanating from the thing, even before his mind recognized the name for it.

The creature was enormous. Its eyes focused on him, black pools under the grey moon. It moved toward him in slow, incremental steps while whispering to his mind.

Mahalel turned to Doris. Her back was arched. Another of the things stood by her head. Its snout nuzzled her ear, twitching. Those scratched voices rose again.

Stricken with cold panic, Mahalel couldn't scream. His feet were heavy, his body unresponsive. It was like trying to rouse from a nightmare.

More of them trotted into the open. There was a wet, sloshing sound, a light smacking. Garments torn. Then the roar of camels.

Mahalel shut his eyes and tried to will himself to move. Something tore at his leg and brought him to his knees. His scream finally came.

CHAPTER 35

BAZUMEL RUMINATING

The Messiah's ministry toured the cities and villages of Israel, rounding the sea of Galilee, skirting the river Jordan where John baptized disciples and castigated the religious leaders of Israel. Through even Samaria. Nearly every Jewish village had the opportunity to see *HIM*. Condescending as a man, it was as though *HE* carried a glowing coal. After mesmerizing a village with his wisdom and feats, the embers were taken on the wind, roaring through the dry and shrubby hearts of men and women, sprouting lush vegetation in the place of the burned chaff that grew there previously. The good news spread.

HE sent disciples to double back, two by two through the villages, preaching about the Kingdom of God, laying hands on his emissaries and granting them authority to cast out unclean spirits and heal diseases.

All this, to Bazumel and the others, hovered about them like an incessant swarm of gnats, pestering without end. They could sense it. Joyous, unbridled worship. A mockery of the throne room itself. The human part of him harbored bitter dregs in the corners of the mouth that tasted sour, a rotten hollow in the stomach under constant strain and pressure, and pounding headaches. He was beyond constraint of any physical ailments of course, but such visceral reactions fascinated him.

Bazumel's ministry concentrated predominantly on the gentile villages. There were Jewish bourgs throughout the region visited by his wrath, some the scenes of slaughter, others targeted once they knew *HE* and his minions were as far from their activities as possible.

The pairs of envoys were a response to their presence. *HE* expected Bazumel and the others to simply sog and decay at the bottom of the Sea of Galilee. The humiliation of inhabiting swine, then a creature as prosaic as a goat–Bazumel shook his head–poor Charuk still stank in the fields as an ox.

Optimism in the face of their eternal foe was increasingly difficult. The Accuser had warned them of further humiliations. The act would seem like a triumph, he assured, but this would gather the sacks of flesh to their fold in a way the Seraphim could only pine for. He found himself in a daydream, reminiscing on the glint of sapphire, glass as expansive as the sea, the repetitive drone they were coerced to sing. *Holy Holy Holy.*

Bazumel wondered how long it would be before he would see *THEM* again. And how long before that possibility extinguished. They'd listened to the Accuser. His every point made sense, his campaign, justifications, the rhetoric sharp, undeniable. It had been the encapsulation of his existence at the time, some fleeting semblance of how the humans burned to sin against their creator. Rebellion gave them what they never had. Agency.

The fall was brutal. The glow of that burning sea, where black rock floated like glacial drifts over waves of cinders and ash lapped shores, bound for eons in chains, gouging the eyes from each other's wings out of sheer boredom. They waited while mountains rose from mantle, the stars burst in scintillating palabras through the black expanse, and inevitably the dusty visage of the creator, molded as they were from lumps of clay, were breathed to life.

In OUR image.

In whose image then, was Bazumel fashioned? How beautiful had *THEY* made the Accuser? Such ferocity and elegance encompassed one being. All that adorned him, his wit, the power of his song that shook the very pillars of the throne room. The indictment was pride.

Pride. From one lauded day and night for distinctness, praised for the mysteries of *THEIR* collective singularity, the source and essence that defined and characterized all goodness. *THEY* are praised for their beauty, gloried in by lesser, finite beings. Were Bazumel and the others not glorious? Did they not stop the hearts of man with their presence?

For every one of the Israelites he killed, he imagined shards of a looking glass, each bearing a piece of their maker's reflection, and each mind they infested, sapped dry like parasites or forced into self mutilation and debauchery, was like crushing those shards to dust and loosing them in the wind, distorting the image their maker imprinted on them into something utterly indistinguishable.

Bazumel sighed. He raised his chin when he realized what he'd done. A tinge of shame passed for this weak display of humanity.

Things were progressing. Belphegor's schemes were orchestrated masterfully. Their influence was already at work in Caesarea Maritima, throughout the populated gentile cities. They had servants in Herod Antipas's fortress. There were even inhabited members of the high priest's family. Belphegor's plan was quite simple: To sow discord, raise doubts, and to establish an alternative for the zealous, where they could indulge in pleasure rather than asceticism.

Bazumel dressed. The tunic was clean, the fringes of his tallit kempt perfectly, elaborately threaded. As a small and petty pleasure for personal indulgence, he'd scrawled obscenities and lewd drawings over the script that filled the phylacteries.

When he opened the door to his chambers, the cripple's mother was waiting. She knelt the moment she saw him. Bazumel approached, leaving his groin decidedly close to her face. He hoped she'd smell the scents of harlotry. Sex was one human trait they indulged in incessantly, denied in their true form. He stroked her hair.

"Back again, child?"

"Master. As you know I came for my son's ailments. His back had sunk into the center of the mat over the years, I'm grateful for all you've done–"

"Dispense with the flattery, there's work to be done."

"Yes. I'm wondering, you see. My son's wife, Salome."

"I've seen her." Bazumel licked his lips. His lower extremities tingled.

"Before, while Samuel lay ill, I'm afraid. Samuel lay crippled for a long time, I stayed with them–"

"Get to the part that pertains to me."

"I believe she's committed adultery."

Bazumel laughed. It made the old woman shrivel. "Of course she found another man. Look at her. She's in the flower of her youth. You expect her to care for an invalid, flaccid and pathetic, *and* deal with her shrewish mother-in-law without release?"

Hannah looked up. Her missing teeth made the hole her open mouth made seem larger. "I..I.."

"Someone had to pluck that flower before it withered."

Her eyes shook back and forth slightly. Confusion, disgust, dismay–all inscribed in the wrinkles of her old face. Bazumel smiled. "But...my son..."

"What would you like me to do about it?"

"I...I wanted your counsel."

Bazumel stood straight. He put his hands behind him. "Hannah, don't you think your nagging has been punishment enough for the woman?"

Hannah, still on her knees, blinked. Looked around the room.

"You're a pestilence to your sliver of the world. Your son, in his healthy days, used his resources to help widows and orphans, inspired peasants to stand up to the Romans and their sacrilege.

Instead of following his example you became one of Pharaoh's plagues."

"I did what I felt was right in my heart." Her voice was a low whimper.

"Your chest is a dank and barren tomb. There's cobwebs where your heart should be." He smiled as she writhed under his words. "How many beggars have you denied alms, Hannah? Oh, but let there be a Pharisee nearby, you'll put a little more into your hobble, make the coins clang."

Hannah tried to speak. Her jaw opened and closed, but words were lost to her. Tears streamed down her face.

"Tears? Tears now?" Her Mashiach laughed. "You sycophants are all alike. Never crying for your sins, but let some embarrassing personal matter emerge and you'll set the Ark afloat."

Hannah was on her knees with her eyes down. Her brow and cheeks as wrinkled as a wadded rag.

"How long did you mourn your husband?"

"No. Please."

"Oh, the widow!" Bazumel's forearm covered his brow, standing contrapposto, he whined, and in a perfect duplicate of Hannah's voice, but smoother, free from the dings and divots acquired with old age, said, "Hold me, I've been so lonely." Then he moaned, and she recognized the sounds and when she'd made them.

Hannah's sobs crescendoed. Her hands were on the floor. Tears pattered the stones.

"You made it your duty to tell your son about your daughter-in-law's infidelity every chance you had. I wonder if Samuel would be interested to know mommy's secret? How you made yourself a widow, then devoted the rest of your pathetic existence to giving everyone else guilt about it."

"No no no no no." Her head shook violently. She reached for Bazumel's sandal and he kicked her.

"You belong on the ground, don't you?"

She nodded, red eyed and leaking from every orifice puncturing her crumpled face.

"You have no idea what it's like for God to turn his face from you."

She looked up, a pathetic supplicant, reaching at the fringes of his garment. "Please, have mercy."

"Mercy." His tone was flat. "You want mercy, child? Are you ready to be free of the guilt that plagues you, so you can be filled with something greater than yourself?"

Hanna nodded, sniffled, and let out another brief muffled whine.

"Good." He cupped the sides of her face. "I think I can make use of this old chamber pot." Bazumel laughed a short, sparing syllable and poured himself wine. "The first thing you must know." He crouched and gave her a disgusted look. 'There is no sin in my kingdom."

C H A P T E R 3 6

B E L P H E G O R

Outside the damp cellar behind the Roman villa, the sow heaved for air. The belly, pink, pricked with coarse follicles of blue and silver, swelled and dented with each breath, like an old wine skin with cracks indicating an inevitable burst. The creature laid against the stone. The body sagged, and the many nipples, swollen and sore, formed two dotted lines over the flesh of its stomach. They trickled sour milk. Piglets scuffled over spigots promising what already spoiled.

Its eyes were dry wells. Deeper than a sane mind cared to explore. Indifferent to the crack of Abaddon's mallet, to the screams accompanying these strikes. It focused inward, the eyes reflecting the black intent of its own machinations.

Belphegor, the router of generals, was worried.

The events had transpired so suddenly, tearing them from a cave full of bones to the cusps of political influence. Besides the days spent in the water, things had moved too fast to stop and ask why any of this was possible.

Why would *HE* not cast them into the darkness? They knew *HE* was near, felt *HIS* presence humming like a nascent storm. Was it a feint? When they were in the man, kneeling like vermin before their condescending foe, Belphegor, in a moment of panic, blurted the first thing that came to mind.

Don't cast us into the abyss.

And *HE* listened.

But why? Why this reprieve now? Surely, *HE* would have recognized any subtlety or dissonance leavened in Belphegor's pleas. It was all very disconcerting. Before this place they were running free into villages, swarms of portly bodies pumping stout legs, blood frothed snouts, black, grey, and pink hair slothing downhill like mudslides. Bloody walls and floors. Bite marks and hunks of flesh.

We've gone undisturbed.

Belphegor felt the organs (what withered remains feigned to operate as such) grow cold, slowly, as if anxiety was thick and viscous, working its way through his veins.

The only reason they were allowed to inhabit the pigs had to be because of some usefulness he couldn't decipher. Belphegor knew this was the case. Couldn't deny it any longer.

There's facets to destiny. Those who act in a manner *THEY* consider righteous, trust their futures are something greater than imaginable. These were the people Belphegor marveled at. Despite the heartache, calamity and loss, despite the bad things permeating their pitiful existence, they achieved buoyancy through trust in *HIS* goodness. Isn't this the tale of the abused? Hope that the bruises will turn out to be kisses. *Heaven.* He spat the word from his mouth, shook its remnants from his scabrous skin.

Then there are those like Belphegor, who know the one who orchestrates the paths of stars, and still defy him. They live with the impending expectancy of demise. Like a spider under a bowl. Prepared for the magma and chains of Tartarus to wash over their necks again.

Is this striving futile?

Belphegor sighed. He stood, scratched his hip on the wall and dropped heavy on the ground again. Dust glinted in the air. Lying against the stones, he thought of dignity. Dignity in standing one's ground against a foe whose strength could not even be understood by its wielder. The gallantry of a warrior who fights without the fear of death. He thought of the Accuser. Another sigh seeped from his snout.

He was numb. There were muffled cries from the wheat fields, monotonous begging. He heard them laughing out there, Abaddon was having fun. That was a good thing. He had done well. Belphegor listened. To the sound of piglets at the teat and their whimpers. Chatter from the idiots in the villa following Bazumel, content as the swine, with no real ambitions for anything meaningful.

The intricacies were maddening. Defying their tormentor was like trying to fool the sunrise into doing something unexpected. Who has the gumption to curse the hands they're molded by? One of the piglets worked its mouth at Belphegor's nipple. It had a black mark covering half its face. Discolored, the dead babe yearned for its mother's milk.

And the analogy struck him.

Belphegor rose, ignoring the squealing underneath. These piglets, they were like man. A dead, festering thing, decomposing in sin and yearning for sustenance. And what did that make him? Men, for the most part, were happy. And did those pigs ever care if their milk was spoiled?

He crossed the yard, thinking over man's predicament. Though their choices were illusions in the grand narrative, they still experienced them as though they were free.

Belphegor's knowledge had been a stumbling block. *No more.* Though he knew everything worked for the good of the elect and the glory of his enemy, while he was here, as short or as long as that may be, he'd allow himself to experience the present moment. Like the humans.

ROAMING THE VILLA

Salome explored the villa by day. Dusty spears of light intersected its rooms, bathing furniture and art in its glow. Salome felt the marble surfaces of busts, the polished wood on the tables, the soft texture of a blue tunic draped over a chair. The banquet hall was foul with the odor of last night's wine. A Roman laid snoring beside a candelabra in the vestibule. Her sandals stuck to the floor.

Elijah described his Rabbi as somewhat of a vagabond. Not these people. They enjoyed their affluence. And from the sounds she'd heard down the hall the previous evening, as well as the evenings before, they enjoyed every carnality imaginable.

The property was immense. It boasted olive and wine presses, fields of grain. Beyond the clearing adjacent the portico, the wine cellar's door was open. The enormous sow laid beside it watching her, as if guarding the place. Salome thought the stench was adequate enough to ward anyone away. About a furlong from the cellar the temple stood. White as bleached bones. The statue of a Greek deity in pieces near its steps.

The villa's buildings were long and tiled, with courtyards annexing various points. On the opposite side from where Salome stayed, a second story overlooked the fields. She'd seen Saul up there, brooding, sometimes with Chuldah beside him. The portico bridged the kitchen and the covered vestibule outside the banquet hall. Palms were bent and broken near the portico and throughout the open area near the cellar. The wheat beyond the cellar and temple was nearly as tall as a man. The time to reap was close at hand.

Salome walked through the portico, cringing at the fetid scents the breeze carried. She entered the second building and passed through the kitchen, nodding to the doleful servants. They seemed relieved at her presence. Salome found a staircase near the kitchen. As soon as her eyes broke level with the roof coming up the steps, she ducked down. When she poked her head up again, the man hadn't moved. He sat mumbling incoherently with his head to his shoulder, propped against the wall in a thin tunic stained with blood. Salome stepped up slowly, greeting him and waving, and stopped when she saw he'd wet himself. Blood trickled from his arms and face and from gashes along the sides of his throat. He held a flat rock in his upturned palm, dark with dried blood.

Salome crept toward the man. His skin had blistered in the sun. Flies dotted his forehead; guests of the dead, early for a man well on his way. She listened. The language he spoke was unlike anything she'd heard. She took another step toward him. Once her shadow covered him, his eyes shifted to her abruptly. They were hazy. Held no recognition for her or the world beyond.

Then, without provocation, the man brought his head forward and ripped it back. Salome flinched at the sound. He began bowing his head forward, snapping it back against the wall. A slab of meat bludgeoned on a butcher's block. She tried to grab him but could do nothing.

After what seemed an eternity of self mutilation, it stopped. He slumped over. Gore splotched the wall, bits of his skull stuck to the residue with a little clump of hair. She stepped back when he raised his head. "Yes Ima." Her own voice had come from his mouth. Salome screamed.

Ephron came to the roof shortly after. Abijah followed. "Grab him," said the boy. The man muttered under his breath and lifted the deranged man over his shoulders.

"What's wrong with him?"

"He's insane," said the boy. "We'll bring him to the master, you'll see. He'll have manners fit for Pentecost before the sun falls."

Salome nodded. Wrenched her garment in her hands.

"What are you doing up here?"

She turned to the boy. What kind of child orders a man around and interrogates women? His demeanor and mannerisms betrayed the roundness of his face, the smooth arms and undeveloped muscles, the cracking alto he spoke with. None of it fit. His eyes made watchful anachronisms. "Why is it your business where I walk, boy?"

Something dark passed over his face. His head tilted forward, bringing the fat under his chin puffing toad-like. He looked up through dull eyes, like a ram ready to charge. "My business is the master's business."

"Where's your mother?"

The boy turned and walked down the stairs without answering.

She stayed, leaning over the wall and taking in the vineyards and structures in the fields. Beyond the temple where the wheat grew, she could make out four figures. Arms stretched to the sides, facing away. *Scarecrows.* Strange, however, there were birds perched on the shoulders, and it looked as though they were pecking at the filling inside. She looked over the portico and the clearing. Stopped at the cellar. The sow near the cellar door raised its head. It stared up at her. Yawned without moving its eyes.

Salome turned from its gaze. Her flesh broke out in little bumps. As she descended the steps, she saw a vulture making wide circles in the sky overhead.

CHAPTER 38

ELIJAH

Elijah rode back toward where he'd left Mahalel and Doris. He couldn't help seeing them in every cluster of rocks, his dread growing as he scanned for more corpses. He dreamt he found them, Mahalel locked around Doris's frail body. In his dream the two were wrapped in a lover's embrace, and their blood fanned into the sand around them. He was exhausted by these visions. They had reached the point where he dreaded sleep. His ass was numb from riding and his spine felt clamped and squeezed top to bottom. The insides of his hips burned from squeezing his legs to stay on the camel. He was nodding off atop the camel.

Elijah found the cistern Mahalel tied to the cart, cracked in half and filled with sand. Shards of cheap pottery laid around it. Mahalel must have thrown it to the ground when he realized he couldn't take it.

The landscape alternated between sepias and verdure, shrubs sprouting modest figs and trunks even Samson couldn't put his arms around. He'd passed furlongs of thirsty land with cliff formations that looked like spikes, and on the same day watched butterflies circle shoots of grass.

The day after he found the pottery he spied some buildings off the road. From the colonnades, the white stone and gabled roofs, he recognized the work of gentiles. Buildings made with the same materials composing the Hebrew homes he knew, but instead of the lopsided bricks packed with mud and shit, their corners were precise.

Elijah turned the camel toward the village.

Whatever had gored Absolom and spurred the warnings about the dangers on the road had visited here. He'd never seen such things. Flies swarmed bodies in the streets. The life source of men splashed walls like haphazard brushstrokes from careless artists. Men and women with digits of fingers and things the creator gave to interpret the world through torn away. He thought of the children of Egypt, the angel of the Lord's visitation. How close instinct brings us to truth without our knowing.

Bloated bodies floated in a limestone pool large enough for several people. Their tunics spread out on the surface. The water a diluted wine color.

His heart wilted, every vital part within him pulsing. His hands shook like one of the old women at the synagogue.

The camel made slow deliberate steps, guiding the pads of its feet and sweeping its head left and right, low to the ground. Scavengers picked at the bodies. He sat frozen for a while. Absalom had been horrible to see, he expected to find him dead. But this…this was Jeremiah's Lamentations. The aftermath of a tangible and prodigious evil. Eradication. The warnings to steer from the road also applied to caravans, perhaps even a marching legion.

His eyes were as blank as the camels'.

For the first time in days, Elijah thought of the Rabbi. How badly he wanted to see him now, to feel safe in his presence. To make sense of this. Elijah stopped when he saw a child against the bricks of one of the houses. One of his chubby arms hung out behind his back.

The Rabbi's words came to mind: *Weeping and gnashing of teeth.*

It seemed fitting. Absalom, now this, the feeling he had standing with his fists clenched as he watched Salome ride off with that bitter old woman twisting her knobbed fingers, opening and closing to pantomime her private conspiracies.

The fishing village had been abandoned, and now this. He'd searched several small villages and had made his way through the synagogue and markets of Capernaum. The Jewish villages were fine. The places the Mashiach would be. Where Salome would go.

Elijah ushered the camel on, tightening his dead legs and setting off toward Jerusalem. The things he'd seen stayed before him. He felt more alone now than he ever had.

He rode the better part of the night, only stopping to eat and to let the camel rest. Elijah laid on his cloak that night without sleeping, staring at the stars, brimming with questions. The next morning he set out early, and by mid day came upon houses. It was as quiet as the last village. The nearest door was open, its black shape threatening portents of every kind. He didn't breathe, watching. Elijah exhaled when a little girl ran out. He sat on the camel laughing.

Once he was farther down the road Elijah climbed down and sat on a boulder. He put his face in his hands and wept.

CHAPTER 39

A HUSBAND'S NEEDS

Who can fathom the loneliness an invalid knows? The cycle of emotion and crooked labyrinths Samuel's thoughts traversed on that mat, gathering each hateful tinge, resentment, and sentiment of ill will like cobwebs torn from the moldy corridors of his mind; all this had accumulated–it must have–clogging a conscience designed to contemplate the divine with putrid thoughts and envy. Lying helpless while the world blurred by and his aspirations sank into the sores on his back. She understood why a man would be bitter. What happens to a mind without a means to alleviate its anxiety? To alleviate anything?

Samuel was subject to gloomy moods when he was healthy. At times he grew pensive. During these introspective spurts, he'd gather wood in great piles, throwing sticks and branches about until he deemed the pile formidable enough for his rage. Salome would hear him outside, grunting, the knock the ax made and the sound of split wood. On those nights her thighs and back were scratched by his calloused hands, which, were she honest, she enjoyed.

Lying on that mat for as long as he did, only his mind moved. No one to share ideas with, no physical relief, no reasoning friend to calm paranoia. Samuel's mind had hacked away at the good qualities. Perhaps even his sanity.

His behavior made sense. And here, seeing the Romans. To drink wine with the men responsible for him becoming an invalid. And then to hear of his wife.

But shouldn't there be *some* joy in his pain? And she remembered, Elijah was downcast after being healed as well. But that was due to whoever had abused him on the road. Samuel's situation had been far worse. He smiled at the others. But she knew. In this place all the smiles people made after they were healed were skewed somehow. As if smiling came at a price.

Samuel stirred.

People change. She wasn't the same woman she was when they married. Salome had waited by his side daily. Putting a sponge to his lips, grinding fruit to a paste and patiently feeding him little chunks. She was there for him. Of course, when she left for a walk or to the market, his mother came and assumed her duties. In most things, she'd been faithful. As much and as long as she could be.

She didn't want gratitude. But she hadn't expected hostility. Hannah must have relayed her suspicions. That could be the only explanation for his cruelty. How curt he was, the rude things he harangued her with. The coldness. His apathy to her emotion. But holding something in was unlike Samuel. Samuel told people how he felt, unbridled, regardless of consequence. Among the many things she appreciated about the man before.

The last time they'd been intimate he scared her. He was rough. He entered her with something like hatred in his eyes. Stronger than an emaciated man should ever be. He'd held a palm to her face, scowling with exposed teeth. She recoiled at the thought.

He moved again. Groaned. Samuel was on his back. Eyes open. They rolled, and the pupils made small specks. They flicked side to side. His body was still, but the eyes…Was this terror?

Only his eyes moved. It was as though…She didn't want to say it. As if the thought would somehow set the omen into motion. Make him an invalid again.

Why would he be frightened?

He laid there while she tried to soothe him, stroking his shoulder. She raised his hand. It fell limp again.

No.

"Samuel? Samuel?" She shook him. His body flopped with the motions. No volition of its own.

The eyes regarded her. Glossed and teary. She shook him again and a spasm passed through him. His jaw bulged to one side. The neck craned, wrenched into motion with a series of clicks. His chest rose, spine popping in an arch that left only the blades of his shoulder and his lower back on the mat, while his stomach made a shallow arc and his bones sounded like wood crackling in fire.

Tik. Tick.

She watched, frozen while his movements gained fluidity. His rigidness eventually left him and he settled back into the bed. That maddening smile returned. The new smile of a new man. The fearful gaze had gone too.

Samuel brought a hand to her knee. His breath bore a hint of the stench from outside.

Salome squeezed her legs and put a hand to his wrists. "I'm sore."

"I spend years living like tree bark, and you deny me the fleeting pleasures I have left?" There was a sharp edge to his tone.

"This tree will be dried up at the roots soon if you keep it up."

"You're my wife. You'll submit!"

"I submitted to you before you slept."

"My appetites have matured in their dormancy."

Samuel had never talked this way. He'd always spoken in simple terms, lacking pretense. And neither she nor Hannah had ever talked in such a way while he was bedridden. "I've been meaning to talk to you about your appetite."

He sat up, she flinched at his movement. "My appetite doesn't concern you."

"I can almost see your ribs through your cloak. You have to eat more.""

"You don't just grow meat overnight."

She nodded, then proceeded carefully. "I was told that when the lame or lepers went to the man they call Jesus, he–"

Samuel sprang on her, grabbing her wrists and bringing his clenched teeth close to her face. "You won't say that name here!"

"You're hurting me!" She tried to pull away.

"Saul bar Azareel is the Mashiach."

"Let me go, you're hurting me!"

"Say it!" He squeezed.

Her wrists burned, ready to crack in his grasp.

"Say it."

"Saul ha Mashiach."

"The stone mason is a magician. He swindles shekels from orphans and widows. The man ministers a brothel for Canaanite gods. And summons the unclean spirits he casts from people." He let her go, pushing her arms away, disgust in his face. Her wrists throbbed. She rubbed them, curling up and turning her back on him. She thought of Elijah. How his eyes had changed. The stories he told her. She shrugged.

Samuel laughed to himself. "Women will believe anything."

Her chest was tight with angst. After some time she turned to him and sat up. "Do you know how many of your friends came to visit you the first few months? What they did after their leader was trampled? Nothing." Her wrists were already bruised. "The men you were put on a mat defending dropped their eyes when they passed our house. *The men* were ashamed of what you became. Remember it was a woman that stayed by your bedside and fed you. That helped you swallow and drink. That wiped your bony ass."

Samuel's hands were around her throat before she could react. Pressure filled her head. "You listen," he hissed. "You'll do what I tell you or I'll fold you in half and feed you to the pigs. But before I do I'll send you down the hall so the Romans can have a turn at you. Do you understand?"

She did her best to acknowledge.

"From here on you'll be like the statues the Romans put everywhere. Your role is purely aesthetic. I'm not with you for your mind, my dear. There's something poetic, something that gets the rocks crying out in me all over again when I see the way you fill a tunic. That's why I'm with you. Your hungry womb. Don't think I don't know about you and the shepherd. I was paralyzed, not deaf. Adorable how you used each other." Veins bulged in her forehead, her face splotched, flushed with blood. Something wild and unrestrained passed over his eyes. He let go.

Salome gasped and pulled away coughing, scurrying off the bed and over to the wall. Her head throbbed and the room waned out of focus as blood returned.

Samuel rose, muttering obscenities, throwing chairs and furniture against the wall, stomping personal items before storming out.

Salome sat and rubbed her neck. She looked at her wrists. His grip left striped bruises there. Likely her throat looked similar.

She sat huddled up, worrying for tomorrow. For herself, for whatever burned at Samuel now, for everyone there at the villa. Wondering about Elijah and whether she'd ever see him again. Whether she could bear to risk his life in such a way.

CHAPTER 40

TWO BY TWO

The two had been on the road for weeks. Their clothes were stiff with dust, beards coated with the debris of Israel's byways. Every joint and sinew in their tired legs cried mercy.

Village after village, monotonous faces. The peoples' need, humming and pervasive, cried from a world in pain. It was constant. Overbearing. They didn't know how the master handled it. It certainly explained his gloomy spells, the many times he'd disappear from under their noses, found hours, or in some cases days later, in diligent, sweat filled prayer, or ministering to some scourged soul privately.

Matthew and Joseph speculated what it must be like to hear all the prayers of the world. To hear the churning brooks, laughing babies, the curses men make to their neighbors before striking them dead. The father knew every sin. Just a fraction of such knowledge would melt their mortal minds.

But they were given a fraction of something else. Whatever kept Shadrach safe in Nebuchadnezzar's furnace, and manna sprinkling from above, was a part of them now. In minute measure, but a part of them no less. This was taken as a grave responsibility, one which could be stripped for incompetence as quickly as it was given.

With the authority they were given, their bodies were now conduits. It wasn't clear how the miracles were accomplished. How something like that could pass from one man's fingers to another. But miracles were performed. And with each miracle, confidence in the inscrutable gift their master gave them grew. All along the roads they traveled, they healed, cast unclean spirits, mended bones. In a village not far from Capernaum, Matthew healed a leper.

The words of the invocation–the name of Jesus of Nazareth–was of little accord. What healed these people was the simple trust in the act's accomplishment beforehand. Faith in the bearer of the name's power. Not pronunciation or style in its utterance. What did the master say near the Shepherd's gate in Jerusalem? "The small seed of faith becomes a giant tree." It has nests, attracts animals, and so on. That's how Matthew tried to view himself. To keep these abilities veiled in humility, regardless of the villager's praises and thanks. It was dangerous, this power. He watched the skin of the leper wither like a snake's molt and had to restrain himself from feeling grandiose after. In believing he was a tree with a huge trunk and thick roots burrowed into the soil through his own works.

"Matthew?" The one that spoke, Joseph, could have been handsome if it weren't for his expressions. He had a thoughtful, drooped face, with pursed lips that became fish-like when musing. These ruminations were quite shallow. But what Joseph lacked in wit he made up for in virtue and faith. And he had an inner strength that provided no little comfort to his companion. A simple, yet righteous man. A better man than him.

Matthew was ugly for different reasons. For when a man pictures himself a way, it will become manifest to the world. The wrinkles, his permanent squint toward the sun, posture decades beyond his age, all stemmed from his lack of self confidence. He cowered and neglected his responsibilities. Years of drinking himself haggard didn't help, and with a shrunken soul taught from early on how pathetic its endeavors were, he lived in the confines of a mind filled with doubts. But he always stood again after he fell.

"Matthew, are you listening?"

He grunted.

"How long will we do this for?"

"Do you think he passed me a parchment while you weren't looking? How should I know?"

"We're just…walking."

Matthew sighed. "Your powers of observation border on omniscience, Joseph."

"It can be exciting though, can't it?"

"Of course it's exciting. God uses us. Some of them would be dead if we hadn't come."

"It's too bad I can't use it for bunions and blisters."

"I've seen the abominations you consider feet, Joseph. You ought to chop them off at the ankle and start over."

Joseph laughed. "I'm not a lizard, Matthew."

"The bugs I've seen you eat do little to help your claims."

"Locusts, Matthew! They're locusts. Even the baptizer ate those." Joseph rolled his eyes, chuckling at his friend and slapping his back.

"At least he was civilized enough to use honey. You just crunch it in your teeth like little vegetables with legs." Mathew shook his shoulders in an exaggerated display of revulsion.

"Civilized." Joseph's cackle sounded mule-like. "I don't think camel hair would get a warm reception in Rome."

"You're just mad you couldn't pull it off. They'd have to skin three camels."

Joseph turned his head sharply. Matthew could see his comment stung. "I'm kidding, Joseph. If you added that, fathers would lock their daughters away from Jerusalem to Tyre. Besides, I would need two and a half." With that he grabbed his belly and shook it, nearly dropping his staff.

"I don't know why the master chose you. You can't even make a bowel movement without a joke."

"Flatulence is a risque, but thriving source of humor, Joseph. And God certainly has a sense of humor."

"I don't know why God chose me either." Joseph looked down at his sandals.

"Ohhh, Joseph." Matthew put an arm around him. "If he can use a dried out wineskin like me, he can use anyone. I think that's the point." Joseph stared off thoughtfully. "Besides," continued Matthew, "if you spend all your time lamenting a gift you'll never take the time to enjoy it."

"Enjoy it?"

"Yes. Doesn't it bring you joy to do these things?" He stopped. Held up a hand. "I couldn't even chop a piece of wood without butchering an angle. Look at me now, straightening spines."

"It's not us doing that."

"Of course not. But there is something about being used, isn't there? And the thrill of his provision. When our stomachs rumble, our lips blister, and some stranger comes to supply our exact need the moment before we need it. The man who gave us water had been walking for two days. If we hadn't met him, we would've fallen over and shriveled up. We could have died."

"It is a unique privilege." Joseph scratched his beard. "But what about the suffering?"

"What about it?"

"He promised us we would suffer."

"He did."

"I guess... I don't see why all that's necessary. Why there's so much of it."

"You've read the Tanakh. You know about Eden."

"Of course. But what does Eden have to do with me? You and the scribes and Pharisees mention Eden like that should be the end of it."

"It's why things are the way they are."

"Because a woman ate some fruit? I've seen my mother eat a thousand figs, Matthew. It never got me kicked out of the house. And talking snakes, Matthew? Talking snakes?"

"You saw a man feed 5,000 people with a loaf and the snake bothers you?"

"Hmmph."

"Besides," he swiped at a bug and leaned on his staff as he walked on. "Why should I know about the origins of our woes? I only know mine. And all that's happened to me, I've been responsible for. And I probably deserve far more than what I've received."

"But what about the children that die in their cribs?"

"Better to not have lived in such a cruel world if it's as bad as you say it is."

"The children born lame? The lepers?"

"What about the beautiful? The mountains, the way a lyre sounds in the right room while a maiden sings?"

Joseph's eyes were fixed ahead. "But there's so much of it Matthew. So much."

"Joseph." He turned to his friend and put a hand on his shoulder. "You have the power to heal the very afflictions you speak of. If you don't like it, walk faster. There are other villages."

Joseph considered this. They turned and continued on.

The road had gradually inclined for some time. Both men huffed and felt their backs stiffen. When the ground leveled out they saw the roofs of another village come into view. Their hearts lightened, excited over the prospect of rest. Food. Witnessing the power of God yet again.

"Hills, hills, hills," said Matthew. Joseph wheezed agreement.

They walked on. Their instructions were clear. They were to stay in the first house they were invited into, not leaving until they were finished with the village. No extra luggage. Eat and drink what was given. Heal and preach. Move on, repeat. Each time they'd stayed just long enough. As though their itinerary was set out before their arrival.

They entered the village and were greeted by several men with weary expressions. After some pleasantries passed, a widow took them in. They were given water, some bread and oil, peas and lentils. The woman, like so many other lonely hearts in Israel, had an attitude as bland as the meal she prepared.

She brought them bowl after bowl. They accepted each happily, wondering if they were too literal with their instructions. They ate past the warmth of the food, until their tunics were tighter and their stomachs anchored them into dreams.

Later, Matthew listened to Joseph preach, planted on a rock telling all who'd listen all he'd seen. Hoping someone would actually hear.

"It's like we're living out the times of the Tanakh... There's nothing the man can't do... He calmed a storm, easy as quieting a dog. No, I didn't see it, but I know a man who did and I trust his word... He walked across the Sea of Galilee and found his disciples' boat in the dark. They thought he was a ghost! He forgives sins."

This brought grumbling. An older man asked, "is he a wizard?"

Joseph's smile dropped. "He's not a wizard. "He's the Mashiach."

Another man added, "the way you describe him does sound wizardish."

Mathew interjected, "he's come to be the light of the world. These aren't a charlatan's tricks. Israel's salvation has come."

"Salvation from what?"

"Rome. Each other. The wrath of God."

These talks often took turns like this. There were archetypes in every crowd, Matthew learned. The doubter, the naive fool nodding to all they heard, nosey spectators, the one who riled up the susceptible ones around him and sucked them into his lunacy. Then, like He'd told them there would be, there were a few with ears to hear. Who made sense of the knowledge they passed. They were throwing seeds at a stony surface here.

Mathew sighed, longing for good soil.

Opinions generally changed once the healings began. It only took one. The desperate mother of a child, an estranged spouse struggling with their lover's mortality. Not that miracles soften hardened hearts. For the roots to take hold, God must intervene. Another miracle entirely. And another point of theology Joseph and Matthew bickered over. But that problem can be addressed in some other scribe's parchment.

They did heal people there. There were shouts of Hosanna and praises. But like so many other places, they only glorified their maker with their lips.

Late in the evening a man came to the widow's door. Matthew woke when he heard him arguing with the woman. His host's voice rose against the caller, and Matthew caught a glimpse of his face over her shoulder, half drowned in shadow. The man's eyes scanned the inside of the house over her shoulder in frantic movements.

"My son," the quaver in his voice stretched the words. "We had to tie him up. He's as strong as a man. The things he says–it says…" His hand gestured toward whatever waited in the night. "That's not my son."

The old lady shook her head, trying to close the door. "Come in the morning. They've had a long day."

"It's alright." Matthew rose and walked over. He placed a hand on her shoulder. She slumped a little, shaking her head and muttering as she sauntered off. At the threshold stood the visage of despair. The circles beneath his eyes rippled like disturbed water. His desperation weighed on him, it brought his shoulders, his expression, his very heart sinking down with it.

"We tied him up…" His chest rose as his voice caught. "My boy…my wife and daughter left, they can't stay near him. My daughter." He sobbed, took a sputtering breath while his face seemed to age in a moment. "The things from his mouth are so vile." He buried his head in Matthew's chest and wept. Matthew patted his shoulder while the man released a torrent of emotions he'd held in. He looked over at Joseph, who was lying on a mat with his mouth open, snoring loud enough to punch the bricks out from the widow's walls.

"Take us to him."

The man lived in another village, not far from the widow they lodged with. Its houses made imposing strangers in the dark. Matthew could see into the open area of one they passed, the family was huddled together listening to the screams coming from up the hill. The lamps in many homes were out, being so deep into the night. Curious shadows moved through the dark shells.

Matthew stopped when he heard it. "Leave me the whore and eunuch, Marduhl, fine. I'll take the scraps. I'm going to pin his shriveled phallus over the threshold." It sounded as though it came from a throat torn with rocks and blades.

"That's him," said the father.

"I thought you said he was a boy?" said Matthew.

"Sour minds and lust driven whores," came the voice again. It was blaring, resonant, impossible for a child. "Where are your mothers? Give us a tit, hussy." He cackled and the laughs carried and echoed from the walls of the dark houses. "Do what you do for the tax collector. When you're dripping over the hay like a braying ass." The voice then imitated a woman's moans, frantic breathing and private things that happen in bedchambers. Matthew saw the father's head drop. He pretended not to notice. "All the thatching will burn. Mud and brick will be rubble. Soon, my pets, soon. Blood to the horse's bridle. Gnats will blot the sun and they'll return to their gods the maggots." An awful burst of laughter followed.

The words, and the pervasive shadows closed in around Matthew. He saw the man's house before them and thought of his master's parable about the city on the hill. The man's house was on an incline, and light shone from it, flickering now and then. Matthew saw the defeat in the father's eyes and was determined to ease his pain. Joseph was groggy, his eyes barely open. Waking him had been a miracle in itself.

It was impossible to believe that voice came from a boy. A son, a young man, perhaps. But a boy?

The house waited on the hill. They could see the light from many candles and their shadows. This provided no small comfort to the missionaries. The prospect of entering the room where those sounds came without light was maddening. There were already black shadows dancing, like demons around a fire. At the bottom of the hill a woman and a young girl held one another, looking up at the house. They turned their heads when they heard the three men coming. She went to Matthew and wrenched her fingers in his tunic. "Help him, please, help him." The boy's father embraced the woman, then placed a hand on the girl's head. They left and walked toward the house without a word.

The three stopped before the threshold. The boy's father lowered his eyes and took a deep breath. His hand rested against the door, for much longer than the affection he'd shown the girl. His hand opened and closed. "Whatever he says–it doesn't matter–he doesn't mean it. Something's wrong with him." He raised his eyes. Joseph put a hand on his shoulder and nodded. *Wide awake now.* For that Matthew was glad.

Before they crossed the threshold there was a great roar. It reverberated through the confines of the little house. Matthew wasn't certain, but he thought it was the sound a lion makes.

"Come to cast me out. Cast *me* out!" Laughter. Matthew's bones chilled at the sound. As they moved into the house, past a retaining wall divided in two waist high sections crumbling apart, the boy began making shrill squeals. The noise, impossible in its own right, replicated the sound of a thousand pigs. The ground trembled. Something in the room fell and broke. The men caught one another's eyes. Both were sweating.

"I've been waiting, Matthew. And what a gift you are. A fitting meal for your maggot gods. You know they came from the sea? Stampeding filth smearing shit and blood over everything clean."

Matthew crossed the retaining wall and stopped. The boy–he really was a boy–barely old enough to walk to the well alone, was on a bed in the far corner. Matthew could smell spoiled meat, garments damp and soiled, the putrescence of death. He smelled excrement, too. The child's chest rose, his back arched like a bow when the string's pulled taut, the limbs bent ways they shouldn't, the angles of grasshoppers prior to leaping. His head craned slowly and watched them cross the room. The eyes had a dull yellow glaze, like parchment worn yellow by the grease in men's hands. He smiled.

The father used everything he could to restrain his son. Sandal straps coiled around one of his wrists. Indentions of red rings circled the forearm. His other hand was tied with a series of scarfs and torn strips of stained garments, cranked tight to the corner of the bed with no room to wiggle. His legs were fastened with ropes, thick enough for the rigging on a boat. The knots bulged, it had wrapped around and in on itself repeatedly. Evidence of inexperience. Matthew stood in wonder over how the boy's body still contorted in such ways.

Matthew swallowed. "He has an unclean spirit."

"You have an unclean prick. Your skin still reeks of shekel rate whores, drunkard."

Matthew tried to appear unfazed, but the words loosened his insides. He stood near the wall. He could feel the spirit. Its malevolence peeling off in waves and telling every primitive alarm his body possessed he shouldn't be there.

Joseph walked toward the boy with his eyes steady.

With every step the boy turned with rigid movements, adjusting his body. He squealed again. Matthew took a deep breath and walked up to stand beside Joseph. He noticed the boy was mottled with bruises. Blisters bubbled over his arms and chest, the skin on his lips and face resembled clay that cracks up once it dries.

"What happened to his skin?" Joseph didn't turn from the boy.

"He leapt into the fire." The man's voice cracked. Matthew's throat squeezed closed.

Joseph roared. "Tell me your name, demon!"

"Father," said the boy. His eyes turned slowly to the man. The voice finally matching the frail body. "You've brought this squeaking thing to make me well?" He threw his head back laughing.

"Tell me your name!" This time Joseph didn't scream as loud.

"The stench of one dying in the wilderness."

"Tell me your name, in the name of Jesus of Nazareth!" The boy laughed. Joseph leaned over him. "Come out of him!"

The body twitched, and after several spasms appeared to lose some of its rigidity. The boy's chest rose and fell with slow, labored efforts. For a few disorienting moments the boy seemed to look out at them. The real boy. Joseph leaned closer, lowering his face to the child's, who breathed and looked off with a blank expression. When Joseph was close, the boy jerked his head toward Joseph and snapped his teeth. Joseph pulled his face away with a cry, bringing a hand to his face. He spit blood in Joseph's face.

He kicked in his restraints and laughed. The ropes squeaked, Matthew was amazed he could move his legs at all.

"What is your name?"

"I am the stench that wafts from the corpses in Gehenna! The piss trickling downstream, bringing fish to the surface. I spill disease in the wells, send flies to cover the fetid water."

"Quiet devil! what is your name?"

The thing chuckled. "Why are you jealous of Joseph, Matthew? You about left him sleeping to come alone. For your glory. Why do you despise him so, Matthew? Because he can do the same things you can, more than you can, without the bitterness? Without the constant need for recognition?"

"I command you to leave this boy, in the name of–"

"He likes you, Matthew." The boy's face twisted in a mock pout. "He looks up to you." When Matthew didn't respond, the child asked, "do you ever worry you'll see one of your old whores gallivanting about like you do? That you'll have to play holy man to a woman you had on her back?"

Matthew's skin was slick with sweat.

"I hear your heart, Matthew. "I'll enjoy eating your insides."

"In the name of Jesus of–" Joseph's voice cracked. The unclean spirit squealed with laughter. Laughter from a thousand voices, as if every unclean spirit in creation had gathered to laugh at them.

"He didn't send us back, Joseph." The voice of a child keeping something from a playmate. "Did you ever stop to think he might want us here?"

"Tell me your name, I command you."

"Even now, your pride is your undoing, Matthew. You're still the same man who clung to the wineskin. Your cup flows with recognition. If you believed I'd already be gone." Matthew knelt and lowered his head. He started praying.

"Yes, call the maggots forth. They wriggle to the surface with your pleas."

Matthew's eyes were squeezed tight, lips in motion.

"Your flesh has grown pale in Joseph's shadow. What does your master think, I wonder? What does he think of the way you look at Mary? He knows, Matthew. Knows you were with her while she was still a whore, knows how your loins twitch watching the women oil his feet. Putting their asses in the air while they wipe their hair across his feet. You wish it were you and it fills you with heat, you braying beast." He laughed again. "How many times have you approached the throne room of God with a hard little lump in your tunic? Hypocrite!"

Matthew continued to pray, trying to ignore it. Shaking all the same.

"What is your name?" said Joseph, lacking any real conviction now.

Matthew opened his eyes. The child was thrusting his pelvis into the air like a deviant recounting his exploits. "Call your maggots, Matthew. Ask for more wine!"

Something shattered. Matthew looked around the room. Bowls and vessels spun from impossible angles on the shelves. He watched, transfixed. A small jar whipped across the room, just past Matthew's face, exploding against the opposite wall. The boy's father stretched his hands to keep a shelf from toppling. Joseph shouted at the laughing spirit to come out. Stone and clay smashed against the floor and walls. A swine's grunts came from the child as everything fragile in the room began breaking.

Matthew fell on his ass, backing away. In the scramble he knocked over a stone jar full of water. It broke and poured onto the dirt floor.

Matthew looked down and screamed.

The water teemed with maggots. Squirming, tiny undulations taunting him from the filthy puddle flowing around him. He felt them on his legs. Crawling under his cloak and tunic and tickling the hairs on his shins.

"The maggots have heard your prayers, drunkard!"

Matthew stood, swatting at his cloak and hands, raising and stomping his feet. They were on his fingers, crawling up his legs and wrists and burrowing into his skin. He backed away.

"What is it?" said Joseph.

The father was shouting. Matthew backed past the wall. The maggots in the puddle were too small to see now. He could feel them. On his back. Turning his skin cold and making him retch. He turned and ran out of the house into the night.

He was down the hill, near the boy's mother and sister, when he heard a man's scream from the house. It was followed by the scream of a child.

CHAPTER 41

AN ALTAR FOR
SCAVENGERS

Swaying with the camel, Elijah put a hand above his eyes and watched dust scrub travelers from the horizon. All was silent save the rustle of fabric where he sat and the animal's plodding steps. Vultures made drunken circles above, wobbling as their cordon constricted. Smoke rose from a blurred shape in the distance. Whatever it was, the carrion altar provided a pleasing aroma to the scavengers.

The travelers had passed what burned and the debris leading to it without stopping. Before he could distinguish its shape he passed a strip of silk with a hole burnt out in the middle, weighted down from dirt on one end while the other curved in waves like a snake held by its tail. A lump filled Elijah's throat. Blurred in the flames, too charred to distinguish beyond the rude suggestion of its shape, was Mahalel's cart. He urged the camel on, clenching his jaw.

Mahalel's livelihood made a trail that veered from the road into the brush lining the side. Clay lamps in broken shards, wicker baskets torn to hay needles, multicolored cloaks that served as frayed and faded imitations of the garment Jacob gave Joseph. A Roman gladius stabbed the world half to the hilt, stone water vessels cracked in zig zagged sections, a broken lyre with knotted hair for strings. In the sand lay food and bent cooking utensils, their functionality only suited scraping chamber pots now. Broken commodities spotted the dirt like fragments of bones.

Elijah scanned the terrain. He had the camel lower itself and slid off with a grunt. The animal protested but he spoke softly and patted its neck. There was a goad in the debris, too old to be Mahalel's. The tip was broken. Dried blood and sand caked the curve of rusted blade remaining.

Round prints near the wreckage, smaller than the camels, and prints of men beside them merged and turned to continue on. Elijah moved through bushes and shrubs and broken fronds of date palms.

He found one of their camels in the brush. The exposed flesh was already browned. Portions were gone from the torso and the humps were partly eaten. Bloody knobs of vertebrae peeked through the exposed fur. Vultures hunched over the portion torn from its side with their wings half open, faces lost in the carcass. One looked up when he got closer and stretched its wings and the sun streamed through its feathers, transfiguring the bird into a creature from a gentile fable. The other raised its head, carrion dangling from its beak, and hissed. Their heads were white as bleached bones, bodies the dirty brown of a traveler's garment. They assessed Elijah with brazen stares, as if to say they would have their turn. They only needed time.

He walked on and found the kiln.

Smoke coiled from its opening. He poked at the ash inside with a stick and steam seeped out. It cleared and revealed the burnt shape of a foot. Elijah brought a hand over his mouth as part of it crumbled away.

Elijah stayed by the road for some time, bent at the waist with his hands on his thighs. He retched. Wept. Screamed. After he stood, he looked back at the brush where they were hidden. Then the direction he came, where he was headed. Both horizons cut into possibilities too terrible to contemplate. How long before he ventured on similar horrors, some vulgar ossuary for Salome? He shuddered at the implications.

Elijah clenched his fists. Scanned the mountains. The red glared cliff sides. The very sun. Any hints of a master curator subject to his inquisition. He stood there for a long time, allowing his mind to adjust to reality as he now understood it. To make sense of the insoluble.

He looked back at the brush as he led the animal on. A hint of smoke still whispered from the cart, potential squandered for the indifferent nostrils of deity. "A pleasing aroma to the LORD," he whispered. He envied them now, cured the plights of life and memory.

CHAPTER 42

THE CITY OF PROPHETS

It took several days to reach Jerusalem due to the stops he made. The Jewish villages continued with their lives. He discovered another gentile village, where the corpses of swine laid about the streets. Blood painted its stones and left the waters of its baths a rose color. There were no people, only traces of what once filled the homes. He salvaged food from the desolate houses, hungry from the road, and tried to eat what was lawful.

The sun rose glinting from the limestone surrounding Jerusalem. Elijah sat on his camel from a nearby hillside. His first visit to the city as a man. People moved around him to get to her gates. He sighed.

Jerusalem. Stones piled on the ashes of prophets. Foundations laid over idols toppled in jealousy. Even now clops of hooves fill the streets from beasts ridden by invaders, as it was when Israel's children were carried into exile, as it will be when all is rubble once more.

Elijah looked on like a man does an estranged lover. He made his way to the north gate. The smell of bread and oil from travelers outside scratched at the insides of his stomach.

He paid the tax at the gate after waiting. The immensity and pace of the city swept him in. Such a contrast to the crass mud and thatchings of the villages he knew. They spoke with a strange dialect, nothing like the fisherman north of Galilee or the rural men near home. Unwashed peasantry milled about, toiling in the relentless sun. The masses made a collective body here, representatives of the city's heartbeat, the way a man's pulse reverberates in his body, he saw its palpitations in sweaty brows and dusty feet. Here was Israel. His people.

Salome would be impossible to find. But she'd left to find the Mashiach. And He could tell Elijah whether she was safe. Where she was.

A woman in a small house near the gate saw his ragged cloak and tired face and looked on him tenderly. She brought him in, served him old smoked fish and vegetables with a paste she insisted restored a man after a long journey. Her husband supplied grain for the camel and let it drink from a basin set aside for their donkeys. Elijah had gathered all he could salvage from Mahalel and Doris's possessions. He gave the couple some seeds and a drum with a strange smelling canvas from somewhere south of Egypt. Part of the bottom was chipped away. The woman smiled at Elijah and he dropped his eyes.

He whispered to the camel and pulled at its fur so it wouldn't snap at passers by. Shoulder to shoulder, bodies clogging alleys and streets, the men's coverings a river of wool. The people smelled of stale sweat, the animal scents of fields and stables. This part of the city carried the stench of ignored latrines.

Over the rows of houses he could see the towers and parapets, the balconies of wealthy men. The old palace was straight ahead on the other side of the large wall bisecting the city. The part of the city beyond the north gate where he stood was smaller than the other side and filled with poor people and dilapidated shanties. Houses huddled close together, built with crude mud and brick like the ones in rural villages, corrupted by the excess of people, the primal business of life here, and their forced proximity. The wall severed the poor from the aristocracy of Jerusalem. The significant meeting places, Herod's new palace, wealthy homes of scholars and members of the

Sanhedrin, including the high priest and his sons, were in the area known as the upper city. The towers and parapets extending from Herod's new palace peeked over the city's western edge.

A path cut through the center of shanties and mud dwellings Elijah now searched. Subtle inclines sloped both directions, leading to rows of homes lining the outer walls. It looked as though a heavy rain would flood the center path. The inclines left some of the architecture skewed. Slanted roofs followed the natural slopes of hills, and many of the beams appeared to lie under the throes of a pressure that could likely be toppled with a gust of breath, let alone a heavy wind.

To the east, another limestone wall sectioned off the cornerstone of Israel and the lifeblood of her beating heart: the temple. Through the persistent odors of refuse and human waste, Elijah caught the scent of sacrifices burning. The memory of Mahalel left him seething.

Elijah cut left to avoid the crowds and followed the inside wall around. The houses skirting the wall had warped the color of the desert in the sun. Some had multiple stories and retaining walls of their own. Exposed vestibules where families gathered while women worked looms, structures where men and women threshed wheat, as modestly as one could in a bustling city, and stables filled with thin animals. Vendors waved and called but Elijah shook his head and moved on.

Elijah inquired about the Mashiach, of course. His questions only concerned His whereabouts, but the people happily divulged opinions and suspicions. A no good swindler said some. Some dubbed him Beelzebub's sorcerer. This came from the austere, dogmatic sorts with first hand knowledge of Pharisaic jealousy. Elijah heard myths of His wonders even the Greeks wouldn't believe. A woman told him Jesus sewed a man together after he was chopped into pieces with a strand of hair he plucked from his beard. Another claimed he dried up a lake to find a drowned boy and revived him. Perhaps the most outlandish, however, detailed how the patient Rabbi resurrected a small army from nearby tombs to descend on gentile villages. They attributed strange parables that were complicated or absurd. Nothing like the succinct profundity of the stonemason. The ones who told these stories were never the witnesses of such miracles or atrocities. Except for one old beggar, who told Elijah he encountered Him alone and received counsel regarding a private sin no one but God could have known. He told Elijah the Rabbi was in the city only a few days before, and he'd probably brushed shoulders with the man without knowing.

Later, a boy offered to store and water the camel in exchange for some money. Elijah haggled with him, giving the boy a hand carved toy and a roll of some frayed twine to cut the cost. He hoped he would remember what the house looked like.

Travelers with cages, animals led by ropes, and whole families of merchants loitered in the streets and along the wall of the temple mount. He found the entrance on the northern side, where many had lined up to tie their beasts. Worshippers stepped into a mikvah to cleanse themselves while a frustrated Levite barked orders. Elijah watched from a distance. Every type of creature permissible for sacrifice could be purchased. He smelled the burning flesh.

The money changers sat at tables, smiling with miserly greed in their quest for every shining metal and ore imaginable. Near the temple's entrance they sold doves in bulk. They sang dirges crowded into wood cages littered with feathers and droppings. The stout man who sold them had head coverings specially made for prayer. The material, according to the man, ensured every supplication was heard. He had a variety of other animals available for purchase, all prayed over diligently by Israel's most respected priests and scribes. Each had grazed in fields where Israel's kings had brought their own beasts. All this ensured a timely and benevolent response from the God of Abraham. He led potential buyers to makeshift pens filled with goats and lambs, and fortified stables for heifers and bulls. The man patted his forehead with a piece of purple cloth and went along to the people in line, encouraging them to remain steadfast, for the line was a worthy inconvenience for the holiness they would soon attain. But of course, if they didn't want to wait in this line, and they didn't mind spending more, he could take them to a shorter line with plump, unblemished calves and lambs with spotless fleeces.

Elijah watched him, fuming. Grime filled the wrinkles of exhausted faces. A man of modest means would work two sabbaths for one dove. He watched a bent old man hold a shaky hand out to purchase a sick lamb.

They've made a harlotry of sacrifice.

Elijah approached the man with the purple cloth. "You have quite the business here, selling sick lambs to old men."

He turned, bewildered, checking to see if the old man heard. "I've sold no sick lambs."

"Look at the scabs behind its ears. On its hip." Elijah motioned with his hand.

The vendor pushed Elijah's hand down, putting an arm around him and turning him from the line. His voice lowered, the jovial airs of the salesman gone. "They're going to be burned before the sun sets. What difference does it make?"

Elijah shook his arm off. He looked around at the people waiting to buy their animals. Then back at the man. He laughed. "What Pharisee would pray over a dying lamb?"

"Are you so righteous?"

Elijah regarded the man. Shrugged. "I suppose it doesn't matter. Have you heard anything about the Mashiach?"

"Which one?"

Elijah stared, dumbfounded.

It was the merchant's turn to laugh. "You haven't heard?"

"No."

The vendor looked around like a conspirator preparing to share a dangerous thing to know. "They claim another man heals and preaches." He patted his brow with the purple cloth. "He has the staff of Moses. His teachings say men should indulge themselves."

"Indulge in what?"

"Whatever the heart desires."

"What of sin?"

"How should I know? Soon the anointed will be as common as farmers."

"I'm looking for the man they call Jesus. The stone mason from Nazareth."

"Haven't seen him. It's almost passover though, he'll be here flipping tables soon enough."

"Flipping tables?"

"You should have seen him. Last time he chased the money changers with a cord, whipped them like horses."

Elijah looked at the money changer's tables. He longed to do the same himself.

The man with the purple cloth yelled to a boy struggling with the dove cages and stormed off.

Elijah talked to more of the onlookers. No one else mentioned any others when the question of the Mashiach was raised.

Thousands of worshippers would pass through Jerusalem in the coming weeks. Finding one man, so that man could tell him the whereabouts of the woman He had warned him against seeing, suddenly struck him as foolish. But it was unavoidable. He felt the dread of a boy preparing to confess to his father what would surely bring the rod.

He sat against one of the walls near a widow begging for alms. She glanced his way several times before rising and hobbling off. The money changers fed their greed while the wards of animals bleated for food. His thoughts were drowned in the shouts of hagglers and hecklers, agitated dickering, the grit teeth voices of men with fraudulent smiles. He watched hope fill the faces of those who could purchase expiation. And the faces of the destitute drain as they sauntered away to remain sinners.

Far from being a holy and sanctifying place, the temple mount was more and more a source of contention. Elijah was a filthy, discarded thing in the eyes of man and his maker. He decided to look around the other parts of the city.

The sun glared from the surface of the western wall over Herod's palace. He followed it past the arches adjacent to the temple. Beyond, a group had gathered around a scribe who taught from the books of Moses. Farther west, the Hasmonean palace was patrolled by Roman soldiers who kept the crowds from the gate with their typical unbothered violence.

Elijah maneuvered through the masses of people and wandered the paths and alleys between the houses there. The homes in the upper city were larger, built with precision that made the dwellings on the other side seem like clay in a child's hands. Elijah circled back to Herod's palace.

Along the walls of the praetorium, Roman soldiers pushed each other, laughing and whistling at Jewish women, calling out to whoever looked their way in their tongue. They didn't stray far from the palace and seemed to drink as much for the onlookers as their own enjoyment. People huddled around trying to see. The soldiers walked in furs and linen they'd sacked from conquered cities.

Shouts rose from the praetorium. Elijah saw a flicker of movement, heard the slap of skin that punctuated the crowd's shock. Screams and wails of pain followed.

He couldn't understand their words. The tone was derisive. Something was repeated by the soldiers. A raucous laughter followed and intertwined with their repeated chants, as though they found their own irony irresistible.

Elijah pushed past hecklers and spectators until he was near the wall. It was a spectacle of corporal punishment. Soldiers took turns whipping a man with a flagrum. The leather, along with whatever little horrors they'd woven into it, slapped and tore the man's flesh, splattering blood with every strike. The Romans chanted and yelled. Jews followed suit. This Elijah found particularly egregious, that these men would join heathens in humiliating their own countrymen. They hushed as one of the soldiers talked. Their tongue had soft edges and lacked the passion of Aramaic. The phrases were repeated in Greek, but Elijah didn't understand that either. Save for one word: crucify.

He looked around. Whether in bewilderment, or to identify some vestige of sanity in the mob he didn't know. They were senseless, swept up in the commotion. Then Elijah saw something move, and spotted a dirty face protruding from behind a beam. It supported a canvas awning where vendors sold tawdry garments. The man glared at the Romans, and when he pushed the sheet aside Elijah caught his profile. There was a stone in his hand, which he held at his side. His every movement was a failing struggle at anonymity.

He looked up as Elijah approached. Leaned to see past once he stood before him.

"What are you doing?" Elijah tried to read his face. He didn't look as old as his posture seemed to suggest. The man was filthy, rank with wine.

"Doing my best to mind my affairs."

"Do you want to be strung up in a tree beside him?"

The drunk furled his brow. "Yes."

"You don't mean that."

"Who are you to tell a man what he means?"

"There will be other opportunities."

"I missed my opportunity." His eyes shook side to side. "My friend died because of it. A little boy."

Elijah nodded and put a hand on his shoulder.

"I was afraid." The man's eyes rose, dropped, rose again. "I know the man they'll crucify."

"There's nothing you can do."

"You don't know that, I–"

"If you go over there, your own people will cheer while the flesh is torn from your back, just like him."

"David killed Golia–"

"You're not David." Elijah saw the man's strength dwindle before him. "And God's not here to help you."

The man shook his head and muttered something about little faith. He tried to shoulder his way past, but Elijah grabbed him and squeezed his wrist until the rock fell and its dust made a tiny protest only the two of them and their silent maker ever saw.

"There's nothing you can do for him."

The man gripped Elijah's cloak. "I need you to move."

Elijah shook his head. He looked over at the Romans. One of the soldiers dragged a forearm across his face. He watched with a curious expression. Then began walking toward them. The crowd continued in their excitement, swept up in the veneration of their golden calf. Elijah grabbed the man's arm and pulled him away.

The drunk's name was Matthew. They sat in a crumbled vestibule in the northern section of the city, not far from where the camel was boarded. In a turn of luck, Elijah learned Matthew had traveled with the Mashiach. He was one of the ones sent through the country to preach. Matthew told Elijah how Jesus found him, in a torn tunic stained with vomit, staggering through the streets of Capernaum with enough wine in his belly to fell an ox. He described the Rabbi and all the wonders he'd seen. He spoke of him the way youth do of early love. Matthew's somber expression became one of rapture as he recounted this.

When Matthew finished with his story, Elijah said, "I've met the man."

Matthew nodded eagerly, then waved a hand, expecting more.

The silence between them, taken with the noise outside in the city, seemed to creep up, to scratch a gnarled finger at Elijah's mind. He groaned. Then decided it didn't matter if this stranger knew his failures. "He healed my eyes. Then He asked me to follow him, told me what needed to be done. I couldn't. I ran in shame."

Matthew laughed. Elijah's face darkened and he held up a hand to comfort him. "Two cowards. I suppose if we put both of our hearts together we'd be a man."

Elijah laughed. "Sounds better than the curse God and die

thing."

Both were laughing now. Matthew pulled a wineskin from some hidden recess of his cloak and they drank.

Once their humor subsided, Elijah rubbed his hands together. "I have to find him."

"I know where to find him."

"You do?"

"Yes. I didn't want to see him. I don't deserve to see him."

"I know the feeling."

CHAPTER 43

BETHANY

Matthew went out alone. Elijah sat in the vestibule's shade watching a mouse dart in and out of a hole in the bricks. Perched above sat a coal colored cat with sparks in its fur, tracking the rodent with a predator's fascination as its tail slapped the dirty bricks. It leaned over the wall slowly, one paw reaching below it to support its body, suspended in an agile line toward its prey. The moment before the cat pounced, Elijah threw a pebble. The mouse disappeared. The cat jerked its head up, leapt from the wall, took a single step forward as if to accuse Elijah for his tampering, then bounded away in a flicker of movement. *If only He did the same for us.* Elijah made parables of everything now.

Matthew returned with a boy. They were led out of the city through the sheep gate. Outside, pilgrims still filed in, haggling fees with the guard. Animals and carts bivouacked in the distance, some in protective circles, others alone. The boy led them on.

They passed a market selling sheep and Elijah thought of a simpler life. Their bleating evoked memories of the hills and rocks of Galilee's northern shore. The closest he'd known to a home. There were a series of square buildings with covered colonnades and porches, which Matthew identified as the pools of Bethesda. With the crowds, the men and women who couldn't find respite under its shaded porches languished in the sun, mostly invalids and cripples, hopeful someone would drag them to the water for its supposed healing abilities. Elijah watched men step over them to enter the pools. An old man who couldn't use his legs held up a shaking hand to grab at a man's cloak as he stepped over his body. His hand stayed in the air, even after the man swatted it away.

They were passed by a garrison of Romans on horseback. The soldiers laughed and motioned toward them with their chins.

The Mashiach was staying at a man's house in Bethany, some 15 stadia from Jerusalem. The boy walked at a good pace, head down, stomping and shuffling and kicking rock and dust the way children do. They traveled the road to Jericho.

Elijah didn't know if the man would even speak to him, much less divulge the whereabouts of someone He'd advised him not to see. If He even knew. Elijah followed the child, shoulder to shoulder with Matthew, scratching the back of his hands as he contemplated what he'd say if denied.

The well worn path ran through the ridge east of Jerusalem known as the mount of olives. The necropolis at the southern end harbored the bones of Israel's nobility. According to Matthew they'd rise in the last days. He gestured toward the white stones in the distance while he rattled off the names of inhabitants he knew. Elijah was quiet.

The boy led the two men into the village. They passed a well where villagers waited with cisterns. The onlookers studied them. Travelers pervaded Bethany too. The boy hurried them on until they reached a fence surrounding a large property with rows of figs and dates accenting its small bushes.

"There," said the boy. They thanked him and Matthew put a coin in his hands. The boy kicked up dust as he vanished through the other houses. A woman came out and met them before they'd crossed the yard. She had olives for eyes and full cheeks resting on the ends of a tired smile.

A strong scent of perfume welcomed them in. They passed a vestibule filled with plants and found the Mashiach reclined at a table listening to a woman. He was focused on her story.

The woman who escorted them waited for a lull in conversation. Once they were announced, the Rabbi motioned them to sit. "Eat while you can. Soldiers shouldn't head to war on empty bellies."

Matthew went to the man and fell to his knees. The Rabbi put his arms around him and spoke in his ear. Matthew's shoulders rose and fell with his sobs as the stonemason continued talking. Two of the others, one a fisherman Elijah recognized from before, came and picked up Matthew, leading him to another room.

Elijah sat and watched in awe. They were affectionate to one another, jesting, laughing at the things they'd seen over the previous days. Everything was done with a warmth Elijah was unaccustomed to. Being near the man brought a great sense of security, like the familial bonds that bring children to their parents' laps. Elijah felt an ache in his bones. He couldn't help but contemplate forgetting everything and staying.

The woman who answered the door smiled at Elijah. He stole glances. Eyes that have seen pain are balm for the sorrows of others, they reflect the victory over tragedies they've seen, and prove the hard road ahead possible. For the first time since any of this had begun, Elijah felt some semblance of contentment. It was fleeting, however.

"Many of you will suffer," said the Mashiach. "Some for my name. Some will kick against the goads until the very end." He addressed them with a stolid expression. The tone of his voice level, every word conveyed as incontrovertible fact. He searched the room around him. Elijah dropped his eyes and put his hands in his lap. "After the son of man ascends to the right hand of the Father, His followers will be boiled and cut, nailed to trees, and flayed in the streets while the children of Babylon rejoice."

"But our reward will be sweeter." The host, a gaunt man with intensity in his stare and grizzled features, looked at the Rabbi with the adoration of a boy showing his father something he made.

Jesus sighed and put a hand on his arm. "Hold to your faith, Lazarus. It will keep you when they come for your head."

Lazarus's eyes widened. He looked down, letting the words settle in, then brought his head back up resolutely. "My body was rotting in a tomb. These bones moved at your command. I'll tear my heart out and give it to you now if you ask."

Jesus turned to look at Elijah. "A young man received a lot as an inheritance. He tilled the soil and gathered wheat to the threshing floor in season. He gave the poor a portion of his grain and his crops flourished. The young man had all he needed to live on. But as time went by, he became restless. One of his neighbors fell ill, and the young man stole his prized calf.

"The neighbor eventually died of his sickness, and all of his property went to a vindictive man who decided to settle all debts and assess the man's property. Tell me, what will happen when the vindictive man discovers the stolen calf?"

"He'll demand to be compensated for his livestock."

"The young man will be stoned."

"He'll kill the neighbor for his greed and condemn himself to gehenna."

"The neighbor will throw him into prison until the debt is repaid."

His eyes never left Elijah's. "He who has ears to hear, let them hear."

Evening came, Lazarus and his guests crowded around the Rabbi. Elijah slipped out, wrapped himself in his cloak and laid in the grass beneath a fig tree behind the house. The wind moaned for all the world's suffering. The parable was his. Salome the prized calf. He smiled at the thought of telling her such a thing.

Elijah closed his eyes and listened to the night. He tried to focus on the sounds around him, refraining from the spiral of his thoughts, the portents from around the table, and the conversation he would soon have. Sleep overcame him before long. He was roused by footsteps.

"Elijah."

Elijah knew before he turned. He went to rise but the effort was waived off. He sat up, pulling the wool over his shoulders. A heaviness accompanied the man, which Elijah hadn't placed until now. Being around him was conflicting, the way the view from a high precipice terrifies and enthralls all at once, that sense of allure and danger mingling as one and settling in the bowels. *That's what it was. This man could have his followers do anything.* But Elijah didn't fear him. For though such a power should rightly be feared, He was good. Before he spoke, the dread of disappointing him again and seeing his countenance falter, if only for a moment, seemed too much to bear a second time.

But His eyes softened. Elijah couldn't tell whether the corners of his mouth rose slightly. He knew this was the closest the man likely came to smiles. Elijah felt something warm in his chest. That the man would expose even a nascent sign of emotion on a flake of dung like him unhitched something inside him.

"I'm not clean."

"Amen. But not for the reasons you think." He sat beside Elijah. After a moment He turned to look at him. "You're still blind."

They were quiet until Elijah spoke. "The view from Mount Ebal is cloudy this time of year."

"If you knew the road ahead you'd save your breath to pray." He sighed. "You're like a man with broken legs who refuses a crutch. You'll walk into oblivion rather than casting aside your idols."

Elijah swallowed and sat with his arms around his knees. "I have to go." Jesus sat, considering this. Elijah thought his eyes watered.

"Follow the road to Jericho until you meet the river. Take it north, you will find an emissary of the Accuser. Ask only his name, don't answer his questions or try to cast him out. Don't let Matthew try either."

"Matthew's coming?"

He nodded. "He believes he owes you something. But now you must listen. The emissary will prophesy and tell you the way. You will find a Pharisee who knows me. Matthew will heal him. He will help you find what you seek. You go to a nest of serpents and vultures. Be strong. I'm telling you not to fear, but truly, you will. Your faith will falter. Even in your suffering I am with you."

Elijah nodded. Jesus watched him. Elijah could only drop his eyes and nod again. He wrapped himself tighter in his cloak.

The Mashiach rose and brushed himself off. "Elijah."

"Yes?"

"You will see things. Things that hold power over sinners. You go to a haven for idolaters, they know only licentiousness and murderer. Although they are strong, remember by whose power they are permitted to exist. You will have a choice when this is over." With this he raised his hand to a branch and gestured with his fingers. Elijah watched as a tiny leaf grew and bloomed into a ripe fig. "Remember who made the land they desecrate. I want you to stay, for I fear you will choose your ruin."

He tossed the fig to Elijah. Then turned and walked away. Elijah watched until he could no longer see His cloak in the dark.

CHAPTER 44

LIFE AT THE VILLA

The villa attracted the refuse of every dung trodden alley and pig stable in Israel. Bawdy and barbarous men Salome expected were thieves, gloomy pilgrims from gentile villages that wanted to meet this Mashiach who championed their lusts. More Romans arrived after the legionary Claudius, who had simply appeared at the table one morning. He sat and ate with a hammer on the table. He seemed to have an affinity for the thing. He arrived with a sick man she'd only seen once, briefly. She heard his laughter every night, and when she asked Claudius about him the smile he made rivaled the shrill revulsion that comes from scraping iron over stone.

Claudius's son arrived with them. A dreamy, conflicted boy. At times lucid, thoughtful with a propensity for speech far exceeding other children his age–much like Ephron, strangely enough. But on occasion, this clarity dimmed. His stare approached something bestial, and he seemed to look out at the world with an elderly man's senility for a time, until finally he would raise his little face, aghast and troubled by some bewildering epiphany, then revert to the intelligence he'd relapsed from, joining the adults surrounding him as if nothing happened.

Earlier that day, the boy suffered one of these spells while they ate. Chuldah sang one of her songs in her pleasant voice. Salome sat across from him. While Chuldah plucked strings and sang, the boy's eyes opened abruptly and he gasped. He looked around the table, mortified at the faces surrounding him. His scream began and died in a moment. As soon as the boy opened his mouth, Claudius struck his son with the back of his hand. The boy fell to the floor and laid snoring with a thin trail of blood running from his nose. No one at the table was bothered.

Salome was convinced the child had woken from a nightmare in the middle of a meal. She'd seen the same bewilderment in Samuel's eyes, when suddenly he hadn't seemed capable of movement for a time.

The boy sat back up a few minutes later. He smeared the blood into the tunic he wore and smiled at Salome. He sniffled and wiggled his nose the rest of the meal.

Others adjusted in their own ways. Hannah spent most of her time in one of the courtyards with a group of old women. The bizarre turn of life they experienced in the villa, and perhaps more than anything Samuel's harsh responses and criticisms, brought a wedge between them. For the first time in her long life she was too frightened to nag.

Samuel remained indifferent to every discomfort and concern. Although it brought her guilt, more and more Salome found herself wishing he was back on the mat. She didn't like how he was cruel to his mother. And his sexual appetite was a fire she couldn't quench. The thin man wouldn't be denied. He'd been with the concubines. Perhaps with Chuldah too. He'd come into their bed late with the scent of their perfumes and efforts. Thinking over what bitterness may have spurred this on provided the relief balm would a severed limb.

She explored more of the villa as the days progressed, but never approached the cellar beyond the portico. The swine made this an abominable place. The air broiled with their putrescence as the animals' conditions worsened. The day before a donkey ran down the portico, braying insults at its creator. When she asked Chuldah why Saul didn't just heal the pigs, who looked to have some pig ridden version of leprosy, she said the pigs remain vile to teach his people a lesson. To gauge a person by the heart, never appearance. "How much more must we strive to tolerate our fellow man in their ailments and lots in life? If we can live around a pig we can suffer any man."

Some days she came down the hill from the villa and walked around the village. She watched their tired faces. More than just the need for rest plagued them, however. It was as if they were tired of their very existence. Each time the people watched her with fearful expressions. When they saw her coming they studied her a moment, scrutinizing her face. She tried to talk to them. Some responded in Koine. Others never brought their faces up from the tasks at hand, or looked nervously to see who watched before leaving. They muttered under their breaths and handled their tasks with a diligence wholly contradicting their dispositions.

The place smothered her slowly.

She stood on the roof many nights. Samuel was never in the bed when she woke. She never saw him sleep anymore. Chuldah gave Salome an herb to drink with a bitter edge that gave a heavy sleep free from dreams. She took this every night now, sleeping well into the next morning. As the days progressed, she wondered whether her face looked as tired as the villagers'. They kept watching, as if they were waiting for her to do something.

The scarecrows had grown in number. They stood small in the distance, wholly ineffective in their duty. Birds lined their shoulders and pecked and tore from their heads. Watching the sun sink past the mountains, she leaned and envisioned another life. A voice startled her.

"The sunset will never be monotonous."

It was Saul. Salome nodded, trying not to blush at being startled.

"Jeremiah said blush is the color of virtue." He smiled. Whatever it masked was impossible to decipher. "Why don't you take off your covering and let the breeze cool your head. You'll feel better."

"I can't."

"Why? Because some bustling scribe said not to? How many things have you been told in your life you later discovered were only meant to control you? Do you know why women wear these things?"

Salome shook her head.

Saul laughed. "Because of the angels."

"The angels?"

He nodded with a hungry gleam in his eye. She crossed one leg over the other while she stood there. "In the early days of man, the sons of God plucked women from the Earth like Enoch." He made a swiping gesture with his hand. "They gave the women pleasures their husbands couldn't dream of supplying. And they birthed incredible beings. A new race of man. Intelligence and strength, beautiful beings who glistened in the sun and sang sweetly."

"The Nephilim?"

He nodded. "The Tanakh would have you believe this race was a perversion of man. That," Saul pointed a finger up without raising his eyes, "the Earth had to be purged from a great many sins caused by their presence."

"You're saying the Nephelim weren't bad?"

Saul nodded.

"So why the deluge?"

"Man was made in his image." He shrugged. "He's a jealous God."

"But we sinned–"

"What are sins?"

Salome looked out at the wheat twitching in the breeze. "Offenses against God."

"And what does God find offensive?"

"Murder, coveting, idola–"

"Everything. The prophets described sin as a war within you. You're at odds with your desires. And in turn we must strive to live contrary to our true natures. Have you ever wondered why the creator would be jealous of a thing carved in stone? Why make beings capable of building something as extraordinary as the temple, capable of songs and poetry, beings given the illusion of volition only to be punished for acting on it?

"How often did the prophets write about God putting things in a man's heart? He punishes his creation after searching their hearts, yet they could never love their maker without it first being instilled in them." He shook his head, slowly. "Man is capable of so much, but he's kept on a short chain once his legs are hobbled by his religion."

"Man is capable of war."

"Yes. And is war always bad? He certainly used war to take this land did He not? I'm sure the Amelekites have a different view than you about your *god's* views on war. Your ancestors came for milk and honey and what did the former tenants receive? Weeping widows and orphans."

"The enemies of Israel."

"Yes. Their children made formidable enemies. Better in Sheol than a warm crib I always say." Salome didn't respond. "Do you really believe the prophet Elijah cleft the river Jordan with his cloak? Have you heard a serpent talk? If so, please. We can bring one to the Decapolis. Imagine how many shekels we'll get for a viper singing the Shema."

Salome smiled. She felt his hand on her shoulder. There was no comfort in his embrace. Instead her hairs stood and a slight nausea crept over her.

"Search your heart," he said at last. "Was your affair a sin?"

She turned abruptly.

"How many times did you contemplate tossing yourself from the rocks in your distress? Your duties as a wife became a pestle that ground you down until nothing was left. The shepherd boy kept you alive."

She tried to dam the torrent in the back of her throat. *How did he know? Could he really?* Pressure built in her cheeks. Then her breath was hitching. Great sobs followed. Salome wept in Saul's arms.

They stayed that way until she regained her composure. Then the strange man who knew her secrets raised her chin with his finger. Smiled. "Let it go. Let your desires call you forth."

Pigs scuttled from the cellar door. Wheezes and grunts accompanied them to the grass. The sow near the door rose and sauntered over to a low palm with trampled branches. Its heavy body collapsed.

"Why the pigs?" she said.

"They were convenient."

For the first time, something about the creatures made sense.

CHAPTER 45

ELIJAH AND MATTHEW

Before the sun rose the disciples gathered around to see Elijah and Matthew off. Their master was already gone. Elijah was given a mat made of reeds, rolled tight and tied off with a cut off sandal strap. They were both given fresh tunics and cloaks. Elijah nodded at faces whose names he'd already forgotten, and when he made his way down the line the stocky fisherman who couldn't control his mouth handed him something wrapped in cloth. It was hard and flat, Elijah thought he knew what it was. He stuffed it in his bag.

Elijah's chest filled with warmth as he said his goodbyes to the green eyed woman. He remembered her name. Mary. He set off toward Jerusalem with a pang of guilt at his slight against Salome. The journey there was a blur. They dickered with the man at the gate and finally bartered entry. It took over an hour to find the little house where he'd left the camel. The sound of beasts and stench of dung helped direct them. Matthew led an ass that staggered along and had to be pulled and slapped on the hip to follow. "He won't slow us down once I'm mounted."

The streets were thick with men making spectacles of the baths and gathering around expositors. Pious chins raised to God and pilgrims flowing through the crowds like currents moving silt down a muddy river. The camel had no desire to push through. Its crooked teeth snapped at everything it passed. Elijah maneuvered through the crowd. He pulled at the camel as its teeth clicked the air near a little girl's cheek. The camel caught her head covering and pulled it away. She ran off crying while the camel chewed and shook its head side to side. "You're a menace," said Elijah.

They left and before long Matthew rode beside Elijah on the mule singing Miriam's song. Elijah rode silently with Matthew in his shadow.

"Must you sing *that*?"

"It's the passover."

"I know what it is. We've yet to even face a breeze pushing against us."

"Yes. But we must claim victory now. We are his people."

Elijah sighed and shook his head. They listened to the animals for a while. "What did you do before you traveled with them?"

"I passed out in alleys and haggled with whores."

Elijah turned to appraise him. "You don't seem the type."

"How should the type look?"

Elijah shrugged. He smiled. "We look ridiculous."

"Oh yes. A fat man on an ass and a vagrant flopped over like a reed on a camel. You're better off opening your tunic and letting the wind take you there."

"You flatter me."

"A man ought to go to his death laughing. It's the only way you can be sure the sorrows of life haven't tamed you."

"What about your master? He never laughs."

Matthew grunted. "He's different."

"He's not a man?"

"Yes, but…more."

"More?"

"More. The measure of a man–whether he falters in tough times, his patience, his ardor when all is against him. Honesty. In all things, He's exceptional. The only man I've ever seen balanced in such a way. And from what He's said He's getting ready to undergo the worst suffering of us all."

"So the sorrows of life have tamed him." Elijah said this conclusively, as if His case was the understandable exception.

Matthew thought this over. "No, I don't think so. I've heard him speak of conquering death. I suppose it's a very somber business."

They rode on. The sun was high and bright when they reached Jericho. They continued, only stopping when their legs were stiff and cramped into the positions they were seated. They cut northeast to link with the river. It was cooler near the water. The day ended with a red sky that reminded Elijah of the baths he'd seen in the village. They let the animals drink and continued well into the night.

They ate fish and bread Mary had given them. After they laid their mats out, Elijah remembered the bundle the disciple had handed him. He pulled the twine and moved the cloth, knowing what it was before seeing. It looked old enough to have been swung at a Philistine. The blade and hilt were fashioned from one piece and wrapped with a deteriorated band that had blackened from the sweaty palms and blood from battle. Dings and chips ran the blade's edge, but it certainly remained capable of its true purpose.

The following morning they set out along the Jordan. Cattails and saltgrass bent in the breeze and the water rippled. There were people dispersed along the river. Mostly cupping water to their faces or rubbing the filth from their bodies. Some of the shrubs were as tall as a man. The banks widened and thinned. They passed villages. Their stomachs rumbled and they ate quickly. Elijah was thankful to be near the water, and for Matthew. It took a man of merit to help carry another's burden. They were told they would suffer. Most of what the Rabbi said was cryptic, some foreboding. At the end of the matter, every man is Job. Lives are antes in a wager prepared for the whirlwind. Satan casts his lots and waits for them to curse God and perish.

Elijah shook his head, laughing softly.

"What's so funny?" asked Matthew. He had a long blade of grass in his mouth that bounced as he chewed.

"Do you think God has a sense of humor?"

"More than you."

"We laugh when children fall. Do you ever wonder if our calamity amuses him? He brought the Romans here. Brought us out and back. Out and back. Sometimes I think the milk is sour and the honey's guarded by hornets."

"You have a bleak eye for the world."

"It's a bleak life."

Matthew nodded. The breeze cooled their sweat. "I think the best we can do for now is laugh as much as we can. Find every flower and shape in the clouds we can and marvel at the beauty around us. We'll need it to sustain us."

"We don't even know what's coming."

"Who did he say we'd follow from the river?"

"An emissary of Satan."

Matthew nodded. After a pause he said, "You think I didn't know that parable was for you?"

Elijah picked at the camel's hair and decided there was wisdom in what Matthew said. He pictured the marsh beside the river soggy with blood. He would be tested soon. Elijah would learn how full or empty his own cup was. How lopsided his scales had become. He reached into the cloak and felt the fig there, rolling it in his fingers.

C H A P T E R   4 6

B E L P H E G O R ' S
O B S T I N A N C E

Belphegor had laid near the cellar door, watching the horizon, planning his future in meticulous detail. Not a whisper in the villa escaped his attention. In regards to the corporeal body he now inhabited, he welcomed the gossip of flies wings, conscious of every bug supping from his body. He knew every sack of larvae and burrowing maggot, allowing the creatures who lodge in the decay of tombs and ossuaries to abide in his putrid body. He considered this an insult to heaven and a stroke of malevolent genius; an entity who once covered his feet and eyes in the presence of the Godhead was now filled with the manifestations of filth.

Occasionally Belphegor raised his sow snout to test the air. Several times he'd circled the yard, only to collapse with a monstrous cloud of dust. He'd lie still again for days, watching, letting mold accumulate over the skin on his thighs and the cycle of larvae to continue unimpeded.

Bazumel took his possession of the pig and goat as a matter of the strictest necessity. To remain in such creatures was an insult to his nature. Thus Belphegor's behavior remained inexplicable.

Acting against Belphegor's advice, they'd cleared the villagers from the surrounding area preparing for the feast. Their bones, young and old, now littered the dung covered floors of the cellar. Belphegor wouldn't indulge. Wouldn't rise to drink from the troughs along the cellar's outer wall. Wouldn't move. It didn't matter to his body, he'd already partially decomposed. But it struck his companions as strange, since these feedings were so pleasurable to the bodies they inhabited. Falling on the victims, blood at a boil in their veins, they could pick a man apart in the span it takes to walk a few furlongs. Their violence often culminated in the herd violating the corpses and one other. Belphegor's cynicism and perpetual ennui left him a repugnant idol. A wretched cadaver at mercy to the elements.

The number of swine had dwindled. The herd had been possessing stray villagers and the occasional tax collector for months now. Two thousand pigs is a formidable herd. Of that number, all of which had run into the Sea of Galilee to drown, quite a few remained. To think they all had taken refuge in one man.

Many of Bazumel's pawns found hosts and took to the winds. Their presence now haunted the shaded corners of gentile cities throughout the diaspora, and would soon seep into the Roman empire like puss from a malignant wound.

The most powerful among their ranks acquired bodies quickly. Bazumel, Marduhl, Abaddon–all but Belphegor. He seemed content in the sow's body, which Bazumel found reprehensible. He watched the cellar from the roof of the villa, pacing, muttering blasphemies.

Belphegor's slothfulness made Bazumel paranoid, so he eventually took to sending candidates to the cellar. Belphegor was brought men, strong leaders with wealth and land. These he denied. Able bodied women, voluptuous, thinking perhaps he enjoyed the female sex he'd found home in with the pig. Rejected this as well. Even the animals they brought were undesirable. Bazumel was exacerbated further when Belphegor refused a bear. The demon inhabiting the beast was delighted to stay, for a bear is a much more formidable dwelling than a pig. It now made residence in the bottom of the cellar amidst the horde of festering swine. Each time they brought a candidate Belphegor raised his head, stares for a moment while they watched in rapt silence, and let it fall again.

"You've grown complacent," Bazumel told him one day, well into preparations for the feast. At this, Belphegor yawned, then snapped his jaws closed. "Do you take any of this seriously?"

"What's serious for you is a wager to *THEM*. The host probably casts lots as we speak."

"You can help us more by inhabiting a body."

"You postpone the inevitable."

"We could be back in the abyss. Then would you be happy?"

Belphegor raised his head, regarding Bazumel through the sow's rheumy eyes. Dry discharge caked black around the lids like flakes of charcoal. "You chase fleeting pleasures. Why, to draw upon while you burn in oblivion? You've stooped to their level." He snorted laughter. "A hedonist."

Bazumel returned to the villa in a rage. He shattered busts and furniture. He rained down curses. In the midst of his tantrum, when his anger crescendoed, stones rained upon the villa. One of the servants had been washing in a courtyard at the time and was struck through the head by a rock.

Abaddon was not much help either.

"You know him better than anyone," Bazumel told Abbadon on the roof, overlooking the cellar where Belphegor laid, undaunted.

Abaddon had returned from Caesaria Maritima, in his own new body, enjoying the prestige and fearful stares that accompany a Legionnaire. He shrugged. "I never know what he's thinking. He broods. He finds it all futile, you know."

"Finds what futile?"

Abaddon looked out at the mountains and swept his hand out. "Heaven and Earth, you, me. All of it."

Bazumel grunted. "Belphegor is shrewd. I don't trust this behavior."

"I think he still feels slighted for what happened."

"For what happened?" Bazumel threw up his hands. "*HE's* here, preaching and healing. And while *HE*'s here, they have hope." He shuddered as though a spider had crawled under his robes. "I can feel it. It's repulsive. Belphegor's wallowing interferes with our purpose."

"What is our purpose? The feast?"

"The feast is only the beginning. We'll have power. People in positions of influence. We'll soak the earth in pitch and dance in the ashes."

Abaddon nodded. "I'll talk to him." He turned to leave.

Bazumel grabbed his arm. "*HE* sent them to squandered land when they fell. They were cursed with pain, with a conscience. Through their restrictions they were granted access to pleasures we couldn't fathom. *HE* gave them pain when the womb breaks. But even in the midst of this suffering, you still see joy in a mother's eyes." His lips curled as though some foul odor had offended him. "Don't forget, when we fell, we were smothered in darkness and flames. Drowned and burned alive for as long as the stars have burned. No beauty, no pleasure. Torment without reprieve." Bazumel raised his eyes to Abaddon. "I want to visit our pain upon them. The land of milk and honey will be curdled and sour." He pointed down at the cellar. "If he won't help, make sure he doesn't get in the way."

CHAPTER 47

IN THE SHADOWS OF THE VILLA

Salome laid in bed that night and listened. Shouts and laughter carried from somewhere close. Someone played a stringed instrument while a woman sang, the clash of a cymbal and claps followed. Then there was a loud scream. It didn't last long. Revelry and laughter filled the lull shortly after.

There was something amiss. This man they called Mashiach spoke well. Could charm the venom out of a snakebite. But something deeper lurked there. The coldness of his stare. A smile that lacked warmth and sanity. There were beetles and maggots behind that grin. And a face so jagged, she wondered if his heart was made of the same rough angles. She wasn't sure what brought these thoughts, but they crept upon her in the quiet of the night. She didn't think there was any mercy in the man and felt dirty having been held in his arms. She cried in his bosom. A man without mercy, what is he? He's no different than a pig. She covered her mouth.

The shouts from the adjacent building remained a steady din. She rose and found the clay lamp on the table against the wall. She took the wick and pressed her thumb to check the tallow. A few strikes against the iron brought a spark and the little saucer sizzled to life when the oil caught flame. She tipped the clay lamp and opened her door.

Her shadow made an exaggerated curve over the walls. She looked in one of the courtyards and found a man sitting. He was a gentile from Sepphoris who arrived a few days earlier. He sat in the moonlight turning his hand before his eyes.

She backed away slowly and decided to go around. Salome cut through the building and went around through the old garden that ran along the side of the villa. Dead shrubs and drooping flowers, vines and weeds reached out in the dark. Wilted petals and fronds covered the ground. Statues stood as sentinels in the dark. She stepped through quickly.

Salome made her way around the far building where Saul and his companions were still engaged in their revelries. She walked through the clearing feeling vulnerable holding the lamp, relieved once she'd finally made it to the portico. Still not knowing what she was searching for, Salome stepped through the columns. She started toward the other side of the villa and froze at a noise.

Movement. "Who's there?"

"Shhh."

Someone was huddled against one of the columns. The light from the torches pooled in the wrinkles of their garment. Salome recognized the bent stature and stale smell of age before her face came into view. "Hannah, you startled me."

She put a finger to her lips. Her eyes darted in different directions and she was trembling. Salome leaned closer and Hannah pointed out toward the buildings beyond the clearing.

"You see them?"

She did. The quick trots of several black shapes. "The pigs?"

Hannah nodded. "They run around the whole plot of land. Like they're patrolling. Watching for something."

"Ima, that's–" but two of them ran into view, legs scissoring. They crossed the clearing and bolted off into the fields toward where she'd seen the scarecrows from the roof.

"You see?"

"They've trained them?"

"I don't know. They're smart. They've been dropping dead in the clearing night after night and none of them seem to care. Last night the boy who led us here dragged something to the cellar bigger than him. It was wrapped in something. He threw it in and I heard them squealing. You'd have thought he'd brought–" Hannah flinched at the sound of more pigs running. Her eyes searched left and right.

"Brought what?"

The old woman's eyes came to meet Salome's. "Food."

"Surely, they must be fed."

Hannah grabbed Salome's arm. She had a wild, skittish look. "We should leave."

"Leave? You brought us here."

"We'll go down to the village and follow the road. We won't stop until morning."

"What about Samuel?"

"That's not my son, my son would ne–" Salome hushed Hannah. The old woman's eyes darted around.

Salome put her hands on her shoulders. "I get the same feeling here. It's…unsettling at times."

"It's unnatural."

"It certainly seems that way. I've thought about leaving. But I can't… not yet. He's not the same man. I think he *has* changed. All those years wasted. I'd be bitter too. And it didn't help, you feeding him rumors everyday, poisoning his mind. But Hannah, he comes out of it sometimes. I see it in his eyes. Like he's fighting against his new self. I think…I think he's still in there."

Hannah grabbed Salome's cloak. "I know I've been cruel to you, and for that I'm sorry. But listen to me. Something's wrong here. We must leave this place."

Salome ran her hand over her face and smoothed her garment. Then she checked the clay lamp, shaking her head. "I can't. If you choose to leave, go in peace."

"You know the servants left? Most of the ones here disappeared?" Salome turned to leave. "And the woman. I don't trust her either." Salome took a step and Hannah's voice rose. "The stench of death is all around."

Salome looked back at her. "The whole country smells of death. If we'd had this conversation three days ago I would have happily ran with you. But I'm not leaving without Samuel. Or at least without trying. I won't give up on him like everyone else has. Like you." Salome left her. When she looked back, Hannah had a hand on one of the columns, watching the pigs while her mouth moved.

Hannah stood in the dark watching the pigs. The commotion from the banquet hall carried into the night. She turned toward it, contemplating her escape with every step, but curiosity proved insurmountable. Beyond the columns and shadows lining the portico a slice of light cut along the bottom of the door. She crept toward the stripe of light, a moth drawn to a flame. The hum from inside was clear. Although she didn't recognize the tongue, it was foul and full of violence. And verified every suspicion she held for the place.

Hannah went to the door. Cracked it open. She moved through the vestibule silently and paused at the end, trying to decipher what she saw. She gasped and staggered back. Condemnation for their debauchery, fascination, and hot blooded shame surged up in her.

This man. Who could do such perverse things and claim to speak in the name of God? Chuldah didn't surprise her. That woman drew the eyes of men in every room she entered. The whore passed Hannah one afternoon with a smug smile and devious look about her. Hannah could smell her modest parts. Harlotry seeped from every pore.

But her son. She covered her mouth. Crying quietly, trying not to make noise.

The dull expressions they made chanting, standing with a child present, watching the unholy consummation as Hannah's horrified mouth opened so far she feared her jaw might crack and her scream would split her in two. They were awful chants, dirges for Molech and Baal. The world pulsed around it. Chuldah enjoyed it, her lips flitting to a provocative smile while they profaned her body. And what was the red substance shimmering on their faces?

She turned and left. As soon as she left the vestibule and walked out into the portico she gave a startled yelp. Someone stood in the path. The torch light from behind traced him in its glow, and she thought she saw the light behind him through one of his wrists. He shook. Hannah stepped forward tentatively. She had a hand out. "You scared me, I'm sorry... I'm on edge. She moved closer. The man moved too, something scraped with his steps. He moved into the light and she stepped back. He had a dark socket for one eye. A mauled grin. He hadn't been shaking. The man was laughing. A tiny string in the exposed tissue in his cheek shook with every cackle. Hannah screamed when he lunged for her.

CHAPTER 48

THE BAPTIZER

Matthew and Elijah fell into the rhythms of their journey. The camel and the ass bemoaned the condition of the road and their cargo with grunts and braying. The stubborn donkey kept a much slower pace. Elijah wanted to leave the animal behind, but wasn't willing to abandon Matthew or ride with his breath on his neck.

The mighty Jordan murmured beside them. Ripples lined the surface and birds flew from its banks. Matthew wiped his brow, looking off at the surface gleaming in the light.

"Elijah?"

"What is it?"

"If we survive this, I may kill you when it's over."

Elijah laughed. "If we survive."

"He certainly gave that impression, didn't He?"

"Yes." Elijah looked down at Matthew. "Did you hear Lazarus? What type of man has men begging to die for him?"

Matthew shrugged. "A great man."

"Or a dangerous man."

"Can you be a great man without being dangerous?"

They rode on, silent. After some time had passed, Matthew dug into the bag at his side and pulled out a wineskin.

"I thought you'd given that up?"

"It's good for the stomach. And the nerves."

Elijah looked down at him. He could see the tension, his struggle for composure. After a swig Matthew handed the wineskin to Elijah. He drank deeply. It felt good to drown their worries for a moment. He tried to hand it back but Matthew urged him on.

"Go on, there's more."

Elijah drank. After a long sip he looked over at Matthew. He was looking down.

"What is it?"

Matthew looked up, wiped his mouth with his hand. "Nothing."

"You're a better drunk than a liar."

Matthew slouched. "Something he told me before we left."

"What did he tell you?"

Matthew's brow raised. "What did he tell you?"

"I've already told you. We're going to meet the emissary of the Accuser, whatever that means. And where we go is a nest of serpents and vultures."

Matthew looked at the water. "I don't think I'm supposed to tell you."

"Why not? I've told you everything."

"A man can't just lay everything bare. He'll have nothing left to chew on when he's alone. Some things are better left between a man and his God."

"Wine makes you a poet. A bad one."

"A poet I am not. But a better drinker you won't find scouring all the cellars of Rome."

"A man must take pride in something."

Matthew narrowed his eyes. "What do you take pride in?"

Elijah considered this. "I've lived more like a goat than a man. Everything has been food or drink. Stomach and loins. I don't remember taking the time to find satisfaction in anything besides the temporary pleasures that come in this life."

"But you're a farmer?"

Elijah frowned. "A Shepherd."

"Good. You'd be a horrible farmer."

"Yes. I'd burn the land. Besides, it's fallow and more trouble than it's worth."

Matthew didn't laugh. The path beside the Jordan was partially shaded by trees. They came to a house built a ways off the water. Several additions had been added over the years and it looked as though the builders added sections only to forget about the last. They called at the door and walked around, but it was empty. There was a dark stain in the front room and shambles of furniture strewn about. Chickens bobbed and pecked through the house and the yard outside. Neither said a word. They climbed back onto the animals and continued on.

"You ever wonder how the nile looked when Moses turned it to blood?"

"Blood is dark."

Elijah looked on. The village, the kiln, and the waiting vultures paraded through his memories.

"I bet Pharaoh could smell it from his house."

"You think *He* could do something like that?"

Matthew shrugged. "I don't think He would do something like that."

"Why?"

"Who am I to say why? He doesn't use his gifts to coerce or frighten."

"Moses was a prophet of doom." Matthew looked confused. Elijah blew air from his mouth and threw something in the water. "It all seems such a waste."

"What?"

"To let this all go on. The Romans are here. They pin us to trees outside our cities over property disputes. Bandits fill the roads. So long as they leave the trade routes alone they continue unbothered. I've been to empty gentile villages, all up and down the countryside. Some filled with corpses. What happened to those people?" Elijah threw his hands up. "Where are we going? He could grind every brick and reed in this nest of serpents and vultures to dust if He's who He says He is."

"God's ways are not like ours."

A grunt. "Men get things done."

"God made that river. The mountains you see."

"Man made boats. Cities, he cultivated the Earth. Forged steel to make weapons. I've heard it my whole life." Elijah's voice rose. "The prophets. Floating ax heads. Locusts blotting the sun. What reason did I have to believe any of it? I went to the Synagogue for alms when my grandmother was dying and do you know what they told me?" Matthew's face softened. "Fear not, The Lord watches over orphans and widows. The glutton sent me on my way with nothing. When my grandmother died I had to steal bread."

Matthew didn't argue, only nodded a worry striped brow at his companion. "When I saw the things he did, I believed everything."

Elijah nodded. "My eyes were healed. But what good does that do our people? Rather I was blind now and avoided the things I've seen. The Son of David comes to tell us we'll suffer. But telling Jews they'll suffer is like telling a rock it's hard."

They stayed silent. The black expanse rolled up from the retreating azure and a few stars already winked. They rode on with the moon, great and grey in the sky and wavering in the water beside them. Listening to the Jordan. Grasshoppers and the occasional clicks of flying bugs carried over the moan the breeze made. Later they tied the camel and donkey to a stake and laid a little ways off from the bank in their cloaks.

The morning brought fog over the river and a somber feeling. A dreadful expectancy settled in their stomachs, their nerves were taut harp strings ready to break.

That afternoon they rode upon a man and a young girl. He held her hand and led, together they waded out into the Jordan. He was gaunt, the curves of bone pressed out against his sallow skin. The girl was in white, close to the age of marrying. The man wore a garment made from camel hair. His arms were hatched with light lines where scars had healed.

"Is it the baptizer?"

"John is dead."

"He took her out rather far, don't you think?"

Matthew nodded.

They watched from their animals, creeping slowly along.

The man placed a hand behind the girl's head, the other on her shoulder. She was apprehensive at first, but he nodded, and whatever he said conjured a smile. The water was calm, lapping gently at the man's waist and the girl's chest. She relaxed and let him guide her. He looked up at the travelers, said something to the girl that brought several tiny nods, and tilted her back until she was fully immersed.

Elijah stared ahead, resolute in his mission. Matthew had lingered. "Elijah!"

He looked back and Matthew was tugging the donkey to turn. Elijah stopped and looked out at the water. The girl hadn't come up.

In the water stood a different man. Snarling from one corner of his mouth, he fixed on Elijah and Matthew as his lips moved rapidly through clenched teeth. The girl's arms broke the surface, pounding at his chest and trying to scratch his face while he forced her under.

Elijah dropped from the camel and ran into the river, shouting. Matthew fell from the ass with a grunt. There were flat stones in the grass where he landed. He grabbed one, stood, and threw with all he had. It was low. The stone hit the water, skipped, and struck the baptizer in the face. His head jerked back and Matthew cheered.

The girl came up gulping air. The baptizer recovered, snatched her by the hair and shoved her down again in the middle of a scream. He leaned in, smiling maniacally with blood trickling over his face.

A crow swooped down over the river and diverted its path just before reaching the baptizer.

The deranged man smiled, "it's not good for man to be alone." He leaned in, shoulders rolling, straining with whatever his hands did to the girl under water. Elijah made long legged strides through the marsh. Matthew was behind him, splashing up water in his path. Water churned as the girl fought, arms thrashing in her futile attempts to claw and slap him away. "Here we are," he said, grimacing. One of the girl's hands stiffened and her fingers spread. With one final grasp at heaven it fell limp into the water. The baptizer's hand emerged holding a curved piece of bone. He held it triumphantly as the other hand still held her down. The water around him was murky with blood.

"Here's your woman, shepherd." He tossed it at Elijah, laughing. It bounced off his chest and plopped into the water. Elijah reached him a moment after. He tried to pull the girl free, but the man was incredibly strong. He brought the back of his hand across Elijah's face, sending him sprawling back. Matthew came huffing a moment later and wrapped his arms around the man. Elijah was up again helping to restrain him. The baptizer finally let the girl go. But she didn't rise.

The men struggled there with the baptizer while he cursed and laughed and lifted them from the water to slam them back down. He dragged Matthew beneath, and when Elijah tried to go for the girl, the baptizer grabbed a fistful of his hair and pulled him back, pushing him below as well. They fought desperately. Matthew struggled and pushed up with his legs. Once his mouth found air, he struck the man in the genitals. Then Elijah broke the surface. He squirmed free, leapt on the baptizer's back and wrapped an arm around his throat, squeezing. The two of them wrestled the man to shallow water, pulling and dragging him to the marsh, bringing fists down on his face and head in the tangled weeds.

"What is your name?" Matthew screamed in the man's face. The eyes rolled back and clouded over, the head shook as the body convulsed. His lips moved.

"Tell us your name!" Elijah tried this time.

Spasms shook the baptizer's body and his back bent to an impossible angle. They heard a pop. The splashing stopped and he was still.

They stood heaving for air.

"The girl!"

Elijah turned, already wading out, but froze when he raised his eyes. Matthew slipped into the water to follow. When he saw, the heavy man scrambled back to the bank with a muffled cry. Elijah didn't move. Couldn't move. The sight turned him stone inside and spread cold panic through every limb.

The girl was on the water. Standing. Its surface rippled where her feet touched. Her head was cocked. Beneath her matted hair glared a blasphemy to all youthful beauty and femininity. Her tunic was torn, exposing one of her small breasts. Crimson spread wide and low down the side of the wet garment. The torn fabric bulged where bone protruded through from her wound.

"He's made plans with your whore, Elijah." Water poured from her mouth with her words. Her side bled in spurts. She looked at Matthew. "The drunk lead the blind."

"What is your name? What is your na–"

"The vultures and serpents are hungry. Even now, they head where the carrion awaits, to sup with flies. He will pick your bones clean and pigs will ravage the holes in your skull once they eat your eyes." The wet tunic bunched up as she moved. Ripples spread in widening circles around each step. They could see bone through the hole in her side now. White and red meat.

She turned her face to Matthew. "Do you like what you see, drunkard?" The girl reached into the wound at her side and moved her fingers. She tore something free, held the red glob of tissue to him like an offering, raising her chin, "eat heifer." The girl threw her head back, laughing. Matthew's mouth opened and moved without words. She looked in her hand and threw it away. Then brought red fingers to her mouth to lick them clean. She moaned and ran a provocative tongue around her knuckles. Matthew retched.

"Tell us your name," said Elijah. The strength had drained from his voice.

Her head jerked up. The girl's tone changed to something childlike, and she spoke in a monotonous, haunted rhythm. "There will be a gentile on the road ahead carrying oil. He'll greet you. Tell him you're looking for the village where the pharisee hid and he'll lead you there. The drunk can heal him, if he finds his faith." When the girl finished speaking, the snarl she'd assumed relaxed, they saw a glimpse of the young woman's true face and she fell with a feeble splash.

Across the river, a white bird flapped its wings to fly but fell into the water. It tried again and spread its wings, dipping toward the surface, then steadied itself, gliding just above the surface before lifting away.

Elijah waded out and pulled the girl to the bank. They covered the man and the girl in branches and reeds where the vegetation was thick. When they were finished, the two set off again without a word.

CHAPTER 49

SALOME

Salome laid with a growing heaviness, musing over implications and sorting the meanings of things. Still in shock at seeing something so private. So intimate. Heat tingled in her cheeks as she scraped her mind for rationale. *How could the man bearing Moses's staff behave in such a way?*

What could offend Addonai, the God of Jacob and Abraham, who she'd worshiped since her mother's breast, more than a woman exposing herself in a room full of men? Fornicating openly, verboten lust, panting like a dog in heat. And the man... the man was a religious leader. Well, he certainly enjoyed the privileges of his office. If the claims his followers made about him were true, why would the son of David commit such vile and atrocious acts? Why would God grant power to such a man? Why would he have the staff of Moses?

Salome had followed their noise in the night. What she found horrified her–Saul and Chuldah fornicating in the open while his followers watched. While her husband watched.

Elijah made claims about another. Whom she'd certainly heard about, though most tales regarding him were too spectacular to believe. But Elijah had been healed by this man, like Samuel. And his eyes, once greyed and lustrous with spots that blocked his vision, were now clear and pristine, with no trace of his former ailment. Samuel, however, still had the legs of a river bird.

Perhaps restoring a man's eyes and restoring a man's legs are different.

She thought of Elijah's words. How he described the healings with such excitement, such life in his eyes. But he had also returned from his journey troubled. This manifested over the days following. He didn't say what pestered him, she'd left abruptly, but she sensed it. His eyes were slow to follow, as if something only he could see drew his vision back, tangled him in its dream. And that's what it's like when a man or woman feels guilt, is it not? Had the man Jesus known? Had he said something? *What a foolish thought.*

Samuel came later after she fell asleep and shook her shoulder. He was firm and demanding, smelled of sweat and lye. She caught hints of ointment when she buried her face in his neck to avoid his fetid breath. The same scent wafting through the halls after Chuldah.

Did they all use her in such ways?

The only time he came to their room anymore was at night. He'd found things to occupy his time. Women, drink–he habitually stank of wine and sex. How long had they engaged in these rituals?

"Samuel?"

"What?"

"When will we go back?"

"Why would we do a thing like that?"

"The servants. Our affairs. The responsibilities we have."

"None of that matters anymore."

She propped herself up. "What do you mean it doesn't matter?"

"Everything we need is here. Are you not happy?"

"Happy?"

"That's what I said. I've been given my legs once again. There's wine and rich food, land for us to share here. You want to go back to that dirty little village and its peasants?"

"You gave everything for that dirty little village."
"And a lot of good it served. They took my legs. My livelihood.
Once the old woman had poisoned my mind and picked me clean,
they took my wife."

Salome turned her head. There it was. Beating at her heart like a
fist rapping at a door.

"You want to go back to your Shepherd boy? Will you bleat for
him again, little sheep?"

An impossible silence spanned between them. She shifted, trying
to move from him. "Samuel... You couldn't move. Couldn't touch
me. It was just me and your mother. She put such foul things into
your ears. Treated me so harshly."

"Did my mother open your legs?"

Salome was rigid, silent. Fear's invalid.

"Do you know the new man, Claudius? Do you know what he
did at Caesarea? He crucified prisoners. Jews, gentiles, men, women,
some children even. Have you ever seen a crucifixion, Salome? Do
you know what they do? They take a nail, not much longer than the
distance between your ear and chin." He ran his fingers over her
throat and a chill swept her skin. "They cross your legs at the ankles
and drive the nail through."

"Samuel, you've never talk–"

"What I'll do," he ignored her, "is drive the nail through the
sides of your knees." His thumb and finger squeezed her knee. "That
will keep your legs from opening." He cackled. It was devoid of
anything resembling mirth or enjoyment, a pitiless sound. "Then
again you could still be bent over." He looked as though he was deep
in thought. "I know. I'll fill your womb with pig shit." His fingers
moved like the legs of an insect walking, traveling up her thigh as he
spoke. "Then I'll shave your head and sew you closed with your
hair." He laughed again. His legs rose and he kicked his heels
against the bed like a child in hysterics.

"Samuel..."

"Samuel," He mocked her. His voice shrill and high. "I don't know why we've let you linger on in your current state. I think your purpose here needs to be made clear to you."

"My purpose?"

"Yes. Are you so foolish to believe we'd keep you here if we didn't have use for you?"

"What use?"

"What did you see the other night?"

"What are you saying?" But as soon as the words left her mouth she understood. The ritual, the strange behaviors and attitudes of the people around her. Their deference toward her. How Saul had taken to her. All this rose and ruffled through her mind with a biting nausea that banished thought and brought animal panic.

Samuel saw the horror on her face and smiled. "Don't worry. They enjoy it. When the children come they'll have places of honor. You'll be revered among the race to come."

"Samuel…"

"When the sons of God laid with the daughters of men, great men of renown roamed the Earth." He turned and regarded her, stroking her face with his fingers. "They were better than men. Fiercer, stronger. Far more clever. But *HE* gets so jealous of these things. Anything that threatens their supremacy. Their image." This he said with disdain. "*THEY* destroy."

She could only shake her head, slowly. Saul had mentioned the same thing.

"They'll be back. The witch begged to be first. It's an honor for her. She served Molech and all the names we used to seduce the Philistines. As did her mother before her. The child will tear her open wide enough for a man to crawl through. But she yearns for this, you see? She's grateful. Men and women will believe in anything if you cater to their indulgences."

She could feel pain throbbing where his hand now gripped her. The skin would bruise like thunderclouds. "Let go, Samuel, please."

"I don't think I will. She's with child now. Soon, so shall you. Have you not wondered why you're not allowed in the other parts of the villa?"

Samuel rolled over onto her. She slid her body to the side. She smelled his breath and felt the swell of his manhood. She tried to slide away but his hand went to her throat. He raised up, smiling. Adjusting.

She reached for the stone pitcher beside the bed. Fingers scrambling. He pressed against her and she twisted and brought her knees up to resist.

"There's fight in you. You'll make a suitable womb." He was too strong. He pushed her legs down. "Show me what you do for the shepherd boy." Samuel pinned her thigh with his knee. She rotated her hips, writhing beneath him. But he shifted her body easily. He lifted her and moved her over and brought her down.

Salome's knuckle hit the table by the bed. Her hand throbbed, but she found the pitcher's handle. She nearly dropped it because of the weight. Before he could enter her, she adjusted her grip and swung for his head. Samuel's face turned with the blow, and in his brief disorientation she brought a knee up to separate them. Samuel seethed. He sneered and squeezed her throat. Pressure filled her head but she managed to raise her hands, holding the pitcher in both, pouring water as she brought it back to strike. A moment later her knees were over him. She straddled her husband, this stranger, raising the vessel and bringing it down on his face, screaming. Grunting as she smashed stone and man. Blinded by rage, bludgeoning the crown of his skull and his forehead. Until his body twitched and stopped moving.

Salome rose, dropping the pitcher and backing away. There was a large gash over his forehead. More blood than she'd ever seen. She breathed hard, trying to think of something. Some plan or course of action, to get away or trick the people around her into letting her go. There was nothing.

Hannah. She grabbed a cloak and her covering and walked swiftly to the old woman's chambers. She knocked. Nothing. She went in but the room was empty.

Salome paced the old woman's room, talking to herself in a low ramble. She searched the floor and Hannah's things. There was a small knife for meat and a stone jug a little smaller than the one in her room. She brought the knife.

The silence awaiting her in the courtyard wrung cold sweat from her back. Shadows of laundry lines and the brick parapets made ghastly apparitions, lurking in the corners with outstretched arms. Following the shadows, she crept inside, then maneuvered around the outside of the building, avoiding the portico, only stopping when she heard voices. It was a group. They descended the hill toward the village laughing and pushing one another. Salome watched the dark shapes of their cloaks merge with the night they wandered into.

Salome headed back, took the side of the villa through the shambled garden once again. This time every dark leaf seemed sharper. She moved slowly, methodically.

She came out into the open, sticking to shadows and praying not to see pigs. She moved past the temple, its stones bright under the moon. There were noises coming from there too. The sounds were profane and utterly foreign. It brought needles prickling through her insides. She didn't dare look in. She ran for the fields.

Before she reached the crops, peripheral movement froze her. Her heart hammered. *The pigs have found me.*

When it moved into view, she sighed. Only a donkey. The ears twitched their strange way as the animal watched her. She stared for a few moments, then tried to shoo it away. It only dropped its head and chewed. She began to walk and the animal moved with her.

"Go." She motioned it on with her hands. "Go. Go." She walked briskly toward the fields and the animal brayed.

Salome ran. The wheat moved aside for her and snapped back. Every rustle or scrape of wool added to the clarion call the donkey made. It brayed as she ran, warning man and swine alike of her escape. There were squeals and grunts before she heard any men. Salome ran, not knowing where, until she tripped in a thin ditch dug out in the crops. She scrambled to her feet, took off again. As she moved from the temple and cellar there came a new stench. Ahead she saw the outline of the scarecrows, high and bloated with straw. Birds perched and picked at them, their wings flapping in the dark, defying their prey's very reason for existing.

She heard men now. Commotion from near the temple. She wondered at the donkey, the pigs, the whole warped society in which she found herself. God's eyes had turned from this place.

She was almost to the scarecrows. Enveloped in the new stench. She looked up when she reached them, the whole morbid row, exposed in the cold dead eye of the moon. The eyes of scavengers stared back. She stumbled. Salome struggled to stand, with choked sobs and hitched breaths she continued. She couldn't look. She followed parallel to the row, not daring to look at their feet, nailed to the boards level with her face. Her mind recounted Samuel's description of the nails. His threats.

She'd been seduced into naivety. The signs were present. Fractions of a puzzle laid under her nose. The guise of this religious community maintained by thespians with the wiles of sorcerers. This was a place where old women were nailed to crosses for running. She staggered on and fought through the stitch in her side. A vulture flew in front of her path, beating its wings and making her shriek.

The pigs caught up to her shortly after. They circled her in, turning their heads curiously. Their desiccated bodies putrid and ghastly in the silver effulgence.

Abijah and Ephron reached the circle of swine shortly after.

"Did you say hello to Ima?" asked the boy. His eyes were set. Cruel and hopeless. His smile an awful corruption of innocence.

CHAPTER 50

THE WATCHFUL EYE OF DEATH

They found the man the following afternoon. He was bringing oil back from somewhere farther up the river. Somber, reposed with deep set eyes and a stare that waited for omens on the horizon, he seemed to possess a grave sense of duty and the wisdom beaten into a man through pain. He was a gentile but spoke decent Aramaic. His name was Jason, and his words were distributed like a miser's last few coins. Elijah got the sense Jason didn't trust them, for when they asked about the Pharisee his chin rose and the meager sociabilities he'd previously expressed withered away. But he led them on all the same. He walked ahead while they led the camel and ass, stooped over, following the thin path through the trees. Branches brushed their shoulders and Elijah had the absurd thought the bushes were trying to hold them back from continuing on.

"How long has he been there?" asked Matthew.

Jason shrugged without turning. Matthew and Elijah looked at one another, and Matthew made a contemptuous shrug to mock him. Elijah shook his head with a slight smile.

The path ended near a clearing. Yellow patches of grass shone gold in the sun. They saw a cluster of houses as they set down the hill. Vultures circled overhead. Matthew looked at Elijah again, this time with no humor in his face.

The first structure they passed was a Greek temple, not much larger than a synagogue in a moderate village. It looked as though one of their gods had struck his dwelling place with a giant club. A headless statue stood at the front with half a spear, its militant pose now comical. The head was on the ground in two pieces, the face turned from them in shame. One of the pillars had broken away and lay crooked on its side and there was a piece of another that had rolled down the hill the temple was built on. Lichen climbed the rest and darkened the stone.

The village consisted of clustered brick structures spread out on the floor of their little valley. Several were black as tar. Well hidden by the trees and depression of Earth that rose up around it, the village was closed off from the outside world. Most Greek cities were large, but this was an exception. Gentiles huddled together in a community no larger than a poor Hebrew village. There was a ravaged vineyard beyond the homes. Dried mud at the center of the village near the well. Eerily barren of people for the time of day. Behind one of the houses a camel stood in a fenced enclosure, chewing.

"What happened here?" asked Matthew.

Jason stopped and turned without expression. "The Pharisee came and my mother put him up. He spoke Koine as well as any of us here. My mother tended to his wounds and waited by him while the man rambled about pigs and haunted children. We thought he was mad with his sickness, since the fever was so fierce. Three days later they came."

Jason's body shook as he laughed without the sound.

"Who came?"

They had a boy with them. Foolish as it sounds, he seemed to be their leader. Pigs, too. Just as the man said." His eyes seemed to be reliving the destruction of his community. Elijah's heart went out to him. "My mother told us to hide him so we put him in the tomb. I told them where he was after they killed Diana. They killed the rest of them anyway." His eye twitched.

"Why didn't they kill you?"

Jason's arms rose and fell to his sides. "The boy said they left him for me." He said this with a casual indifference, as though describing the color of clouds. "He was in there three days. I heard him crying and praying. I didn't know what to do with him. When I took him out his wound stank and had turned yellow."

"I'm sorry," said Elijah.

Jason clenched his teeth. "Say that to my mother. See if she stirs."

Elijah swallowed. "Can you take us to him?"

Jason let out a snide breath. "I thought of killing him. He's in pain. My family died for him so I wanted him to feel it. To know what he did." His eyes hardened looking at Elijah. "To suffer."

"What did you do?"

Jason trembled. His red eyes fought back tears, and Elijah knew the man only indulged in cruelties to allow his hatred to keep him from feeling. A man can function with hate. Desolation will eat him bone and gristle. Jason wiped at his face with his hands and slapped his cheeks with his hands. He turned and headed toward the houses.

They smelled old fires. Beneath the burnt scent, death. It grew as they moved near one of the houses on the far end. It was half charred, as if a painter had given up before finishing a black coat.

"Is that him?" asked Matthew. His cloak was to his nose. Jason passed through the threshold without answering.

The stench was offensive enough from outside. Inside, it became unbearable. This was a grave's redolence, with the acrid touch of charred materials. Matthew gagged. Elijah felt the back of his throat pulse as saliva gathered in his mouth.

"What's this on the floor?" Matthew's eyes looked to be in pain. Dark smears ran from the front door to the back of the room where Jason stood beside an entryway. It was covered in smears, dark brown, burgundy, black.

Elijah followed Matthew, who gasped when he stepped into the room. The large man ran from the room to the front door, nearly slipping on whatever filth coated the floor, covering his mouth and heaving. Elijah heard him vomiting outside, his warnings not to go in there. Elijah ignored him. Stepped inside and stood on wobbled legs.

The Pharisee was bound. He lay naked on a mat. His bandages were brown and his bald head had blistered, exposed by the sun spilling in through a hole in the roof. It outlined him in light. Elijah moved in and saw what made Matthew run.

Across from the Pharisee, positioned so he was forced to look, were the bodies of the villagers. They were stacked like timber. Several had fallen over, and the corpse of a large woman was bent from the pile, contorted so part of the forehead laid on the Pharisee's mat. She was close enough for him to reach over and stroke her hair if he desired. Were he able to move. The bodies were stacked high, almost to the room's low ceiling. Some were caked black, skin flaked and bubbled from burns. Others bloated. The pallid skin of the gentiles were like bones already. The pinks and light coloration from the less severe burns made the thought of ever eating meat again repugnant.

Elijah stood in horror. He didn't move until he heard a hiss. A wing flapped from the top of the pile as a scavenger buried its face in spoiled treasure. There were vultures in the house.

"What is this?"

"I want him to see them."

Elijah's hands were around Jason's throat before he could react. He shook him, moving him to see the piled corpses, slamming him against the wall. "Your pride is more important than burying your dead!" Elijah spat on the floor and shook his head, disgusted. "You think this is what your mother wanted?" He let go of Jason's throat and turned slowly to the room again, covering his mouth.

Jason's eyes were wide, his brow raised as he trembled. Then, as if processing the feelings Elijah's rebuke stirred, his face tightened. "You don't get to talk about what she would have wanted." The tone was flat. "Her wants died with her." A contemptuous glance at Simeon. "When he came."

Elijah ignored him. He walked over to the Pharisee and draped his cloak over his exposed body. The man laid in his own filth. His chest rose and fell with rapid, shallow breaths. Elijah kept his head raised, pretending not to notice. After he went outside to find Matthew they dragged him out of the room while Jason sat against the bricks in the burned part of the house with his arms around his knees, rocking and singing something in koine.

They brought the Pharisee to one of the nearby structures. Its bricks were burned black and the smell of fire was strong. But nothing could be as foul as the room they'd left. Matthew laid hands over the Pharisee and shut his eyes. Elijah watched his lips move and the man stirred. They unwrapped the soiled bandages, which were now stiff as palm fronds and the color of old clay. His skin was smooth and without scars. The man opened his eyes and sat up slowly. They gave him water and stale bread with some oil, then left him alone.

Elijah and Matthew walked to the top of the hill beside the village and stood looking at the country beyond. Both mens' faces had aged in the few days they'd spent together. After a long silence, Matthew shook his head. "I've never seen anything like that."

Elijah raised his eyes, nodded, and looked back at the houses. "Even a good man, if you put him through enough..." Elijah's face was haunted and haggard. He sighed. "He's capable of anything. Even something like this."

"That's not a good man."

"Probably not. I thought he was a normal man, though."

"Did you see their eyes?"

Elijah looked at his feet and nodded.

"Why would he do that?"

"He wanted him to feel them there. Watching."

Matthew shook his head. He took a few steps off and stood with his hands on his hips. The sun had set a burning lavender, but its beauty seemed an insult to the horrors they'd seen. Mathew raised his hands and slapped his thighs. "It's only been a few days, Elijah. I've seen demoniacs, and I've seen real, hate filled vengeance. I don't know what's worse." He pointed toward the village. "What will we do with him?"

"Let him bury his dead."

Before they left the next morning, Elijah and Matthew, after looking around outside, went back to the house to check on Jason. The door was open. They entered, and a vulture stepped through the hall and hissed. They stood to the side as it hopped and waddled out. There were more inside. They would come and go until the food spoiled beyond even what they could tolerate. They put their cloaks over their faces and went in.

"Jason?" The house had a hungry silence and seemed to drain something from them the longer they stayed. All the deaths pulled at their vitality. They took shy steps into the room opposite the horrors they'd seen.

"Coward," said Matthew.

They looked on, listening to the soft squeak of rope rubbing on the beams overhead. Jason's eyes were open.

They took the camel from the enclosure and left Matthew's donkey to save time. The three set off and said little.

After being on the road for some time, Simeon thanked them with a dry and languid demeanor. He moved as a shell of a man. The eyes of the dead villagers in that room seemed a fixture in his memory. Regardless of who he addressed or what was said, his voice barely carried farther than his shadow fell, and his soul seemed just as devoid of light. Simeon's eyes fixed ahead like a sailor hopeful for land.

"Simeon," said Elijah, early on their first day. The Pharisee sat behind Elijah. He grunted. "Do you know where they are? The ones who came looking for you?"

Elijah could feel the old man shift his legs. He sighed and slumped down as if he'd gained the weight of another man. "Yes."

"You'll help us find it?"

"We're all going to die."

Matthew laughed. "A true scribe." He brought his camel beside theirs, and handed a wineskin to Simeon. Simeon sniffed. He made a face and tilted his chin, felt it heat him up from within. "There's more, found a cache near the temple. Drink as much as you like."

"Don't suppose they'll be needing it," said Simeon. He laughed, and before he realized, laughter was coming out in waves, making him shake. He couldn't stop. But once his mirth expired, Simeon rested his face against Elijah's back. Silent sobs replaced the laughter. Later, he asked for more and Matthew obliged.

They rode forever, it seemed. Simeon drank until he was singing psalms and telling them stories of the ridiculous questions he'd been asked in synagogues. One boy asked what God ate. The boy insisted the creator of the cosmos had an appetite, and Simeon finally told him what his heavenly diet consisted of: "boys who ask foolish questions." The mother came to chide him after. He'd felt bad. Simeon sang psalms and began talking to a woman that wasn't there.

He drank that whole day, trying to shake the calamity that stained his soul. They ate cold fish while riding. Simeon fumbled his fish and tried to lean over and grab it. He fell from the camel and laid in the road laughing.

"Matthew," he said. Both hands raised to him. "Come down here and heal me again, I think I've broken my ass."

Matthew looked at Elijah and frowned. The cloak they'd found for Simeon was up by his waist. It wasn't the worst they'd seen in recent days. Elijah lowered the camel and got off to help Simeon to his feet. They convinced him to get into the river and sober himself. He did. Later he berated them both when they refused him more wine.

That night Simeon woke up screaming. He sat up, heaving. He

walked off alone in the night. Elijah went to search for him but heard his sobs, so he went back and rolled up in his cloak.

When Elijah woke up, Simeon was still gone. He found him standing along the bank watching the water. Elijah called to him but Simeon didn't move. He called him again, but he continued to stare, entranced by the water and whatever thoughts held him hostage. Elijah put a hand on his shoulder and Simeon whirled. There was bewilderment and confusion in his face.

"Are you all right?"

Simeon only shook his head slightly. Red cracks lined the whites of his eyes, the bags beneath pooled where sleep had tried to fasten him to the world, but he refused. Jason's work was thorough but incomplete. There's no reprieve for a man who can't find solace in sleep.

"Have you been out here all night?"

"Yes."

Silence passed between them. "I can't imagine what it must have been like. Either place. I'm sorry he did that. I'm sorry we didn't get there sooner." He put a hand on his arm. "We need you to take us to where they are. He said you'd take us."

"Who?"

"Do you know the Nazarene?"

Simeon nodded. He smiled.

"He told us how to find you. Said you would take us to a nest of serpents and vultures."

"Serpents and vultures?"

"Yes."

"Pigs and children."

"Why are there dead pigs everywhere something bad happens? What do they have to do with any of this?"

"They fill the pigs."

"Fill the pigs?"

Simeon nodded.

"What do you mean?" When Simeon didn't answer, Elijah sighed and put an arm around his shoulder to lead him back. "You know where they are?" Simeon nodded again. Elijah led him back to where they'd slept.

They had a small breakfast and let Simeon sleep a while. They set out again in the heat of the day. Simeon didn't want any wine. Before long he broke their silence. "I was bitten by them. I'm unclean."

"Who?" asked Elijah.

"The pigs."

"You'll be alright," said Matthew. "It won't matter soon."

"They're smart. They watch you with their little black eyes. I don't know how to explain it, but...I could hear them. They speak to you."

"Talking pigs?"

"Not the way men talk. It slides into your mind. You feel dirty after."

"It had to be pigs."

"The gentiles say they taste good," said Matthew. "I've always wondered." Elijah frowned at Matthew and he raised his hands. "Just curious. I'm an Israelite, through and through." He struck his chest with his fist. "Our father Moses commanded what he was told."

"He has the staff," said Simeon.

"Who? What staff?"

"Saul, that swindler. He has the staff of Moses. He serves the goat."

"The goat?"

Simeon didn't respond. Later, he asked to stop. Once they lowered the camels he walked off and stood staring out with his hands on his hips.

"He's gone," said Matthew, shaking his head. "To think a goy pig could ruin a mind like that."

"He's not ruined."

"Listen to him. The staff of Moses? Serving goats?"

They were quiet when Simeon returned.

He rode behind Elijah. "The pigs whisper in your ears," he mumbled. Then, in a loud voice that cracked and broke mid sentence, "I brought them there." Elijah felt his back rattle as Simeon began to sob again.

They looked ahead with a gnawing dread that grew and bit down harder as they rode.

CHAPTER 51

INVITATIONS

Envoys were sent through all the highs and lows of Israel. They carried invitations, transcribed on a thin and peculiar brand of parchment none recognized, written with the steady and practiced skill of a master scribe. The ink was a dark and rich sanguine approaching black, and rose from the parchment in a manner pleasant to the touch. Each seal proved odd as well: a goat with curling horns and eyes scattered to the winds, on each the wax glob surrounding the indentation a near perfect circle.

Men of considerable prestige and influence broke these seals. Roman dignitaries with privilege to the governor's ear or ties to Senators in Rome, religious authorities with influences on the midrash or seats in the Sanhedrin, tax collectors with economic pull, advisors with places at Herod's table. The man who took John the baptist's head to give Herodias's daughter received a formal invitation, which he declined due to a prevailing madness he'd suffered since the incident.

The invitations read as follows:

The sons of Israel invite you to attend a feast in

commemoration of the prosperity of Israel and

her union with Rome. There we will discuss plans for a prosperous

future, that our progenies may flourish,

and our enemies shudder at our names.

Peace be upon you

As any respectable Israelite is aware, invitations are normally passed along to the recipients twice. The first, given through servants, allows the potential attendee to assess the guests and environment in which they potentially find themselves. This allows the recipient to inquire upon the breed of guests projected to be in attendance, and discover any unfavorable deterrents beforehand. The second proceeds after the invitation is formally accepted or rejected.

In this regard, these invitations were unconventional. Gossip is an alluring sedative for the people of the Tanakh, despite its many admonitions against it. The feast's coordinator, in his great wisdom, spread word of these feasts some time prior. Rumors took flight of a clandestine society, where the elites and socially revered enjoyed lavish and extravagant exhaustions in hedonism, and were instructed to vehemently deny its existence thereafter. The result was just as the coordinator intended. The invitations came, and the circulating gossip worked like a parasite of the brain.

It also helps, in such events, to employ messengers with influence over the hearts of men. To such, second invitations, or details concerning the particulars, become irrelevant. Their words have the power to fester in minds. They take root and germinate until volition is choked by the weeds of doubt and the guest's minds are supple in the messenger's hands.

CHAPTER 52

PREPARATIONS

Chuldah was radiant. She walked their land singing an old dirge her mother sang when she was a little girl. She'd gathered plants and spices from the wilderness beyond the villa and boiled them in a cauldron. It helped with the pain. The child in her womb, growing at an alarming rate, sent shudders through her body and its kicks nearly brought her to the ground. She could already feel its strength. The toll it took on her faculties and energy. It would tear her apart with its arrival, but her life was inconsequential in her service to them.

It was incredible to think. The Nephilim would walk the Earth again, like the days of old. And would condescend to mortal flesh through a direct descendant of the witch of Endor. *From the old Saul to the new.*

Preparations for the feast were well underway. She laughed. There hadn't been a playful aspect to her life in years. Isolation, contempt, derision. Her heart was a frigid thing, there was never much warmth, one doesn't prosper in the business of child sacrifice with pity and kindness; but the years had sapped her humor, left her soul empty as a grave and likewise bustling with every crawling and creeping thing. Every divisive look, each murmured suspicion, the skewed compliments of well to do women with their cracking tones, thick ankles, and skin striped with measures of growth from child after child after child. What was all that now?

Funny. It was funny.

How many of their children had she brought to Molech? How many babes cried out under dull blades, as blood and tears splashed Baal's altar? And how many more would come?

The world would soon catch fire. Fan the flames, pour oil where it rages! There was a place for her. Chuldah laughed and laughed and part of her reverted to childish wonder. To see her belly bulging, the growth beneath stretching the skin in its shape, her arms stretched, spinning in the fields of grain–an observer may think she was a normal woman, rejoicing in a fruitful womb. But in her mind she tread on ashes; splashed the horses' bridles with blood.

She danced in the shade of the trees that rose above the grain. Their fruits were nailed to their trunks, spoiled and distended crops that scream in blossom. Some fresh and ripe with suffering, petals of viscera falling, others long expired, picked apart by worms and birds. The carrion's banquet. Their agonized faces looked after the grain, watching the crops fall victim to time. The old bitch that came with the woman writhed above her only hours before. Her body finally grew too tired, and surrendering to the Earth's pull, she slumped forward and ceased struggling.

Where would she have gone? The slumbering masses try to escape the inevitable, they're rodents under a cat's paw. She loved to watch them squirm under the weight of impending death. There's no greater spectacle than a man or woman preparing for their demise. Being privy to the intimacy of these supplications is like a snippet of omniscience, where a mortal can get a glimpse of every sin a soul tries to drag down silently to sheol.

The old woman's confessions were delightful. As were the others, all down the line. Chuldah stood behind her cross and listened. So quiet, moving with the soft steps of a predator, standing just far enough to hear the old woman's breathing. The whimpers. But her confession came, they always do. Slowly. Much had to be deciphered, and was drawn through labored breaths from wet lungs. Chuldah sifted it all like grain on the threshing floor.

"I used my son," she said. "Tormented his wife. Stole from him while he was healthy. And after. Acted unfaithful toward my own husband, yet came down righteously when I heard the rumors of her and the Shepherd."

Oh, to know their sins! To tap into the subconscious and witness the vileness of a man or woman. To see them lower their masks and expose their ugliness to the world.

While the old woman breathed and wept, Chuldah came around so she could see her. Her eyes were closed. She pressed her heels into the block below her feet so she wouldn't suffocate. Chuldah pulled her toe. Giggled when her eyes opened.

"H–h–help."

"Should I call them to break your knees?" Chuldah turned her body, smiling. "Your son hates you."

Her face wrinkled in anguish. Her wails were cut short by the pain.

"His body is no longer his own. He abides in everlasting darkness."

Chuldah stood beneath her. Waiting. She spoke softly. Enraptured with the liminal state of a life near its end, each time she watched the soul in a person's eyes snuffed out, her arms rippled in little bumps. After the old woman died she waved, warmth filling her chest, then turned from the row of trees to find Abaddon.

Abaddon was near the cellar, holding counsel with Belphegor. She skipped over as a young girl might head for a drink on a hot day.

"What wicked things are you two devising?" she said as she neared.

"If you knew," answered Belphegor, "you'd tear your ears off and stuff them into your mouth."

"Oh tell me, lord." She pouted to the sow, a hand to each lobe. "I've never been fond of these things." She turned her head and shook her hair. "I can hide them."

Belphegor made a low rumble.

"Will you be at the feast, my lord?"

"I'll be *here*, wretched as ever."

"If only you'd have taken a body. This seed in me could have been yours." She held her hands to her stomach.

"What makes you think being a man is any better than a pig?"

Chuldah turned her head, thinking. Then her face brightened and she held up her thumbs, wiggling them for Belphegor.

"If only you could have saved yourself rather than playing the whore."

Chuldah laughed. Belphegor laid his head down, turning away from her and Abaddon.

"Is it time to gather the wood?" asked Abaddon.

She nodded, smiling.

Abaddon walked with Chuldah to the fields. He enjoyed his work. In each of them there were remnants of the people that once inhabited the bodies. Abaddon assumed the flesh of a cruel man. The Roman Claudius had raised up trees of men like a woodsman righting what he'd cut from the world. A glint of joy shone now in the demoniac's eyes as the hammer rang, its metal a sweet bell ushering their reign over all things.

They walked to the crosses. He looked over his ornaments, each frozen in its rictus of pain. Chuldah watched him pull the wood from the holes in the ground as easily as a man lifting a single brick. He set the pole on the dirt and let them fall back. Wood cracked and dust filled the air. Bodies laid disjointed and twisted from the impact. One after another they fell like trees in the wake of some great beast barreling through a thicket.

Ephron and Abijah came. Chuldah didn't turn or flinch as they pulled the nails and gathered them into a matted patch of wheat. The men carried the rigid bodies under their arms to the cellar.

Chuldah spoke sweetly to the pigs outside and ran a hand over the hairs on their backs as their snouts tested the air. She'd come to them daily, making conversation and lauding them like a lonely woman does her cats. They opened the door. The men tossed their bloated parcels and Chuldah leaned against the jamb watching their heads snap left and right and swarm around the damp enclosure clicking hoof against stone. Grunts and snorts rose and echoed in their narrow confines. She sighed.

"Soon we'll have you out in the world."

Chuldah and her masters were a spreading sore. The masses would pick and scratch in their frail attempts at justice, but the world would be a raw and bloody thing soon. She put her hands to her belly. A sharp pain flared low in her back as the child shifted. The skin on her stomach bulged when it moved.

Would it be a boy? What would it look like? Would it have her features? Would the father's face show in his true form or the Pharisee he inhabited? She pictured the structure of her face imposed on the new race to come. They would call her mother.

Witches rarely became mothers. They're known for their disdain for children. She supposed one could almost feel sympathy for the bastards, dashed against rocks or expelled violently with home mixtures. But children had always meant a sentence to servitude. After their birth, the woman was declawed, resigned to wipe excrement and fluids from dirty crevices, to burp, to coddle. Chuldah had never desired children.

But now, despite the pain and cravings, a warm affinity grew. This wasn't some farmer or fisherman's baby. Her child would share the bloodlines of Molech and Baal. A part of Ha Satan.

Chuldah returned to the villa and entered the building housing the women. In a large room stripped of everything save torches, mats were lined up along the far wall, positioned in such a way that the sun would fall over them when it rose high enough to angle down from the windows.

The women were tied and manacled, confined to mats of battered reeds atop soiled linen. The air was pungent, almost as suffocating as it was near the cellar. Their faces would have surely haunted a lesser woman. The mind of each was now a smothered wick, the smoke and ash left in their ruin snuffed the vibrance once animating their expressions. Another spectacle, nearly as fascinating as death, was watching sanity wither. They begged while they had their wits. She put damp rags to their heads. Whispered in their ears. Ensured the dread of each was private. Intimate.

She left when they came for the women. She didn't pity them, but it was something she only needed to see once. Women were commodities. Watching them have their pleasures reminded her that she would have been as expendable as the rest were not a womb needed. And the only reason she wasn't lying on a mat beside them was her willingness to bear their child.

Beyond the room where the women were tied was a smaller annex with wet stones along the wall. Inside, the woman, Salome, laid low, with only the blades of her shoulders propping her against the wall. Beside her head a pig licked her ear. Its nose twitched. The black eyes rolled up to Chuldah and she smiled.

The woman on the floor's mouth moved. Only slightly. The pig spoke sweetly to her.

All in time.

CHAPTER 53

MACHINATIONS

On the morning Hannah was crucified, a Centurion at Caesarea Maritima opened a sealed letter delivered by the courier. He broke the seal with his knife and unrolled the parchment. After he'd read the contents he stood for a moment, tapping the paper against his leg with his eyes down. Then he rolled the parchment and walked briskly to the guard. He waved away the startled man's salute and held up the message. "Who brought this?"

"A young man. thin…" The guard swallowed. "He just left, sir."

"Go find him."

The guard stomped down the footpath leading from the house, then disappeared through an arched walkway. Shortly after, he returned with the thin man flailing his arms like a feral cat. He couldn't do much against the larger guard.

"That's enough."

The man stopped struggling.

"He's a liar, sir."

"Let him go."

When the guard released him, the man shook out his cloak and glared at the guard. He spoke in Aramaic, swiping the air in wide gestures as he spoke.

"He spoke the lingua latina when he brought the message. Claimed it came courtesy the cursus publicus. His rhetoric was perfect. Like a senator. Look at him now, barking like a Jewish dog!"

"You've heard a senator speak?" The soldier shrank under the Centurion's gaze. The Centurion paused, then turned to the thin man and in his own language said, "We enjoy making whores of your mothers and daughters." No subtlety flared behind the eyes. "I'll give you to the men. They'll make a woman of you." The man looked around, tugging his cloak and shrinking into himself. The Centurion frowned. He then said in Koine. "Can you understand me now?"

"Yes, understand, understand," said the courier. He pointed at the guard. "He struck me." The man spoke horrid Koine, but the Centurion understood.

"You've never seen this man?" asked the Centurion in a slow and condescending tone.

After no small effort, he learned the courier's last memory was watching the water. He didn't know how he'd arrived there.

"What are you doing at a Roman outpost?"

The man looked around. It seemed as if he'd only noticed the stones and pillars after the Centurion's remark.

The Romans spoke among themselves while the man turned from one to another. He shifted his feet and rubbed his arms. "I'm a fisherman." His eyes went from the Centurion to the guard, then back.

The Centurion sighed. An hour later he walked along the water beside the Tribune explaining the letter and the courier to his superior.

"Did you have him flogged?" asked the Tribune

"I wanted your advice."

The Tribune threw up his hands at the incompetence of such an oversight.

"I don't think he's lying."

"Something you'll learn soon enough. When enough of the fluids in a man come out, the truth soon follows."

"I understand sir. There's just…things about him that don't make sense."

"What's that?"

"His appearance. The worn sandals, cracked lips. He walked for days to get here.

"To lure us into a trap."

"Who would send a Jewish peasant and expect us to believe? That's just it, it's counter-intuitive. Were the message spreading lies this would be the worst way to pass such a thing."

"Perhaps the setter of such traps is one step ahead of you." The Tribune smiled.

"We would wipe them from the earth. Where would they hide? They're not guerillas. They have no Hannibal."

"What about this anointed one the letter mentions?"

"That's what has me worried."

"And this isn't the same one we've heard about, the one preaching in Judea?"

"According to the letter this one was a Pharisee."

"It will be the Maccabees all over again."

"So we'll send men?"

"I'll talk to the Prefect in the morning when he returns. But I think I know what he'll say."

"And if this is a trap?"

The Tribune turned to the Centurion and smiled. "We'll send men who are used to traps."

C H A P T E R   5 4

P R E P A R A T I O N S   I I

Over the following week, a great many travelers ascended the path that wound through the village and led to the gates of the villa. Compared to previous weeks, a conspicuous number of residents dallied outside their homes. All seemed receptive and amiable. They displayed a lighthearted congeniality, waved at strangers, engaged in jovial conversations when addressed, and appeared otherwise focused with projects that kept with the appearances of mortal routines.

If one were to inquire further into these villager's pursuits, they'd soon discover a fraudulent world. Empty buckets were lugged by women returning from imaginary wells. Scythes swung at nothing over dead grass, the wielders never flinching, even after nicking their own shins. Families reclined making atrocious comments on the Law and Prophets, while the visitors watching from afar assumed their lively conversations were wholesome signs of rural life.

Once they'd ascended the path, The villa's gates opened like the yawn of a great iron beast and swallowed them into the yard. Hospitality continued inside the villa, of course. Guests were brought wine and bread until they were warm and immobile. Women were sent. Blinded by opulence, with every hedonistic desire appeased, the many guests were lulled into tranquility in preparation for the feast.

Bazumel made his rounds. He showed the Israelites the staff of Moses. When dusk rolled up everything visible beyond the fields, he raised a large man with red hair from the dead. Every interaction between host and guest, each performance of the miraculous, when Saul Ben Azareel's staff transmuted into a viper–all transpired according to plan.

In order for the guests to do what was required, a faith in Saul's power had to be cultivated. They needed participants who had strayed. Whether through the obstinate path of a prodigal, or in the blind righteousness of men and women who falsely believe themselves holy, the same effect could be achieved. A man's sin makes him clay in wicked hands.

Saul's hands began molding the moment the first guests arrived. They were shown to their quarters. The rooms were adorned with elaborate furnishings, soft beds, grapes, bread and oil. Lye soap and buckets of water to wash were set inside. Servants soon came to wash their feet.

The villa itself was made presentable, of course. The banquet hall needed more light. The stones scrubbing. More importantly however, were the smells they had to contend with. The cellar had been inhabited by swine, and as their many bodies expired, the stench grew. The villa retained its livestock odor, but the scent of death needed to be masked for the time being.

They planted scented flowers and placed rows of stone pots with sweet smelling herbs all around the cellar and temple. The insides were scrubbed. The stench remained, but only as a subtlety their noses sought but couldn't quite recognize.

Everything was as Bazumel planned.

CHAPTER 55

BY THE FIRE

With their traveling finished for the day, Elijah and Matthew built a fire while Simeon sat on a rotting trunk. They spoke from time to time to keep the pervading silence at bay. The quiet sense of dread had become their fourth traveler.

Simeon's eyes glowed in the flames. Elijah offered him some of the stale bread he had left. The Pharisee took it with a shaking hand. Since the village, he'd looked older every day, like all he'd witnessed compounded on him.

"What do you plan to do when we get there?"

Elijah looked up at him. The old man seldom spoke besides the directions he provided. Until then it seemed as if his worth as a man had been stripped to the simple act of pointing north or west. Elijah shook his head. "I have no idea."

Simeon laughed. It was a healthy, deep sound from his belly. "We don't need a plan. We need Michael and a flaming sword."

"I'm glad you find this amusing," said Matthew.

"You'd go to your tomb weeping? There will be wailers for that. Let others weep, we'll go to sheol like men, laughing. Bellies full of wine."

"You're a crazy old fool." Matthew spat into the fire.

"Let him be." Elijah turned to the old man. "Do you have any suggestions?"

Simeon looked at the flames. "I don't know what we can do against them. These are not men, who you seek."

"What are they, then?" asked Elijah.

Simeon scratched at his beard. "Do you remember when God sent a lying spirit to Ahab?"

"They're spirits?"

"Yes. I believe so. Something like that. Older than these mountains. Older than Adam."

"They're unclean," said Matthew.

"Yes."

"But you can cast them out," said Elijah, turning to Matthew. "He gave you the gift. You went with the 70." Matthew was quiet. Something popped in the flames. Elijah furled his brow and kicked at the sand. "You have some of whatever he had. You healed him." He pointed to Simeon.

Matthew closed his eyes. "I couldn't help Joseph. Or that boy. He's saying this place is filled with them. What can I do against that? What can any of us do?"

"Nothing if your mind's already convinced," said Simeon. "Where faith is dead the body's soon to follow."

"Spare me your mantras, Pharisee. You could barely climb onto the camel when we pulled you from that house."

"And you were pulled from a puddle of vomit, Matthew. Isn't that what you told me? At least another man put him there. Does your fear make you cruel, too?" Matthew dropped his eyes. Elijah went on. "Where we go we need one another."

It grew quiet again. They sat idle with thoughts of other places and people. Until Matthew laughed.

"What's funny?"

"Do you know why Joseph died?" Matthew's eyes were low, fixed on the flames trying to lap up the night sky. "I ran away. I saw the thing, it…made me see things and I fled. The demoniac went into the boy's father and killed my friend. Then the boy." He dragged a hand down his face. "I didn't heal you, Simeon. And the gift wasn't given to me because of some noble trait I possess."

"You're drunk, Matthew."

Matthew laughed again. "I am, but these are a sober man's thoughts. I laughed because I realized there's no reason to be afraid." Elijah and Simeon sat back. "We live for the future. To see the dreams we put out in the world come to pass. But what is it like to meet the future? It nearly always fails our expectations. This was true even for the prophets. God put big dreams in such wretched little hearts. And his favorites always felt the fire. What do you old scribes say? You've suffered much, God must surely love you. Now consider the past. It fades as life goes on, and it's either not as bad as the horrors you remember, or not as good as the memories you cling to when your present situation upsets you. When you think back on those things you understand how much our memories lie to us. We cast these illusions ourselves. Once we learn the future disappoints us."

"What's your point?" asked Elijah.

"We dream, we fear, we reminisce, because we fail to accept the present. We cherish ideas more than things. We're so worried about things we can't control, that we lose sight of what we *can*. Right now. We are finite. Our fears and worries are desperate attempts at timelessness. To put ourselves in the place of God.

"I saw a girl standing on the water holding her organs in her hand. The fear that's crept into my sleep the last few nights has nothing to do with wanting to be like God."

"The Mashiach said once, 'don't worry about tomorrow, today has enough problems.' Or something like that." Matthew burped and spat. "We know there's many things to worry about in the next few days. But what will our worries accomplish? Maybe you're right, old man. We should go to our graves laughing. If for no other reason than to frustrate our enemies and make us more effective in our mission."

"You're smart for a drunk," said Simeon.

"So I've been told. But wine puts courage in frail hearts and songs in shy lips." Matthew took a deep breath. "I suppose I'm ready now."

"We're not going anywhere until the morning."

"I mean I'm ready to die."

"I hope you live all the same."

"Me too," said Matthew, and they were quiet.

After sitting with their thoughts, Elijah broke the silence, "I don't understand why he couldn't have come. He could have just cast them out, sent them back to wherever they came from. It would have been easy."

"It's not his path," said Simeon. "What he must do has already been written."

"Why is he confined to what's written on some scroll?"

"Every word of God proves true. He is a shield to those who take refuge in him."

"I've heard it before. We're here. We go to a nest of serpents and vultures, like He said. He roams the country healing and having women pour perfume over his feet. While villages pile with bodies and children become demoniacs."

"What the prophet's have written is final."

"Well, I can't read," said Elijah. A short breath of air left his nose. He looked at Simeon, and after a pause pregnant with tension both men fell back with laughter. Soon all three were laughing.

Matthew took a big swig of wine that trickled down the sides of his beard, then passed the wineskin on. Elijah drank next. Then Simeon.

"You know what old man," said Elijah. He leaned forward with his forearms on his knees. "I'll write my own stories."

"You can write?"

Elijah smiled. "No. It's a parable."

"I don't think you realize what a parable is," said Simeon.

"It's when someone tells a story in a roundabout way instead of telling you what they really mean. If you're confused after, it means it's a very good parable."

"He who has ears to hear," said Matthew, laughing. The wineskin came back to him. "He who has lips to drink, drink." He raised his wine. They laughed at the shadow of death looming over them.

CHAPTER 5 6

DESCENT

The lights fade into blurs of colors that run and merge together. At times, it's like I float without form. My mind exists apart from my body and I'm tempted by an abiding darkness. There's voices in the dark. They beckon and make sweet promises. There's an animal foulness, the stench of beasts that chew the cud, of soil that's run fallow, the rot of death. Voice's call from over me. They hover overhead, as though my tormentors walked on the ceilings and called down from stalactite perches.

I'm not afraid while I'm here, only faintly aware that this is not my true place in the world. My only fear is what's being done with my body. Sometimes I hear things. Real things. There's movement in the villa, a budding excitement, and I catch some of the strange words that are said. Words are said to me, to the body beyond my reach. And I hear the clever things I say in return. Vile and hateful things I'd never say. Sometimes the words are directed at me. The me here. By those who know I'm gone. They're vile.

I've had glimpses of coherency. The first time, my eyes opened and the sun was warm on my back. Shards of dappled light covered the courtyard. My hands were cool. After my disorientation wore off, I was roused by frantic screams, arms pulling me. There was a loom in shambles and splintered wood scattered the ground.

Then I looked down. I'll never forget the feel of her hair in my hands. I leaned over one of the basins they use to dye garments. The ground around the basin, the back of the woman whose head I was holding in the red water, and the front of my tunic was soaked. She twitched and I rose and backpedaled, covering my mouth, shaking my head. I tried to scream but the thing in me—-that vile thing, kept me fixated, watching the results of the work of my hands. The ladies pulled the old woman out. Slapped at her face. Her skin and hair had a red tint from the dye. As did my hands. In the brief moments my mind returns to the physical world, I think of her. I look down at my hands and they're red. Dark, wet, blood red. A beacon of my iniquity. I see that and I want to return to the darkness. God help me.

CHAPTER 5 7

B A B Y L O N   A D V A N C E S

Days of marching bring familiar pains. Knees become a whetstone for aches they've picked up on their travels. Every step sends a knell of pain ringing through shins. Lower backs protest the weight of the world. There's an odor too, like some motley pack of predators redolent with acrid sweat and stale urine. Bodies press forward, regardless of temperature, terrain, or enemy. The sounds of jostled belts and the nails biting the earth beneath their soles herald their approach. The hollow clang of shields, spears tapping armor, and each man's gladius, secured in scabbards fit to their preference, swing in stride as leather and wool hum melodies of a war machine. They sing morbid cadences learned around fires after battles. Perversions spawned from babel's fall pass among them.

These are the seasoned among them. Grizzled warriors, whose skin itch for the collision of ranks. Eyes of hard flint and sun leathered skin, roughed over with healed scars. Men who paid death's dowry in blood, wed to the catacombs of glory, who Mars smiles upon with clouds of arrows.

Their eagerness consumes them, whets tongue and blade. The longer these warriors are idle, the more their proclivities for battle manifest. Scabbards come loose. Spears grow wings. The Earth calls for blood.

They approach the coming skirmish with confidence. They think they go to fight men.

The detachment from Caesarea Maritima departed two days after the Prefect received correspondence from an old friend. A retired Roman officer he served with under Germanicus with property in Judea. The message bore his seal, and its contents attributed the source of the information to a network developed among affluent Jews paid off to inform the Romans of surreptitious activity.

The message promised just that. This meeting would bring together wealth and political influence, social elites and men of power. And a good deal of Romans–whose omission of these matters to any governing body struck the Prefect as peculiar enough to investigate further. The letter urged immediate action. Another of these "Messiahs." Their names moaned through the teeth of widows, and whined through the cracks in villager's houses. Rome already had its eye on the rabbi who'd ravaged the money tables in Jerusalem. Although one could certainly sympathize with him. Still, they couldn't afford another rebellion. And the last thing the Prefect wanted was a blunder in his time there.

They would be dispatched quickly and efficiently, with whatever brutality was needed to quell insurrection and beat swords to plowshares (to borrow a phrase from the occupied). The crucifixions and flagrums deterred morale. Messiahs seemed positions of rhetoric, rarely praxis.

But according to his old friend, and Herod's spies, those scurrying rodents, this was real. The Centurion assigned was given his charge and the location, with a stained copy of one of the invitations for the feast (provided by the Prefect's personal guard). They would send their very best. No rebellion would sully his tenure.

Two of the men had gone ahead for reconnaissance. All were anxious. They were roughly a day from the villa. The men ate behind a nest of boulders and rested for a while.

While the Optio conferred with the Centurion about their plan of attack, something crashed out from the brush. Legionnaires sprang to their feet, gladius and spear at the ready. A man staggered into the clearing. Over one shoulder, he held a pole of some sort. There was something on the end, and when the wanderer turned they got a clear look. It was a goad, skewered at an odd angle through a severed head. It was black from rot, maligned in a decaying scowl. Dried blood stuck the long hair together in thick clumps.

The man didn't seem to care that he'd stumbled upon several hundred Roman soldiers. He whistled, oblivious.

They yelled for him to stop in Latin. He glanced their way but kept moving. One of the soldiers screamed a warning in Aramaic.

"I heard you," said the man. His Latin was perfect. This struck them as strange since he dressed and looked like one of the Israelites.

"Take another step and you're a dead man."

The wanderer's eyes rose. He took the goad from his shoulder and held it straight in the air like a torch, so the head was facing the man who addressed him. The legionnaire who warned him staggered back when Its eyes opened. "If you go there Gaius," said the head, in a low wheeze. A beetle crawled from its mouth and fell to the ground. "Your head will be with mine." The wanderer laughed, high and shrill. The head joined, black tongue rolling out. The soldiers looked at one another.

"He's mad."

"He's a sorcerer."

"A demon!'

"Like the stonemason."

"Are you the one they call Messiah?"

They surrounded the wanderer with spears, shields raised. The Centurion was making his way over to handle the situation when the two legionnaires who had been sent ahead for reconnaissance returned, panting. Their faces flushed.

"Sir, you need to look at this."

The Centurion ordered them to detain the man and followed his men.

The Centurion stood a ways off, staring. He wiped his mouth and spat in the sand. A row of men and women were raised there. They'd been impaled and crucified without precision, with pieces of their carts and some of the nearby trees. Arms dangled where victims had writhed and pulled free. Some were burned, whether it came before being nailed in place or after, none could say, since every beam was burnt. A woman had torn her hands free and fallen forward. She hung inverted by one foot, which was still nailed in place. She was a large woman, and the beam they used leaned toward them with her weight. Farther off they found pikes. Jutting from the ground, they ran through the bottoms of severed necks, and continued like great horns through the tops of the victim's heads.

"What monster did this?" asked one of the men, looking down at the remains of a boy. The body swarmed with specks of green where flies busied themselves with their good fortune.

"The monsters we've come to kill," said the Centurion. He turned and walked back to where the men were still huddled around the wanderer.

The strange fool still had the goad over one shoulder. He was humming to himself. The men hadn't touched him, but were still holding their weapons.

"What is this?"

"A nest for serpents and vultures." The wanderer threw his head back. The head on the goad laughed too. The Centurion's skin prickled. Beneath the whine of wind he heard more laughter. The Centurion knew where it came from but didn't want to believe. The world itself was laughing at him. He closed his eyes, and gave orders to kill the man and move out at once.

CHAPTER 58

THE VILLAGE

They reached the village late afternoon, ascending the path in the shade of clouds. Simeon pointed to the top of the hill. Matthew and Elijah looked on at the villa's white stones and got an impression of its size. Still enormous with half its structure obscured by trees. He'd expected the place to appear more ominous, and somehow its grandeur added to the tension. Simeon shifting behind Elijah didn't help. The smell of livestock hung about the place.

Life here had stopped abruptly. The houses seemed stale, swallowed in silence. One of the camels kicked a pail that had rolled to the side of the path. Garments were crumpled on the ground beside abandoned laundry lines. Matthew's camel groaned.

"There's something there. Between the houses."

They looked into the alley where Matthew pointed. They could make out only curves at first. Once his eyes adjusted, he saw the curves and swells of fat bodies piled over one another. Their mass rose and fell collectively. They listened, could hear the breathing; a collective wheeze interspersed with snorts. One of the pigs came out of the dark and stared at them. Others watched with their heads low in the dirt, huddled together on the mud and shit packed ground, eyes glossed and rheumy enough to shine in some cases.

"What's wrong with it?" asked Matthew. "Is it a leper?"

Elijah asked Simeon, "can pigs be lepers?"

"I'm a Jew, what do I know about pigs?"

Elijah stared at the decrepit animal until Simeon urged him on. They moved up the path, past more desolate houses. Some of their doors were broken off, the spaces they once filled open maws. Elijah thought of the other villages.

"This place was full of people," said Simeon.

Elijah nodded. He looked back. Another pig had walked out and sniffed the pail. . It raised its head to watch them.

The camel Matthew rode groaned. "They sense it. I feel it too."

One of the pigs squealed. Its echo made them feel exposed. More squeals and barks answered from higher up the hill.

"At least they'll know to set out bedding for us," said Matthew.

"They should probably just start digging." No one laughed at this.

The path curved with the incline, and once they were nearly level with the villa they could see the fields behind it. Elijah touched the hilt of the sword concealed at his side. Then sat higher. He stopped and turned the animal. "You see that?"

Matthew and Simeon shook their heads. Elijah could see them clearly. A chariot pulled by two horses pounding its way through a grass covered path adjacent the fields. It wobbled on shaky wheels while a tall man tugged the reins. There were two of them, jostling with the shape of the road. Elijah described them for the others.

"Romans?"

"I don't think so," said Elijah. "They look like Jews."

"Are they...with them?"

"How should I know?"

"Are we just going to walk right up to the gate?" asked Matthew.

"They already know we're here," said Simeon. The pig stood a ways behind them in the road. It turned to where they were looking, as though contemplating, then glanced back at them. It grunted and trotted back to the others.

"What should we do?"

"We'll ask for her."

"Don't be a fool," said Simeon.

Elijah looked back over his shoulder. "What do you suggest?"

Elijah and Matthew waited for the men in the chariot. Simeon slipped away past the villa and away from the pigs, toward a decline in the path ahead. He would find another way in, since Saul or any of the others would immediately recognize him. Elijah had offered Simeon a camel and told him he was free to leave, but Simeon only frowned and shook his head almost imperceptibly. After Simeon left they stood and waited. Elijah raised a hand when the chariot pulled near.

"Peace be upon you."

The man who wasn't holding the reins was tall. One might consider him handsome if not for the way his mouth hung open while he was idle. The stout man holding the reins came to his companion's shoulders and had a face like a lump of wet clay tossed at a wall. He wiped his forehead with a cloth and frowned. Elijah didn't think it possible for that face to have any more wrinkles. The short one's eyes were not much different than the ambling pigs. "We don't have time for formalities. I'm afraid we must be on our way."

"Are you headed to the villa?"

The dark eyed stranger had been patting along his creases absently. His eyes shifted to Elijah after the question. "What business is it of yours?"

Matthew raised his hands. "Just a greeting. Can men still ask questions?"

The tall man eyed Elijah like a wealthy man would an unruly

slave. "Where are you headed?" The eyes moved from one man to another. Then back.

"The Villa."

"You were invited?"

"Of course."

"The whore of Babylon's cup is full," said the shorter man with a smirk.

Elijah and Matthew were silent.

The tall man snorted. He shook his head and muttered under his breath, snapping at the reins so the horses pulled away. Matthew and Elijah looked at one another. The chariot's wheels squeaked as it wobbled off. The laughter of the two men faded with the drone of their complaining wheel.

"What will we do now?" asked Matthew.

"We'll go."

"Do you think they'll say something?"

"I don't think a man like that cares about anything but himself."

Still, they decided to take a different route than the carriage, which had gone toward the rear of the villa. A wall ran along the side. They made their way to the main path. They looked back and two pigs were lying in the road.

"They don't seem that bad when you get a good look at them," said Matthew.

"Go scratch behind its ears."

Matthew looked at Elijah, then back at the pig. "If I touched that thing I could never step foot in a Synagogue again."

The villa's gate was unattended. By the time they worked up the courage to go it was drizzling. The rain pelting the palm fronds rose to a droned shush. They lowered the camels, climbed off and tied them outside the gate.

Matthew and Elijah sloshed through the grass. Matthew pulled his cloak over his head to shield from the rain. Elijah walked just as he did in the sun. Outside of the building was a stone bowl with brown film at the bottom. Water streamed from the roof.

They made their way past a vestibule and paused at the threshold. Elijah took a deep breath and dropped his eyes. He stood in front of the bronze double doors while his lips moved. He stood that way for a moment, then sighed and rapped on the door. Noise came from inside. The door creaked open. A woman peered through the gap.

They waited for her to say something. Nothing came. Elijah said, "All hail the whore of Babylon." Matthew mouthed something to him from where she couldn't see.

She pushed the door open and Elijah winced. Her lips were stitched closed. The skin was pink and scabbed around the punctures. Elijah caught himself staring, but she was undaunted. Her eyes weren't far from one of the corpses they'd seen a few days earlier. She looked them over and the warnings they'd received passed from myth to reality.

"What happened to you?" said Matthew. Elijah cast him a sharp glance.

She lowered her gaze. The corners of her lips and eyes drooped and wrinkles rippled the skin around them, as if the features of her face were sinking. She hunched over at the neck, looking down, rubbing her hands together. Her every mannerism and expression made her appear smaller. She stayed that way for some time, until Elijah asked, "Is there a man named Samuel here?"

The woman motioned over her shoulder then back at them.

"Can you take us to him?"

The shake of her head was almost too subtle to notice. Her eyes were wide and for the first time displayed some life. Elijah watched her. He had his hand near his waist feeling the sword under the cloth.

"I need to see him."

She flinched at a noise from behind her. The door opened wider, and Elijah's stomach turned as an enormous silhouette moved from behind her into the light. The man was immense. Red as Esau. There was something unsettling about his expression. The smile seemed forced, a practiced charm put on to please.

"Peace be upon you." He stood beside the woman with his chin high, regal in manner. His wide shoulders rolled back with the posture of a soldier.

Elijah motioned toward the woman. "What happened to her mouth?" asked Elijah.

The man nodded, pursing his lips as if it was a regrettable but necessary fact about life there. "I'm afraid this young woman is a blasphemer." He looked at her and gave a solitary cackle. "Was a blasphemer."

"That's your punishment for blasphemy?"

"Would you have it so the servants said whatever they liked?" He smiled. "It's not as though she stubbed her toe and cursed." He looked at Matthew then, and Elijah thought his eyes narrowed slightly. "But you're at our door. I'm the one that should be asking questions."

"You're the only one here that can," said Elijah. He was smiling now.

The man laughed and placed a hand on the woman's shoulder. "You're quick. I'm thankful we have someone here to mend our split seams. One can only tolerate so much filth. If a man desires quiet, he keeps the cocks far from his bedroom window."

"I hear pigs fare better." Elijah tried to read the man. He struggled to keep the muscles in his face relaxed.

"I'm Abijah." He put a hand over his chest.

"Elijah."

"Matthew."

"You've come for the feast?"

"Yes."

The man stared at Elijah. He tilted his head, brows high expecting more.

"Oh," said Matthew. "How careless of us. We've already addressed your servant." Matthew stood taller, and in his best rendition of an orator said, "The whore of Babylon's cup is full."

"May her womb be ever fruitful."

Elijah did his best to hide his revulsion. The pigs, the imagery, the woman's lips–everything added together to dizzy him. How would Salome be when he found her? *If he found her.*

Abijah opened his arms in an elaborate display of hospitality. "You've come to see the Mashiach."

"The Mashiach?" Matthew blinked.

"Surely you've heard." The man's face looked surprised, but again, seemed forced. Elijah felt a gnawing sense of panic rising up. "Saul Bar Azareel."

"We've heard. It's been a long journey."

"I'm sure you'll want to bathe? You look as though you've been traveling for some time."

"Oh yes," said Matthew, with the voice of a man finally able to relieve himself.

Abijah smiled, delighted with Matthew's response. Just as he'd been delighted to explain the woman's stitches. He poked his head out through the door and scanned the vestibule and grass beyond.

Abijah ushered them inside. "Take heart." He turned to lead them on with a finger in the air. "Come, I'll take you to meet the Mashiach's wife." They followed, leaving the woman with the stitched lips near the door. Elijah looked back at her. She watched them walk off with a worried wrinkle through her brow. Her hands curled together on her chest. Elijah felt for the sword and followed.

They were led past some bronze sculptures and a marble bust of a hook nosed Roman with the paint peeling from the eyes. Abijah mentioned the name, it had an ius at the end, like all the other

Romans. The fresco of a phalanx of warriors spanned one of the long walls, their shields raised against raining arrows. Jupiter, Neptune, and a host of demigods watched over the figures from above.

There were women in the first courtyard they came to grinding stones over garments and scrubbing them with lye. One worked at the loom, slouched over a Roman stool. A thin woman worked a strand of wool with fingers that looked like they belonged in an ossuary. They were grinding dyes and bringing water to a boil. Cloaks soaked in a basin filled with blood red liquid. Elijah's mind drifted back to the baths again.

It was odd seeing them work without words. Activities like this were normally ripe with laughter. The jests and gossip of old women at work is as pleasant to the ears as birds in the morning. They never looked up from their tasks.

They passed room after room, courtyards, corridors. A small vestibule with a sofa opened to the portico. Its stone floors had a few palm fronds that had blown in. Green fuzz caked up in the grooves of the columns lining the way.

In a clearing beyond the portico, to the rear of the villa, there were men carrying tables and carved poles. An old man stood in the center, directing them where to put things. All of them worked undaunted, impervious to the rain. Elijah and Matthew followed Abijah through the portico. The stable smell was strong here. There was a foulness too, fleeting in their nostrils. Elijah thought of the pigs.

"Abijah," said Elijah. "Is this your villa?"

"It's all of ours.' We share everything."

"You're a religious sect? Like the Essenes?"

Abijah laughed and shook his head. "The Essenes would have a man deny the few pleasures he gets in this life."

"A man must have pleasure."

"Pleasure *is* our worship."

Elijah thought of all he'd been told to deny. All his failure led him to. A snippet of a life he'd never attain, of pleasure at no cost, swelled up and through him, opened his soul to possibilities that struck fear into every pore they opened, and sealed closed in an instant.

They were led back into the villa, down a corridor and through another courtyard. Empty besides some large plants. There were shields tilted against the wall and splintered racks of swords and spears.

Abijah led them through the doors and into a tiled room. Filled with sundry faces. Heads were uncovered, even the women, and Matthew made an audible gasp at the shock of what he saw. As they made their way across the room a woman rose and approached them. She walked with strict posture and an air of affluence. Her hair was slick with oil and the scent of perfume lingered about. Elijah noticed a slight swell in her stomach.

"Welcome."

"Peace be upon you." She reminded Elijah of this whore of Babylon. *May her womb be fruitful.*

"I'm Chuldah. The master won't return until later tonight."

Abijah introduced them.

"Where have you come from?"

"I'm from a small village north of the Sea of Galilee," said Elijah. "I'm sure you've never heard the name."

"You'd be surprised by what I've heard."

"I'm from near Capernaum," said Matthew. "I look forward to meeting the Mashiach. I hope he won't be delayed by the rain."

"I wouldn't worry," said Chuldah. "With a word he could seal the floodgates of heaven."

Elijah looked around the room. "You speak very highly of him."

"A woman ought to speak highly of her husband."

"My apologies. How many of you are here? This place is much larger than it appears from down the hill."

"Our family grows by the day."

Where Abijah's smile had a fraudulent quality, Chuldah's possessed a malevolence. Elijah pictured the serpent in the garden smiling at Eve. Lulling whoever listened with venom disguised as honey.

"I hope the road's been kind to you."

The kiln, the villages, Simeon trapped in that festering room under the watchful eyes of the dead. Elijah lied with a smile. "It has."

"Excellent. I suppose you're weary from your journey? It's not a mikvah, but we do have baths. Roman baths. I can't say what they've done in there. And even if I knew it wouldn't be appropriate for a woman to say. Would you like to ready yourself for tomorrow?"

"Tomorrow?" asked Elijah.

Chuldah's smile widened. "The feast."

"Of course. I'm weary, forgive me."

Chuldah laughed. "You'll find no forgiveness here." Meant to be a joke, neither man found humor in her words. "Now go. Cleanse yourselves and I'll see about getting you something to eat. Tomorrow will be a trying day for you."

The baths were as impressive as everything else they'd seen there. Matthew and Elijah sat submerged to their shoulders, weary of every foreign sound and growing increasingly nervous. Elijah's clothes were just beyond the steps, within reach. He left the hilt of the sword facing him with his clothes heaped over so he could grab it if needed.

The clamor of little bells drew their attention. They looked up to see a Pharisee. After a condescending perusal of the bathers, he walked into the water with his chin raised. He rinsed in their prescribed methods, looking around tentatively and humming supplications. The man came and left without a word to either man.

"They're a friendly lot."

"All smiles when the Tzedakah is light."

Matthew laughed. "You know what he said to them." He looked around, the other Mashiach being a dangerous topic here. "He called them sepulchers. Right in their noses. Clean on the outside, full of death and decay inside." Matthew chuckled. "You should have seen their faces. You'd have thought they smelled the very rot he spoke of."

"He can seem harsh at times."

Matthew shrugged. "The truth can feel tortuous to a man at comfort with his lies. We take offense at what we don't wish to accept."

"For a man that wears bells, it must be near impossible to accept you're dead inside."

"Sometimes he tells the truth to drive them away," said Matthew. "So they won't have any trouble with the choice." He looked over at Elijah. "That woman's lips."

Elijah nodded. "Quite a sight to meet at the door."

"What kind of thing could be blasphemy in a place like this?"

"Probably the things we were just talking about. The Shema."

A silence fell over them. "We shouldn't have come."

"A nest of serpents and vultures."

Elijah was looking straight ahead, working through these things in his mind, when another man stepped into view on the other side of the bath. His clothing fell behind him. Elijah sat thinking, staring without focusing until the man's legs drew his attention. Thin and brittle, knobbed knee caps and sallow skin. Elijah followed them up and then sat upright abruptly, disturbing the water. Standing across the bath, naked as Adam before he ate the fruit, was Samuel.

The shriveled man waded into the water on shaky reeds for legs. Then sat on the opposite steps and moved his hands around over the surface.

"Hello Elijah. I'm glad you came."

"Samuel…" Elijah fought to control his voice. "You walk."

Samuel smiled and brought his eyes up, settling in and leaning back on the steps. He had a large scab on his forehead. "I can. And Salome will attest with pleasure, these legs are not the only things that stand on their own."

CHAPTER 59

SIMEON

They were wrong about the village being empty. Simeon had walked down the hillside, past the villa to where it descended again, checking over his shoulder every few steps for swine. The rain had stopped and the sun shone faintly through a cover of clouds. There were more pigs moving about.

Farther down from the villa he followed an offshoot from the path. His intention was to go around the wall to see if there was a way to enter from the other side without being noticed. He found a well, and a collapsed shelter that looked as though it may have been used by merchants. The structure and its tarp were stomped on and tattered, half standing at a slant while rainwater rolled off in a slow stream and pooled in the middle of the material. He heard a noise and looked up. Someone was lugging water down the hill in a wet cloak. Simeon followed.

Labyrinths of cleft prints cratered the mud. Their puddles shimmered. The figure brought the pail to a nest of houses near the bottom where the hill leveled out.

Simeon looked back up at the villa. Its position provided an excellent vantage of the village below and the path leading in. The houses were nestled in a small valley. Any attack from the path–by far the easiest point of access–was hopeless. There were inclines beside the road leading up, clusters of trees, not to mention the dark alleys between houses. Favorable spots for an ambush. Well beyond the villa were mountains, and the flat terrain stretched far enough to make an advancing party conspicuous from multiple directions.

The figure hunched over in the cloak, kicking through clumps of mud, stopping at the last house hugging the vessel without spilling water. Two knocks, then a moment's pause, followed with three more knocks. It took several moments, but the door opened quickly and the figure disappeared inside.

Simeon approached the door. Something was smeared over the threshold. He thought of Moses and the children of Egypt as he repeated the knock's pattern. No one answered.

He did it again. Simeon waited, then crept around the side of the house. Its bricks were laid poorly, packed together most likely with mud and excrement, as were so many other peasant homes. The animal scent was strong, as well as the stench wafting from what he figured was either the wall, holding it together, or worse, seeping out from the inside. Before he circled the house something crunched behind him. As he turned he was shoved into the wall. His cheek touched cold brick and Simeon, repulsed by its feel and smell, went to shake free but froze when he heard the voice.

"Move and I'll make you a eunuch."

It was a woman. Simeon stopped struggling, but pulled his face back from the wall.

"What do you want?" A small knife was in her hand. Its point pressed low on his back.

"I saw you by the well. I'm not here to hurt you. I need to get into the villa."

"You'd be better off gutted here than going anywhere near that place."

"I need to find a way in." She stopped pressing her elbow into his back. Simeon turned. Her hair was knotted, wild with burs and small pieces of twigs where she'd been able to keep it dry. Streaks of dirt smeared her cheeks. She carried with her a sour pungency, as though her time had come and she hadn't bathed.

Her eyes moved left and right rapidly, searching Simeon's face. "You can't go there. No one comes back. And if they do they're not the same."

"I know… And I must."

The woman sighed and lowered the knife. She ran her hands over her face and moaned. "Come inside you old fool."

Inside was filthy. The woman had a son as dirty as her. One foot was missing and his stump was wrapped in filthy rags that had turned black and hardened. The boy scurried back when he saw Simeon. His mother held him and spoke softly. Simeon looked around at their squalor. Bile burned the back of his throat. He felt ashamed when he thought over their predicament.

"We weren't always here. We lived up the hill, past where the market used to be."

"How long have you lived like this?"

"Since the preacher came."

"The preacher?" The boy's shoulders shook. His mother noticed and waved the question off.

"Is there anyone else here?"

She shook her head. "We were told there was work in the fields and vineyards. Sewing and mending for the ladies." She shook and her voice quavered. "Only days ago this place was filled with people."

"It's just you two now?"

The woman sighed. "My husband went to work in the vineyard. He came back three days later." Her eyes were low. "It wasn't him."

"I've seen them."

"Then why are you here?"

Simeon looked at her a moment, thought over her words, and nodded solemnly. The woman's face contorted in anger. Simeon shrugged and raised his hands. "This can't go on. I'm here to–"

"What can you do?" Her hands were on her hips. Her lips curled, brow furled.

Simeon ached for the woman. For the whole desolate place. "If there's still a God in Israel, perhaps He'll show his face."

"God has abandoned this place."

"I need to get in."

"Don't go near that place. Look what happened to my boy." Her voice quavered, she pointed at the severed limb.

"There's a hole in the wall." The boy's voice was weak, raspy. His eyes didn't move from what they were fixed on. "You might be able to squeeze through."

The mother turned to her son with her mouth open. "You speak!" The boy raised his eyes to meet her's. He shrugged.

"You haven't spoken a word in weeks, now you open your mouth to send this stranger to his death."

"What's there to talk about?" Simeon recognized the boy's struggle to admit his helplessness. His heart broke for him. The mother's face softened and she brought her hands to his face. He shook her off.

The boy turned to Simeon. "Follow the wall that goes along the right side of the house until you see a tree. The hole's blocked by its trunk. It leans against the wall. Pass the tree and look back and you'll see it. The hole should be big enough for you to crawl through… I think."

"And then?"

"There's space between the house and the wall. It was a garden before they came. Follow that to the back. Behind the villa there's other buildings. Hide in the temple if you can. You can see most of the villa from there."

Simeon nodded and stood. "Thank you."

"Be careful. The pigs walk there. One bit my ankle and held on until I hit it with a rock. I climbed a tree. They stayed under it all night, licking up the blood that dripped. Looking up." His eyes went to the soiled cloth around his shin.

"I had to remove it." said his mother. Her eyes were somewhere else, haunted by memories.

The boy shrugged. "I wanted to find him. He's still there."

"Your father?" asked Simeon.

The boy nodded. "It's not him. Not anymore."

"If I make it out of this I'll come for you. I'll take you both from here." The Mother and son didn't react. He understood. "You're a brave boy. Thank you."

"God be with you," said the woman. "God be with you."

"Let's hope."

Simeon left thinking the boy looked uncomfortable with his mother's words.

CHAPTER 60

THE BATHS

Elijah watched Samuel cup water and tilt his hand to pour it back. He repeated the movement until its repetition was maddening: palm rising, a corresponding swish as if fish agitated the surface, and the stream and trickle of the cycle's completion. Samuel displayed a child's immunity to monotony. Years of inactivity begets patience, Elijah reasoned.

Samuel's presence brought questions. Elijah's astonishment only grew with their implications. And although Samuel's response was crude, even if merited, he didn't appear bothered. He was nothing more than bones wrapped tight in parchment. Muscles gone, withered from years on his back. Elijah wondered how legs that frail, and a walk that wobbled like a wood tower in the wind, could actually support standing. "Healed" seemed a cruel description for the man's state. But he was walking. And what did that mean for the man these people called Mashiach? Could there really be two? Could the man behind the terrors on the roads and the pigs and the woman with her lips sewn closed be Jesus's equal? Or was he the anointed for whom God abandoned?

Elijah looked at Samuel and thought of the crippled girl he'd seen healed by the Nazarene. She got up and danced after. And when she rose, her legs were whole. Even the fat in her face had been restored. She appeared a healthy child with none of the effects of her prior infirmity.

Not like this.

"You look surprised to see me."

"I am."

"Why?" He gestured, hand up from scooping water. "Hannah told you she was going to see the Mashiach, did she not? Were you not healed?"

Samuel was never a consideration while he'd been with Salome. In his state, the man's feelings simply hadn't occurred to Elijah. He was a solid, soulless thing. A face with no life behind it, like one of the statues around the bath. Elijah sat upright, leaning forward slightly. "It's just... surprising to see you walking... talking. It's been so long."

Samuel nodded. "But didn't you tell Hannah?" Samuel's brows were high. His mouth curved slightly. "Why would it be any different with me?"

"I'm not sure I could get used to something like this. And if I ever did, it would cease to be miraculous."

Samuel nodded and smiled. Elijah didn't trust it. "I can't wait to see Salome's face." He rubbed his hands together.

"Samuel, I..."

But Samuel held up a hand. "Your problem is you still blush. What's done is done."

Elijah remembered something his grandmother told him, gleaned from some forgotten passage in the Tanakh. *Blush is the color of virtue.*

"Truly. What could I have done for her? A woman like that has needs few men could meet, even while healthy. You would know." Samuel's arms stretched out beside him on the steps. "Can you imagine? Watching that woman every day while your body sinks into the earth. Not being able to touch her. To feel her." He shook his head and let out a huff of air. "The only movement I could make was to roll my tongue. Left, never right. And swallow. I could make a moaning sound, but the vibrations in my throat made it itch until I couldn't breathe. The actual sound killed the little manhood I had left." Samuel laughed. "Don't look so forlorn. I hated the Romans. Myself. God. You, of course. Though much later." He laughed again, shaking his head slightly. "I hated you. Especially with my mother in my ear." He looked down, smiling. "But that's no longer a concern. Imagine how it must have been for her." He took a long hard look at Elijah. "Longing for the touch of a *real* man. Having to resort to a shepherd."

Elijah stared at the water. In his heart he wondered whether Salome had ever felt as strongly for him as he did. Whether he was just something to bide time with. His fantasies of happiness had died. He felt foolish being there. But the rising hope she'd look back at him fondly and feel an ache for his skin against hers, or think of some private joke or moment and sigh into her old age somehow comforted him. He'd take what he could from her as he would alms. Salome would remain an altar in his heart to defend fiercely. And would burn up all else striving for room there.

Elijah looked up, Samuel was studying him. He didn't seem anything like the man he'd been. The strength, assertiveness, willingness to fight for the principles he held dear, the absence of all this made a conspicuous hole in the personality before him. This man seemed smug. Glib about his wife's affair. Plotting.

But hadn't Elijah changed when he secluded himself from the world? And again when he first spoke with Salome? All the things he'd seen recently had certainly changed him. Elijah's life seemed a torn sail, thrashing over rising billows any way the wind carried.

"Aren't you happy for me?" Samuel flicked the water. "I can get on to living my life now."

"I don't want to see any man suffer."

"Ahhhh," said Samuel. "Yet your sorrow is unmistakable. I've gained and you've lost. You've lost so much, Elijah."

Elijah stayed quiet. He ignored the pressure in his cheeks. The bile rising in his throat. He answered once he composed himself.

"I've never had much to lose."

"Who's tending your flock while you're here?"

Elijah shook his head.

Samuel's eyes rose. "How will you eat when you return?"

"We live by faith," said Matthew. "Our food is not the food of this earth."

Samuel's shoulders rose with his laughter. "But what it comes to smells just as foul in the end."

It took Matthew a moment to understand. "You insult my religion?"

"Your religion makes fruitful men Eunuchs."

"We give in this world to gain in the next."

Elijah warned Matthew to stop, placing a hand on his arm.

Samuel smiled. "He repeats his master like one of Sheba's parrots."

Matthew's face twitched. A groove formed above his brow, a lone crack in his frail patience.

"Will you be eating real food tomorrow?" continued Samuel. "Or do you plan on gathering manna from the fields in the morning?"

"You belittle my faith. Yet you live as a cult here. And your Mashiach's work is incomplete?"

"All things are incomplete."

"Matthew," said Elijah, but his friend raised a dismissive hand.

"He couldn't restore your body to what it was."

"A man with the breasts of a nursing mother criticizes an invalid who walks!" Samuel broke into taunting cackles that echoed and amplified through the baths.

"I've seen the real Mashiach. I've seen a man whose hand was crushed by a millstone. It hung limp at his side with nothing but a thumb remaining." Matthew held a hand open. "Every finger was restored. But you. You're something children step on in the woods."

"Matthew," said Elijah, with irritation bleeding into his tone.

"You'll see signs and wonders," said Samuel. "You'll fall on your knees and beg to be a son of Israel."

"I know whose son I am. And I know whose son you are."

Samuel's beard was against his chest. He stared down over his nose, eyes in a narrow squint, malice shaping every bone and wrinkle of his face. "Will your father hear your cries, drunkard?"

"The LORD watches over those who fear him."

"You'll watch your mouth or wind up like the woman at the door."

"Tell me your name."

Samuel's head snapped up. A snarled rictus of hatred. "The tricks you used on the road will get you nothing here."

"Shut up, Matthew," said Elijah. He did. For a while there was no sound but Matthew's grunts and discontented breaths. The sounds of displaced water as he shifted.

Samuel seethed. "You play with things you shouldn't."

A figure moved behind Matthew and Elijah. He made no sound, but stood over their clothes and prodded the cloaks like a cat pressing its paw into something questionable to stand on. Samuel never moved his eyes from Matthew. Never blinked.

Matthew stared back at him. "I'm not afraid of you."

Finally, Elijah raised his head, letting the air from his body as he slouched. "Will Salome be at the feast tomorrow?"

Samuel smiled wide, which pulled the skin back on his face. Excitement filled his eyes now. "You really are a fool."

"You said you couldn't wait until she saw me."

"You know the punishment your God prescribed for adultery?"

"Whatever punishment I deserve will come."

"Did you bring stones to pass out to the guests?" Samuel cocked his head. He stayed that way, until some cruel epiphany brought a smile. "That's what you want." The terrible laugh returned. "To make a myth of yourself."

"I want to make sure she's safe."

"You want to die for an ideal. To be remembered valiantly. It's what mortals do when they can't obtain their desires."

The figure behind Matthew and Elijah was raising one of the cloaks.

"Mortals?" asked Matthew.

Samuel's eyes closed and he breathed deeply. "It's the same reason my back was covered in sores and my wife was gallivanting with sheep herders and farmers." His eyes opened and he turned slightly to Elijah.

Elijah shifted.

"You think you were the only one? Eight years. A woman like that needs it. Her legs can't stay closed any longer than your fat friend's mouth."

"Don't speak of her like that."

"You'd tell me how to speak of my wife? Your view of the world is skewed. You see shapes behind the fog, never things as they truly are. The chastity of women is a foolish notion. She'll be a proud concubine of the true Mashiach."

"Blasphemy," said Matthew.

"What you call blasphemy we'll make doctrine. The only sin is restraint."

"Tell us your name, demon." Matthew shook with what Elijah hoped was rage.

Elijah tried next, bravado in his voice. "Tell me your name, I command you in the na–"

Elijah screamed when he noticed his hand.

Pointing at Samuel, the change came instantaneously. The white stones were abruptly cast in scarlet tints and shadows. Elijah leapt back and splashed some of the red froth the water had become on Matthew's beard. Matthew wiped his face, dumbfounded with Elijah's reaction. *He doesn't notice.*

Elijah turned his hand before his face. Crimson droplets fell from his stained hand. He brought his fingers to his nose. "Blood."

"Elijah, what are you talking about?"

"He who has eyes to see," muttered Samuel.

The water, now dark and sloshing vermillion, gave the marble and limestone a ruby's resplendence. Everywhere the water splashed was now stained with gore. Rivulets and droplets splattered the faces of the statues along the baths, the bloody visages of these idols stared on with ichor prints stamping their heads from the hands of patrons climbing from the water. Elijah's movement disturbed the water, it lapped at the edges of the bath and brought a tiny red tide washing over. A heavy metallic scent filled the air. Elijah looked at his hands, red and stained skin.

When he looked up, Samuel was laughing, rubbing his hands as if molding a ball of clay and rocking. He shouted, "signs and wonders! Signs and wonders!" As quickly as it came, the water was normal again.

Metal sang and clanged from the stones behind them. Elijah spun, and froze at the sight before him.

On the edge of the bath, holding Elijah's cloak, stood the apotheosis of every child in Israel's nightmares. The demoniac stared through one sepulchral white eye, his other socket a dark void lacking form or substance, smirking down at the sword with a hilarious malignancy only he was privy to. His head tilted, daring Elijah with his teeth exposed through the torn flesh on the side of his face. Unhealed holes passed through each wrist, as if a plug of flesh was punched out. Impossibly propped on an ankle bent to the side, he motioned for Elijah with his chin.

Elijah lunged. But the bent foot struck out, connecting with Elijah's chin and sending him sprawling into the water with a heavy splash. Before Matthew could move, he'd picked up the sword and shook it free from the tunic. "Move and a slab of your belly goes to the pigs tonight."

Matthew pulled Elijah's limp body from the water while the mutilated figure looked on, and Samuel's laughter echoed from the stones.

CHAPTER 61

VISIONS OF THE FALLEN

Simeon watched the wall from behind a house near the well. He crept toward the villa, cautious of movement, watching for the pigs and listening for signs of their presence. When he did move, he tried to use the shadows and trees to his advantage. He knew nothing about sneaking. The faithful Pharisee, and there are so few, has no need of subterfuge. He thought over what he would do if he crawled through the hole and met the snout of some snarling unclean beast.

You would die. Silent cackles shook his belly. The firmament would peel away to darkness soon. Shadows stretched farther as night approached. The way the black shape of trees fell over the path reminded him of teeth.

He moved through pools of shade, flinching at the twigs he crushed in the weeds and grass. Moving between the houses carefully, sniffing the air for signs of pigs. Simeon crossed the path and climbed an incline using his hands to level himself. He lost his footing and grabbed a patch of weeds. It tore free and he slipped into the sopping grass, soaking his beard and cloak and wetting the garments beneath. The old man grunted and cursed, slapping a puddle and splashing his face again. Then he exhaled and rose, doing his best to scurry uphill again toward the villa. His legs and side already burned from the effort.

Simeon reached the top of the incline panting. He waited, crouched, then crossed the grass toward the wall. He followed the wall until he saw the tree. A juniper. The trunk twisted up and over the wall at an angle a man would make squeezing out of a hole. Some of the branches extended over the wall. Once he'd passed the tree he saw it. Just like the boy said.

Simeon stared at the missing portion of the wall. *What could punch a hole through limestone?* This was the entrance to another world. A living man crawling willingly to Sheol. Simeon wanted to laugh but couldn't muster the strength.

He listened. His heart rattled in his ribs and brought jolts of pain. Simeon said a silent prayer, then lowered himself to crawl. Tired old bones cracked their complaints. There was a puddle beneath the hole. Cold water met his knees and thighs. Fitting through wasn't difficult, there was plenty space. Even for him. Had the boy really thought he wouldn't fit? He smiled to himself and made a silent resolution to move about more and eat less if he made it from this place alive. Once he was on the other side and he'd scanned about he stood. The wall of the villa wasn't far from the wall he'd passed through, and in the clearing, only as wide as a small shanty where he stood, but wider ahead, it led through the shambles of what was once a garden. The pigs had surely been through here. Crumbled statuettes, upturned and overripe things, vegetation sparse and barren and as drooping as the wisps of hair falling from his bald head, all attested to his suspicions.

It was noticeably colder here, with a new depth of darkness on account of the proximity of the walls. He crouched and lurched along. To Simeon, every dark curve and shape in that garden was a pig. Every sliver of light the gleam of an eye.

Simeon recited the Psalms that kept him strong. He attributed their remembrance to his sanity now. His meditations in that room had kept his mind from crumbling completely. The eyes of those dead villagers had watched morning and night. He was left with their glare in the darkness, the transfigurations of horrid shapes in the shadows, intensified by the flickers of movement from the hungry birds. They saw through his weaknesses, brought every vestige of cowardice and failure up, reeling to the surface like a bucket creaking to the light from a dark well. He found solace in the fact (with hysterical laughter at the irony), that his God's eyes never closed. But when he'd laid to sleep since, when his mind wandered, and over the previous days if he caught Matthew or Elijah's eye, the others came to mind. They haunted his dreams. Watching. Knowing. Blinking in horrible unison.

The wrecked Eden before him provided fleeting comfort. He remembered what was written, *Fret not yourself over evil doers... they will wither like the green herb.* The ravaged garden served as the vision of what his enemies would become. Whether he'd be alive to see such things providence would decide. *Look to the LORD and his strength. But now the wicked prosper... How long, LORD?*

Something stirred ahead.

Adonai is with me. Sweat trickled down his back and another stab of pain flared in his chest. He ignored it, grimacing. His body, his life, his health–no longer mattered.

Most of what lay ahead was hidden. The shadows seemed to undulate, and he couldn't tell whether it was only a breeze shaking some of the branches and leaves filling the space between the villa and wall, or if something was really there. He picked up a branch he'd nearly tripped over. It was about as thick as his wrists. Simeon walked on, wrenching the limb in his hands.

There was a rustle in the dead fronds just ahead. Simeon swung the branch. He grunted, bringing it down, bludgeoning the perceived threat, pounding the brush in sweeping arcs to ensure nothing would escape.

Simeon's breaths were heavy. His hands were clenched and it was difficult to open and close his fingers around the branch. *Fine way to summon the swine, you old fool.*

He crept along the side of the villa. Passed under a high window and heard voices. The soft notes of a lyre rising up like a prayer. A discordant note followed, Simeon heard strings break and a woman scream. Laughter.

When he reached the corner he stopped and leaned against the stones. He closed his eyes and breathed, praying and thinking about the weak fools God used through the ages. Simeon gathered courage from those stories, held the branch to his chest, and poked his head around the corner.

There was a large sheet and tables set in a clearing. People loping about, servants bringing things across and driving stakes into the ground. If Simeon had to guess they were half a furlong away. He noticed a large box against the rear wall of the villa. He turned to look behind him where he'd come, then looked again, trying to get a better view. He recognized what it was and took cover again.

Simeon clenched his jaw. His cheeks were hot, temples pounding the same cries for help his heart made. There could be no mistake. The points of horns extending from the corners, carvings he couldn't decipher in the shadows. They'd built an altar. He shuddered thinking what their sacrifices would be. And to whom they'd be made.

With his back to the side of the villa, Simeon could look left and see a stone structure in the distance. What the boy had mentioned. In the moonlight its surface shined white like the underbelly of a great fish. Shadows flickered over the stones from distant torches. He couldn't move toward the clearing. That building really was his best option, just as the boy had said. He counted slowly, breathed full and deep, then moved toward it.

Don't run. Walk as a normal man. Casual. Once he'd passed the sheets and workers he saw the fields behind the stone building. Beyond, the black mountains jutted from the edge of the world, traced in the dark blues of a day that had already fled from this place.

He walked past the sheet they'd set in the clearing. Past the shapes of poles and the outlines of tables. When he cleared the sheet he stopped. There was another building to the left, its structure considerably smaller than the other. Beside the door lay the largest pig he'd ever seen. Its face was turned to him.

Simeon froze. Conscious of his heart now, the discomfort accompanying his quickened pulse. Cold terror climbed his back, he focused on remaining calm, breathing, but his leg was shaking. His sandal tapped in rhythm with his bouncing leg. His pulse and the rub of leather were the only sounds in the world at that moment. The pig stared at Simeon with dead black eyes.

Eyes.

Simeon watched the pig's head tilt, as though the animal had noticed something strange in him. It moved, shifting its weight, the belly jiggling as it slumped in the grass. The flesh was pale. He watched as slits appeared. Like the jots and tittles of writing. Simeon moved closer, terrified and unable to turn from the spectacle before him.

The slits opened.

Black and glossed, rheumy, every one. They were eyes. Lined in rows across its enormous gut, peering from the ribs, glaring along thigh and neck. Even from the center of its head. Open, staring. Accusatory. And although they were black and shined, he could make out the faint traces of the grey irises. Simeon staggered back, dropping his branch and nearly falling. His legs trembled more violently, and a shudder passed through his viscera, disturbing his bowels and clenching his testicles.

The eyes shimmered, became slits again, opened. Simeon whimpered.

He brought his palms to his eyes, wiping vigorously. When he brought his hands down, the pig's skin was smooth and pale again. Its head slightly raised. It yawned and laid its chin over its crossed front hooves.

Simeon stood bewildered. Trembling. He eventually found the resolve to walk again, but kept his eyes on the other building. With a silent prayer of gratitude, not daring to look back, he ventured on.

The building was a steep gabled Roman temple. Columns lined the front of the porch and the statue of an armor-clad idol lay in several pieces near the steps. Simeon thought of how strange it was for the boy to direct him there. The doors were opened slightly, light from inside splashed the sides of a column and spilled over the steps. He climbed to the porch and listened.

Voices. Chants in strange dialects. Not Aramaic, certainly not koine. Simeon recognized an archaic quality, like the forgotten words that fill the old scrolls in the dusty jars of Jerusalem's archives. But there was something distinct about the voices. Something strange in their resonance. They filled the empty space, both of the temple and his mind. Floating words dispossessed of bodies, spoken to the substrate of conscious thought.

The brass door was surprisingly cold. His breath left in plumes, puffing in sporadic little clouds as he made his way through the vestibule. He approached a large curtain. Simeon moved it aside slowly, and stopped when he caught something looking back at him.

Multitudes of things.

The dread that sight provoked broke something in him. All the angst, terror, every foul sight and frustration he'd experienced over the many weeks since he'd seen Saul, all of it tried to rush to his lips at once. The need to scream welled up, but muted by the horror before him, all that came to his lips was a gurgled sob.

Eyes.

A burning aura emanated from each. Bathed in prismatic color, they shone brightly, set in the glow of metal heated in a furnace, all through the thing's body. A burnt smell foreign to his nose inflamed his nostrils. Rows of eyes stared into him, some looked at other things, darting left and right. They were set in burning feathers that had charred black in some places, sending flakes of ash floating around the room with their movement. The pinions of its great wings, razor sharp and burning too, were likewise covered with eyes. It stood on long legs ending in hooves, three times the height of a man, domineering and cloying with sulfur. Sapphire and beryl, undulating iridescences, the likes of which he'd never seen, illuminated the room in bright sequences of color. But he was fixed on the intelligence in the eyes, as they flicked about, some locking onto him. Each was flecked with spots like burning brass, and as he looked up to see its head–no, heads, faces–fracturing mentally all the more, he recognized what the creature before him was.

The four wings opened, they flexed and it stood taller. The eyes changed colors. The faces blurred and contorted and the smelt iron metal gleamed as smoke filled the room and wafted out, stinging his eyes. The ground shook. The heads, one of a pig, another of a goat, a snarling and ugly man–

No no no no no…

Simeon fell hard on his tail bone. He ignored the pain, sliding back on his hands all the way through the vestibule. Down the steps, tumbling into the grass. He shook his head and planted an arm to rise, gasping for breath, but fell again. Simeon no longer cared about who or what saw him. He was ruined. He crawled, digging his nails in the earth and trying to scream through burning tears and finding no strength to do so.

He didn't think there could ever be a worse sight than the corpses in that house. But this. A creature from the very throne room of God. Perverse and malformed. Eyes that had seen his maker. Wings that covered its feet in the LORD's presence. Now burned and smoldered, corrupted by whatever punishment had been justly meted upon it. How could men, these wayward sinners, stand against such a thing? Dread curdled in his throat. He saw the eyes everywhere. Wrapping the pillars of the temple, gleaming in the distant mountains, all focused, all possessing a deeper knowledge of him than he'd ever possess of himself. All drawing him into something.

Simeon stood to run. As he did, something crashed behind him to his right. Several pigs tore from the other building and were now squealing behind him, sprinting and pumping their hooves as they neared. They caught up quickly and circled him, snapping their jaws and digging into the ground, letting out grunts.

Bazumel had walked onto the porch to watch. The part of him that now lay dormant, the conscience that once belonged to the Pharisee that despised and envied this panicked Pharisee writhing on the ground, was quite pleased.

"You have a dangerous curiosity, Pharisee. Did you like what you saw?"

"You're…you're…" his lips moved like a rodent nibbling at crumbs. " an Abomination."

"Did not God make the angels, Simeon?"

Bazumel watched him. The foulness that had assumed the names of a thousand forgotten deities, lost to incantations and time, descended the stairs. His robe trailed over the marble steps behind him. "Allow me to show you." Bazumel stretched his hand to Simeon's forehead. The old man's eyes were wide. He trembled and moved his lips as Bazumel showed him great and terrible things.

CHAPTER 62

ELIJAH

Elijah woke disoriented. Streaks and blurs of color and pain deep in his head. Sparks danced in the corners of his vision.

"Do it. Are you so weak you let her choose?" A low and sonorous voice he didn't recognize. A voice for stories.

His head was propped at an uncomfortable angle. On something soft.

A face loomed over him. He blinked.

Blinked.

Slept again.

"Do it." With laughter now.

Elijah blinked. The distortion waned and he stared up until he saw her. Her head wasn't covered. He was on her lap, bent at the neck. Trembling fingers stroked his head. Elijah laid still, listening to the rhythm of her breathing, the hitches, her broken efforts to inhale. Her body jerked with a hundred little convulsions.

No. No no no. Under her breath. He understood when he watched her mouth.

Something cold touched Elijah's temple. A hard point scraped near the corner of his eye.

He tried to speak but the pain in his head intensified.

Elijah reached for her arm. Found her wrist. Whatever she held fell with a soft thud and slight clamor.

He moved to look. Her jaw shifted, head shaking no while her body swayed like a palm leaning slowly with the wind. Her eyes looked off in all directions, never focusing on any one thing longer than a moment.

Elijah felt along the ground and found what she'd dropped. It stuck to his fingers as he rolled it in his hand. He didn't contend with his fading confusion long, a look of disdain curled his lips upon recognition. A nail nearly the length of his hand. Dried blood caked up under the flat part one strikes. Elijah sat up and slid back from her. He sat up from there and saw her entire profile. Jutting from behind her kneeling frame, the heavy end of a hammer angled up so its handle perched in the pocket of her knee. Her eyes moved from the hammer, once she saw his reaction after seeing it, to him. Beset with confusion. Terror.

Salome glanced at the hammer. Elijah. The nail between them.

"What are you doing?"

"I...I..." She came forward, hands extended pleading her harmlessness. Elijah flinched. The handle of the mallet knocked against the stone.

With her closer, the room felt smaller. Elijah finally noticed his surroundings. Slick with mold and mildew, rank with generations of sweat and something acrid that had soured the air just as long. They were in some sort of dungeon. Its door was a series of flat iron bars crossing in square patterns. Against the opposite wall, beneath a high window striped with bars, lay the carcass of a small pig with its legs curled from its body. Flies hummed hungry ballads of death.

"You were going to drive that into my head?"

Salome looked from the hammer to the nail in Elijah's hand, then his face.

"I came for you."

She trembled. Soon her cheeks shimmered with tears.

"How long have you been here?"

"You shouldn't have come."

"I should have come sooner."

Elijah went to her and put his arms around her. Her arms were stiff to her sides and she shivered with little sobs.

He laid Salome's head on his lap now.

She was at the cusp of becoming like Samuel. Like the girl treading the Jordan. Elijah held her. At last. Bitterly. Wallowing in frustration over every broken dream, the rote assurance offered by holy men his whole life, the numb acceptance of misfortune he'd grown accustomed to; holding her now, like this, only bolstered his gripe against Heaven.

"It is his fault, you know. All of it."

Elijah's spine went rigid. He'd forgotten the voice.

Clad in the garments of the High Priest (which Elijah had never seen, like most Israelites), stood who could only be their Mashiach. Adorned with replicates of the divining stones Elijah had long forgotten the name of, the breastplate laid over a scarlet garment with elaborate embroidery, with a blue tunic beneath all. As the Tanakh described. Elijah could recognize all this even in the dim light of torches. He'd made a parody of the highest glory Levites could attain. For if rumors bear truth of any sort, this Pharisee was a Benjamite. And the way the shadows pooled in the beveled angles of his face suggested a grim potential for wickedness.

"I'm Saul Bar Azareel. Here they call me Mashiach." Saul appeared quite pleased with himself. He stood tall with his shoulders back, as if to give the viewer a grander display.

"I met the Mashiach. He's Judean. And doesn't dress like a priest."

"I hear he didn't approve of the woman you're holding."

"What did you do to her?"

Saul clicked his teeth. Finally, he shrugged. "She's been through a lot, your little hussy. Ran and played the whore while her poor husband festered on a mat in his own waste."

"You did this to punish us?"

"I'm not your judge. I can't punish anyone."

"You were telling her to kill me."

Saul smiled. "But she didn't. So I don't see the need for consternation."

Elijah was quiet for a while. "What do you want?"

"We appear to feel very similarly about our divine conspirator." He gestured above.

"You have no idea how I feel."

"How you feel isn't difficult to decipher. You're angry with your maker. Because he made you and placed you in a position to experience continuous sufferings and hardship. Your parents, the old woman with her spindle, and now, after finally dangling a sliver of happiness before you," he lowered his eyes to Salome, "*HE* snaps it up in his greedy jaws. Alas, the price for your joy is desolation."

"I'll have my reward later."

"Why would you assume the one who's heaped misery upon you from the womb," his voice rose and carried in the confines,"would only extend benevolence in the next life? Even now, *HE's* left you desolate. It's his pleasure to do so. For his glory."

"What do you want?"

"To offer you rest."

"You have a strange hospitality."

"You and your friends have a strange way of imposing yourselves. I thought I'd watch her play with you. Now that I've seen what's in your heart, I see we're not so different."

"We're very different."

"How so? You don't think I've suffered?" He stepped forward. Elijah saw fury in his eyes. "I've put my passions, my wants and needs, the purpose of my very existence forth on the altar so that your *God*," his eyebrows rose, as if all he sacrificed was incomprehensible, "the source of blessings, plagues, and pestilence, would be pleased?"

Elijah looked down at Salome. "Where are my friends?"

Saul smiled. He didn't answer.

Salome shifted and moaned. "What's wrong with her?"

Saul shrugged. "You ask the same questions. You're a species at war within yourselves."

"She couldn't do it."

"Your kind can't do anything with a sullied conscience."

Elijah stared, confused.

Saul sighed. "The consequences of Moses. A culture overwhelmed with guilt. Everything you do revolves around wrongdoing. Everyone in Israel is fixated on punishment. Your ineptitude leaves you begging for mercy from your invaders. Otherwise able bodied, intelligent men are subjected to sackcloth, sprinkling ash over their scalps. And for what? Acting in accordance with their true nature. Foolishness."

"Your ideal world is one where women drive stakes through the heads of men they love?"

"In my ideal world women do what's right in their own eyes."

"And how do you know what's right?"

"What a stupid question. How do you?"

"I know the commandments."

Saul laughed. "You can't even read the scrolls they're written on, Elijah."

"I know what they say."

Saul was smirking. "The commandments don't matter to you if

they're at odds with your desires. You broke those commandments to fulfill your needs. With this woman. How did you feel during those months in the hills? Rolling around like animals while the sheep watched?"

Elijah looked down at Salome.

"The commandments are always at odds with your desires. That's why the priests' goal is to change your desires to what aligns with the commandments. But once that happens, there's nothing left of the individual. Your mind has withered and you've snuffed out any real volition." Saul shook his head. "You're a fool. The best your life's ever been was in violation of the rules you're defending now. Some sorcerer tells you to leave her and you fall into deeper squalor than before."

Elijah was looking down. "What do you know?"

"I know more than you think, Elijah. More than your feeble mind can comprehend. Do you really think something that brings that much joy can be bad? Why would these feelings be a part of you? Who put them there? The one demanding your unquestioning loyalty would have you part from her. And what does he do for you?" He laughed. "He calls what's transpired between you sin. Why? Because your mother ate the fruit and allowed you all a silly thing like a conscience. Then a madman raised in luxury brought a rock down from a mountain. Says it's carved by a God's finger. You believe the lie. That you were given everything and fell. The truth is simpler. Obvious to even a child. You could have everything if you'd but reach for it.

"But, alas, Your God made no provision for your happiness." Saul laughed. "Think of who he blesses. Who he leaves without. Consider Job, his family and livelihood wiped out over a wager. His wife and children's lives were of no consequence. Tell me, Elijah, do you really believe no man was worthy of his life during the flood? Were the babies in Egypt wicked enough for the avenging angel?"

"We're corrupt from the womb."

"Your mind's polluted with Pharisaic filth. Who rules this land? The men who weave tedious laws into the fringes of their garments and worry about the steps you take on the sabbath, who heckle you over how to wash your ass? Or the ones who indulge in wine and orgies? War? Who does your God truly bless?"

Elijah stared down at Salome. Saul's words made more sense than he cared to make provision for. His open irreverence seemed dangerous. "What do you want?"

"I want you to open your eyes. I want you not to fear your desires. To really live. You can have the woman."

Elijah turned to him abruptly. His mission, the resolution fortified along the journey– undermined in a few words. What would life be like if he returned with her? No, they would go somewhere else, somewhere far. What *could* his life become. The prospect teased him. He tried to keep his feelings abated. A tremor bled into his reply, "she has a husband."

"Her husband is a man who understands desires. Yours. Salome's. His own. He's indulged since his arrival here." Saul had the smile a tax collector makes after settling debts. "You have yet to see the concubines the Romans brought."

"So you condone adultery?"

"I condone a man choosing his own way. Tell me Elijah, why is what's forbidden so enthralling?"

Elijah remembered their times together in the hills. During one of these encounters, they heard movement nearby and froze. Elijah had been on top of Salome, whispering indecencies and praising her in the quiet confidences lovers share. She had her legs around him, pulling him closer. Both were naked. Both froze at the sound. Elijah stared at the shaking brush. A bead of sweat fell from his nose onto Salome's exposed throat and she flinched. Leaves shook, crunches and scratched foliage quickened their hearts. Until they heard the bleating. Elijah rose and walked over. One of the sheep had his wool tangled in the bushes. After their laughter subsided, they returned to their task with vigor. The risk of exposure only pulled them deeper into their passions. And there were other examples he could draw from.

"Because we're sinners." Elijah said at last, dropping his eyes.

"You lie to your God and to me. Yes. You're sinners. But only because you refuse to decide right and wrong for yourselves." Saul turned his head down the hall and nodded. Elijah heard steps and shuffling. A guard came muttering silent apologies and fished a key from somewhere beneath his dirty cloak, bowing reverently, raising his head and lowering it again and again like some obsequious bird. Saul stood impervious to these gestures. The bars clicked open on screaming hinges. He stepped inside. Stood until Elijah set Salome's head down and rose. "Why is there a pig here?" Elijah motioned toward the carcass. "They're everywhere. Why?"

"Because of what they represent."

"Filth?"

"Moses declared pigs unclean because of diseases in the camp. Our people have despised them ever since. Some Pharisees go so far as to bathe if they even see one, lest its image tarnish their purity. But the pig is intelligent. And cleaner than the cow and goat. Perhaps even the sheep you keep. They're loyal creatures, capable guards, and their meat is good. But most of all, they symbolize what's been rejected. And that which was cast down I seek to liberate from bondage."

"It's dead."

"She was ill. It's given its life that she may live."

Elijah looked from Salome to the pig, then back at Saul. He had the expression of a man who'd left something valuable around thieves.

"Come, I'll show you."

Elijah left the cell warily, walking just behind Saul. The man changed the mood of every room he entered. Perhaps the greatest difference between the two men claiming to be the Mashiach was in relation to their followers. Both men commanded respect, and both were shown great reverence. But Saul's relationship to those he surrounded himself with depended on fear. The man Jesus's followers had been loyal out of love.

Elijah walked on, internalizing everything. Conscious of the woman with the stitched lips, the atrocities they'd seen along the road, Mahalel and Doris. *Pigs*. Saul's shadow spilled into it all. The bleak path there and this darkness merged, eclipsing everything. But then, the words came back, breaking the gloom like the first rays of light at dawn. *You can have the woman.*

They passed through halls and rooms and out a courtyard again. The women dyeing garments still labored silently, but when Saul approached they sat higher and lowered their eyes, "Saul Ha Mashiach." Inside the halls, servants backed against the walls and lowered their heads to let them pass, muttering the same. All expression and personality had been extinguished. Elijah remembered the Mashiach (the other Mashiach, who warned him of this place), telling a parable comparing faith to the glow emanating from a lantern. Whatever light these people once had seemed snuffed out. Their hopes were wisps of smoke now. Elijah held his tongue. Turned his mind back to Salome and her current condition. *You can have the woman.*

They passed through the portico. In the clearing there were tables, and the men and women sitting there, Romans and Israelites, Pharisees and businessmen, were eating, engaged in lively conversation. They passed through a vestibule, then a wide room with tables and people sitting silently with dead faces, eyes open yet inattentive. This opened to a room lit with standing lanterns and candelabras. Bronze and soft wood teased the light along edge and curve, and the apprehensive faces of the people waiting shone where sweat met wrinkle in the soft light. There was a throne on the far end of the room cut from grey stone. It stood on a small platform with steps on all sides. A rug stitched with scenes from the Tanakh ran in line with the seat beneath it.

The man and woman waiting were dressed well, garments sewn with detail, rare material dyed vibrant colors. Their clothing belied opulence. But their faces were haggard, which brought a dull ache to Elijah. Misfortunes visit every walk of life.

Before them were baskets. Incense, fruit, frankincense, silk robes, and a mat with piled tunics and rags. Everything else was arrayed neatly, set aside near the steps. Saul strutted past and sat back on the throne. He motioned for them to come, and for Elijah to stand off to the side. The woman greeted him, then bent down and brought up a small flask. She broke it open, and as the perfume inside filled the air she fell before him. She doused Saul's feet with the contents of the flask and rubbed her hair across his feet, wiping with fervor. Saul smiled at Elijah while she did this. Then hushed the woman once she started to pray, grabbing her hands and pulling her to her feet.

"What is it you want?" He leaned forward. The woman was high on her knees, tears glistening in the light the candles cast.

"My mother." She motioned toward what Elijah previously figured for a pile of tunics. The grieved daughter wept, so downcast with sorrow her wrinkled skin resembled the folds in the heaps of clothes. She sniffed loudly and whimpered to Saul, "she didn't make it. We came as soon as we could, but she only lasted a day. The third day... she started to smell. So my husband wrapped her in herbs and the normal spices for burial." When Saul put a hand on her shoulder she broke into violent sobs. Saul nodded to one of his servants and he scurried away. The woman and her husband (Elijah watched in awe, fascinated with the parallels he now saw between the healers) stood silent, staring at their clasped hands, taking note of art and peculiar furniture throughout the room, and occasionally looking up at Saul with timorous smiles. When the servant returned, a pig with brown spots trailed him. Elijah could smell the animal before he heard its snorts or hooves. Man and swine wheezed in tandem. Saul reassured the woman, who flinched when the pig nuzzled up beside her mother's ear. The pig's nose wiggled. Elijah cocked his head, thinking he heard words from somewhere. A moment later the pig fell over, twitched and laid still.

The pile moved.

Garments shifted. One end of the cloaks rose, layers of soiled rags and garments slid and flapped open. The woman and her husband rushed over to free her. Pulling the burial shroud, tearing strips of linen from the woman's face, shouting triumphantly at this miracle. Saul rolled his eyes as the woman praised God. The woman's mother sat up. As they tore more of the material from her face the smell invaded the room, a subtle punch amidst the pig and perfume. The effect was nauseating.

Saul watched, one leg down with the other heel on the seat, a thumb and forefinger stroking his beard. "Get her to the baths."

The old woman smiled through her remaining teeth as the man and woman held her arms and pulled the rest of the filthy linen from around her. The eyes were fixated on another world when they led her away.

Elijah thought of Lazarus. His surprise when the man said he'd been resurrected. He thought of what Simeon said about them entering the pigs. Of omens regarding serpents and vultures. But above all, the voice of Saul rang clear. *You can have the woman.*

CHAPTER 63

MATTHEW

The mutilated man plucked Elijah from the water as a father would a small child. Then he came for Matthew, nearly tearing the shoulder from his stout body as he raised him up. Matthew was by no means a tall man, and while he dangled, submerged to the ankles, suspended for an incomparably potent stretch of time with the mauled intruder's lone milky eye scouring the recesses of his soul, he understood the moment would be another humiliating ache he'd recall for as long or short as life endured. Matthew gripped his other wrist, kicked to find the edge for support, but slipped and slid and stubbed toes on the wet stone as his captor yanked him forward, irreverent to the shame burning in Matthew's cheeks as his manhood shamefully flopped about, and Samuel's laughter suffocated the trickle of water and noise from outside.

Despite their frail appearances, the scarred maniac and invalid possessed an astounding strength. Samuel brought Elijah over his shoulder with no trouble. Matthew soon discovered the scarred man was in command of not only Samuel (who Elijah mentioned was a landowner, the top of the rural hierarchy in Elijah's village), but the red haired Abijah as well.

The scarred man's insanity was obvious. As horrific inside as outward appearance suggested. The crossed scars on his neck looked like the feet of birds trying to push their way out from inside. Matthew wondered how far into his torso, and to what other scabbed topography they led. His mangled snarl opened with a string of tendon running vertically through his exposed cheek. It vibrated as though plucked from an instrument when he found new evils to delight in.

Matthew was told to dress under threat of the blade. Then led away by the man. Who prodded him along by the point of the sword, drawing blood, gifting Matthew his own scars and scabs. His fingers bruised Matthew's arm where he'd held him. His shoulder burned.

He brought Matthew to a room where several people ate. The scarred man approached the woman they'd met earlier, Chuldah, and asked whether she'd seen him. She said no, absently, without raising her eyes from her nails. He left Matthew under her care, with a quick snap to a Roman nearby, who sauntered over grinning. The mutilated man walked off, swinging Elijah's sword in circles at his side and singing a perverse version of a children's hymn.

Matthew stood before her, conscious of his constricting throat, the instability in his voice. Tremors coursed through his body and he prayed she wouldn't notice. "What do you want from me?"

She raised her eyes. "What makes you think you could offer me anything I'd want?" She smiled, then attended to her nails once again, as Matthew stood being prodded by the Roman.

Samuel came, and Chuldah and the invalid exchanged conspirator's smiles. She waved her hand in a motion fit for warding off a bug. His protests were useless. Matthew kicked his legs as Samuel, with his thin invalid frame, pulled Matthew's large body along the passageway. Matthew swung and clawed. Struck him in the nose and brought blood, grabbed at his groin. Samuel grabbed Matthew's wrist and squeezed. There was a pop as the two bones met, and a flare of pain shot through his fingers and up to his elbow. Matthew buckled at the knees. Then followed willingly, clutching his wrist.

They brought him to a room where he was stripped and beaten by two guards. They left him in the dark. He heard claws scratch the floor. Bristled hair pricked his foot as something scurried past, making him scream.

He stayed there in the dark. Every few hours someone came to the door with a torch. They spat into the room, and he'd hear it on the cold stones. They cursed him and his God, called him a drunkard and a coward. "Tomorrow you'll see your friend Joseph again," said one. He sat in horrified wonder at what seemed to be omniscience.

Matthew languished in the dark. Later, whether night or day he didn't know, the door opened and banged against the stones outside. Matthew tried to move along the wall, scraping his back. There were two people. One held a torch. The scarred man stepped forward with a cistern, smiling. The other, just a boy, held a torch and lit a candle on the wall. The boy wore a bag that rattled with the clang of metal where he walked. The scarred man brought the cistern over to Matthew. He flinched, covering his head with his hands, preparing himself to be bludgeoned with the thing. The scarred man dumped sour, fetid wine over Matthew. Then threw the cistern against the opposite wall and staggered, laughing. The crash was close and terrible in his confinement.

"We thought you'd be thirsty," said the boy. They were drunk. The boy walked over. He teased Matthew with the torch, bringing it slowly to his face until his beard and lashes were singed and his eyes watered profusely. The boy laughed. When he stood again, he bumped into the scarred man and fell on his ass. Something in the bag fell to the floor. The door slammed shut. Laughter faded down the hall with them as they left.

When he was sure they were gone, he found what dropped from the bag. It was a large nail. He tried to find a place in the door where he could work the lock, but the iron was far too thick. He threw the nail against the wall.

Matthew's resolve soon wavered. He tried to focus on all the good he'd seen in his travels. What he'd been able to accomplish through the gifts he was granted. He sat there, hugging his broken wrist between his knees. The sour smell and scurry of feet, as well as the light trodden insect movements in the dim light, eventually wore him down. The candle expired. He prayed for strength. For his wrist to be healed. Nothing. He moved along the wall where he sat and felt pooled liquid where the floor was uneven. When he brought his hand to his mouth, he tasted the sour wine.

Matthew wept.

Some time later, tears and faith spent, he knelt and lapped from the wine puddles like a parched dog.

There was laughter from the hall.

CHAPTER 64

ELIJAH AND SALOME

Elijah was brought to a room by one of Saul's followers and told to wait. He asked the man how long it would be. "Until you're useful." The man laughed and closed the door. Still laughing as something slid into place behind him and his footsteps left down the corridor.

There was a bed against the far wall that came to his knees, set on thin pillars. He sauntered over and sat, testing the thickness of the material on top and patting the cover. He'd never slept in a bed. He laid back and stared at the ceiling. Compared to his mat on the filthy floor where he laid as a child, or the rocks pressing up from under his cloak in the fields when he herded, it was soft and inviting. His weight sank into it.

Elijah thought of the old woman. His impression of her resurrection was mired with doubts and apprehension. When they tore the cloth from her body the skin was already discolored, and her smell, although partially masked by the burial spices wafting up when the cloth peeled away and the perfume her daughter doused Saul's feet with, had the subtle tang of sweet and wretched death. Death had become a familiar scent over the previous weeks. Except, in her case, she'd been moving.

Are there bad miracles?

He recounted the scene. The pig had flopped over dead. Then the woman rose. Simple. A life for a life. She didn't thank Saul, just followed the servants and her family to the baths with the precursors of a smile, as though she'd known some secret they didn't. Her family hugged her, pretending not to notice, turning their heads so she wouldn't see them twist their lips from the stench and recoil at the feel of cold flesh. They fell to Saul's feet in rapt worship. Sobbing, with faces Elijah thought looked unsettled between alarm and jubilance. Elijah wondered whether that scent could be removed with lye and water. He pictured them scrubbing her. Scrubbing until wrinkled flesh peeled to gristle and meat, wailing at their impotence as tendon and bone were exposed, helpless against the all encompassing odor the woman would carry with her forever. What defilements would a walking corpse add to the baths?

These people didn't care about being unclean.

Unclean. He hadn't thought about ceremonial washings or cleansing rites these last weeks. Washings, food, the law. He'd seldom bathed even. He handled corpses. When he thought about the Levitical mandates, the washing and breaking of pots, the stonings reserved for so many infractions, prohibitions against mixing fabrics, seafood, the natural ways of women that made them filthy–it all did seem foolish.

You're giving him space in your mind.

He focused on the reason he'd come. Foremost in his thoughts, Salome's face kept coming back. Wide eyed, cold dry skin and trembling lips. The far away stare so many seem to have in this place.

The hammer in her shaking hands.

He closed his eyes. What if she came while he slept? Sly crooked smile, one eye raised slightly on the same side, fixing her in one of those indecipherable expressions, where you never knew what she was thinking, holding the nail to his temple with a smirk and lowering the hammer with a single strike.

How long had they worked on her? He'd been here a day. One day, and the prospect of being with her drowned out every cry for precaution. The still small voice screaming this was wrong.

It's Moses's law.

How else could an Israelite think? The world around you, its strange people with the same urges and desires, similar needs for love, worship, justice; all were unclean. Their food, the way they make their garments, how they make babies–unclean. And if they didn't cut the skin at the end of a penis on a certain day, they were out. Unclean. Hadn't God tried to kill Moses before Zipporah intervened? She'd circumcised their son with a piece of flint before God struck him down, then touched his feet with the bloody foreskin.

That didn't seem very clean.

Elijah considered the things Saul told him. Could God be capricious?

King Saul, for example. This Saul was ordered by the prophet Samuel (Elijah laughed at the irony, laughed longer than reasonable for a man in his predicament), to slaughter every Amalekite. Man. Woman. Child. Even their beasts. But what did king Saul do? He spared the king. As well as some of the choice livestock. And why had he been ordered to commit this genocide? Because the Amalekites opposed Israel when they possessed the land. And that was centuries before King Saul or the prophet Samuel were even born. Sparing the king and animals was a grave offense to God. Samuel hacked the Amelekite monarch to pieces in front of Saul as an act of reverence. God turned his face from Saul. He went mad, lost his sons, and killed himself in battle to avoid capture by Philistines.

Then there was David. He was given the kingdom, the promise of the Mashiach was to come from his blood, but ultimately, he'd committed greater offenses than Saul. He had Bathsheba's husband murdered so he could marry her. David committed adultery and murder, and surely that's worse than sparing a king and some livestock, no? No. The Lord loved David. And the son he made with Bathsheba also became king of Israel. God did seem to love people by choice. He chose their calamities, supplied their blessings, sent deceitful spirits to confuse, unleashed the accuser on the righteous to prove his glory; when poor Job dared complain after everything he had was destroyed and his children were killed, God went into great detail about the wonders of his creation. And miraculously, that made everything better with Job.

He could hear him now. Although his mother, father, and sister, all perished, his grandmother suffered to the bitter end. Though he'd slept hungry with his stomach wrenched in pain while slowly descending into blindness. And his love was taken away at the threat of God turning his face against him like King Saul, he could see dark clouds descending, thunder and quake, and in a big booming voice: Thus says the LORD: *Did I not make the mountains? Did I not fix the stars to the firmament? Who can unbind Orien?*

Elijah laughed.

He wanted to say it aloud. Scream his renunciation, but the thought of such blasphemy, to state the matter outright and boldly, bothered him. When the temptations came, at least they could be blamed on powers outside his own volition. Deceitful spirits, perhaps sent by the maker himself to test him.

He sat up on the bed, inspecting things around the room. There was a parchment stretched and drying along the wall. He'd never seen a scroll before it was written on. Elijah traced his finger over the thin material. He found another laid across a flat board in the corner beside a stool. The scribe had written in even and straight rows, until a large blot of ink spilled and spread over the middle of the parchment. Pieces of the jar the ink had been in crunched beneath his sandals.

What a beautiful parable the scene made. The spot, his sin. Blotted and permanent, marring the story of his life. And he couldn't even read the writing. More laughter. Wasn't this exactly what Saul had reminded him? He'd been subjected to the futility of living for words he couldn't even read, following a story told to him by people whose actions never matched their admonishments. But again, like the parchment, marred by mistake or whatever negligence splotched the words, they still said *something*. But how could one ever make sense of the tangled story of life? He laid back on the bed and put an arm over his face.

I think I'm going mad.

After some time he slept. He dreamed of the creatures again. For the first time in weeks. Eyes covering wings, faces of oxen and men connected to one another. Brilliant and resplendent colors too bright to stare into. Then a choking dread and darkness.

He was shaken awake.

Elijah sat up, searching wildly. He was drenched in sweat and his heart pounded like the steps of an advancing army drawing near.

It was Salome. Cooing, stroking his face. She spoke sweetly. "Only a dream."

"Salome… You…"

"I'm fine."

"You tried to kill me."

"They thought you were one of *HIS*." She said "His" with the same virulent warning an adder gives before it strikes. "*HIS* scent is on you."

"Who?" But he knew the answer. "But what happened to–"

Her hand went to his lips. "I'm here." She slid next to him and pulled him close, draping a leg over him and pulling his shoulder so they were face to face. She ran her hand over his garment, found the opening, and searched his back and chest with warm hands. Slow circles, warm caresses igniting his skin. "I'm with you now." His heart brimmed. *You can have the woman.*

"And Samuel?"

"With the whores." Her words had a melody, as if setting her woes to music would relieve some of its bite. Her nails searched his skin. "Making up for lost time."

"Lost time?"

"What would you do if you'd been lying on a mat for a decade?"

"I'd want to be with my wife." He looked toward his feet, embarrassed, and added, "if she was you."

He'd seen her face from this angle countless times. They'd laid on his cloak in the hills while the sheep bleated. He'd taken an artist's profile in his mind, immortalizing every detail of the face before him now.

Was there something different?

"You're sweet." Her lips curved and her nose crinkled.

It wasn't an unsightly expression, he didn't think Salome capable, but it seemed foreign to the mannerisms he knew. He feared he'd forgotten something, as though the light he'd refused to turn his eyes from only existed now in the burnt colors of an after image. She'd changed somehow. Was it sadness? Had stress lengthened the lines in her face?

No. The curves and dark color of her skin were just as he remembered. The length of her lashes, the way a strand of hair slid free of her covering in the heat. The change consisted of something deeper. As if whatever breathed life to dust did so to her with foul breath. Some harbored burden rippled the surface from deep within her. He feared he was the source.

"What is it?" he asked.

She smiled. The way her eyes swept over him, taking in the panorama of his being, searching and scrubbing him thoroughly, spread warmth through him.

It's easy to feel the heart beating and misconstrue the feelings at work. The machinations of paranoia, what sober minds call intuition, Elijah ignored and attributed to the flustered excitements of love.

"I can't believe we're here now. That we can be here now. We're free."

"Free." They interlocked fingers and stared down their garments and skin of her exposed leg, which was over his and pulling him close.

"We don't have to hide any longer."

"What about your husband?"

She brought a hand to his cheek. "Why are you worried about

him? Let him play. I intend to do the same."

She brought her lips to his. Elijah shuddered. She brought her hand down, caressing and teasing. He hardened in her grasp. Then rolled onto her and slipped the covering from her head, breathed in the fragrance of her hair, searched along her body for all the things he'd lost.

She moaned as he entered her. Whispered mirth in his ear.

Elijah fell asleep shortly after they'd finished. He dreamed of the eyes once more, while the stranger in the bed beside him whispered in his ear. Her eyes were open, lifeless and dull.

CHAPTER 65

ANOTHER, LIKE MOSES

Once they cleared the crucified from the field, the bodies were pried free and the wood was set aside. With chisel and adze, the blood stained beams were whittled into idols. Though the detail and craftsmanship were undeniable, what they carved was abhorrent to religious minds. Each was shaped so wings wrapped toward the other side, and carved so the tips of the feathers curved into the air slightly. Every feather had the rakish lines and breaks of a real bird. Eyes ran all along the wings, through wrist and feather, with the irises and pupils etched in meticulous detail. Their collective gaze seemed to follow the viewer's eyes.

At the tops of these poles, they fashioned a man to look east, stern faced and smooth eyed. Facing north was a goat, and the tops of the poles were chiseled into segmented horns which curved over and back. Finally, the sun set on a snarling pig's face. Defilements of the prophet Ezekiel's vision.

There were twelve in all. One for each tribe in Israel.

Rather than the local custom of floor seating, enormous slabs of wood were brought forth, lined with high backed chairs with cushions. The tables were set with thin stone cups, sculpted with bizarre scenes from the Tanakh. On one the Levite's harlot was chopped into twelve pieces to be sent to the tribes. Others depicted Elisha's bear attacking the boys who called him a baldhead, Nebechednezzar's guard burning out the eyes of king Zedekiah, and naturally, the serpent tempting Eve.

Seeing the stone cups and bowls would put the lawful minded guests at ease, since cleanliness was such a grave concern. This would make the surprise that followed sweeter.

The grassless area between the portico and cellar was cleared and packed down with water. A sheet sewn together by the servants, almost the size of a Roman merchant ship's sails, cast its shade over the tables that were placed there and a large portion of the clearing. It was staked low behind the tables to block the view of the temple and the entrance to the cellar. The sheet rose in a gradual slope, fastened tight to prevent fluttering or collapse.

In the center of the clearing was a raised slab for the altar. They made the altar with horns curving away from each corner. On its side, a winged creature fell with a smoking trail in its wake.

This took months of preparation, of course. They'd hired masons and carpenters with promises of gold and silver. The artisans were possessed in short order, and those who resisted were killed. They commenced crafting and continued without exhaustion. Seeing four men gathered around each beam of wood, every man chipping away at his section, served as a true marvel of collective ingenuity.

On the day of the feast, the guests made their way to the tables as the sun was setting.

Chuldah wore the Jerusalem of gold. She was wrapped in a thin purple garment that shimmered as though wet and thrashed elegantly in the wind. A Roman landowner who had retired as an officer stood near her with his wife. They made small talk for a while, until Chuldah put a hand on his arm and dismissed herself.

Chuldah was introduced to the guests as Saul Bar Azareel's wife. The witch already exuded a particular radiance through her powers, but satisfaction in her newfound role, along with the glow from the life growing rapidly in her womb, gave her a glory rivaling the very stars. It would not be the only enchantment of the evening.

Marduhl sat with a tax collector from Tyre and Sidon who had arrived in a chariot with a gentile he did business with.They brought spices and a box of sweet delicacies as tribute. The wealthy Sadducee, Ruben Bar Irabin (he owned lots and livestock from Jericho to Capernaum), smiled under the slow hypnotism the wine provided. Some of the Romans had been in Caesarea Maritima. A few recognized Abaddon and whispered among themselves. It wouldn't matter.

And there were others. Whose positions, once attained, would spread the fallen's influence throughout the land. They would return to these roles as new men. With wit and strength unimagined previously. And they would amass followers. Through signs and wonders, miracles and preaching. Had they not learned this from *HIM*? A new race of Nephilim was soon to come. They were nearly ready, nestled in the wombs of the women in the villa, as well as Chuldah's, whose belly grew larger by the day. No deluge would stop them this time. Bazumel saw this future now, anticipated their enemies' screams, the heaped ash and rubbish left behind.

Bazumel looked out at his guests from the portico. Wealthy men conspiring, harlots orbiting tables like profane celestial bodies. The cattle shoved bread into their mouths, sopping up oil as crumbs fell with words. Men were no better than pigs.

When Bazumel entered the clearing, conversation died. They stared, sitting high, craning their necks to see him. He wore a blue tunic with pomegranates along the hem, and over that the ephod. The breastplate glinted in the light of the torches, its 12 stones representing the tribes, every one brilliant in their setting. The white turban was high and clean. Bells chimed with his steps, and phylacteries dangled (which he'd stuffed with little blasphemies). He walked slowly to his table with the staff of Moses and scanned the guests, drinking it all in. His people smiled, those soon to join his fold looked down or whispered.

Bazumel took his seat. Chuldah came to his side and put a hand on his shoulder. "Are you pleased, lord?"

He looked up and smiled. "I'll be pleased when the meat is put to better use."

She rubbed her hand over his back in circles. "Soon."

"Don't try to encourage my patience. I've seen stars fizzle and die." Chuldah nodded. "They're watching," he said. "Put your lips to mine." Chuldah leaned over and mouths searched. Whispers hummed about the tables. Bazumel looked up at her, smiling. "They're scandalized."

"Wait until they see the main course." Chuldah laughed and sat on the arm of his chair. Their antics would offend the Jews, as intended. The Romans, no strangers to orgies and lascivious displays, wouldn't care.

The Sadducee Ruben Bar Irabin was foremost among the gossipers. After some time he rose and approached Bazumel and Chuldah. They ignored him at first.

Ruben came near and cleared his throat.

Bazumel looked up. "Ruben, I'm so glad you could attend. I hope you're hungry."

"Hello, Saul." There was condescension in his voice. Bazumel despised the quiet outrage of cowards.

He smiled at the Sadducee. "Ruben, does something trouble you?"

"It may be more appropriate to speak privately, old friend."

"Old friend." Bazumel nodded, already bored with the subtleties and guile of the lesser species. "Anything you say to me is more than appropriate for my wife's ears."

Ruben grunted. Cleared his throat again. "It's only...well... I don't mean to impose..."

"Certainly you do. Otherwise you wouldn't have strolled over after your little denouncements from the table. On with it, there's things to do that don't involve you."

Ruben was jolted slightly. He'd been accustomed to the old Saul, a man trying to curry favor from the Sanhedrin for years. "Well," he said, smoothing his garment in an effort to compose himself. "We were wondering–"

"We?" The tone was low and irritable.

"We know you, Saul. Know your wife." Chuldah shifted and raised her head. Ruben's hands went up and he bowed slightly to her. "I'm just curious," he looked back at the man he thought was Saul. "I saw Netanya only a few months ago. Healthy. In high spirits. Now you sit here with a young new bride. I wasn't invited to the wedding, nor any of the others I've spoken to." Ruben looked back toward a group of Jews standing near a table. Their eyes found everything but Bazumel's. "Did you divorce her? We've known you for years. And your conduct here–"

"Netanya's dead." Ruben's mouth hung open, then snapped shut when he saw Chuldah's grin. "And my conduct with my new bride is none of your concern. You weren't invited to our wedding because you're a condescending pissant." Bazumel smirked watching the Sadducee wither. "A proprietor whose wealth stems from a father with two divorces, the nerve, and whose stewardship has left the abundance of his inheritance sparse and dry as the womb of your drunkard wife."

Ruben's fury quivered through his little body. He stepped back, fists balled at his sides. "You're no Mashiach, Saul. You're…you're a second rate scribe…" He held up a finger when another insult came to mind. "And a groveling sycophant! Who plagued the Sanhedrin for years."

Ruben flinched at Bazumel's laughter. "Please, old friend. My donkey is more knowledgeable in the Tanakh than you. The only reason you have a seat in the Sanhedrin is because of the gold you've squandered from the fields you govern. And shall I tell your wife the names of your mistresses, hypocrite? Of your illegitimate sons?" Chuldah laughed too now. She slid her hand over Bazumel's groin and smiled at Ruben. "This is the new covenant, Ruben. You can't tell a sin from a toad."

"You're no prophet, Saul. I don't know how you know any of this, but I'll expose you. When I get–" He had his teeth exposed like a wild dog and his finger jabbing toward the ground. He noticed the people at the other tables, and the ones standing around staring. Ruben stood straight and exhaled.

"If I'm not a prophet, Ruben, then why would I have this?" He held up the staff to Ruben.

Ruben couldn't hide his disgust. "Your little walking stick may be old, Saul, but it never touched the sands at Sinai."

"Here." Bazumel gestured for the Sadducee to take it. "See for yourself whether there are prophets in Israel."

Ruben glanced down, skeptical, then finally reached for the staff. He held it to his face, rotating it and running his thumb over the wood. He looked at Bazumel, then Chuldah. Ruben had the face of a man subjected to an impossible question.

Ruben held the staff and touched the bottom to the ground. The chatter around them stifled when the rod shifted in his hand.

The staff went slack and the bottom curled. Ruben tried to let go, shaking his wrist to fling the thing away, but it had already wrapped around his arm. The thick coil changed from the dark muddy color of the staff to a deep black with subtle iridescence. The wood transfigured before their eyes, as it had before Pharaoh's court, and a sheen of scales flashed over its surface while the head changed and contorted. Ruben made a series of low, panicked moans as the head of the serpent took shape, rose and paused in front of his face. Its hood was wide and the eyes possessed an intelligence unheard of in such creatures. Man and serpent stared at one another. Its tongue searched the air.

Ruben looked around at the guests watching, confused, trying to muster some courage. His quaver nearly broke his words. "I don't believe my eyes. I've lived to see the work of God." He looked at Bazumel with a skittish smile. "Saul Ha Ma-"

The snake struck. A black flicker of movement. Spots of blood blossomed over his nose and brow. Ruben stood, unsure of what transpired. He took several drunk, hobbled steps, still holding the serpent. Then muttered to his God and fell.

"Could it really be Moses's staff, Ruben?" Bazumel clapped and stood. The guests didn't move, their mouths agape in horror.

The serpent crawled over the dust on its belly, as was its lot in life, and made its way to Ruben's head. Ruben twitched, already frothing at the mouth. The snake's hiss could no longer be heard once the gasps and moans began. The shriek the Sadducees's wife made broke above it all. Its jaws opened wider than their minds could fathom, and the creature, in incremental movements, began engulfing the man. They all watched as it slid forward, bit by bit, until Ruben was enveloped and his girth distended the serpent and its scales bulged and spread.

The reptile, satisfied with its meal, laid there a moment. Only its tongue moved. Then the shape of its meal shrank inside. Like watching a bloated wineskin deflate. It returned to its normal size, slowly, while the horrified crowd watched with their hands on their faces. Once it was finished it flicked its tongue and slithered back to its master.

Bazumel stood with his hand out. The serpent wrapped around his leg and slid up and around his body. It moved over his torso, then wrapped around his arm and toward his hand. Its tail went straight to the ground from his palm. It straightened and its body turned brown and became a staff once again.

Bazumel looked over his guests and a stillness settled over them. The sobs Ruben's wife made rose, but fell silent when he looked at her. They heard the faint huffs of swine and wind beating against the sheet.

"You know how the prophets of old proved their merits," began the dark Mashiach. "Signs and wonders accompanied prophecy. Moses was given the staff as a sign to anyone who doubted his charge." With that he held the staff above his head in one hand. He turned, watching them unravel under his gaze. "This man's blasphemy has wrought his destruction. When a man tests a prophet he tests the one who sent him."

Chuldah, full of pride and stirred by the moment, rose and shouted, "Saul, Ha Mashiach! Saul Bar Azareel is the son of David! The savior of Israel!" Tears shined in her eyes. After a moment of apprehension the crowd clapped and their voices rose.

Bazumel let them praise him. He raised a hand when he'd heard enough and they fell silent again. "Is it not written, 'Will not his majesty terrify you? And the dread of him fall on you?'" Bazumel turned to Ruben's wife. She was on her knees, weeping while one of the women comforted her. "Do you think the Sadducee believes in spirits now?"

"You're a devil, Saul!" she screamed. "You've always been jealous of the scribes. I know you murdered Netanya. I hear things!"

Bazumel smiled. "A loyal wife to the bitter end."

She stood slowly, looking around at the others and clenching her garment. Then she made a face as if she'd suffered a wave of nausea, twitched, and bent at the waist, heaving. The woman attending her backed away. When she stood she brought her hands before her eyes. She screamed, but her wailing was stifled into a muffled grunt. The crowd seemed to collectively inhale, partaking of the moment's terror as one. When she stood again, straight as she could, her fingers were twisted and gnarled, the thumbs only nubs. Sores and lumps covered her exposed skin. She stumbled to a nearby table with hands stretched for mercy and the Jews seated there scattered. The poor woman fell to her knees, pleading with them.

"Who else denies there are prophets in Israel?" No one dared so much as cough. He turned back to her. "Go woman, your false sense of righteousness has made you unclean."

She looked around in search of sympathy. For courage. The people turned in disgust. The leper rose from the dirt and sauntered away, sobbing.

When she'd gone from their sight, Bazumel began again. "Now is the time to rejoice. You've been invited here to partake of the new covenant. No longer will the children of Israel worry whether what they eat or wear will sully their holiness. My message is one of indulgence. My elect will trample the oppressors beneath their heels. I know you. I've chosen you. I know the sins you hide from the world. And there lies the problem. What you conceive as sin, is only sin because you allow your conscience to convict you. Your holiness is a cloak to cover your true natures, the desire that burns within you. I ask that you remove these filthy garments and move in the world as you were meant to. Rise from pretenses, tear the sackcloth, shake free the ash bestowed to you on Sinai. Sup with me and be like

God."

"Blasphemy!" The items on his table rattled as the protester brought a fist down. His name was Jacob, a failed scribe turned money changer. He'd made a fortune extorting pilgrims outside the temple and badgering peasants who couldn't pay debts. He stood, chin jutting forth defiantly.

Bazumel appeared overjoyed with his defiance. "You'd lecture me, Jacob? Blasphemy is a harsh word for a man who pries the last mites from widows. What do you charge for a dove now?"

"I'm not a righteous man, but I would *never* speak profanely against the God of Israel."

"But you'll do his devil's work and spend the money on whores and wine." Bazumel held out his arms. "These people honor me with their lips."

Jacob stormed over to Bazumel. "I'm not afraid of your snakes. Our heels will crush the serpent's head."

"What great faith, Jacob. You'll have a martyr's reward."

Jacob's consternation softened at the roar that bellowed from the other side of the sheet. Grunts and squeals followed. They began low. Beating hooves and their disjointed clamor followed a trail of shadows moving along the sheet. The torchlight from the other side cast them as enormous apparitions. Snorts and barks and high shrieks prickled Jacob's flesh as the first of their putrescent bodies rounded the corner. They flooded into the open with a cloud of dust, bellies shaking, mouths snapping. Hooves flinging clumps of dirt. The ground shook with their strides. Their eyes black as the abyss they'd come from. Jacob held his robe to run but didn't make it far. Overtaken just beyond the guests, the pigs swarmed over him, tearing flesh and crunching bone and gristle. His screams drowned in gargles of blood. The dust their havoc brought provided a brief mercy for the people watching, as the fat bodies rolled and wrestled over the money changer's flesh.

The dust eventually settled and the swine finished. Pigs ambled lazily, scratching and smacking their teeth. Jacob was nothing more than a boiled hen picked to the bone. Fragments of his robe and sandals lay in trampled bloody strips.

The pigs roamed the clearing, sniffing about. Some collapsed, full with the short meal they made of the big man, sending up plumes of dust as they fell. Others approached the tables and sniffed at the guests. The sounds of their labored breaths and snorts ebbed. Every Israelite's face filled with disgust and confusion. Even the Romans and other gentiles were flush with shock.

Abijah and Marduhl fell to their knees before Bazumel, just as they rehearsed. Abaddon came shortly after. Bazumel made his way to them and gave his blessing. He stood patiently, watching an old man seated nearby. A Chaldean trader who resided on the Eastern shore of the Sea of Galilee. After some time, the man's discomfort prevailed and he walked over on weak legs and knelt before Bazumel.

"Follow me," said Bazumel. He raised the man's chin. "Saul Ha Mashiach." The old man looked up with apprehension and eventually nodded. Bazumel grabbed his cloak and pulled him closer. "Say it." The old man acquiesced. "They can't hear you." Sparks of malevolent joy lit Bazumel's eyes as the old man stuttered his confession through tears.

Bazumel raised his head to the others. A few rose and approached where he'd stood. Some stayed at the tables. Mostly the Jews, still repulsed by the pigs. They looked at one another.

"You worry about who chews the cud and the splits in their hooves because Moses commanded you. This was done to set your hearts against the Philistines and Amelekites. To keep the camps healthy. I hold the same symbol of authority Moses was given and I tell you now, just as it was in the beginning, every living thing is good." Bazumel's voice rose. "Come to me and rekindle the dead embers of your hearts. Come to my fold and sin will have no need for expiation. I will make your vices virtues." Bazumel stood with outstretched arms.

Many of the guests remained apprehensive. Some made their way with postures stooped over. Others deliberated. One moved, then another. Before long there was a row of kneeling men and women.

Stragglers lingered near the tables. One of the large pigs ran around the table squelching and drove them forth, snipping at their heels while they ran past the others to fall in line. One man fell and a piglet tore a chunk from his calf. They closed around them, squealing low and horrible, as though great tears had opened deep in their throats.

Bazumel laughed. "The one they call Mahiach in Jerusalem has stated unequivocally, 'he who is not with me is against me.' I share these sentiments." The ones on their knees shut their eyes as the sounds of excited pigs rose and rang in their ears.

Bazumel addressed each of them, moving in slow, ceremonial procession. He told them their private sins. Shameful and obscene secrets they only whispered in their prayers for absolution, things they'd resolved to take to Sheol untold. They wept and confessed. Looked up gratefully through tear soaked eyes, muttered, "Saul Ha Mashiach" through sobs, and reached for his hem or caressed the breastplate on the ephod with hesitant fingers. Bazumel blessed them all, encouraging man in his quest to be like God. He promised sweeter fruits than Eden, which bore no consequence, and accepted their oaths hungrily.

"You see," he told a woman who admitted to drowning her infant son. Her tears fell at his feet as she wailed. "You did what you had to. You'll hold your son when you're safe in Abraham's bosom. If you want. Or you can throw him to the beasts in paradise if it suits you." The woman's face pruned with worry. "You have freedom to do as you desire. I release you from your guilt."

After he had addressed each of them, and their hearts were tender for change, they returned to their tables. Some of them seemed lighter, having these burdens exposed. Murderers, cheats, those who had brandished the chastity of children. They felt at ease, since a man with such intimate knowledge of gross personal sins, and capable of such terrible signs and wonders, must have spoken face to face with God like Moses. If these wretched souls only knew the truth and horror of their suspicions.

Wine was brought in great cisterns. Women came with tambourines and drums and danced and sang. The guests drank.

Harlots walked among them, running hands over shoulders and enticing with smiles and crude whispers. Sitting on some of the Roman's laps. They drank as though trying to forget everything they'd seen, and before long some of the Romans fornicated with the concubines behind the tables, in front of them all. The wife of one the Jews, whose shameful secret had been rampant adultery, engaged with two soldiers. Her husband busied himself with a prostitute, glancing over at his wife in angry fits of jealousy as they bent her over the table. Some of the Roman men fornicated with one another. This made the Jewish men uncomfortable, and some irate, considering the law's prohibition and their lifetime stigma against sodomy. They didn't dare speak a word to the contrary for fear of the man they called Mashiach.

Wine spilled and soured breath. They were brought more bread and exotic oils to dip it in. Delicacies from foreign lands, sweet to the tongue. Fish was served. After some time and mingling among the guests, Bazumel and his disciples convinced the Jews to try shellfish. It was served in a sweet red sauce. They did. Some even went back for more.

It was working. Soon they would be ready.

A stout Jewish man from a wealthy family sat at a table with gentiles. He'd never been as drunk. He eyed one of the girls and grunted, "Aaron was onto something with that golden calf."

"Your Moses ran them through for having a little fun, ehh?" said the Roman beside him.

"God has condoned all of this. How would he have Moses's staff otherwise?" The stout man didn't seem convinced of his own words, however.

A young Benjamite wiped sauce and shellfish from his beard. "How could Moses forbid something this good?"

"Wait until you try the pleasures of a man," said a defected legionnaire, laughing and bringing an arm around him. The young Benjamite moved his shoulders from him, blushing.

After some time, even the Jews ignored the pigs that laid about. Some wandered near the tables to eat scraps that fell. Those eating gagged at their smell at first, but the wine and aromatic plants Chuldah had the servants hang helped.

Chuldah was a great help to the fallen ones. Not only her charisma as a beautiful host, but the sorcery she used to coerce them to debauchery. It served as the additional nudge needed for complete and utter hedonistic degeneracy.

It was dark and the torches blazed when the boy who arrived with Abaddon came from the villa accompanied by the lunatic. They stepped into the open space beyond the tables. The boy had a horn in his hands. He raised it and breathed a hollow note. "Distinguished guests. I present to you Saul Bar Azareel. To the Jews, Mashiach. To the Greeks, the Christ. To all who oppose him, an iron heel."

They erupted.

Bazumel stepped forward with his eyes set. The altar was brought into the clearing, horns sharp and menacing, curving from its corners. It was carried forth on rods and set in the slab at the center of the clearing. There were 12 holes positioned around it in a circle. One for each tribe of Israel.

Bazumel approached the altar. He called them forth. The new worshippers came, urged on by the boy, Abaddon, and the lunatic. They were terrified of the lunatic at first. But he laughed and laughed and soon they tried to ignore him. Some even joked with him. One of the Romans called him handsome. The lunatic brought the hole in his wrist over his remaining eye and winked. The Roman walked away, clearly unsettled.

They stumbled drunkenly, confused, herded through the clearing until they knelt in a line beyond the altar. The boy that came from the villa held a long blade, smiling. The men and women looked at one another. Jokes passed between them. The young Benjamite vomited–the Roman still lingered behind, comforting him–and a pig came over to lap it up.

The carved poles were brought and placed in the holes around the altar. Bazumel motioned with his hand and one of the pigs came and sat on its haunches beside him. It scratched its side and a scab fell to the ground. Then it snorted and shook its head like a wet dog.

The boy handed Bazumel the blade. He held it up, turning it so all could see. He raised the pig's chin. Stroked its head. Then he grabbed its scruff and pulled it off its front hooves so its snout was straight in the air and its bruised belly was exposed, with the hind legs dangling over the ground. Bazumel thrust the blade into its throat and tore into the surrounding flesh with swift violence. Its throat geysered crimson. The boy gathered its blood in a bronze bowl while Bazumel held the pig. Once the bowl was full he tossed the pig aside and the rest of the swine fell upon it in hungry triumph.

The man and boy made their way along the line of worshippers. Bazumel dipped his fingers in the blood and sprinkled it on their heads. Then smeared some on their ears and made them remove their sandals to put blood on their toes. Those who were Jews, especially the scribes and Pharisees, recognized the event's significance and bit their lips or squeezed their eyes closed. A few squirmed as though the blood stung their flesh. One man began to sob, but the boy slapped him. Bazumel smiled wide when he sprinkled his head. When he was done he made his way back to where the remains of the sacrificed pig littered the clearing. The area around it was dark where blood had pooled.

During the ceremony, a figure in a tattered cloak stood beyond the reach of torchlight. He knew each member of their legion by name. Pleased with the proceedings, he turned and walked off into the wilderness. To roam about the earth, testing the hearts of men.

Bazumel had chosen his priesthood well. Spineless men. Silent workers of iniquity with self interest at the seat of their desires. They were consecrated.

They were his.

He sent them back to their tables. They watched Bazumel lift and bleed another pig, this one much larger. He carried it as though it was a bag of grain. He cut its leg free and tossed it onto the altar. Smoke rose. Fire followed. The guests smelled burning pork. Servants brought plates and set them before the guests.

The Israelites looked at one another, alarmed. Their bloody faces were rigid with shock, fearing the inevitable.

Bazumel brought the meat from the altar with his hands and put it on a tray one of the servants brought. Chuldah seasoned the cuts with a dark mixture of herbs she prepared the day before. Bazumel sprinkled blood over the horns of the altar, as well as the flat portion where the offering was placed. The boy presented him with the severed head of one of the pigs. He held it over his head and spoke while it dripped over his turban.

"Your life is no longer your own. You are high priests of the new covenant. Sealed in blood. That which you once considered unclean, sanctifies you. You no longer walk in sin. In Eden the fruit promised knowledge of good and evil. With this meat, every man will decide what's good for himself. All is permitted. The only sin will be a failure to impose your will on the world. The failure to define your own good. Amen."

Bazumel lowered the head, then raised it again and said something the guests couldn't hear. He tossed it into the fire. The altar erupted in a high column of flame. The garments of everyone standing near it were blown back as if by a strong wind. The head sizzled and the boy, Abaddon, Marduhl, all of the wayward sons of God, began chanting in a forgotten tongue. In the distance came squeals, the roar once again, followed by the long bray of a donkey.

Bazumel was presented a tray. He sliced meat and brought heaps of undercooked flesh to his guests and placed it on their plates. One by one, each of his new priests bit down, retching on the spoiled meat and rancid juices invading their palates, trying to nullify the war raging in their minds. The dark Mashiach rejoiced in the scandal at hand. Pious men eating sanctified pork. His own abomination of desolation.

Bazumel watched until each had finished their portion. Many did this under violent coercion from the lunatic. One of the Pharisees refused to eat. Bazumel shook his head and smiled. The lunatic carried him away to the other side of the curtain, laughing. The roar bellowed once more from somewhere out in the dark, amidst more excited squeals.

Bazumel stood silent. Watched until they began to hallucinate. They rose from the tables and walked in circles, with their hands in front of them like the blind, clutching their stomachs. Finally they collapsed. They writhed and grabbed their sides. Took the positions of children curling up to sleep, spewing blood and food from their mouths. Violent convulsions dislodged joints and tendons. The backs of their heads struck the ground and they clawed at the earth, screaming in pain. The pigs were worked into a frenzy at this, snapping the air, screeching and barking. High pitched yelps came from their mauled gullets as they mounted the suffering guests and humped their writhing bodies.

Eventually all was still. They lay covered in Bazumel's sanctifying blood. Many in their own waste.

Later, their eyes opened. They sat up, seeing the world anew. The sons of God shook the dust from their clothes and tossed their soiled garments onto the altar. They stood naked and bloody, with understanding smiles.

"Now," said Bazumel, smiling at his Legion. "Milk and honey."

CHAPTER 66

MATTHEW AND SIMEON

Matthew woke to the sound of muffled breathing. He was naked, cold where his skin touched the floor, and a sharp pain welled in his temples. His wrist throbbed, but the pain had subsided since the night before. Someone had come and lit the candles. Gummed residue and crushed chunks of grapes reminded him of the splashed wine. Of his pitiful condition. He held his face. Slapped the ground in frustration with his good hand.

"They see... See see…me…see you... See see see…Eyes, eyes everywhere."

Mathew rolled over to look, startled. Huddled against the far wall with his knees tucked to his body, Simeon trembled and mumbled to himself. Matthew rose quickly to approach his friend, and felt as though his head was drained of blood when he did. He stood and waited as the world returned to order, then took a step and felt a sharp pain scream through his foot. He cursed and dipped with the pain, then regained his composure. He'd stepped on a piece of the cistern the scarred man threw against the wall.

"Simeon." He grabbed him by the shoulders and gave a slight shake. The old man continued muttering about eyes. That they could see him. See everything. He looked worse than he had in the room where they'd met. "Simeon, what did you see?"

Simeon grabbed for Matthew in a violent lurch that made him fall back. He leaned on his broken wrist when he did, and pain exploded through his arm.

The old man's eyes widened. "They see." Simeon looked up, and in a brief moment of clarity, seemed to notice Matthew for the first time. He looked at his eyes then quickly down at the floor. "Cherubim."

"Cherubim?"

Simeon's hands trembled as they made a slow path to his face. One eye was bruised closed and purple. His mind appeared completely desolate.

"Simeon, what's gotten into you?" The old man's mouth opened wider. His eye twitched and subtle spasms shook the loose skin on his face. He stayed that way, breathing rapidly into Matthew's face. Reliving whatever nightmare brought about this state of mind. "What did you see?"

Simeon's scream was low and weak, and tapered off before carrying any volume. Soft rasps of a hoarse old man.

Matthew tried to pray for him. To heal the wounds as he'd done before. Nothing came from this. The sense of abandonment cast his soul in shade then, as if the face of God had finally turned from him.

Simeon slapped his head. Raking his fingers down his forehead leaving furrows that beaded with blood. Matthew grabbed for the old man's wrists when he tried to claw at his eyes. Pain spread again when he squeezed. Matthew slapped Simeon. A sharp, distinct sound that startled the old man into focus. The old man nodded and slowly lowered to lie on his side.

After praying for him, trying to soothe him, Matthew eventually left Simeon there, trembling like an infant.

Matthew muttered to himself as he sat against the wall. Some time later he drifted to sleep.

He was roused awake again by a groan, slowly increasing in

panic and volume.

The old man had found the nail. Simeon was pushing the point through his eye, the agonizing moan rose the farther he pushed. He toggled the flat end around to destroy it all. When Matthew pried the nail from the old man's fingers, he'd already wept torrents of blood.

"You damn fool!"

Matthew took the nail and tossed it out through the bars. He tore strips from the old man's tunic. Wrapped them tight around Simeon's head, leaning him back to push what had fallen back into place. Simeon hugged his legs, moaning "eyes," over and over and rocking slightly. Blood soaked through the cloth almost immediately. The curves of his face shone in the blood as the light slowly died.

Simeon stopped moving after a while. He breathed in shallow, slow breaths.

Matthew sat against the wall with his head back to the ceiling. He thought of Elijah. Hoped he'd made it alive.

CHAPTER 67

BELPHEGOR

Belphegor had lain with a far away stare Bazumel and the others mistook for longing.

The clothing the women dyed in the courtyards were brought for the guests. Each donned the garments with affection, treating their new appointments with grave solemnity. A number of peasants had been gathered up in preparation for the feast and stuffed together in an old stable in the village, guarded by a small group of swine. Forced to sleep with the stench of dead livestock, they were eventually hungry enough to taste the flesh of the animals that expired there. These unfortunate souls were brought in a procession, already mad with hunger and desperation, tied together and poked with goads while Bazumel's companions laughed, threw stones, and flashed their genitals at the terrified villagers. A decadent orgy ensued. They gorged and fornicated well into the night, past the metallic luster and sanguine hues of dawn. They rejoiced in the novelty of their new anatomies, sang terrible dirges and performed blasphemous renditions of the prophets' writings. They drank great quantities of wine and mocked the heroes of the Tanakh: blood and shit were smeared over thresholds in the village, a woman was tied to a tree by her hair with stones draped over her neck and fastened to her feet, so the body slowly separated from the scalp while the throng chanted, "Absalom! Absalom!" in David's actual voice. Crucified men and women screamed while demoniac dances mocked their passions. They were sacrificed alive to the fire and dedicated to the false gods whose titles the demons had assumed over the years.

Belphegor listened without interest. Before morning, the cloaked man came from the wilderness and they spoke softly together. After the morning cleared, Belphegor rose up a little from his position of rest.

On the horizon, glints of metal flashed in the shimmers of heat. The sow huffed and stood. They were coming.

CHAPTER 68

BAZUMEL AND BELPHEGOR

Bazumel watched as men materialized from the dust. They'd been an amorphous blur, teetering at the edge of the world in the heat's chrysalis. Armor and cloth of sundry colors bloomed into clarity, spears and helmets traced in heaven's effulgence heralded the sun.

Bazumel looked out at the sow, now standing off to the cellar's left. The pig turned its face from the approaching soldiers to Bazumel.

Belphegor.

He surveyed the remnants of the previous evening. The altar was heaped with grey ash, the vague outline of a final sacrifice suggesting what was now only memory, a slow victim for the breeze. The sheet had torn in two after the guests relinquished their bodies. This struck Bazumel as intensely symbolic, for reasons he couldn't decipher. And like all reminders of his fallibility, it infuriated him. The poles were discarded haphazardly, some now charred black, striped lighter where shards of wood chipped from the faces and littered the ground.

Many of the guests left at first light. Disappeared in the trails at the foot of the mountains. Others took the path that ran through the village, or headed the opposite direction of the approaching soldiers.

Obedience with enthusiasm spurs pleasure from the least of rulers, and Bazumel had smiled sending his apostles into the world. He suspected whatever roused him so early stirred in them as well. The ones who remained would be enough. He'd looked on from the roof as morning broke and saw the smart ones leaving, scowling at the naked bodies and open robed fools. The smell of their fornication and revelry, the stench of pigs and the bodies of the crucified repulsed him.

Bazumel woke the fools, enraged at their complacency, a bleak sense of helplessness threatening. They prepared for what was coming. He sent Chuldah inside to protect the mothers. After this they would head north near where he found her, regather and wait to build their strength. This time, they would exercise caution. He couldn't leave here yet, not with the Nephilim so close.

Belphegor was waiting. The sow appeared smug. Scabbed skin, slobbering jowls, glaring black olives that flashed pleasure.

These men wouldn't be scared off. He could sense that much. War throbbed in every vein. Fear had succumbed to the numb diligence of battle long ago, adrenalin and lust for Mars's riches fueled the gallantry with which they stepped to their destruction.

Bazumel made his way to the cellar. His shadow fell over Belphegor. The sow looked up. "Whatever you're planning will fail."

"You're oblivious to reality. You won't know it's too late until you're burning in the dark again."

"You think I fear these men? You think they could stop anything that's been set into motion here?"

"You think they'll stop when their men don't return?"

Bazumel looked down at him. Fists clenched, the human body vibrating with the rage of the being inside. Fury older than the stones at their feet. "Why couldn't you help? We needed you. But you'd rather use your mind to tear down your brother."

"The great cherub has family now?" The sow's lips smacked after a yawn. "I thought the Accuser was your only kin."

"That's why you've done this, jealousy?"

"There is no why. Not for us. The souls here, the children you're hopeful for, *HE'LL* never let them leave the womb. The world sings a dirge for you, Bazumel. You plug your ears and ignore the melody. Man is born to die slowly, that they may be *HIS* playthings later. In Gehenna, or in his throne room. Blame your father for the futility of your existence. I seek one simple pleasure, and all will be fulfilled soon."

"And what is that?"

"To watch your demise before I return to the void."

Bazumel, trembling with wrath, looked back at the villa to those who hadn't left. The few remaining were lying about the yard in contorted positions, with blood smeared about for effect. "I should have cut you up to feed the others."

"I should have led them. But if you could eat your regrets you'd have a bigger body than mine."

Marduhl came and stood behind Bazumel. "We're ready." He cast a snide glance at Belphegor.

Belphegor snorted and laid on his front legs.

CHAPTER 69

BLOOD TO THE HORSE'S BRIDLE

The Centurion and his men approached. The crunch of feet and shake of iron droned and swallowed all humor as the sobriety of their mission took hold. In the final stretch of their march, the villa well within sight, they heard a noise. It floated overhead, like whips a blade makes through the air. One of the men out front fell forward. Plumes of dirt rose in jagged patterns, bronze sang from shields and helmets made sharp twangs. The men shouted "archers!" as geysers of dirt and rock burst skyward around them. The legionnaires interlocked their shields and made a roof of bronze. On the ground before them were stones, roughly the size of a fist, lying in the craters they'd made. More fell, thudding hollow and metallic from their shields. Some were large, and their phalanx tore open temporarily, until the men could move together once more to clot the wound. The whip the stones made falling and the horrible clang against their shields persisted while they inched forward.

They laughed to one another under this strange artillery.

It eventually stopped. The mens' hearts were beating, spines rippled cold from this new sorcery. But no man faltered from his course. They were resigned to the inevitability and imminence of death. Warriors.

The soldier who fell had a small hole in his face. Others were grazed, one lurched on with a chunk missing from his thigh They marched on, undaunted.

They neared, surprised to find only desolation. The villa welcomed them with enveloping silence.

Quiet save the murmur of flies and the flaps the sheet made beaten by the wind. They'd expected a fight. To run in with spears at the ready, met by the crescendo of violence every man burned for. Iron and bone, soft flesh and fashioned edge. Adrenaline subsided in the still heat. The pervading silence, all the more jarring, settled in their blood and brought their hearts pounding.

The legionnaires broke formation to inspect the area. Scouts went to the adjacent buildings, toward the fields. The clearing was littered with corpses. It seemed they'd been poisoned. Perhaps some mystery cult's last act of defiance. Their final moments were spent in agony, the grimaces contorting their faces proved this much.

"What happened?"

"How should I know?"

"They're all dead."

"Every time you speak I'm in awe of your deductive powers."

"Look alive, men."

"We're the only things that look alive here."

"A lot of dead pigs."

"And?"

"You found Gaius's mother, Marcus?"

"You'll be lying in–"

"Jews don't touch the things. Their god says they're dirty."

A soldier named Aulus approached the body of a woman. Her robe was stained with blood and half opened. With the head of his spear he moved the garment away to reveal more flesh. Aulus smiled. He turned his head to tell his companion, who had already caught the woman's eye rolling to where Aulus stood over her.

Before either could react, she leapt up and swiped at Aulus. He stepped back, wide eyed, staring down at the blood splattered sand, holding his throat while hot blood rolled over his knuckles. The woman held a red chunk of flesh in her hand. She crouched, bearing teeth like a cat with its hackles raised.

Raising his shield, his companion roared and charged the woman. A jolt of pain shook his bones from the impact. Her strength was astonishing. She grabbed the side of his shield and tried to take it from him, but he brought the side of his spear across her fingers. She let go and he raised his spear and charged again. The blow punctured her chest. She screamed. He let go and watched as she began to pull the spear from her body. From where her heart should be. As she did, another legionnaire approached from her flank and swung his sword. The woman's head bounced along the ground. The face twitched into an angry scowl as the mouth opened and closed, as if it would bite the air until its prey wandered into her mouth. Her body fell after and threw dirt into her eyes and mouth.

"Take their heads!"

A few of the Romans were momentarily paralyzed by this nightmare unfolding, and were struck down before they could react. Legionnaires charged with their shields hurling spears.

The fallen advanced despite their wounds, no longer subject to the pain and inflictions men succumb to.

Spears flew, blades slashed. Shield against bone, the hack of metal cleaving flesh, and the agonies of mortality. The throes of war pulsed and surfaced around them.

One of the fallen stooped over a soldier. As the demon clawed and tore at his writhing victim, the Centurion caught him unaware, lifting him from his feet after colliding with his shield. The Centurion brought his gladius down and claimed the head, still seething and hissing as it was repeatedly stomped. The Centurion roared after. He ran among his men, rallying and directing them, running headlong into any who approached, spurring them on with vulgar encouragements.

"Hold the line. Look at the sky boys, it's a beautiful day to die!

Shields tight, shields tight! Backman, fill the hole when it opens! Charge through when you see that gap like the whore you think awaits you on the other side! I want shields tight! Like a temple virgin!"

They formed a line. Marduhl collided with a fury that left the phalanx reeling. He ripped a shield from one of the legionnaires, pulling the man forward with the momentum. Marduhl raised it overhead, a foul parody of Moses holding up the commandments, and severed the man's neck as he brought it down. Blood painted the shield. Marduhl charged and swung it in great arcs, displacing the air in its path, knocking any who weren't behind the line to the ground.

The Lunatic's laughter wrung courage from their mortal hearts. He fought off a handful of legionnaires closing their shields on him, crashing together and slashing with their swords after contact. He dropped the sword he took from Elijah the first time they smashed together. Then the Lunatic waited until a shieldman was about to connect, and kicked, knocking him off balance. The Lunatic scrambled over him. Climbing on the shield, laughing maniacally, he pinned him down, then squeezed the man's helmet until the skull and brain beneath submitted to his grip.

Pigs darted around the clearing, proving a veritable nuisance. They rounded each phalanx (while separated, they formed several) snapping at heels and calves.

Abaddon held a sword in one hand, from the other his flagrum dangled. Its jagged bone and metal, with Abaddon's strength, stole the expressions from many a man's face that day. Leather whipped the air, and Abaddon snatched their skin while his blade gathered limbs and coated its edge in blood. Some were shocked to see their former comrade, Claudius, but by the time they registered the change it was too late.

O' Israel, to have seen such things! The bastard sons of Adam and the sons of God reenacting the Cherub's rebellion. Poetry in viscera, tinting the world vermillion. Blood sizzled in the heat.

Abaddon and Marduhl held fast. Many of their number, the weaker ones among them, lay headless. The soldiers rallied and strategized. The men fought hard. Many were maimed by the fallen.

The Centurion shouted orders. Abaddon's flagrum had torn a chunk from his arm, but he still held his sword, and fought as fiercely as any of his men. They'd closed around the Lunatic. He laughed when struck and cursed them to the end. His head rolled over the grass, now muddy with gore. The face smiled with blissful senility. The Legionnaires' nail studded soles ensured that image would never haunt another soul.

Marduhl and Abaddon were back to back, torn and emaciated, skin and garments painted the colors of war. Bazumel felt a cold swell in his chest watching from the roof. *The man's chest*, a sensation he'd assumed he'd never relive.

He summoned the rest of the herd.

The soldiers turned their heads to the commotion that followed. War Cries from hell. Amplified in the confinements of the musty cellar, squeals pierced the air, frantic snorts reverberated. A shrill bray pounded their ears. As did the terrible roar of some unseen beast they knew was large. And coming. Ascending the stone steps, the hooves sounded to the men like the clicks locusts make in a swarm. Swine poured forth from the cellar. The rent sheet flapped over their dark shape, and the herd pushed and tore through easily, spilling into the open, stumbling, snapping jaws and sprinting forward with excited yelps.

The legionnaires had regrouped. They shouted to one another and formed a line interlocking their shields. The Centurion backed them to the portico and held the phalanx there, rotating the line so their backs would be to the wall along the side of the villa. Were the herd to split and take their shields and backs, all would be lost.

The men watched as those who were maimed or injured were overtaken by the stream of tainted flesh. They stampeded through. Bloated and mangled, ghastly with decay, only moving slower than their stench, which had already met the men's noses before even a pink ear could poke from the other side of the half torn sheet. A brown bear with a scarred muzzle and huge patches of scabs ran behind them, growling. An ox with one of its horns snapped off bucked and shook its head as it caught up with the others. Saul's old donkey, Balaam, brayed behind with black eyes and gaping nostrils.

"Hold, boys, hold! This is our stand! Our children will worship our memories and they'll shout our names at the triumph!"

They braced themselves.

Pigs collided with the phalanx. The men kept their shields to the ground and knelt to brace the bottom, while the second row pushed against the tops. The creatures threw their bodies against their formation, some breaking their necks colliding. The men kept the first wave back with a coordinated effort. They began to advance in this way, pushing and beating them back, until the bear leapt on one of the shieldmen near the center. He brought the man down with his weight as part of the formation collapsed around it. The bear closed his jaws on the soldier's screaming face while the frantic rear ranks hacked and stabbed at the monster. Some of the pigs flooded in after the bear. The ox collided with their left side shortly after. Men were tossed back by its broken horns, stomped under its hooves.

Mayhem.

One of the Roman soldiers had crawled over to where the sheet fell. It draped him as the pigs ran through, and its soiled material hid his body. He waited for the earth to stop vibrating beneath him, then dug his fingers into sand and grass to pull forward. He crawled until he couldn't. Until the shadow of an enormous sow eclipsed the azure above. Its snout twitched in his ear and made promises and told him truths about himself he'd been scared to acknowledge his entire life.

CHAPTER 70

BEDLAM

Elijah fell from the bed, startled by noises. Raucous outside the window, commotion through the halls. Disoriented, he opened his eyes to blurs, and for a moment feared all he'd gone through to keep from blindness had been a dream.

He rubbed his eyes, wiping furiously until he could distinguish shapes and colors again. Then remembered where he was. Recognized the parchment and table. There was a jar of ink on its side spilling a trail to the floor, torn parchment, and what appeared the aftermath of some stubborn bird interrogated feather by feather.

Salome pulled him to his feet and shoved his cloak in his hands. He looked down at the garment, then up at the window. The clamor out there made the room seem smaller. "What is that?" He glanced back at Salome, arm still raised behind him toward the noise. Salome was rolling parchments. His arm lowered slowly as her fingers worked, dexterous and practiced, her movements a mechanism directly correlated with the lever of his arm and his faltering confidence. She tied a thin rope around the parchments and shoved them into a bag.

Elijah stared at the sunlight streaming in. Listened as metal scraped and clanged, and mens' screams explored the spectrum of suffering and valor. Animals roared and bellowed like Noah's cargo protesting their voyage.

"What is that?"

She was gone. He stood blinking, alone with motes floating in and out of the light piercing the room, ushering with it the intonations of malice and war from outside and above.

What a fitting parable.

Elijah grabbed his bag. When he walked into the hall he was immediately struck by the change.

The villa's grandeur and affluence had completely corrupted. Grime and squalor reigned now. Stains caked the floor and stone walls, banners of cobwebs entwined the dust coated cylinders of candelabras. Marble and art suffocated in catacomb staleness.

A tumultuous roar from outside startled him. It was followed by a small eruption of triumph, hopefully from whoever had to deal with such a beast.

Elijah slipped the cloak on. His sandals were missing. Unsure of where to go, wondering about the parchments, he walked toward noises he heard from deeper inside.

Cold stone taunted every step. The debris of furniture and art sent hateful messages through his feet. How long had he been asleep?

There was a crash. Shouts in the halls. He ran through the corridor and stepped on the shard of a bust that shattered. Elijah pulled it from his bleeding foot, limped into the light, out the threshold past the shambled stone fountains and benches of the courtyard. Where he'd previously seen women soaking clothes, tatters of red and blue material now clumped together in soggy piles beside a broken loom with strings hanging out like the disheveled hair of beggars. Spilled dye stained the bleak world. The body of an old woman laid beside a broken cistern. Elijah fixed his eyes ahead, swallowed hard, and moved on.

He reached the banquet hall. The door beyond, past the vestibule, was barricaded. The tables and chairs, a sofa from the room where he'd witnessed the old woman's resurrection, broken racks for weapons, and the throne where Saul had sat were shoved against the doors. The old woman who'd been resurrected stood staring at the barricade. Her shoulders shook. From just outside, noise roared, discordant and unpredictable, and the pile of rubbish keeping the door in place shook as something slammed against it. The commotion was louder here, imminent, and he could hear the voices outside. They were speaking the language of the Romans. The sounds squeals, a great multitude it seemed, made Elijah back away slowly. He turned back. Crescents of blood stamped the floor from the direction he'd come.

He made it through the courtyard, down the hall past the open room he'd woke up in. Trying doors along the corridor. Empty or locked and quiet. The heat in his gut provided an unstable center now, trembled in his limbs and shook his hands. Another rounded corner brought more evidence of struggle. A corridor fragmented with destroyed furniture. The next courtyard had rows of statues broken at the shins. It made Elijah think of Adam returning to dust.

The size of the place dawned on him, heating through viscera and rising in slow, awe inspired panic. He might not find her. Elijah passed an open space with a fountain, crossed an annex and found himself back where he'd entered the villa. The doors were open, an opaque wall of light cut the room in half. Elijah stepped in something wet and warm. Blood. Several bodies laid outside the door. Servants and some of Saul's men. Footprints ran in several directions through the blood. Farther down the corridor were dark shapes of people crossing the hall in a hurry, and farther beyond there were screams. Something broke.

Elijah headed that way. He reached into his bag, partly to occupy his hands, but in hopes of finding something useful. He recognized everything by touch. A dry piece of bread, half eaten fish wrapped in dirty cloth, a clay lamp that wasn't very useful any longer–but then, something round, hard, that gave to the touch. Elijah pulled out the fig the Mashiach gave him. Nearly too ripe to eat now, it provided a brief sense of comfort.

Farther down the hall he found a large room with its door torn free. Inside there were rows of mats, and the light leaking in divided the room in bright bars. Beside the door lay Chuldah. Her purple garment was stained and torn, dried blood covered her throat. Her legs were twisted behind her, with her face cruelly illuminated in a stream of light, tilted back so she was looking at Elijah. New networks of lines carved her cheeks and eyes. Impossible hatches and wrinkles that should only come with age. Her smooth skin had withered, as though all the vitality had been sapped from her body upon death.

"You shall not suffer a witch." The voice was low, flat.

Elijah spun to find a woman slouched against the wall with her hands on her lap. He approached and her head rose slightly. It was the woman he'd met at the door. The stitches torn free from her lips.

"It had to be done."

With where he now stood, Elijah could see the other mats. He was thankful for how dark the dusty room still was. "What she carried… What they all carried." Her words quavered. "It had to be stopped."

He looked at Chuldah. "She was pregnant."

"They all were." She kept her eyes on him, awaiting his judgment. "But not with the children of man."

"What was this place?"

She laughed. "A nursery for the damned." Her eyes raised and she closed her mouth, staring across the room at the women on their mats. The ends of the stitches still poked out around her lips. "These women were to carry their seed." She motioned to Chuldah with her chin. "That one did it willingly."

"Did you do this?"

"I helped. What was growing inside them was unholy. They would have spread from her. Consumed us all."

"How?"

"Birth would have killed them, anyway. Then countless others. I heard them crying in here at night. All I could do was listen."

Elijah nodded. "You should leave here."

"There's nowhere to go."

"The doors are open. Out there is better than here."

"Everything has been taken." Her head turned to Chuldah and she scowled. "They made my brother one of those things."

He tried to console her. To convince her to leave with him, pulling gently on her arm. Ultimately, he understood. He left after pleading and headed to the voices.

In a sitting room with toppled furniture the servants he'd seen making preparations for the feast stood in a semicircle, armed with spears and swords and scythes and sticks. Samuel was backed against the far wall. He was covered in blood with a broken shard of wood in his side, hissing and swiping at them. Others laid on the ground nearby. Whose men had fallen Elijah couldn't tell.

Samuel looked at Elijah. Elijah stared back, and raised a hand. He walked away from Samuel's screams.

They let Elijah pass. He kept moving. Down a dim corridor with candelabras spilled over with wax, he passed a woman scrambling for the way out. He guided her back. He passed the baths and looked in. The water was dark, a film had settled and a woman floated facedown.

When Elijah rounded the next corner he nearly knocked over Matthew and Simeon. Their arms draped each others' shoulders. Matthew was wheezing. The men embraced. "I thought I'd never see you again!"

"If we don't get out of here we'll see Elohim," said Matthew.

Elijah saw the soiled cloth around Simeon's head. "What happened?"

"Let's just get out of here."

"I'm not leaving without her."

Matthew grabbed Elijah's arm. "She's been here too long."

"This is why I came."

"She's like the others now, Elijah." Desperation brimmed in his eyes. "God has turned his face from her."

Elijah ripped his arm away. "I haven't."

Matthew's shoulders dropped. He looked away and shook his head.

Simeon moaned. Strips of the saturated linen hung from the side of his face. He resembled some sightless prophet of doom.

Matthew put his head to Elijah's, embracing him. "Come now, Elijah. Please. Forget this madness. You've done everything you could."

"You go," said Elijah. "Down the way we came. We'll meet where we set up camp before coming. If I don't get there before dark, head to Jerusalem. Go to him. I'll find you."

Matthew put his arms around Elijah and kissed his cheek. "Go with God."

Elijah returned an irritable nod.

Then they were down the hall and gone. Elijah was left with distant screams, sounds like stern commands, and the rumblings from outside. He was on the other side of the villa now. He passed frescos of battles and demigods. Then stood in the largest kitchen he'd ever seen, still tracking light red prints with his steps. Beside the kitchen was a dark entrance basked in shadows. There were doors on the far side of the kitchen, and he could see light through the center where they connected. They opened to an annex leading to the portico. Vine wrapped pillars lined the stone walkway. Farther on, its covered path surrendered to darkness. He could see a pig lying ahead of him, as if the animal had come in from the heat to rest in the shade.

An enormous clearing spanned to the left. The portico was higher than the clearing, which declined in a mild slope. Elijah took a few steps out from the shadows and stopped. Corpses of man and animal spread across the ground. The scene was both horrific and surreal; how an artist would render a visit from the angel of death. On the opposite side of the villa, a band of legionnaires with their shields huddled together fought back swine. They were surrounded by corpses. The bodies of their comrades, some of Saul's favorites, pigs in all manner of size and color. There was a huge mound of fur near the wall with spears jutting from every angle imaginable. In the center of the clearing stood an altar with a man impaled on one of its corner horns. On the ground lay all manner of things: tunics, red capes soaked in splotches of bloody sand, helmets, a great number of shields which were in some cases miraculously broken, spears; but the worst was the limbs and bodies flayed and mauled. Elijah's hand was shaking.

The Romans screamed to one another in their tongue. Their shields locked together, occasionally opening the ranks so pairs of legionnaires could run out and dispense with swine. The shields closed behind them and the men that ran forth swung their swords at the pigs trying to dig under the shields. Whoever commanded these men called out in a hoarse, worn voice. Elijah was in awe of their choreographed precision and swiftness. From where he stood, he could see another group of Romans behind the shield bearers. Their shields were down and they were sitting against the wall resting behind the safety of the phalanx and the men just beyond. Their armor was on and several had spears within reach.

Who would believe the sight of Romans could encourage an Israelite? Still, stranger things had happened in recent days.

He spotted a Roman lying not far from the portico. He wasn't in armor like the ones fighting. Elijah found a blade near his body and picked it up. He looked down at the man. "Sorry." He unstrapped his sandals and crouched to tie them on.

The puddles of blood near the soldiers glared red in the sun. With the heat the battle's offerings steamed up and hovered a faint pink mist. Elijah shuddered. *Where are you?* He ventured along the wall in the opposite direction of the soldiers and pigs. There was an enormous cloth of some sort, stained with all types of filth. Beyond that was a set of buildings spaced fairly wide apart. Across the clearing, a lone legionnaire made his way toward the villa, sword in hand.

Once Elijah passed the side wall he could see the stretch of thirsty desert and the shadows of clouds cast from above. She hadn't gone that way. The mountains stood menacing, blocking the other direction, as they would to the end of time.

Elijah looked back at the soldiers. Behind the shields stood a man with gold in his helmet, adorned with red plumes of feathers. He shouted orders to the line. Another soldier pulled on his shoulder and pointed toward Elijah. He watched two of the resting soldiers rise when their leader beckoned. The Roman motioned in his direction, but it looked as though he'd pointed above him. Elijah turned and looked up. Saul stared down at him from the roof. Beside him, Salome's large eyes were dark blots on her stolid face.

"Salome!"

Saul said something to Salome. She nodded, neither with any lines to indicate expression. Elijah ran inside. He searched the nearby rooms, finally resorting to the dark passage near the kitchen, nearly tripping in the dark as he entered. Stairs. After the first set of steps he could see a thread of light overhead. Taking them by twos he bounded up until he came into the light. He could see the village when he came out, and turned to see Salome and Saul watching him.

Salome's eyes were impossible to interpret. The side of her lip turned slightly, the playful smile a brazen reminder of everything he'd risked. A leather strap crossed her chest and Elijah could see the parchments sticking out from the bag over her shoulder.

Saul had shed the priestly robes for the common brown cloak a traveler might wear. He held the staff and stood tall. Undaunted by his faltering kingdom. "Do you still want to be my disciple, Elijah?"

"I'm no one's disciple."

"You were ready for her sake."

Elijah gestured toward the fighting below. "I've seen what happens to your followers. Your former servants won't let you leave here. It's over fo–"

"Nothing's over. They can destroy this body. I'll rise again."

"I saw Chuldah. I don't think your door woman wanted to play midwife. If you hurry, you might be able to bring her back."

Saul's lip twitched. "Wombs are plentiful in Israel."

Elijah looked at Salome, unable to hide his worry.

Saul stood tall and laughed, tapping the staff down as he did. "You'd follow." He turned to Salome. "We'd make him a cuckold like he did your poor Samuel."

Salome smiled. She didn't have a head covering, and as Elijah watched her hair in the wind something softened inside. He'd help her be rid of whatever controlled her now. No matter the cost.

Saul looked at Salome again, and something dark crossed his face that made Elijah's gut twitch. He turned back on Elijah with new resolve. "It's not fitting for the Nephilim to return through her. A well worn road runs through this one." Saul sighed.

"You're full of bile and sulfur," said Elijah. "Tell me your name." Surprised by the strength in his voice, Elijah squeezed the handle of the blade in his hand.

"And by whose name do you demand such a thing?"

"Jesus of Nazareth."

"The stone mason?" Saul smiled. "A man you lack the faith to follow. He would have you abandon this woman."

"And I would if it brought her home safely."

Saul shook his head. "Fool. You scorn your chance at freedom. He'd have you cut your prick off as soon as it twitched to life."

"It's him or a cheap sorcerer who fills dead women with unclean spirits."

"I'll enjoy nailing your tongue to a tree."

"Not as much as I enjoy seeing your ruin."

The deep furrows and angles his brows made professed Saul's hatred without words. "You don't know who you tempt, boy."

"Surely I do. He who fills his wine glass from a chamber pot."

Saul raised his head. He seemed to weigh the insult a moment before regaining his composure. "There is more hope for a fool than one who speaks in haste." He looked at Salome, she smiled when he did, then he motioned toward the mountains with his head. She slipped the bag from her shoulder and handed it to Saul. Without dropping her smile she turned and climbed onto the ledge. The blade clanged down as Elijah ran, but she had stepped off before he could reach her.

He didn't hear her hit the ground. Didn't hear the world shatter. Elijah looked down and quickly turned away. Plucked from flight, a broken bird. A void tore open in him. Its shape the absence of all she'd filled. Hot tears stung his eyes as he screamed.

"Sweet music you make, little cull. I think I'll eat your eyes. She'll be the last thing you see."

Elijah lunged for him. A breath later his feet dangled and pressure filled his head. Both of his hands clenched Saul's wrist. He couldn't make a sound.

This is how it ends.

Sparks and flecks of different colors dappled his vision. Darkness spread. Saul's teeth were the last thing he saw before the black.

Misfortune had clouded Elijah's life the previous weeks. Bazumel's hold brought him to the gates of Sheol, but providence finally smiled–subtle as the grin remained. The Roman had walked from the cellar toward the villa with a purpose. Foremost in that great mind the subjective emphasis on the commandment against murder.

He wore no helmet and his armor had plates of iron missing. The tunic below soaked through with blood. The heart beneath a drum whose rhythm ceased. But an ancient and iniquitous enemy had stirred the flesh. Sinew and organs twitched to life and the creator's image rose anew from unholy dust, breathed to life from brimstone breath, fueled by epochs of hatred and deceit.

Belphegor crossed the clearing and headed to the wall. Glad to be rid of the sow.

The scabbard brushed his thigh as he walked. Behind and to his left, Saul's remaining comrades threw their heavy frames against the shields. There were more. Nearly a hundred, loyal to Belphegor, huddled in the belly of the cellar.

He would gather them under his wings. He sought a greater influence. To dwell among the lesser species and scheme. Bazumel's anger and pride had ruined him. The others had followed. As they had into the lake. As they had after the Accuser.

It amazed him. An astounding fact really, that the entities hurling into the shields, which were so much smarter than the favored race, with the experience of time and such immense capacities for reason, when together, somehow reverted to the intelligence of normal pigs. He looked at them disdainfully. Abaddon laid farther off. His fault was in his faithfulness. He'd tried to please both of them. There was no tinge of pity. Unfit sentiments for a demon. Still, Abaddon's return to the void was unfortunate.

Before Belphegore reached the villa, he saw the woman take the ledge. Watched her drop. He heard her paramour's anguish over the commotion. Looked up as he peered over and quickly drew back. He hadn't seen him. Belphegor stepped on her writhing body as he passed. She made slight, languid movements and reached for his leg, but he continued indifferently.

Belphegor climbed, scaling the wall with the competency of an insect. Some of the baffled Romans watched and pointed. When his head finally peeked over the ledge, Bazumel had the mortal by his throat. Just as Bazumel turned and noticed him, Belphegor raised the sword and hacked the arm at the elbow.

His nemesis screamed. The sound of rage, not pain. Blood poured from the severed limb. The mortal fell in a limp heap. The staff thudded to the ground as Belphegor hopped over the ledge and ran the blade through Bazumel's heart. The foul Mashiach grabbed for a dagger hidden in his waist, but Belphegor was fast. He gripped the hilt of the gladius and kicked Bazumel's chest, freeing the blade with a stream of blood that lapped skyward. The false prophet fell back, and Belphegor swiped the blade at the arm holding the dagger.

Bazumel stared up at his foe. With lips turned back in his blood flooded mouth, he said through clenched teeth, "we could have had everything."

"Half of everything leaves much to be desired." He stomped a nail studded sole into Bazumel's chest and pulled the blade free. "We'll meet soon, great cherub." Bazumel's severed limbs flailed as he tried to back away. "We have all eternity to bicker."

CHAPTER 71

EXODUS

Elijah woke under a bruised sky. He sat up abruptly, head pounding. The mountains were traced in a red glow, as if those responsible for the debauchery had moved beyond their peaks and lit new fires to conspire by. Something near the ledge drew his eye. Elijah stood and looked around. Slow steps. He could make out an arm at first. He stopped when he noticed it laid alone. Then he saw the rest.

Saul's head was gone. What remained beneath the ruined cloak had been hacked with malicious intent. Whoever had done such a thing hated him. Elijah spat. "Good."

He leaned over the edge. Salome was there. Half swallowed in shadow. Her leg was broken and an arm bent beneath her.

She moved.

Something leapt in him. He rushed down the stairs and through the kitchen. Raced along the wall, stumbling and rising again. The fear that nothing had really moved, that the twitch she made had been a hopeful delusion, solidified into a certainty by the time he made it to her. He fell to his knees. Her eyes turned to him.

He saw her mouth move. The movement of her lips, the tongue's pause between her teeth on the second sound, her groan. Her lips spoke the shape of his name.

"I'm here." He took her in his arms, stroking her hair and whispering to her.

He looked her over. Feeling her body, parts of her that used to be firm were malleable now. Soft and broken.

Elijah made a splint for her leg and arm with the broken shaft of a spear. He tore a garment from someone lying nearby, careful not to take anything defiled with blood, and tied it in place once he'd torn the strips to use. Salome groaned as he fastened it to her leg. He lowered his body over her's and spoke softly. He was fairly certain her back was broken.

Elijah searched the area. The soldiers wanted nothing to do with him, since they had so many of their own dead and wounded to attend to. They had prevailed, but at great cost. Elijah staggered around the field in a daze, searching for something he could use, slipping in and out of a walking dream. Some of the servants were outside. He saw the woman with her lips stitched crouched over a body in the grass, crying.

Elijah found a lamp in the kitchen. Fortunately, the soldiers had lit some of the torches in the portico. He picked up one of the Roman's swords from the clearing.

On the far side of the villa he found a stable where the guests kept their animals. The chariot they'd met on the way was there. The horses turned their heads and shook their manes. Horses made him nervous. But there was a donkey. A small cart with weeds sprouting near the wheels was positioned against the outer wall. It would be just large enough for her. He searched its contents, most of which he shoved to the ground, saving only a rope curled over the wood and an old stone water jug. He pulled in the donkey and made a clumsy effort to secure it to the cart. Then he lined the cart's wood with cloaks and tunics from the villa so it would be as soft as possible.

He knew where he'd take her.

He wouldn't refuse if he came in faith. He couldn't. Desperation built. It rang in his ears, stubborn resolution drowned out any excuses the weak part of his mind tried to make on his behalf. This was why he'd come. He'd see it through. Some time later, he passed where he planned to meet Matthew and Simeon without a thought. Their faces didn't cross his mind until well into the night. He listened to the cart's wheels creak along the road while he sat atop the donkey until his legs were numb.

That night Elijah built a fire and sang to her under the tendrils of dust and flickering host, while stars burned trails through the heavens. A dull coin moon loomed half eaten by darkness. That was how he felt.

The following morning was one of the most beautiful he'd seen in some time. There was a stretch of open desert to the side of the road, and when the sun rose the sand glared like water. He thought of the stories he'd heard of people seeing lakes when they were thirsty. He looked back at Salome, who hadn't moved, hadn't shown the slightest sign of life other than a groan and what he thought were twitches from the corner of his eye. In moments of weakness he wondered whether all he'd seen had even happened.

By the afternoon Elijah's mouth was dry and his lips were peeling badly. Salome had started to smell. Hunger began as a dull ache, spreading through his insides as the need grew and squeezed his stomach.

Elijah started talking to her more. Confessed things he'd never mentioned in mumbles. Fantasies of smothering Samuel once their affair began. How long he'd waited to meet her in the mountains again after the first time he saw her there.

"I could see us," he told her, "Old. Greeted at the gate. Dowries brought for our daughters. Cisterns of wine and grandchildren on our knees and tugging on my beard. Your hair silver." He laughed and looked back at her. "It wouldn't grey and thin like the others. Yours would shine. You would be oiled, the women at the gate would praise the grace you aged with."

He prayed too. It had been so long. Once he started it was hard to stop, like some part of him cracked open, leaking everything he'd held in. While he prayed she rocked back and forth, moaning weakly.

Thus went the cycle of conversation: Supplication, then

assurance and clarification to her, so she wouldn't misconstrue how the series of rash oaths he made would affect her. He told her about the Rabbi. "There's no guile in him. You wouldn't think he was anything remarkable. He doesn't look much different than any other Jew." Her eyes fluttered. "But he speaks and tells you things you always knew were true but couldn't say because you weren't smart enough. Or weren't observant enough. And he can make an invalid strong. Restore broken legs. Open deaf ears." Tears welled. "He's not like Saul. Saul used wounded vessels and filled them with unclean spirits. He was evil and only sought to do evil." As he said this something cold searched along his spine.

They reached the Jordan that day and drank. He poured water in her mouth from the jug and she coughed.

He slept on the ground so he wouldn't roll onto her broken body and damage her any further. He woke late in the night and walked out to relieve himself. When he turned back to the cart, Salome was sitting up. He walked back slowly. Quietly.

"Salome?" Her eyes were open. He stepped closer, watching. She slumped over and fell off the side. He ran to catch her before she fell to the ground. Again, he was too late.

The third day was hot. They were traveling slowly, for both the donkey and Salome's broken body. At midday, he pulled the cart to the side of the road and slept. Elijah laid against her despite his worry. Despite her smell. He fell asleep to her breathing, and woke to a nasal voice greeting them.

"Peace be with you."

Elijah raised his head and reached for the sword.

The stranger raised his hands.

Elijah looked at Salome, then back at the stranger and nodded. The man flicked his hand toward Elijah, beckoning. Elijah slid to the ground and followed him to a larger cart pulled by oxen. The old man's wife had made bread for his journey and he had oil in some little vessels. Elijah ate all he was offered. The old man offered him some for Salome and he folded it into his cloak. When the old man offered more for his journey he felt ashamed. He refused several times but accepted in the end.

Later he mashed it in his fingers and fed it to Salome in small chunks. She'd become the invalid.

They'd been on their own for a good portion of the afternoon when Salome spoke for the first time.

"You should have left me."

He turned back. "To die?"

Her eyes shifted away. "With them."

"Them?" She coughed and when she turned back there was blood on her teeth. Elijah stopped the donkey and tended to her. He dabbed her face with the end of his tunic. "Salome. Who are they?"

"Take me back." He could hear the irritation in her voice.

Elijah climbed into the cart and sat beside her. "I'm taking you to someone that can help."

Her eyes shifted as her head faced the sky. The networks of veins had burst in some places and spilled into the whites. In a harsh, low rumble she asked, "Who?"

"Jesus of–"

Salome grabbed his forearm and rolled onto him. Her breath was foul and hot, her tone unlike anything he'd ever heard in a woman. "His disciples are sodomites. He forces the women to wash his feet with their hair. He'll kill me and leave me in Gehenna."

He shook his head. "Whatever festers inside you will be driven out."

"I've heard of his wonders. Sorcery for alms. He baits widows out of their money."

"He's not a charlatan, he knows–"

"He was conceived outside of marriage."

"Since when did marriage matter to you?"

"Now I'm your whore? You'll keep me to do as you please?"

"If I don't take you, you'll die."

"I feel better now." She rolled from him and slid from the side of the cart.

Elijah hopped down after her. She used the cart to raise her body after nearly toppling over, but her foot couldn't hold any weight and the wood in the splint went crooked after a few steps. She fell. Her hands clawed and dug into the clay as she pulled herself forward. She used the broken arm with an impressive dexterity for such a wound. When he put his arms around her waist to lift her she thrashed, and her elbow struck him above the eye. They wrestled there in the road, until finally he was able to carry her back to the cart.

He raised the blankets and used the rope, frayed as it was.

Salome–or whatever dwelled in her body—began haranguing him as soon as they were on the road again.

Elijah tied her wrists and ankles. The splint, a picture of disarray, was reapplied. He'd wrapped a piece of his tunic around her foot before tying it off because she complained of the pain. "Untie me. Help me to relieve this pain."

He stared ahead, concentrating on the hooves and the sound of the wheels.

"You're going to let me suffer?"

Salome moaned, rolling her neck around slowly. Sensually. The bones popped and cracked with her movements. "Elijah, make love to me."

He didn't look. His throat worked hard to swallow.

"Fuck me."

He turned sharply, and the Salome thing burst into cackles. She rolled onto her stomach, moaning still, raising her backside slightly, then rubbing herself against the piles of garments with lascivious moans, panting. Her back looked crooked. "I'm ready for you."

"Shut up."

"Give me something to fill my mouth."

"Shut your mouth, demon." He continued on.

Its laughter seemed displaced from the body behind him.

Elijah struggled to maintain his poise. When she moaned again he turned, "Another word and I'll tie you behind the cart and drag you."

It didn't stop. He didn't tie her to the cart.

They traveled beside the Jordan. Fish stirred the surface and birds fled from the tall grass along the bank as they passed. As if the animals knew his cargo.

"Elijah."

Her voice. Her real voice. He didn't look.

"Where's Samuel, Elijah? I'm afraid…Why are there ropes on my wrists? Elijah?"

Elijah suppressed the flicker of hope stirring in him. He turned, and when he saw her face that hope sank, became almost too heavy to bear. The thing's smile was repulsive. He realized she would never be free until he found Him.

"What's your name?"

"Salome."

"Tell me your name!"

"Elijah, you're scaring–"

"Quiet devil! Tell me your name, in the name of Jesus of Nazareth."

"No." The voice was flat. A subtle smile curved the lips.

"Tell me your name!"

The thing spat in Elijah's face. He raised his fist, and as he did, it extended its face forward. Elijah groaned and put his face in his hands.

"It's hard to destroy what you love. Except for your God. He destroys what he loves and cites love for the very reason he does so. You love me," it teased.

"Not you."

They rode on. The wheel's squeak, and the vulgarities from the Salome thing tested his sanity.

That night he pulled the cart in from the road. He built a fire and fell asleep on the opposite side, away from her. He fell asleep to wood crackling, shrill moaning wind, and the blasphemies rasped from the cart.

Sleep was short lived.

The rustle of his modest fire was disturbed by sand and cinder thrown about. Elijah woke amidst glowing coals, swiping at one eating through his cloak. A shape writhed and rolled about in the flames. Screams of pain were amplified in the night's stillness. He rushed to take her out. The smell of scorched skin and the heat opposed him, and he burnt his hands pulling her free.

He gathered her in his arms, brought her to his cloak and smothered her burning hair. Orange embers made new seams in her tunic. She wailed. The flames blistered her face and chest. An eyebrow was gone. Much of her hair had burned away.

The thing had left Salome in control of her faculties once it leapt into the fire. It wanted Elijah to hear the pain in her voice. For him to know she suffered.

Elijah sat with her cradled on his lap, listening to her cries. He cleaned her wounds with a trickle of water. She seemed both plagued and relieved by this. After, he tore parts of the garments in the cart and wet them. Then laid the strips over her burns. It was a long time before she slept. And when she did, she frowned and occasionally shuddered. Elijah smothered the fire and kept watch. He had no desire for sleep.

Morning came and they set out early. Her lapses in clarity confused him, varying from helpless pleas to cutting insults. The garments applied to her wounds were soiled, stiff and cracking where they'd dried.

Elijah set out with dusty skin and lifeless eyes. The thing came back to taunt him and his heart ached seeing the burns.

The demon drew from the conversations they'd had together. In Elijah's voice, it asked, "would you still love me if I was blind, Salome?" Then burst into laughter. "Would you lead me through the village? Could you care for an invalid and a blind fool in your best years of life?" Elijah had to wrap her body in the garments so she wouldn't rub her face against the wood. It sought destruction. Delighted in her pain and his torment.

That day a covered cart pulled by oxen came alongside them. The man guiding the beasts looked at Elijah's face, then the filthy garments behind him in the cart. He slowed his cart and took a good look at the donkey. Its lice ridden fur clung to the bone and its head drooped. He put a hand up. "Peace."

Elijah looked at the man, nodded, and faced the road ahead.

"Are you hungry, friend?" A boy's face stuck out from the covered cart behind the man. The stranger turned and tickled the boy. He squealed and disappeared inside. When the stranger turned back Elijah was facing forward. "My son," he said with a curt nod. A proud smile on his face. "Asher."

Elijah frowned and gave a minuscule nod.

"He won't last much longer. You can't depend on an ass to pull you very far. Or fast. It's why I caught up to you."

"When he dies I'll walk."

The stranger nodded thoughtfully. "We could pull off and take a break. I can spare some food for it."

"I don't have time to mingle."

The stranger nodded. "What's that?"

He was pointing to the mass of garments in the cart. Salome's body stirred and she made a low groan. Elijah's heart beat furiously. "My wife. She's been burned."

The ox driver frowned and shook his head. He tugged the reins and pushed his animals harder. They passed Elijah's cart with ease, and once the cart was past the donkey he pulled hard right to cut him off. The stranger hopped down and grabbed the donkey's reins. He looked down at how it was fastened, then raised his head to Elijah with a wrinkle cleaving his brow.

"Who tied this?"

"I did."

"You've never tied an animal in your life."

Salome groaned. The stranger walked over. "And look at these rags. You would have your wife in this?" He pulled at a loose fold. Eventually, the stranger's face softened. "Let me at least get you some clean linen. I have some in the cart."

Before Elijah could stop him, the stranger pulled back the cloak covering her. He gasped and staggered back, bringing a forearm over his mouth. "Why is she tied?"

"I didn't ask for help."

The stranger raised his brow, and in a deeper tone, as though he spoke to an imbecile, repeated slowly, "Why is she tied?"

"She has an unclean spirit."

The stranger exhaled and stood taller. His head was canted, arms crossed over his significant belly. "Who is she?"

Elijah sighed and got down from the cart. He came around to where she lay and covered her again. The stranger saw the blisters on Elijah's hands and grabbed his wrist.

"Did you put her in the fire?"

Elijah pulled away. He turned, rummaging for something buried under the piled cloaks. "She threw herself–It threw itself in the fire."

"Help…me." Elijah looked back over his shoulder. The stranger leaned to Salome so he could hear. "He threw me…held me down." The voice was weak, words left its mouth scratched and muffled.

The stranger's brow was striped with worry and his nostrils resembled the black sockets of a skull in his bulbous nose. He reached to untie her but Elijah had the sword out and to his throat before he could pick at the knots.

"I saw it in your eyes," said the stranger. "You're a man with no conscience."

"A conscience doesn't survive long here."

"You'll kill me here? With my wife and son in the cart behind me?"

"Keep your voice down." Elijah brought his face closer. "I'm taking her to Bethany to get this thing out of her. If you try to stop me. I will."

"What's in Bethany?"

"A prophet."

The wrinkles in the stranger's brow smoothed over. "The Nazarene?"

"He can heal her. He can drive that thing out of her."

The stranger's shoulders slouched and he relaxed. He looked at his cart. Then the exposed portion of the coverings where he could still see part of Salome's head. "My offer stands. I have plenty of grain and food." He looked Elijah up and down. "You look like you could use a meal too."

Elijah took a step back. He stared at the stranger, then finally lowered the sword. "I'm not going to hurt her. But I can't let you untie her. You don't know what you're dealing with."

He nodded and brushed himself off. "I've heard the Nazarene is a great man. My brother in law told me he can pull fish from nothing."

Elijah huffed and his head bobbed slightly. "He can do all sorts of things."

"Have you seen him?"

"I have. And I curse the day we met."

"That's new." After a silence, he said, "I'm Zachias."

"Elijah."

"A prophet's name." The declaration came with a solemn nod.

The donkey brayed weakly. Elijah turned. The animal shifted its legs and collapsed. The cart nearly toppled over as it fell.

Zachias was silent for a long time. "We'll pass Bethany before we get to Jerusalem. We can take you."

Elijah resisted Zachias's offer. He was prepared to push forward with her over his shoulder, to drag her if need be. Later, he thought of the donkey's collapse and laughed. *Impeccable timing, as always.* Providence's every turn hinges on comedic intent.

They abandoned the cart. It wouldn't be needed once they found Him.

Zachias's wife had a smile that invited you to join in its mirth, bright as the crescent moon on a dark night. Elijah found his mind wandering. Coveting, not for her physically, but for the bond they shared and the life they cultivated. Her name was Saphira. Like her husband, she seemed suspicious of Elijah's story about unclean spirits. She was hospitable, all the same.

The boy was curious. Naturally, he wanted to know all about the woman tied up in the back of their cart and why she smelled the way she did. He asked about unclean spirits and what had happened to her. Elijah told them part of the story. Most of the horrors were omitted for the boy's sake.

The thing in Salome appealed to the traveler's generosity. "Help me," it said in a whimpering voice. "He threw me in the fire. It burns. Ohh, it hurts."

Elijah told her to shut up, Saphira cast a concerned look at Zachias.

The men traded places periodically, driving the oxen along the road. At times they would sit together, and Elijah would listen to see if the thing would try to talk to Saphira or the boy. When Elijah was at the front, and Zachias and Saphira were deep in conversation, the thing in Salome would wink at the boy and make faces until he blushed.

They stopped somewhat frequently for Zachias's business. Elijah was irritable, but it was still faster than the donkey. They moved along slowly and engaged almost everyone they met to peddle their wares or to offer some hospitality. On the morning of the second day, Elijah went out to the water to wash off and relieve himself. Zachias went off with his wife to talk. An argument over Elijah and the woman broke out. Saphira's skepticism was taking its toll. The boy was behind the wagon, chasing a butterfly's lazy path through the air and watching the wings flutter when it landed. His pursuit brought him around the far side of the cart.

"Asher."

The boy froze.

"Asher."

He walked over and cracked the covering open, looking back at his parents. Their voices rose and fell, his mother pointing to the wagon with rigid, stabbing motions as their arms moved about. Asher peeked in. Light fell on the woman inside. She turned her face over and he got a clear look at the skin where she was burned. He gasped.

"Asher."

"Here I am."

"Don't be afraid, Asher."

"I'm not afraid."

"A brave boy. Bring me a stone, Asher. A flat stone. Go to the bank and dip your foot in the water, it will be there."

The boy stood listening. He looked left, then over his shoulder at his parents. His father was hugging his mother and rocking, patting her back and talking in her ear. "Elijah said not to speak to you. Not to even look at you."

She sighed. "He would say that." She dropped her eyes. Then raised them with a hurt expression. "Did he say why?"

Asher looked down at the grass. "He said there's something evil in you."

Her expression rivaled the actors in gentile theaters. To a boy, the anguish there appeared genuine. "They say those things because I'm ugly." She turned the half of her face that wasn't burned into the light again so he could see. "But I wasn't always so hideous," she said with a sigh. "Not until I met Elijah." Asher saw tears pool her eyes.

"Elijah did that?"

Another exaggerated sigh. "He didn't want anyone else to look at me."

"What did he do?"

"He threw me in the fire," she made a sob and her voice cracked. "He held my face against the embers with his foot."

"That's awful."

She nodded. "Bring me the flat rock. If you put your feet in the water near that tree with the big knot and wiggle your toes you'll feel it. Just pick it up and slide it into my hands from the side of the covering. Do it when no one's looking. Our secret." She winked at him.

He turned to walk away then stopped and looked back. "What do you want a rock for?"

She looked off to the side a moment. "I want something to remind me of the Jordan. I don't think I'll ever see it again."

"You will," said the boy.

She smiled. "Yes, I think you're right."

They would reach Jericho the next day. Elijah began to feel comfortable around these people, and in the long stretches of road and wilderness he fantasized about Salome beside him, traveling the Roman trade routes with the breeze in their faces. Past Tarsus, Neapolis, perhaps even venturing to the Acropolis. He'd heard stories from gentiles about the Greek shores and their philosophers. "They founded their religion with their minds," he remembered one saying.

Saphira made the best of their travels. Her disposition met potential hardships smiling, any doubts or grievances from her family were overcome by her indomitable optimism. Zachias drew strength from his sanguine bride. They appeared to live a happy life. Elijah wanted to soak this in while he could, hoping to model his own family in their likeness. But now he felt his presence cast a shadow over their lives.

Elijah laid his cloak out that night to sleep under the stars. Asher went to the bank and Elijah heard him trying to fill the river. When the boy walked back Elijah patted the Earth beside his cloak. "I saved a spot for you."

The boy stopped. Shook his head. "I'm going to sleep by myself."

Elijah stared up at him, surprised. The boy had slept beside him the previous two nights. "Alright, Asher. Good night." The boy had seemed distant for most of the day. Perhaps it was in his mind.

The boy nodded and sauntered off around the other side of the cart.

Elijah laid there looking up at the heavens. For the first time since he could remember, he was optimistic about the future. About their future. In a few days, this nightmare would finally be over.

Asher.

He opened his eyes. The shorn morning greyed along the edges, like white ash gathered around soot.

Asher.

He wiped his eyes and looked around at the shapes of trees swaying in the dark. He rose. The dirt was cold and hard beneath his feet. Wind blew and chilled his skin. He looked at the glossed path the moon made on the Jordan beyond the brush.

She was standing there. Asher's heart beat hard. The yips of wild dogs were a far whisper, his father's snore buzzed somewhere close. Grasshoppers and frogs sang. Somehow, even with the cacophony of creatures, his name rang clear.

Asher. Come to me.

His feet obeyed while his mind lit with warnings, erupted in fiery points that begged to push out from his skin. She stood to the waist in the dark water, beckoning him closer with elegant sweeps of her arms. Her body moved with a dancer's grace.

"You're free."

She brought a finger to her lips. Nodded. Then her body heard the music again and she moved.

Asher squealed with laughter. "What are you doing?"

She brought a finger to her lips again, then pantomimed a pulling motion. Her hands were out. Hair wet, slicked back. Tunic torn to reveal the glory of her womanhood, which his mother had kept from his eyes for several years now. Asher touched his foot to the water and drew back. She motioned again.

"I can't swim."

"You don't need to."

He liked her voice. He stepped in. The cold Jordan numbed his feet, his flustered mind temporarily stifled by the water cooling him as he moved. Rising as he waded out. She backed away and lowered herself until he could see shoulders and arms, reaching but retreating. He stepped forward, teeth chattering. He reached and she backed away. "I can't."

"Come little fish. Kick. kick." She giggled.

He did. And she took him in her arms. Smiling. Wiped the hair from his face. Cooed at him. They moved into the Jordan together. Past the shining ripples in the budding morning.

Elijah woke to shrieking. The sound raised birds from branches and their spots along the banks. The lament carried with their beating wings.

Saphira.

He sprang to his feet, ripped the cart's cover open.

Empty.

The screaming stopped in the middle of a long wail. The abrupt silence that followed was worse. He ran along the bank, searching. More screams followed. It was *Zachias,* yelling the names of his loved ones.

Elijah ran toward them. He heard Zachias's grunted curses, a woman's laughter that chilled him inside. Splashes. There was movement through the branches. Flailing limbs and water arching. The flash of skin and hair as Zachias and Salome wrestled in the water. Past the trees, where the bank cleared and he could see Zachias and Salome struggling, he stopped.

They were there.

He looked down at what brought the screams, what his reaction hadn't allowed him to consider. Saphira's mouth was open, her head bent awkwardly, hair wild as the marsh beneath. On the bank beside her, Asher appeared deep in slumber. As though he'd lain there the night before and fallen asleep to the hush of the river. The sight numbed something in Elijah. Barricaded all feeling.

Zachias was facing the bank. Squeezing Salome's broken arm, fury in his face, frothing with spittle as the other hand pushed her face down. She bent the way a body shouldn't.

Laughing. Laughing at the havoc she'd caused, at the calamity suffered the world over under the watchful eye of Heaven. At the futility of life's struggles.

Elijah felt it rumble up from his chest. The invitation to join, to laugh instead of striving. To let that impulse that smothers reason take control. Forget the bodies on the bank, the things he'd seen, laugh at all of creation's daunting wiles.

They turned in their scuffle. Zachias almost had her face in the water. Elijah stood where the water met his shins. Half of her face was submerged. The burnt half was exposed, charred and gnarled. Her eye rolled to him. It was her.

Salome.

In a moment, the guise fell away. The thing inside recoiled, and the graceful simplicity and expanding loveliness that first captured his attention surfaced.

"Let her go," said Elijah. He'd wanted it to sound more like a plea.

Zachias's head turned to his shoulder slightly, then he looked down again, forcing her head all the way under.

"Let her go!"

She clawed and tore at Zachias's face and chest. He wouldn't relent. Zachias spoke through clenched teeth. "She killed them…Saphira…Asher…my boy."

"Please." Elijah's voice was weak.

Zachias was hunched over her. Elijah could see him from the side.

Elijah moved forward. Kicked something. It cut the bottom of his foot. He reached down. Pried a stone from the muddy bottom. Elijah sloshed through the water toward them.

"Let her go."

"She killed them."

"It's not her. It has her. Please."

Elijah gripped the stone in his palm and swung. After the awful thud it made, Zachias fell into the water. Elijah pulled Salome to the bank. She was breathing. He fished Zachias out next. He mumbled his loved ones' names over and over as Elijah dragged him out. Elijah left him there, bleeding from the side of his face and shaking his head making little twitches. He put Salome over his shoulder and went to the cart.

Elijah found another stone beside the pieces of rope where she'd lain. He threw the rock away and tied her up again with the pieces. Then covered her.

Once he'd collected himself, he went for the oxen. He led the first to the cart and tried to tie it the way Zachias showed him. The ox was excited. Elijah's frustrations left his hands shaking. *Please,*

441

just let me leave here let me take her away, please it's not her fault.

The reins were horrendous. Salome stirred in the wagon. He closed his eyes and breathed. Then went for the other ox.

He led the animal back to the cart with his head down. A noise ahead caught his attention.

No.

Zachias stood beside the cart, glowering. The wound over his eye a puckered lip, murmuring the color of roses. Salome was at his feet, held by the hair, with the edge of the Roman sword to her neck.

Elijah held his hands out for mercy.

"She drowned my son. My only son. She killed Saphira!" Her name echoed from the mighty Jordan and brought more birds skyward.

"She put ointment on her wounds! She laughed when I asked what she'd done. Laughed at my boy!" Zachias shook her as he spoke. Salome's limp body appeared to convulse.

"It wasn't her." Elijah stepped forward.

Zachias watched with patient cruelty as he neared. When Elijah reached the first ox, Zachias raised the blade and let go of her hair. He swung. Elijah fell to his knees.

He saw it fall and roll.

Zachias stumbled on something, landed on his backside. He dropped the sword and laid there, belly rising and falling.

Elijah screamed.

He scrambled over on his knees and picked up her head. Stroking its features, struggling to remember every curve as his tears splashed her face and her blood poured over his lap. Sobs shook through him. He saw the waste of his life clearly. The errant striving to forge his own destiny when this was the only possible outcome all along.

It started as a tremor. Small, like the spark that ignites a liquid hungry for fire. Heat danced in his head. Churned in his viscera. He found the sword, stood over Zachias, who still laid on his back. He looked up at Elijah and nodded, then turned away. Elijah brought the blade down. Struck with everything he had. Again and again, until the hilt burned in his hand, his knuckles ached from squeezing, and every joint in his fingers felt jostled loose. Every blow was a recitation of a wrong received. He swung until he couldn't raise his arm anymore.

Elijah finally dropped the weapon and sat against the wheel, breathing in great heaves. He looked over his work. Felt nothing.

Elijah sat on the bank later. Covered in blood, hair matted and coiled, knees to his chest. He had Salome's head in his arms, stroking her hair and muttering. He laid on the bank beside it for a long time. Eventually, he slept. When he woke, the sun was high and he heard his name. He looked around. He was alone. He raised her face to his, stared in awe, then put her lips to his ear.

He could hear her. Not the thing, but Salome. *It was her.* She had so much to tell him. Her words were sweet as honey. All he had to do was listen. Listen and they could be together. He put her lips to his ear again, nodding. Closing his eyes and savoring her voice.

E P I L O G U E

He never bothered to put on sandals. He dumped the contents of his bag, found a fig, and stood looking at the Jordan for a long time before throwing it into the water. He watched the ripples spread and calm. He walked, feet coated in dust. The skin on his feet were soon peeled and blistered raw. It didn't matter. The bag he wore had a dark stain at the bottom. His desolate eyes watched the road ahead.

He traveled north. From time to time he sat and opened the bag, looking around to ensure he was alone, putting an ear to the opening. She told him what path to take. Where he would meet up with the others. The voice was faint, distorted. Like deciphering the whine wind makes through a hole in the wall.

He didn't greet anyone on the road. Several times travelers tried to hail him, but when they saw his face they continued on. Tried to erase him from their memory.

When he arrived at the village the wailers were out. Proprietors of grief. Faces furrowed by age and outlandish feats of mourning, the grooves in their cheeks rinsed with the brine of their sorrows. They put rags to their faces as they rocked and waved their arms. When he passed they fell silent. He walked right through their funeral procession. They nearly dropped the dead girl from the litter they carried.

He climbed a steep path, past the dead trees, away from the village. They were waiting by the tomb. The boy, the red haired man, and the Roman. They stood beside an idol near the opening. Pigs laid about, flesh foul and wasted. An ossuary had fallen from the shelf inside the tomb and pieces of bone covered the floor.

The Roman smiled. A pike jutted from the ground near the entrance, close to where he stood. The pike ran through a head with an austere face and high cheekbones, looking up for a mercy that never came. The red haired man stuck a pike into the ground and smiled.

The Roman nodded and extended his hand.

He reached into the bag, pulled it out, and held it so he was looking into her eyes. He rubbed his thumb over the smooth half of her face, raised it up like an offering, then brought it down on the pike.

Yelps and snorts rang from the tomb. The Roman poured something over the idol. Then over the heads.

"Here she'll be with you always. My will and your desires will never be at odds."

He nodded and knelt.

About the Author

Chris lives in San Diego with his girlfriend, daughters, and their horde of feral cats. He enjoys unsettling people with words, reading, and perpetually failing at basketball.

ABOUT THE
PUBLISHER / EDITOR

Dawn Shea is an author and half of the publishing team over at D&T Publishing. She lives with her family in Mississippi. Always an avid horror lover, she has moved forward with her dreams of writing and publishing those things she loves so much.

Follow her author page on Amazon for all publications she is featured in.

Follow D&T Publishing at their website,
www.dandtpublishing.com, or search for their Facebook Group

Or email here: dandtpublishing20@gmail.com